CHAPTER 1

The first annoyance came when, ready to sit and relax for the evening, he discovered he didn't have any beer. So, in spite of the eight o'clock hour, he determined to go out and get some.

The second annoyance came when he was walking to the store to restock his supply of man's favorite beverage and it started to rain.

Now, as a third annoyance, he realized he was being stalked. He felt it before he saw it which was good because, as a cop, he should have a sense for these things. What was interesting was that the stalker was in a car. So Detective Mike Brennen stopped, the steady rain dripping off him, and turned to give the car a hard look.

It was a gray Mercedes Benz moving slowly just behind him. When Mike stopped, it stopped. He frowned. Now why would a Mercedes be following him? He couldn't remember dealing with anyone lately that could afford an expensive Mercedes. For that matter, he couldn't remember ever dealing with anyone who could afford a Mercedes.

Just then the car unexpectedly pulled over to the curb and the driver reached over to open the passenger's door.

"Need a lift?" asked the man.

Mike bent over and looked in. The light wasn't great, but he was pretty certain the driver wasn't anyone he knew.

"My mother taught me to never get into a stranger's car," he told the stranger. "Even if it's a Mercedes Benz."

"Even if it's raining and you're getting wet?"

"I'm already wet, so what's the differ--"

A horn blasted. The Mercedes' rear end was sticking out into the street and someone wasn't as impressed with it as Mike was.

"Detective Brennen, would you please get in the car," urged the driver. Then added, "I promise to bring you back home."

Mike's curiosity was peaked. "How can I resist such a friendly invitation. But, if you know my name, I think I should know yours."

"Tommy One Bears."

"Tommy One *Bares*? What kind of...?"

Several horns blared.

"Please! Just get in the goddamned car!"

Mike decided what the hell, and got in. As the guy pulled back into traffic, Brennen gave the Mercedes' interior an envious once over.

"Wow," he said.

"Glad you like it."

"I'm getting it wet."

"Wet won't hurt anything."

Mike switched his scrutiny to the man behind the wheel. The light was still bad, but the stranger looked to be in his middle-to-late thirties with rough features and black hair that reached almost to his shoulders.

"What kind of name is Tommy One Bares?" he finished his question.

"It's B E A R S. I spell it because most people immediately think 'b a r e s'."

"No kidding? Bears. So are you some kind of an Indian?"

"Native American. I'm half Sioux. That's why my parents saddled me with the One. For one-half."

"Clever. What's the other half?"

"Italian."

Mike's eyebrows went up. "That's kind of different."

"It works for me. You want to discuss your ancestry now?"

"New York City...probably for the last hundred years or more," said Mike. "Now I want to discuss who you are and why I'm in your car."

"I'm just a messenger and delivery boy. There are some people who want to see you."

"Really? Who? Why didn't they just call me?"

2

"Mr. Panelli thought it would be better if I just came and invited you in person."

Mike Brennen's eyebrows had shot all the way up this time.

"Panelli? We talking Anthony Panelli?"

"We are," said Bears.

He had Mike's attention. The Panellis had been, in years gone by, one of New York's most powerful crime families. When Anthony Panelli was sentenced to a dozen or so years in prison, his sons Thomas and Joseph had taken over and cleaned things up. They were still a rich and powerful family, but now dealt in successful, legitimate businesses. Mike had also heard that many of his police counterparts were not all that convinced of their shift to honesty and still kept a wary eye on them.

Mike, however, had never crossed paths with any of them in his twelve years on the force. Not even in his four years as a homicide detective. So why the hell would the Panellis want to see him?

He asked, "Why the hell do the Panellis want to see me?"

"They'll explain," said Bears.

"Right," said Mike. "Is your Italian half related to the Panellis?"

"The Panellis are Sicilian."

"Whatever."

"I am in no way a part of the Panelli family."

"But you handle messages and deliveries for them."

"I hire out by the job."

Brennen sniffed. "They're actually paying you to deliver me to them?"

"Why don't you sit back and enjoy the ride in my brand new Mercedes. That way I won't have to tell you to shut up and quit asking questions."

"Ouch."

With further conversation having been squelched, Mike entertained himself by watching the skillful way in which Mr. Bears drove his Mercedes through the city. The man was very good. Mike wondered what else the man was good at. If he was a free-lance operator, he'd have to be good at any number of things. Especially if the Panellis hired him.

When they reached the ritzy neighborhood of large and stately homes, Mike Brennen did not get to see the front entrance to the Panelli household. Bears turned onto a narrow, black-topped road which had no street name or lights. After half a mile or so, the man pulled off the road to stop at a vine-covered, heavy wooden gate. In the dark and rain, Mike would never have seen it.

The hired messenger flicked his lights once and the gate swung open by an invisible hand.

"The Panellis have invited me to visit, but they don't want me to come in the front door?" allowed Mike.

"The reason the Panellis want to see you is sensitive. They didn't wish for you to be seen visiting them."

Mike frowned. "They don't want anyone to see a cop visiting them and it's sensitive. I find this all very peculiar, Mr. Bears."

Again, "They'll explain."

"Okay," sighed Mike.

The Panelli homestead loomed in the dark and rain. Brick and stone, it was most certainly well over a hundred years old, with at least twenty or more rooms. It sat in the middle of a lavish lawn with a lot of trees and bushes around it. Nearby was a two-story guest house of probably a half dozen rooms, surrounded by its own trees and bushes. Somewhere in the dark were a pool and tennis courts. The entire estate was surrounded by a six-foot-high stone wall.

"I have to admit, I'm impressed," said Mike. The closest he had ever gotten to the Panellis, or their estate, was whatever he had seen in news photos or television. So again he asked, "You're sure it's Detective Mike Brennen they want? I mean, I do dead bodies…"

Tommy One Bears stopped the car near a darkened rear entrance.

"You don't mind getting a little wet going to the door, do you?" he asked.

Mike glanced down at his wet clothes and said, "You've got a great sense of humor, Mr. Bears."

"Please, just Tommy."

"Okay, Tommy."

Someone opened the back door before they got there. Ducking inside, Mike found himself in a cloak room with a long, open closet to the right. A small bench and table were on the wall straight ahead. A lamp on the table provided shaded light. When the detective turned to see who had let them in, he recognized Joseph Panelli.

The youngest of the Panellis was at least as handsome in person as he looked in any photo or on television. Dressed casually in a yellow polo shirt, brown slacks, and tan socks and loafers, the man could have been a professional model. His black hair was trimmed short and expertly styled. Impressive, well-toned arms left no doubt that the rest of the body would be in equally good shape. He sported the perfect suntan, even though it was only mid-May. Obviously, the man had seen more, and warmer, sun the past winter than the city had. About Brennen's height, just over six feet, Mike happened to know that they were both thirty-two years old.

The detective also had his first clear look at Tommy One Bears. He was taller, at least six foot three. His hair, its length not quite reaching his collar, was even blacker than Panelli's. With high cheek bones and sharp, black eyes, he very much favored the one-half Sioux. He was in blue jeans, a black tee-shirt, black Western boots, and a black leather jacket. Real leather.

Mike's practiced eye also didn't fail to notice that Bears' expensive jacket covered a holstered gun on his right hip. For his trek to the store, Mike was carrying a thirty-eight Smith & Wesson in a holster clipped to his belt at the small of his back. He carried a Glock on the job.

There was a definite contrast between the two well-dressed men and Detective Brennen who was in his faded and worn jeans, white tee-shirt that had black cat paw prints on it along with the words MY CAT WALKS ALL OVER ME and worn sneakers. His brown, fake leather jacket was as faded and worn as his jeans. All of it was soaking wet.

Joe Panelli was giving Mike Brennen a return once-over, his dark eyes probing the detective, looking for...for what? Mike wondered.

"Good evening, Detective Brennen," said Panelli, his tone polite but guarded. "One. We, appreciate your coming."

He did not offer to shake hands, which suited Mike just fine.

"How could I refuse Mr. Bears' invitation to ride in his brand-new Mercedes Benz? Especially since it was raining."

"It does look like the weather has gotten the best of you. Let me get you a towel."

"I'd rather hear why the Panellis sent a hired gun to get me. I find it a real puzzler."

"Hired gun?" said Tommy Bears with some amusement.

"I'm not stupid," said Mike. "You look a lot more expensive than a plain ol' delivery boy."

"You're right," said Joe. "He is expensive, but we've always found him worth it for certain...jobs. Tommy is discreet and trustworthy, and we needed both to keep this visit quiet."

He stepped to a cupboard at the end of the closet and opened it to take out a towel. Handing it to Mike, he said, "If you'll follow me, we will explain why you are here."

Panelli ignored the obvious doorway, instead leading them through a smaller door inside the closet.

"Fuck", moaned Mike to himself. "What the hell am I getting into?"

They walked along a narrow hallway that had a couple doors leading off of it. Mike eyed them curiously but concentrated on toweling off his face and neck along with his short, straw-colored hair. A third door was at the end of the hallway. Joe opened it and led them into an even narrower hallway. This one had only one door off it. Panelli tapped lightly on it but entered without waiting for any response. Inside, Mike found himself in one of those smart looking studies that most people see only in movies and on television, himself included. He also noticed that the three-by-six-foot opening that they had just come through was hidden behind book-laden shelves that pulled away from a wall filled with bookshelves.

"I don't believe this," muttered the detective as he turned to take in the rest of the room.

The wall directly across from him had a fireplace large enough to roast a pig and it was surrounded by a dozen or more framed photographs. In one corner of the room was an ornately carved, wooden cabinet. In another, a four-by-four-foot, ornately carved, wooden table, which held a good-sized bronze sculpture of an eagle in flight. The detective detected that wall number four had windows in it since there were dark gold and green drapes pulled across it. Sitting in front of the drapes was more ornately carved wood, this a large desk. Except for a couple of gold-framed picture holders, aimed away from him, and a gold and black telephone with almost a dozen buttons on it, there was nothing else on the desk. Behind it sat a gray-haired man.

The Anthony Panelli. At one time his father's right-hand man in one of New York's hard core crime families. Now, with sons of his own who had turned it around, he looked tired, the years in prison having aged him more than his seventy-six years. Also casually dressed in a dark blue polo shirt, the eyes behind his glasses were still sharp.

Sitting in a chair to one side of the desk was Thomas Panelli. In an open-necked, long-sleeved white shirt and dark green slacks with dark green loafers, he appeared skeptical, even angry. Three years older than his brother, he wasn't quite as handsome, or as tanned, or as muscular. Where Joe handled the legal end of the businesses, Thomas handled the running of them along with his father's help. From what Mike had read and heard, Thomas Panelli was a talented and clever man.

Though Mike found himself wondering about a man who wore green shoes.

Neither of the Panellis stood up to offer their hands to the dripping man before them. Nor did they offer any smiles or pleasant greetings. For a meeting they had arranged, they seemed unusually uncomfortable. Which made Mike feel more at ease. For a couple of moments, all three of them did the scrutinizing thing.

"Detective Brennen," said Anthony, his tone generic. "We appreciate your accepting our rather mysterious invitation. I hope your being wet isn't a result of Mr. Bears'--"

"Actually, you could say that Mr. Bears rescued me from drowning," allowed Mike, hanging the towel over his left shoulder.

Standing off to one side, Tommy Bears showed a hint of a smile.

Joe Panelli, who had moved around to stand beside his father, even looked slightly amused.

Mike went on, "I do agree it's a mysterious invite. On our little trip over here I tried to figure out why the Panellis would want to see a homicide cop. I'm pretty sure none of my current bodies are related to any of you, and..." He glanced around the room. "...I'm not seeing any bodies here. I also don't think we've ever 'bumped' into each other before. I guess I should mention that I'm a disgustingly honest cop, so I'm not open to bribery if you still deal in that. So, why am I here?"

Thomas looked disgusted. "He's a smart mouth, two-bit cop. This is not a good idea."

Joe smirked. "That's just another part of Detective Brennen's personality, Thomas. The smart mouth. More than likely, it's why he's had his problems over the past twelve years of dedicated hard work on the job."

Mike finally bristled. "Okay. You seem to know about me. So tell me, what the fuck do you need a two-bit cop for?"

Anthony Panelli said, "You named one of the reasons, Detective. You are 'disgustingly honest'."

Joe added, "In spite of, or possibly because of, your sometimes pit bull approach to your job, you actually have a reputation for incorruptibility."

Mike blinked and looked from Joseph to Thomas to Anthony.

"So what exactly do you want?" he asked with some coldness.

Anthony Panelli looked at him carefully, and said, "We need your help to--"

"Shit. You want police help, call 911," said Mike gruffly. "Or hire Mr. Bears here to--"

"This isn't going to work," hissed Thomas.

"Shut up, Thomas," said Joe sharply. "You, too, Brennen. We are faced with a serious problem that is also the NYPD's problem."

The detective eyed Joe and then Anthony. He purposely ignored Thomas.

"So, I'm listening," he said.

Anthony Panelli leaned forward, his hands clasped on the desk in front of him.

"We have very reliable information, please do not ask about our source, that Police Chief Andrew Macklin will be assassinated sometime in the next week."

CHAPTER 2

Mike Brennen's eyes narrowed. "What?...The hell you say."

"And," Anthony resumed pointedly, "the assassin will be a police lieutenant."

"What?" said Mike again. "That's nuts. The Panelli family is telling me that the police chief is going to be killed by a police lieutenant? And why would you even care?"

"I really hate this," rasped Thomas.

"Even in the old days, Detective Brennen, the Panelli family was never involved in the killing of any police officer," said Anthony crisply.

"Though I'm feeling a temptation now," muttered Thomas.

Mike sent him a razor-sharp glare.

"If you'll pay attention, Brennen, we'll fill it in for you," said Joe with some irritation.

"Fine, fill me in," rumbled Mike.

Joe started, "What we are facing here, besides the assassination itself, is the man who would replace Macklin. Captain Earl Nimmer."

Mike frowned. "Nimmer. I've heard and read about him. He's a big shot cop. Likes to brag about his accomplishments. Are you worried that if he moves up to police chief, he might give the Panellis a hard time in spite of your cleaned up image?"

"We're worried about him," stated Anthony impatiently, "because he is controlled by the Rezzoro family."

Mike's eyes got wide. "Now you're telling me that the Rezzoros are mixed up in this party, too?"

"They are hosting the party," said Thomas. "Much of Nimmer's successful career has been staged and built by the Rezzoros. For him to become police chief would cause irreparable damage to the police force and..."

"...and maybe to the Panellis..." started Mike.

"We have bad memories with the Rezzoros, so yes, it would affect us," said Joe. "But however you look at it, it's bound to get sticky for everyone if the Rezzoros get a hold on a position that high. So we need someone inside the police force to do some poking around to find, and stop, whichever lieutenant is the assassin."

"Preferably revealing the plot in the process," said the patriarch Panelli. "It would do no good if Nimmer stays in contention."

Joe went on, "And we thought the best way to avoid the Rezzoros finding out that we are aware of their plan, was to choose an everyday kind of cop. One, if you will, who's dedicated, honest, and trustworthy--" A slight smile.

"--if undisciplined--" slipped in Thomas.

"--with that pit bull determination to get the job done."

"A two-bit cop." Thomas again.

Mike ignored him to say, "And I'm the best you could come up with? Give me a break. I can name a dozen, extra good cops, right off the top of my head. Including my partner."

"Name them, and then name the ones who will also work willingly, quietly, with the Panellis," challenged Anthony.

Mike scowled at him. Then shrugged and admitted, "Okay, that makes it harder. But tell me, why am I supposed to work willingly and quietly with the Panellis? I mean, besides the dedication and honesty stuff."

"Why not?" countered Anthony.

"It's not like you have a flourishing career to worry about, or a family to protect," Thomas pointed out insolently.

"Thomas!" His father sent him a warning glance.

Beginning to feel a touch ornery, Mike said, "Okay, but give me a break here. You must have made some connections in the police force over the years. Why don't you just ask one of them to do it?"

Joe said, "To be blunt, we can't be sure they wouldn't go to the Rezzoros."

The honest, dedicated cop stared at him and said, "I'm getting a headache." Then, "Do you know that I had a memorable run-in with Nicholas Rezzoro about a year ago? He killed a teenage hooker and I spent some time trying to convince him to confess to it."

Anthony gave a nod. "We are aware of that. We're hoping it won't become a problem."

Mike snorted. "Well, hell, let's all hope it doesn't become a problem."

"Since you were unable to convict him, he probably has only good memories of you," said Thomas.

Brennen snapped him a dagger look. "I don't like you." He returned his attention to Anthony. "You say this is supposed to happen in the next week. By what miracle could I, or anyone, come up with the dirty lieutenant in that short period of time?"

"We've already narrowed it down to three," said Joe. "Each one has some part of their life they would prefer to keep hidden or a desperate financial situation, or both. This makes them potential targets for blackmail and/or a payoff. We don't believe it's likely that the shooter will survive once the hit is carried out. If the police don't get him--"

"...or her..." injected Thomas.

"...the Rezzoros will. If there is any payoff, it will go to the lieutenant's family."

"What her?" Mike had picked up on the her.

Joe said, "Lieutenant Anita Sheffer."

"Sheffer?" said a startled Mike. "I've heard about her. I've heard she's a good cop. I find it hard to believe someone like her could be bought that easily."

"Her fifteen-year-old son, Randy, has a nasty drug habit," Joe told the detective. "So far she's managed to keep it under wraps, but she's spent a great deal of money buying him out of trouble."

"And even more trying to get him cured," said Thomas. "He's in another expensive drug facility right now. Mothers, especially single mothers, can get very desperate."

"And leave it to you bastards to dig it all up," rasped Mike

"If we can, so can the Rezzoros," allowed Anthony.

"I'm starting to feel real cranky," said Mike. "Just tell me about the other two finalists in this fucking assassin's game you're trying to sell me."

"Lieutenant Marvin Polinski..." started Joe.

"Polinski!" Mike lit up. "He's Internal Affairs!"

"We are also aware of that," said Anthony.

"Are you also aware that the two of us have butted heads? Wait, I know, you're hoping that it won't be a problem. Right?"

"Yes, we are," said Thomas with a thin smile.

"Your confrontations were minor, Brennen. The man has bigger problems than you," said Joe. "His wife has cancer and his insurance no longer covers all her needs, so it has been a severe drain on his finances. Add to that two teenage children to raise and we figure he could be open for negotiations."

Mike's mouth twisted sourly. "The stench in here is getting thick."

"You defend even Polinski?" asked Joe.

"Even Polinski," returned the detective firmly.

"Honesty and loyalty," said Anthony. "We did pick the right man."

"So who's the third one?" grouched Mike.

"Lieutenant Dick Corry," said Joe.

"Hardball Corry in Vice? He works out of my precinct, but you're probably aware of that, too, and you don't believe it will be a problem," said Mike. "And let me guess...from the rumors I've heard about his gambling, the man is up to his eyeballs in debt, probably to the Rezzoros."

Thomas said, "You have to admit, he is in a unique position for someone who likes to gamble. Working in Vice, he knows where to go whenever and whatever he wants to play and he can be bribed. Usually to warn the right people of impending raids."

Joseph said, "But, as you noted, he is a big loser to the Rezzoros and bribes won't begin to cover the large amount he owes them."

Mike sighed and closed his eyes, saying, "And if the Rezzoros ask him to do Macklin, Lieutenant Corry won't have many options."

"Not if he cares about his wife and two boys," allowed Joe.

It fell quiet for several moments.

"Goddamnit," exhaled Mike, eyes coming open. "You must know somebody with influence and connections that could handle this a whole lot easier than me."

Anthony slowly shook his head. "We simply do not know anyone in a position to handle this, Detective Brennen. No one we can trust. As you have taken the time to point out, we are somewhat new to the legitimate business world and, well, life." A thin smile. "But we do trust you."

"Shit!" said Mike with feeling. "So, all you want from trustworthy, smart mouthed me, is to grill these three lieutenant suspects and pick out the one that the Rezzoro family is paying...pardon me, blackmailing...to kill the police chief, and then stop him, or her, from doing it. And I'll do this because the Panellis tell me it's going to happen and because I'm an honest, dedicated two-bit cop. And, in the process, I could very possibly get my dumb ass shot off by the Rezzoros."

Joe shook his head at the dissertation, while Thomas gave the detective another pained look.

Anthony Panelli was openly amused as he admitted, "That about covers it, Detective Brennen. Except Joseph and Tommy, one or both, will be nearby if needed."

Mike blinked. "Pardon me? Joseph or Tommy will be nearby if needed?"

"As backup," said Joe. "Hopefully to keep your dumb ass from being shot off."

"They'll keep a sharp eye out for you, Detective," said Anthony.

"I bet they will. Makes me feel lots better," said Mike. "Today's Tuesday. So I've for sure got a week to endear myself to three lieutenants by sniffing around in their lives?"

"We can't say a week for sure," said Anthony. "Our source could do no better than that for now. If we get more information, we will, of course, pass it on to you."

Mike sighed. "Thanks so much." Then, "Speaking of sources, how do you know the Rezzoros don't have a source in your camp?"

"No one has a source in our camp," stated Thomas.

His father said, "It is inconsequential. The three of us, and Tommy, are the only ones who know about the assassination threat and about you. We'll do our best to keep it that way."

Mike glanced at Tommy Bears. The half Native American, half Italian gave him a small smile.

The detective smiled back. "You sure Mr. Bears is trustworthy?"

"Very."

"Why don't you have him visit the lieutenants? He looks like he could intimidate information out of just about anybody."

Bears' smile broadened. "Why, thank you, Detective Brennen. I work hard to hone my looks."

"I'm afraid Tommy would attract too much attention if he were to pay visits to police lieutenants. We'd prefer to keep this under wraps if we can," allowed Anthony.

"Not for long once I start sticking my nose in it," said Mike.

"Yes, things could start happening then, but we're hoping we'll have some control over it," said Anthony.

"You're just full of hope," sniffed Mike. "With my neck sticking out there. Fuck. You know what a shit job this is. I should tell you to shove it up your--" He stopped and gave another disgruntled sigh. "What if I need to get in touch with you?'

"I'll be around," Joe reminded him. "Or Tommy."

"That's right. How could I forget so soon."

Detective Brennen shook his head in frustration and then wished he hadn't. His headache was getting worse.

CHAPTER 3

Brennen's mind itched as he was driven home and he wasn't able to come up with any good ideas to scratch it.

At first Tommy Bears left the detective to his thoughts, but finally he said, "Guess you're not enjoying my Mercedes anymore."

Mike looked at him dully. "I'm not sure I'll ever enjoy anything again. Probably because I'll be dead...or get fired."

"You must be good at what you do or the Panellis would never have picked you," noted Tommy.

"The way they put it, it sounded to me like their choices were limited."

"Don't sell yourself short. You can be sure they knew what they were doing before they settled on you."

"Right. Thanks so much."

They were quiet again for a few minutes until Mike said, "I'll bet Rambo's wondering what the hell happened to me."

That caused Bears to raise an eyebrow and ask, "Rambo?"

"My cat. You mean you ferreted out my history and missed the fact that I have a cat? That's an important fact."

"I wasn't the ferreter," said Tommy.

"I keep forgetting. You're the messages and delivery guy. But I bet you back it up with a bang now and then."

Tommy smiled his small smile. He said, "Tell me, why did you name your cat Rambo?"

"Because he's a tough guy. You really interested to hear his story?"

"Sure. It will be a new experience for me. I've never heard a cat story before."

"Couple years ago, I was walking home from the grocery store when I heard World War Three going on in an alley. I checked it out and there was this black and white cat surrounded by three dogs. He'd gotten some good swipes in on the dogs, but he was a bloody mess. Even had a front paw dangling. He looked like he was at the end of his ninth life. Guess I thought he deserved a chance at a tenth one, because I chased off the dogs with a can of beer and--"

"Stop," said Tommy. "You know I'm going to ask. Can of beer?"

Mike wore a half smile.

"Anybody who hears my Rambo rescue story has to ask," he said and went on, "The hounds from hell wouldn't run when I yelled at them and the NYPD frowns on shooting off your gun in the air to chase off dogs. So, I got my six-pack of beer from my grocery bag, shook one up, and gave the hounds a beer shower. They took off never to be seen again."

Tommy grinned. "You are a clever detective. And the wild alley cat let you rescue him?"

"He knew a sucker when he saw one. I wrapped him up in my jacket and took him to a vet a couple blocks away. She told me she wasn't sure if she could save him or not but made me promise I wouldn't dump him back in an alley if she did. Rambo survived, minus a good portion of his left front leg and his tomcat jewels, and now he rules my apartment, and me. End of story."

Tommy Bears nodded in approval. "It's a good story and Rambo's a good name. First chance I get, I'll pass it on to the Panellis to add to your life's history."

"Good. Rambo's an important part of my life. He's a great watch cat."

"I'll bet."

Several minutes later, Bears pulled up in front of the five-story apartment building where Brennen lived.

"I'm curious," said Tommy. "I was on my way here when I was lucky to see you walking. Where the hell were you headed in the rain?"

"I was going after some beer, but I think I need something a lot stronger now." The detective opened the car door to get out. "Thanks for an unforgettable evening. Let's not do it again."

"Good night, Detective Brennen," said Tommy politely.

"Good night, Mr. One Bears," said Detective Brennen.

He shut the door and turned toward his building without bothering to watch the Indian drive off. It was still raining, but Mike was long past caring. He crossed the sidewalk and entered the lighted foyer, pulling out his door key to let himself in. This less than-middle-class building did not have a doorman. His third-floor apartment was next to the stairs and he usually walked up. Tonight the detective took the elevator. Unlocking Number 302, Brennen flipped the light switch and paused, looking at the small living room and the kitchenette off to the left. Through the dark doorway straight ahead was the small bedroom with a tiny bathroom. Mike had lived there for over six years, but it all seemed incredibly tiny now that he had been in the Panelli mansion.

The living room furnishings were second hand, or maybe even third hand, and consisted of a sofa couch and a sofa chair. They didn't match, the former being brown and the latter a drab yellow. An end table and lamp stood beside the sofa and the same stood beside the chair. The three-way, pear-shaped, yellow-colored lamps and lamp shades actually matched. They had been a Christmas gift from Mike's favorite aunt a couple of years earlier. Then there was his thirty-two-inch flat screen television sitting on a small table. In the bedroom a two-drawer bedside table and lamp sat beside the medium sized bed. A brown, slightly marred, five-drawer chest-of-drawers was against the opposite wall. A high counter between the kitchenette and living room, along with a couple of high stools, was his dining area. The air conditioner in one of the two living room windows belonged to the apartment. Whether the ancient machine would work again this coming summer remained to be seen.

"Mansions and Mercedes," muttered Mike. "Fuck 'em."

The seventeen pound, long haired, black and white Rambo, bounded off the sofa chair in the corner of the room to greet his human. The shortened left foreleg didn't curb his movements in the least. He rubbed hard at Mike's wet legs and bumped them with his head. When he looked up at Mike, it was with complete adoration. A melodious meow would have completed the picture, but instead there came a sound much like a squeaky hinge.

"Ah, shit, Rambo. Give me a break," griped the detective. "I've got a bitch of a headache."

Mike's sneakers squished as he walked across the thin, green-brown carpeting into the bedroom. There he took off his gun and holster to lay them and his cell phone on the bedside table next to his watch. It took more effort to pull out his wallet and ID, including his badge, from the rain-soaked pockets. Lastly, he peeled off all his clothes, leaving them in a soggy pile on the floor, and stepped into his bathtub to close the shower curtain. Adjusting the water to mostly hot, he let it beat down on him. It felt wonderful.

While he was toweling off, Mike gave a look at himself in the bathroom mirror. With a shrug, he admitted he wasn't in the category of the handsome model type like Joe Panelli, but the detective thought his looks were okay in a kind of rough and rugged way. At least, he had never had any problem attracting women, and he was positive it wasn't his money they were interested in since he had little. He did lack in the tan department. Mike couldn't remember ever having much of a tan. Beaches and tropical vacations were not part of his life. Some outside basketball and baseball in the summer was the closest he came to it. His muscles, on the other hand, were in good shape if not as pretty as Panelli's. Besides playing on the precinct basketball and baseball teams, he tried to work out at least once or twice a week at a small gym a couple of blocks away. Plus, he did make an effort to keep his beer and pizza intake to a minimum.

"Fuck Joe Panelli," he muttered.

Opening his medicine cabinet, Mike took out his aspirin bottle to tap out two, then three, pills into his hand. He downed them with a swallow of water from his cupped hand.

Rambo was stretched out on the bed when Mike came out of the bathroom. The cat's slanted, cave black eyes, followed his human around the bed to the chest-of-drawers where Mike took out a clean pair of briefs and pulled them on.

"Move over, buddy," he said to the cat.

Rambo didn't move, his expression saying, 'Make me'.

"I have not had a good evening, Rambo, so don't push your luck," Mike warned him. Both Rambo and Mike knew that the warnings never went beyond the verbal stage. "If you knew the mess I've been sucked into, you would be looking for a new home. Hell, in a week I might be dead and bur--"

A light knock came at his door. There was a doorbell, but someone had chosen not to push it.

With a squeak, Rambo leaped from the bed to run to the front door.

Mike frowned. "Who the hell...?"

He glanced over at his phone. It was after midnight. Who would come knocking at this hour? Feeling a tiny bit silly, the detective took his gun from its holster and patted barefoot out to the door where he put an eye to the peep hole. His frown deepened. It was Tommy Bears.

"What? You got more bad news for me, Bears?" said Mike through the door.

"I brought you something," said the Indian.

Mike opened up and Rambo immediately began sniffing at the stranger's feet and legs. Bears held out a brown sack.

"Hated to see your entire night spoiled," he said.

Rambo began rubbing on Tommy's legs and the man looked down at him.

"So this is Rambo," he said. "You're right. This ferocious method of attack makes him a great watch cat. He scares me."

Mike, standing there almost naked and holding a gun, was more than a little mystified. He stared at the sack.

Tommy said, "It's not a bomb, or a bribe. Take it...with my blessings."

Mike took it and then watched the man return to the elevator, which he had locked open.

"See you," said Bears as he flipped the switch and the doors slid shut.

Mike blinked and finally closed the door. Rambo, his hinge squeaking, stretched his neck in an effort to sniff the sack. Mike went to the sofa where he sank down, laying his gun aside. Rambo was instantly in his lap, anxious to examine the package. Pulling the grocery sack open, Mike had to peer around the cat's head to see inside. It was a six-pack of Buds and a bottle of Jack Daniels.

CHAPTER 4

It was pouring rain and someone was chasing him. Several someones. And while he was slipping and sliding in thick mud the someones were not having any trouble at all, so were closing in on him. Then there was a loud buzzing and Mike Brennen sat straight up in bed with a loud grunt! The buzzing came again. The phone. Mike grappled for it in the dark, looking at the time as he picked it up. It was five-eighteen. Ugh.

He punched it and grouched, "Yeah. What?"

"Wake up, Brennen, I want you in my office by six," said a brusque, male voice. "I've already called Thorn."

"Huh? Why? What's happening, Lieutenant?"

"You know about the Calamity Jane Gang," said Lieutenant Carl Grands. "Well, we've just inherited them. They killed somebody this morning. Be here at six."

Grands hung up. Mike fell back onto his pillow, still holding the phone.

"No!" he said desperately.

It had been a short night for him. He'd enjoyed one shot of the Jack Daniels followed by one Bud to keep it company and gone to bed. Where he then lay staring up at the dark ceiling. He didn't have to sleep to have a nightmare. He had a wide awake one with the Panelli-Rezzoro scenario.

The Rezzoros. Not as big as some of the crime families, but they had their fingers in the usual money-making operations -- gambling, prostitution, neighborhood 'insurance' racket, probably drugs. And they were not afraid to use violence. Like killing off police chiefs. Or hookers. It was maybe a year since Brennen had tangled with Nicholas Rezzoro. There had been no doubt that the middle brother of the three Rezzoro siblings had killed the seventeen-year-old street girl. The man, in his mid-thirties, enjoyed being a big shot. Enjoyed throwing around his power, and his weight. That night he had thrown the latter around too hard with the girl, but he had cleaned up after himself. There just wasn't any substantial proof for a conviction. Especially with expensive lawyers waiting with all kinds of tricks to keep the scumbag from seeing any jail time. So Nicholas had walked, leaving Mike not only with the dismal task of telling the girl's parents that she was dead, but also that her killer could not be tagged. The detective had made it a point to keep an eye on Nicky since then, but the slick bastard had continued to stay out of reach.

The head of the Rezzoro clan, Antonio Rezzoro Sr., had recently died. That made Antonio Jr. top man. At forty-one, Junior was the oldest of the brothers. He was sharp, but not as sharp as his father had been, and he had a stubborn streak that kept all of his lawyers hopping when it came to business -- legal or illegal. If Captain Nimmer was a Rezzoro man, it had to have been the Senior Antonio who had put the idea together. Neither Junior nor his brothers would have the patience to wait, a reason why they might be going after Macklin now. There was no telling what kind of shit the family would be able to pull off if Nimmer made it to police chief.

Then there was Sylvester 'Sy' Rezzoro, the youngest brother at twenty-eight. Really a half-brother, his mother being the second wife to the senior Antonio. Sy's main aim in life seemed to be spending money. At least, it was the only thing he was good at, and his half-brothers were quite satisfied to let him do it as long as he stayed out of the Rezzoro businesses.

Brennen's mind had bounced back and forth between the Rezzoros and the Panellis. Who was he, Detective Mike Brennen, to be in the middle of this shit? Against such odds! How the hell was he supposed to figure out which of three lieutenants might be an assassin? If there really was an assassin. If there really was a threat on Police Chief Andrew Macklin's life.

Cripes! No wonder he had a headache.

Lying there in bed, Mike had toyed with the idea of taking it right to Macklin himself. The fifty-two-year-old cop had a cool-headed reputation and seemed to be on top of things. But Mike had absolutely nothing to show the man that would prove this was a credible threat. Somehow, telling him that the Panellis were accusing the Rezzoros of owning the highly regarded Captain Nimmer, and that a highly regarded lieutenant was going to assassinate him, didn't seem like a terribly sane idea.

Mike didn't remember falling asleep, but the exhausting dream and jarring phone proved he had. He sure as hell didn't feel rested. He lifted his phone to look at the time again. 5:22. He groaned again as an annoyed squeak came from under the blanket at the bottom of the bed.

He rolled out onto his feet, stumbling over the wet clothes lying on the floor and into the bathroom, where the first thing he did was take several more aspirin. He decided to skip his morning shower, especially since last night's shower had almost been a morning one. He quickly ran his electric shaver over his face. Combed at the cowlicks in his hair. Brushed his teeth. Pulled on a tan shirt. Climbed into his brown suit. Checked inside his tan sneakers to make sure the duct tape was still in place and put them on. Wearing sneakers were his one rebellious act against suits and shirts and ties. The questionable footwear had long ago become part of his image and he was seldom called on it anymore.

Hanging a brown and yellow striped tie around his neck, Brennen slipped his belt through the pants' loops. Taking his Glock 40 and holster from the top of the dresser, he clipped it to his belt on his right side. Took his handcuffs and hooked them at the back of the belt along with the collapsible baton. He clipped his badge to the front of his belt. From the bedside table he took his ID and wallet to put them in back pockets. He took the holstered thirty-eight and put it on his right ankle. Slipped his watch on his right wrist. His phone went into an inside pocket of his suit jacket.

When he got to the kitchen, Rambo was waiting. Mike could leave without eating if he wanted to, and often did, but the black and white cat always made sure he got his breakfast no matter what time it was. Mike opened a small can of Fancy Feast with Rambo's squeaky hinge giving instructions on how to get it done faster. The detective spooned it into a dish with the threat FEED ME OR ELSE printed on the bottom and added a handful of crunchies on top of it. Tossing the can, he refilled a large bowl with fresh water.

Then, with a, "I'll see you when I see you," he was out the door.

Rambo was too busy eating to wave good-bye.

It had stopped raining, but everything was still wet. The dark streets had not begun to come to life yet. Not in this neighborhood, anyway. Mike walked a block to where his ten-year-old, dark blue Buick was parked. He unlocked it, slid behind the wheel. Hanging from his rearview mirror, a fuzzy Garfield cat grinned at him. Mike ignored him and started the car to pull into the street.

"The Calamity Jane Gang," Mike muttered out loud as he drove. "Fuck."

Of course, the detective had seen the reports on the television news and read about them in the newspapers and on the internet when he bothered with it. He wasn't sure who had given them the cutesy name, but the public had liked it and the robberies had become an interesting conversation piece. The Gang consisted of three girls, who witnesses had agreed were teenagers, and a driver. No one had ever gotten enough of a look at the driver to guess age, or even sex. The young ladies were hitting places in the wee hours of the morning, targeting restaurants that had just closed or all-night businesses. They dressed in fancy-fringed, western outfits. Jackets, gloves, jeans, and boots. They even wore western hats over black, pigtail wigs, colorful bandanas over their noses like the western outlaws of old, and gun belts with six-shooters. So far they had pulled off their jobs and galloped away into the night, escaping any and all posses. It was all sort of unique. Kind of cute. Neat to read about. Except now one of the six-shooters had spit fire and someone was dead.

"The Panellis, the Rezzoros, and now the Calamity Jane Gang," moaned Mike to the world in general.

Garfield grinned.

Several minutes later, Brennen pulled into the precinct parking lot, where he took time to tie his tie. A glance at his watch told him it was 6:04. Not bad. For him.

The building that housed the busy precinct was three stories and a basement. It was old but had been renovated to some extent. Such as better lighting and new paint on the walls and no more leaks when it rained. It did still creak and groan. When entering the front door, there were desks and a couple of offices to the right. Straight ahead was the large desk behind which sat the Duty Sergeant. On duty right now was one Jim Hansen. Jim's mouth dropped open when he saw Mike come in.

"Holy cats!" exclaimed the black man, purposely emphasizing the cats. "Are my eyes deceiving me or is that Detective Mike Brennen coming in the door at this early hour?"

"Not possible," said another officer. "Must be some kind of clone."

"Who'd want to clone Brennen?" asked a third officer.

Several applauded as Mike walked across the room to the stairs.

"Very funny," said the detective. "I'm glad to see you all have such a wonderful sense of humor at this dismal time of day."

He took the steps two at a time to the second floor and entered the detective's squad room. There were seven cubicles with desks and one partitioned office. The latter belonged to Lieutenant Carl Grands and wasn't all that big, so right now it was looking crowded.

The hefty Grands was standing behind his desk. Approaching fifty, his thinning brown hair had hints of gray. Bushy brown eyebrows lined deep brown, intelligent eyes. His expression was looking tighter, his forehead more deeply wrinkled than usual this morning.

Mike Brennen's partner, Sergeant Clark Thorn, was leaning against the glass and wood partition just inside the door. Forty-three, Thorn would go under the description of 'average man'. Average height, average weight, average looks with dark hair that was always neatly trimmed. However, if you paid attention to his sharp, gray eyes, you would know that you were up against a diligent cop.

A third man, rangy and partially bald, Brennen didn't recognize. He did recognize the fourth person, and the detective had to work to compose his face as he joined the group.

"Not bad, Brennen," said Grands with a glance at the wall clock. It could have been an amused quip, but the Lieutenant's gruff tone was void of any amusement.

"Sorry, Lieutenant. I--"

"Never mind. This is Lieutenant Anita Sheffer and Sergeant Don Pragg," Grands introduced. "They're the ones with all the dope on the Calamity Jane Gang."

Mike gave Pragg a nod and, still hoping there wasn't any undue surprise on his face, produced a small smile for Sheffer.

Anita Sheffer returned a polite smile, her bright green eyes giving him a quick survey. The woman was more than a little attractive, her amber hair cut short and stylish. A gray, well fitted pant suit, set off a trim figure. A little shorter than Mike, she had to be in her late thirties.

"Actually, we don't have all that much on the three, charming young ladies," said Sheffer. "They've hit eight times in the last four months and we still have no helpful leads on them. Even video from the places that have surveillance cameras have been of little help. Their disguises work much too well. Putting it bluntly, gentlemen, it's been a bitch of a case. Now, with someone dead, things have turned much worse."

"Who is dead?" asked Mike.

"A pharmacist name of Arlen Evers," supplied Pragg. Wearing a gray suit almost as rumpled as Mike's, the man looked and sounded tired.

"It was an all-night drugstore and, according to the check-out clerk, Evers refused to take the girls seriously. By all accounts, they've got real bad manners and foul mouths, but the man couldn't see past the fact that they were only girls."

Sheffer said, "We are talking about a heavy gun here, in small hands, we can't be sure if she really meant to shoot him or just to fire off a warning shot. The only surveillance camera did not show the shooting, because it was aimed at the front of the store and the check-out counter. But it hardly matters. The girls have killed now and there is no telling how they will react to it. They could be scared enough to call it quits or they could use the killing to take on larger, more profitable targets."

"The outfits they wear aren't run-of-the-mill," Thorn spoke. "Have you been able to trace any part of them?"

"That seemed a good route to us, too, Sergeant," said Sheffer. "But my people and I learned a hard lesson about the popularity of Western clothing. With the mushrooming interest in Country Western music and dancing, this Eastern city of ours has gone West without leaving town."

Pragg took it up. "The clothing the girls wear can be bought at dozens of places, from department stores to specialist stores to say nothing of online sources. The bandanas they use can be purchased all over the place. Most of costume places also have black pigtail wigs, or the ladies could have bought wigs of any color anywhere, died them black, and braided them themselves."

"That leaves the guns and gun belts," said Mike.

Sheffer said, "Most traditional gun belts would be too large for the girls' waists. From what we can see on the videos, they're using regular belts, which can be bought at thousands of places, and then attaching full-sized holsters to them. Holsters easily found online or at most gun shops. We have, of course, checked stores and shops for all of it, but without success. No one remembers any teenage girls buying that sort of thing. We figure it's the driver who is their leader in this and has done all the buying. So far we don't know if that is a woman or a man. And we haven't fared any better with the guns. Until this morning, we weren't absolutely sure they were real. Now we know at least one of them is and we have a bullet to work with if we ever get the gun to compare it to."

"From what we've seen and heard on the videos, and from some of the witnesses, none of these girls seem bright enough to have hatched this idea," said Pragg. "So we're pretty sure it is the driver of the getaway car who is the one who put the bunch together and provided the accessories. Like Lieutenant Sheffer said, we don't know if that is a man or a woman."

"Getaway cars are stolen?" asked Mike.

"Borrowed is more like it," Pragg grunted. "We've only been able to track down three of the cars used. In all cases, the owners didn't even know that their cars had been gone. The way we figure, the Gang takes them, uses them, and then puts them back where they got them. It's the middle of the night, who's gonna notice? Every car was wiped clean. Still, we're pretty confident it is an adult. What kind of kid would do all that?" The sergeant slowly shook his head. "I must be getting old, because these gals are wearing me out."

"We can all sympathize with that," said Grands. To his detectives, "I want you two to bring yourselves up to date on these girls and to interview that clerk witness from this morning while things are still fresh in her mind. The press is going to be hot on this. No more cute little cowgirls. What's at the top of your case load right now'?"

"Jason Reed is a nasty one we'd like to drop on," said Clark Thorn.

Mike Brennen winced inwardly. How could he have forgotten Jason Reed? Shit! He didn't need Reed, too!

"Damn," grunted Grands. "We need to stay on his ass. We do know he's too stupid to leave town. Did you come up with some places to look for him?"

"Yeah. We were going to check them this morning." said Clark.

"You'll have to do that. Maybe we'll have some luck and drop on him right away," said Grands hopefully. To his visitors, "Thanks for coming by, Lieutenant...Sergeant. We'll give you our best and together maybe we can run these girls down before that gun goes off again."

As Mike watched Sheffer leave, he had a lot of trouble picturing her as an assassin.

Clark Thorn went to sit down at his computer.

"I think I'll go ahead and make a list of the victims and witnesses on this Calamity Jane thing," he said. "Then..."

"Good idea, Clark," said Mike. "While you do that, I think I'll run up and see if Lieutenant Corry's here. Maybe he can give us some information."

Clark frowned at him. "Corry's Vice. What the hell could he...?"

"You never know," said Mike and went.

CHAPTER 5

Vice was on the third floor. As he went up the stairs, Mike couldn't decide if he wanted Corry to be there or not. If he was, and Mike talked to him, the detective felt it was his first unsteady step toward accepting the scenario the Panelli's had presented him with. Once started, Mike knew it would be almost impossible for him to back off. Yet, each step could get him deeper and deeper into the mud of his dream and probably into irreversible trouble.

"Fuck."

The five desks in Vice were all deserted at this hour. The door to Corry's small, corner office, was closed, but Mike could see Lieutenant Dick Corry through the glass top. The man was sitting behind his gray, metal desk, staring blankly at the piles of folders and papers in front of him. Right now, his image as a police lieutenant could have used some repair work. The man's brown hair was drab and dirty and much in need of a comb and a trim. His rounded face was on the puffy side and his eyelids drooped. He looked disheveled and cranky and his looks didn't improve any when Brennen walked in.

Mike tried a smile. "Morning, Lieutenant."

The eyelids barely lifted and Corry had no smile. "Brennen, isn't it? You're on the wrong floor."

"I'm here on purpose," said Mike, dumping his own smile. "I picked up on something yesterday that I'd like to pass along to you, as a lieutenant. You know...get your opinion, et cetera. Maybe you can sort of give a listen to your people on the street, in case they hear something that could substantiate it. Guy I got the tip from isn't on my reliable list and when you get a tip from somebody like that, you want to be careful."

Corry leaned back in his chair. He showed no interest and even less enthusiasm.

"What's wrong with your own lieutenant?" he asked dully.

"Hey, nobody's got better connections than you...sir." Mike tried another smile. "I'd just as soon wait and see if you hear anything. I wouldn't want a tidbit like this to get passed around when it's so iffy."

"So what the hell is it?" asked the lieutenant. Still no enthusiasm.

Mike moved closer to the desk to say in a lowered voice, "I was told that somebody is planning a hit on Chief Macklin."

The detective watched Corry's face, especially his eyes, to see if any lights came on or if there was even a brief spark. The man continued to show nothing. His eyelids opened perhaps another eighth of an inch, but the eyes themselves didn't look like they had sparked in a long, long time.

"Bull shit," was Corry's mustered response. "Why?"

Mike cocked an eyebrow. "Why? Maybe because he's a police chief?"

"Somebody would have to be one crazy son of a bitch to kill a police chief. The whole fuckin' police force would come down on the bastard." The lieutenant gave a snort. "Was I you, Brennen, I'd file this bad ass tip away and get back to real police work. With your habit of stirring things up, this kind of shit could screw you good."

Mike frowned. "Stirring things up? Is that the kind of reputation I've got? That kind of hurts my feelings."

Lieutenant Corry finally reacted. Coming forward in his chair, he glared at Brennen across his desk and growled, "I don't have time for you or your fuckin' fairy tales. I've got plenty of other bad asses to keep me busy. Get out of my office."

Mike thought of several tempting responses, but decided that with his reputation, he had better keep them to himself.

"Well, thanks for your time and input, Lieutenant," he said politely. "Have a good day."

He turned and walked out before further damage could be done to the friendly work relationship he had with Lieutenant Corry. As he went down the hallway, Mike wondered if he could count Corry's negative attitude as a positive reaction to the assassination plot. It was a tough call considering that the lieutenant's entire attitude seemed negative.

"I wonder if I've got any aspirin in my desk," he muttered, rubbing at the back of his head and neck.

When he got back to the squad room, the only one there was Detective Harry Muller. Small and wiry, with a pile of black hair, the thirty-eight-year-old man was sorting through some paper work.

"Where'd everybody go, Harry?" asked Mike.

"Everybody who? The place was empty when I got here," said Harry without looking up. Then realized who was asking and did look up. "Brennen? Is that you? Am I late? I thought I was early. Is maybe your clock broke? Or maybe mine?"

Mike, rummaging through his desk drawers, said, "Don't be cute, Harry. They already did that downstairs." He found an empty aspirin bottle. "Shit. You got any aspirin?"

Muller opened a drawer, took out a bottle, and tossed it to him.

"But really, why are you here so early?" persisted Harry.

Brennen popped a couple of the pills into his mouth and swallowed, tossing the bottle back.

"I'm feeling dedicated," he answered. Sitting down at his computer, he called up records and tapped in the name, Tommy One Bears.

"Bull shit," said Harry. "What's the real reason?"

"Try this. Early this morning, that cute, news appealing Calamity Jane Gang killed somebody. The slick, teenage gun-toters are now at the top of mine and Clark's bad guy...bad person...list. Right up there next to Jason Reed."

"Damn!" said Harry.

"Yeah," said Mike. "Damn."

The computer screen flashed and a picture of Tommy One Bears appeared along with his particulars. There weren't many. It was simply noted that Mr. Bears was licensed to carry weapons and was often hired as a bodyguard by the rich and famous. He had, on two known occasions, been involved in shootings, but had been exonerated of any wrongdoing in both cases. Mike wondered how many unknown shootings Mr. Bears might have been involved in. He closed the file without feeling all that much smarter about the half-Sioux, half-Italian who fetched and delivered for the Panellis.

Now he shuffled the papers on his desk around looking for something. When he couldn't find what he wanted, he shifted to his partner's more orderly desk. What he wanted was right on top.

"Look, Harry, tell Clark he can handle the interview with the clerk witness without me. I'll start checking this list of possible hangouts for Jason Reed."

Muller frowned. "Is that a good idea? I mean, looking for him by yourself? The bastard's got a real hate on for cops. And might be hanging out with some bad assholes."

"If I find him, I'll call for backup," Mike assured his fellow detective as he headed out the door. He wanted to get out of there before Thorn or Grands returned from wherever they had gone.

"He's a real bad ass!" Harry emphasized.

"I hear you!"

Brennen made it to his car without running into his partner. His real destination was Lieutenant Polinski and he had absolutely no explanation for such a visit to give Clark and didn't need Clark asking questions he couldn't answer. It would have been some relief for Mike if he could have shared the responsibility of this craziness with his partner, but the Panellis had been right in that respect. Sergeant Clark Thorn fit the dedicated and honest cop description, but there was no way in hell the man would work with the Panellis. Even if Clark sat still long enough to hear the assassination theory, without the Panellis' mysterious source, it was unlikely the sergeant would accept it. Even with the source, he might not accept it. Besides, Clark Thorn was a family man who needed his job. If Mike found himself out on a limb because of this fiasco, he didn't want his partner and friend climbing out there with him.

"What the hell," he muttered. "If I get kicked off the force, I can get a job with the Panellis. Unless I get killed." Mike glanced at the dangling Garfield. "Do you suppose the Panelli family would come to my funeral?"

Garfield grinned back.

CHAPTER 6

Detective Mike Brennen's sometimes overzealous approach to law and order had brought him to Lieutenant Marvin Polinski, Internal Affairs, twice. By the end of the first visit, both men were sure they would never be friends. By the end of the second, they were sure they would both be much happier if they never saw each other again. But, thanks to the Panellis, Brennen was walking in to see the man he didn't want to see again. A man who didn't want to see Brennen again. A man who would probably hold Mike over hot coals if he found out the detective was involved with the Panellis.

It was not a pleasant thought.

Polinski's office was in one of the newer city headquarters buildings. Mike had to show his ID and badge to get in and then faced a fifty-something sharp faced woman in a crisp uniform at the front desk.

"State your business," she told him briskly.

ID still in hand he showed it to her and took note of the name plaque on her desk.

"Morning, Sergeant Helms," he said politely. "I need to see Lieutenant Polinski. Is he…?"

Sergeant Helms checked the identification.

"Oh, yes," Helms nodded and gave him a critical look. "I remember you. You've been here to see the lieutenant a couple of times."

"You remember that?" said Mike, honestly impressed.

"I remember repeaters."

Mike scowled faintly, not so impressed.

"It was only twice and neither one of them was a big deal."

"Three times now," stated Helms.

"This time it's my idea," said Mike defensively.

"Better learn to keep your nose clean, Detective," the sergeant said pointedly. Then, returning the ID, waved him on. "Go ahead. He's probably expecting you."

Now Mike was pissed. "He's not expecting me. I'm here on a special case that--"

But Sergeant Helms had moved on and was already busy with someone else.

His scowl deepening, Mike turned away, muttering, "How did I get this reputation? Hell, the Panellis think I'm an honest, dedicated cop, and the cops think I'm a troublemaker with a dirty nose."

When he reached the Internal Affairs Department, Mike found Polinski's office door open, but no Polinski. It was a real office, not a partitioned one like Grands', and roomier. The wood desk was neat and tidy, a computer and keyboard sitting on it. The in-and-out files were on the right hand corner, their few contents neat and tidy. A small stack of different colored folders was sitting neatly to one side. A pencil holder next to the computer held pencils and pens and one red felt pen, the latter undoubtedly for putting red checks behind questionable officer's names. In a corner of the room, at one side of the desk, was a gray metal, four-drawer file cabinet. There were two cushioned visitor's chairs. There wasn't a speck of dust visible anywhere. The whole room was intimidating even when Polinski wasn't in it.

Mike turned back into the hallway and saw Lieutenant Polinski coming toward him.

Slender almost to the point of being skinny, the six-foot-three, forty-five-year-old man, had bony facial features that reminded Brennen of Ichabod Crane of Sleepy Hollow fame. Polinski's piercing, coal-black eyes, were made for boring into a person, making the guilty squirm. At times, even the innocent. The lieutenant's dark hair was short, with every hair in place. His pink face was clean-shaven. His brown, three-piece suit was impeccable, and his pale yellow and tan tie carefully knotted. His shiny brown shoes matched his suit. It could easily be said that

Lieutenant Polinski was the direct opposite of Lieutenant Dick Corry. Mike found himself equally repelled by both men, which, for a brief moment, made him question his own status. On seeing Brennen, Polinski's expression turned sour. Along with the numerous other reasons he didn't like the detective was the annoying fact that he had not been able to make him visibly squirm.

"I wasn't aware that you had instigated another problem, Detective," said the lieutenant curtly. "Or have you decided to resign and save this department, and the New York City Police Force in general, further grief?"

"Glad to see you're having a good morning, Lieutenant," said Mike and immediately wondered why he continued to make remarks that were not in his best interest.

Polinski glowered at him and brushed past to enter his office, giving his door a hard push to close it. Mike stopped it and followed the man into the room.

"All fun aside, Lieutenant," he said. "I really do have something you should hear."

"Get out of my office, Brennen. I don't enjoy your company."

"It concerns Chief Macklin."

Polinski sat down in the chair behind the desk, his eyes narrowing in on Mike. He said, "Ten seconds."

"Right." Mike closed the office door.

"Seven seconds."

"I picked up a tip you might find interesting. Unless maybe you've already heard it."

"Four seconds."

"Someone, possibly a cop, is planning to hit Chief Macklin."

The lieutenant's narrowed eyes opened.

"That's bullshit," he said flatly.

At least he didn't say Mike's time was up.

Mike said, "I guess that means you haven't heard anything about it."

"Where would any street snitch pick up an insane story like that?"

Mike couldn't resist pointing out, "Maybe it wasn't a street snitch."

"Really? Who else would talk to you?" quipped Polinski.

"You'd be surprised, Lieutenant," allowed Mike with a thin smile.

An understatement.

"Would I? Then surprise me and bring whoever it is in here. They can tell me this piece of absurd information in person."

"You know I have to guard a source...sir," said Mike politely. "And why is it so absurd? Lots of people might want to kill a police chief."

"Don't use that wise-ass attitude with me, Brennen," warned the lieutenant. "If it were some kind of personal revenge, I'm sure the chief would already be aware of it. Other than that, there's very little point in killing a police chief when someone else would immediately take his place. Hell, I wouldn't put it past you to think up a crazy story like this just to piss me off."

Mike bristled. He was not using a wise-ass attitude. Yet.

"I resent that," he said. "The attitude thing and the idea that I would make up a story like this. You want to ignore it, fine. I've done my duty in reporting it."

Mike should have stopped there and he knew he should have stopped there. But, if he was going to be accused of having a wise-ass attitude, what the hell.

With the smallest twist of a smile, the detective said, "And we both know I could get you pissed off without thinking up some crazy ass story."

Mike held his breath and waited for the ax to fall. Why did he say these fucking dumb things? He grinned inwardly.

Polinski glared at him silently with those piercing, black, eyes.

Mike met them without wavering. When the lieutenant spoke, he was remarkably calm.

"Bring me your source, Detective Brennen, and maybe I'll listen. Otherwise, I don't want to see your face again. Ever."

Mike sucked in a deep breath and said, "I'll see what my source says."

"You do that. And keep your mouth shut," ordered Polinski firmly. "We don't want any crazy ass rumors getting started. Do we."

"No, sir."

"Leave."

"Yes, sir."

Mike turned, opened the door, and started out.

"Detective Brennen."

Mike stopped, turning his head to look back over his shoulder.

"In your past visits here, I believe I told you to lose the sneakers," the IAD officer reminded him. "They are not part of a detective's dress code when on regular duty."

"Yes, sir," said Mike.

They both knew that the detective would not lose his favorite footwear.

By the time Mike got back to his car, his head felt like there was a juiced up drummer inside of it. Getting in, he leaned his forehead on the steering wheel and took another deep breath.

"Why me?" he exhaled.

No one, including Garfield, answered him, and the headache didn't go away.

CHAPTER 7

After a couple of minutes, Mike started the car and aimed it toward Lieutenant Anita Sheffer's precinct. When he got there, he found a newer, more modern building, four floors of glass and steel. Inside the front door, straight ahead, the uniformed Duty Sergeant sat behind a large, gray metal desk, which supported a computer and three, small, surveillance screens. To the left, two more uniformed officers, one woman and one man, sat at two more, smaller gray metal desks with computers. There were offices behind the desks, with busy occupants visible through a couple of open doorways. It was all a little too efficient looking for Brennen's taste.

The detective presented his ID to the sergeant, again checking the name on the desk plaque. Sergeant Benjamin Abbott.

"Morning, Sergeant Abbott," he said.

Sporting a shiny, bald head and bushy blond eyebrows with a matching bushy blond mustache under a wide nose, the sergeant took Mike's ID from his hand to scrutinize it with dedicated thoroughness.

"What is it you need here, Detective?" he asked brusquely, holding onto the ID.

"I'd like to see Lieutenant Sheffer."

"Do you have an appointment?"

"Appointment? Can't I just pop in for a quick question? We're working on--"

"She's a busy lady. She likes appointments."

Mike tried again, "We're working on the same case. The Calamity Jane thing. I'm from Homi--"

"That case has been going on for several months. I haven't seen you here before."

Mike resisted the temptation to use his wise-ass attitude and just said, "I'm Homicide. The Gang killed someone this--"

"Oh, yeah. I heard that. Well, just a minute."

Abbott took up his phone and punched three buttons.

"Lieutenant, there's a Detective Bremmen here who says he's on the Calamity Jane case. Wants to see you."

The man had scrutinized his ID but still couldn't read. Mike reached out to tap it, saying, "The name is Brennen...n's...not m's."

The sergeant scowled back at him, but said into the phone, "That's Brennen." Then, "Okay, Lieutenant."

He hung up and grudgingly told Mike, "Second floor. Office is straight ahead from the stairs."

Mike took back his ID and, losing out to temptation, said, "Thank you so much, Sergeant Babbott."

Sergeant Abbott glared and did not say, 'You're welcome'. Mike sadly noted that efficiency seemed to take the friendliness out of the job.

Up the stairs and straight ahead was a roomy, half panel, half glass, enclosed office. There were no outside windows, but on the one solid panel wall, there was a handsomely framed print of a bright, summery, meadow scene. There was a wooden desk with a computer, and a four-drawer wooden file cabinet. Also a wooden coat rack. And carpeting. Wow.

Standing up behind her desk waiting for him was Lieutenant Sheffer.

"I didn't expect to see you again so soon, Detective Brennen," she smiled and actually offered her hand.

Wow. No way could this woman be an assassin. He took the hand and received a firm handshake.

"Please, sit down," she said.

Triple wow. No one ever asked him to sit down. Not lately, anyway.

"Thank you." Mike and sat in one of the two cushioned chairs. He said, "Right off, Lieutenant, I'm not here about the Calamity Jane Gang."

"Oh?"

35

"I picked up a piece of info yesterday that troubled me all night," said Mike. Where he hadn't necessarily cared about how honest he was with Polinski and Corry, Mike now found himself a little uneasy giving Sheffer the half-assed truth. "It seems kind of far-fetched to me, but I decided that maybe I should mention it to an officer. To see if they might want to check further on it."

Sheffer arched an eyebrow. "Why didn't you take it to Lieutenant Grands?"

"I was planning to, but after meeting you this morning, I thought you might be a little more receptive." He smiled crookedly. "My lieutenant sometimes gets kind of, well, hard-nosed when it comes to me."

The woman gave him a light smile. "I have heard that, on occasion, you can get...shall we say...carried away, on the job."

"Really?" Mike was taken back. His reputation really was going to hell. "You heard th--"

Sheffer waved a hand at him and gave a laugh.

"Don't get stirred up, Mike," she told him. "When I heard you and Sergeant Thorn would be coming into the Calamity case, I admit I took a minute to find out what kind of cops you are. In your case, there may be a couple of little red checks behind your name, but I also discovered that you're a damn good cop. Both you and Thorn. As far as your reputation goes, as I see it, you simply need to show more restraint at times."

Mike had to smile, too. "That's not exactly how Lieutenant Grands puts it."

"Maybe not, but you notice he still keeps you around," said Sheffer. "So, you've roused my curiosity. What is this troublesome bit of information?"

Without preamble, again watching for reaction, Mike told her, "I heard from one of my sources that there might be an attempt on Police Chief Macklin's life."

Lieutenant Sheffer lit up more than Corry and Polinski together. Which, admittedly, wouldn't have taken much. Both of the woman's eyebrows went up as her eyes widened slightly.

"Whew," she breathed. "That's a dandy bit of info, Detective. I can see why you wouldn't want to spread that around. Just who was your source? It seems unlikely that a street snitch could get wind of anything like that. Are you sure it's not someone only looking for a handout?"

Mike gave a shake of his head, saying, "I'm sure it's nothing like that, but you can see why I was reluctant to say anything. I'm not quite sure how to go about corroborating it. Or if Chief Macklin should be told."

"I agree that corroborating it is most important. The Chief is a busy man and there should be substantial proof before interrupting his schedule."

She was thoughtful for several moments and Mike studied her, feeling uncomfortable. Damn it, he wasn't a goddamned psychic! All he could decipher from her expression was concern. Whether it was concern for the police chief or because Mike Brennen knew about the Rezzoro's secret plan, he had no way of telling.

Finally, the lieutenant said, "I think, Detective Brennen, that you should let me look into this for now. I do have more avenues to pursue than you do, with probably a better chance of finding something out. If, indeed, there is something to be found. It would help move my inquiries along, however, if I knew where you heard it."

"I wish I could be more specific, Lieutenant," said Mike, "but you know how it is when it comes to sources."

Anita Sheffer gave a shrug. "I understand. I've certainly been in that situation myself. You were correct to bring it to an officer. If I find anything solid, I will take it upon myself to warn Chief Macklin immediately. Of course, I will also ensure that you receive credit for originally bringing this to our attention."

She stood up and again offered her hand. Mike quickly got to his feet and accepted it. The woman's smile seemed genuine, her handshake still firm.

"Thank you, Detective Brennen. You did the smart thing. It increases my confidence that we'll soon catch up to those gun-slinging, teenage girls."

As he left the building, Mike found himself hoping that she really would find out what was going on and who was behind it. Then it would be up to the lieutenant to handle it and he would be free of the mess. As far as Sheffer being a suspect assassin, the Panellis could stuff it!

As he climbed into his car, Mike felt the throb at the back of his head let up a little.

CHAPTER 8

As Brennen pulled into traffic, he spotted a worse headache. The gray Mercedes Benz was parked, illegally, across from the police precinct. It did a U-turn, illegally, to fall in two cars behind him.

"Fuck," grumped Mike. "Maybe if I ignore him, he'll go away."

He didn't go away. Bears worked his way past the two cars and when he was right behind Mike, he tooted his horn. If you want to call the sophisticated sound of a Mercedes a toot. So Mike found a suitable side street to turn into and pulled over. The Mercedes pulled over behind him. Mike did not get out. Bears could damn well come to him. Except it was Joe Panelli, who got out of the passenger's side of the Mercedes to come up to his car. Mike reluctantly unlocked his passenger door and Panelli got in, closing it. Wearing stone washed jeans, a tan leather jacket over a blue polo shirt, and Nikes, the man was disgustingly cool and handsome.

"Let's drive while we talk," said Joe. It didn't exactly come out sounding like a suggestion.

"Yes, sir," said Mike with a particularly sour note, and drove.

The Mercedes continued to follow.

"How am I supposed to maintain my reputation as an honest, dedicated cop, when a member of the Panelli family is sitting in my car? After waiting for me right in front of a goddamned police precinct, no less."

"The Panelli family is well thought of in high society these days," said Joe, his tone somewhat sharp. "And it could work both ways. For someone of my stature and prominence to be seen in the company of a two-bit cop could damage my reputation as well."

"Fuck you," said Mike. "This buddy system is your idea."

The detective pulled back into heavy traffic on a main street.

"The buddy system is my father's idea," corrected Joe. His eyes fastened onto the grinning Garfield. "I bet the bad guys are impressed when they see that."

"I don't care if they are or not. I like Garfield. He's my kind of guy." Then, "Do you even know who Garfield is, or are the society pages too far from the comics for you to be acquainted?"

A sly smile touched Joe's mouth. "I did hear about your Rambo cat. I admit to being impressed with your solution to scare off the dogs."

"I'm glad I could impress you."

"Impress me some more. Tell me what you've learned? You've talked to all three of our suspects and…"

"You've been following me all morning? And they're your suspects, not mine."

"Don't give me that shit. We told you we'd be around. Besides, you don't really expect me to believe that the great Detective Brennen didn't see us tailing him?"

The great detective shrugged. "I have a lot on my mind."

"Un-huh. And I suppose, if it will ease your conscience, we can call the suspects, the Panelli suspects."

"Thank you. That does ease my conscience."

Unexpectedly, Mike zipped around two cars with only inches to spare. Joe almost gasped but caught himself. Mike's phone buzzed and he ignored it.

"So tell me, did you pick up on anything from the Panelli suspects?" pressed Joe, watching with growing apprehension as Brennen attacked the traffic. "What approach did you use? I trust you didn't come right out and ask them."

Mike sniffed. "Maybe I should have. Better yet, I should have told them that the Panellis were pointing fingers at them. That would have been more fun for me."

He dodged into the left lane, into a space that hardly looked big enough to be dodged into. Joe fastened his seat belt.

"If you get me killed in a traffic accident, we're both going to be embarrassed as hell," griped Panelli. "Are you going to tell me what went down or not?"

"My...approach...was to tell them that I'd picked up a tip about a possible hit on Macklin and decided it was important to report it to an officer."

"Sounds like a workable approach," allowed Joe. He winced as they almost piled into the back of a bus.

"Gee, I'm glad you approve," said Mike. He continued to ignore Panelli's concerns over his driving.

"Come on, Brennen! I feel like I'm pulling teeth here. How did they respond? What did they say?"

"Get off my ass! None of them surrendered, if that's what you want to know! Hell, Corry and Polinski didn't act like they gave a shit one way or the other."

Mike gunned it around the bus. He paid no attention to Panelli's grimace, nor did he look to see if Tommy Bears and his gray Mercedes were staying with him.

"Lieutenant Sheffer was at least professional about it. She even shook my hand. Twice. If it's her, she's a very nice potential assassin. There is an unexpected wrinkle with her. As of this morning, I'm working a case with her."

"Oh?"

"You must have read or heard about those cute teenage girls that were dubbed the Calamity Jane Gang? Well, they're not so cute anymore. They killed a pharmacist early this morning. My lieutenant called me at 5 a.m. with that good news...on top of the good news you laid on me. Then there's that scuzz ball, Jason Reed, who bludgeoned a guy to death last--"

"Brennen, stick to the Macklin case. Okay."

Mike snapped him a dirty look. When he looked back at the street, a yellow light had turned red. He zipped on through.

"Okay, for what it's worth, according to Dickie Corry the tip is bullshit and I'm crazy to believe anybody would shoot a police chief. If I had to pick one, though, I'd pick him. He looked like dog shit in a mud puddle.

"Polinski also suggested it was bullshit, but then, he wouldn't believe I was fucked if I was the one who told him. He said there was little point in killing a police chief when somebody else would step right in. That remark seemed kind of suggestive to me, but he said it with a straight face. Of course, he says everything with a straight face. He told me to bring him my source, in person, and maybe he'd listen. Otherwise he's not interested in ever seeing me again. So, do you want to set up the meeting or should I?"

"If you don't mind, could we do this without the wise-ass humor?"

"Sorry, but it's a package deal. You want the help of the two-bit cop, you get the wise-ass humor along with it," the detective told him gruffly. "Anyway, by the time I left Polinski, he was probably thinking about assassinating me. If you're interested in my opinion, though, I can't believe that man would ever dirty himself by killing a cop. Other than me. Sure as hell not the police chief. It goes against everything the man stands for. And if he's a worried family man, it doesn't show on the job."

Mike gave Joe a glance.

"You know, when it comes down to it, I'm still not sure how much of this scenario I even believe. But, neither can I come up with a logical reason why you'd want to make up this kind of story. Or why you'd bother coming to a two-bit cop like me. Are you sure this isn't something the Rezzoros might have leaked to you on purpose? To maybe get your family in deep shit with the cops or something?"

Impatiently, Joe told him, "If that was what they were after, there are a lot easier ways to get it done. This is something they don't want anyone to know about. Killing off the police chief is secondary. Putting their man into the vacated position is what's most important to them. They can't let Nimmer get pinned as a Rezzoro puppet, because that would be the end of it, whether Macklin was alive or dead."

Another light changed red. This time Brennen stopped and Panelli was visibly relieved. The phone buzzed again and again Mike ignored it.

"Why shouldn't I tell the chief that the captain is a Rezzoro puppet?"

"With the reputation Nimmer has built up with the help of his sponsoring family? That's not much of an option either. Our best bet is finding out who the assassin is and--"

"...and what?" said Mike. The light turned green and he was off. "Who do we turn the dirty lieutenant in to?"

"We'll cross that bridge when we get to it."

"We better have some idea who that's going to be. Especially since I'm the one who's supposed to finger whoever."

"Try to look at the bright side, Detective. There is a chance you could end up a hero on this. Picture in the paper. Name on the evening news."

"A funeral because of a Rezzoro bullet in the head. Or worse, the NYPD would take away my sneakers because of my new image."

"Huh?" Panelli looked down at Mike's feet. "Sneakers on the job?"

"I wear the suit and the tie."

"Yeah. I've noticed what a sharp dresser you are."

"...but I reserve the right to wear my choice of foot gear. They are much better for chasing suspects. Besides, I do have more than one color so as to better match my suits."

"I don't even want to know how many suits and colors that might be," said Joe.

"None of your business, anyway. I can--"

Mike's phone buzzed. One hand on the steering wheel, Mike pulled it out. "Hey, Clark."

"Well, well, I'm glad you finally found time to answer me." Sergeant Thorn's voice was annoyed. "Would it be too much for me to ask where the hell you are and what the hell you are doing?"

"Sorry, Clark. I had a couple of important errands to run and they took longer than I thought they would. Where you at? I'll come pick you up."

"I'm still at the precinct where I've been boning up on the Calamity Janes. You may remember from our little meeting this morning, with two lieutenants, that this is one of our cases now and--"

"Clark, I--"

"And then I understand from Harry that you took the possible addresses on Reed and ran off like the Lone Ranger. Did you--?"

"I'll be there in ten minutes, Clark." Mike ended the call and dropped the phone in a pocket. To Joe, "If you're through interrogating me for the moment, I've got real police work to do."

"You won't forget to keep track of our...of the Panelli suspects?"

"Me keeping track of three lieutenants. Piece of cake. And when one of them breaks down under my intense surveillance and confesses that he/she is an assassin, I'll give the Panellis a ring," said Mike, looking for a place to pull over. "Oh, by the way, I punched up your Mr. Bears on the computer this morning. Just curious. Wanted to see if the law had ever been interested in him and in what he does. Whatever it is that he does. Didn't find much. He seems to know the right people, some even more important than the Panellis, but he's never been in any trouble. At least, none that hasn't been resolved. He is a mysterious man that keeps his mouth shut."

"Like we told you last night," said Joe. "He's trustworthy and very selective about the jobs he takes. He'll be glad to know you cared enough to look him up."

Mike spotted a fire hydrant and quickly pulled in beside it. "If I may suggest, the next time you want to talk, Let's do it in a place with some privacy. My friendly IAD officer would like nothing better than to catch me in my car having a secret get-together with a Panelli family member. My sneakers would be out the door with my feet still in them."

"You do have my promise we won't meet in your car again," said Joe as he gratefully unbuckled and opened the door. "And as a Panelli family member, I am a concerned citizen trying to save the city from a dangerous possibility."

"Right."

Panelli got out but then leaned down to look in at Mike as he said, "The way you drive, Brennen, you're going to get a ticket someday."

Mike gave him a smirk. "Right."

Joe shut the door and stepped back onto the curb. Mike pulled away and Tommy Bears' Mercedes pulled in almost immediately to pick up Panelli. Mr. Bears obviously had not been left behind by the detective's erratic driving. As Mike continued down the street, he kept glancing into his rearview mirror to see if the Mercedes continued to follow him.

He couldn't tell and that bugged him.

CHAPTER 9

Sergeant Thorn was waiting in the precinct parking lot, leaning against the back of his car, arms folded across his chest. He had the indignant look of a father displeased with his child. Mike Brennen put on a friendly smile as he stopped beside his partner.

"Hi, Clark. Hop in."

"No. We'll use my car," stated Clark firmly, leaving no room for argument as he walked around to get in behind the wheel.

Mike muttered under his breath but gave Clark room to back out so he could pull in. In a moment he slid into the passenger seat.

They didn't move.

"What?" asked Mike.

"Don't you want to bring your vest along?"

"No. Don't nag, Clark. Let's go."

They still didn't move.

"Now what?" griped Mike.

"Seat belt," said Clark.

"You know, Sergeant Thorn, sometimes you wear the hell out of me," said Mike wearily, putting on his seat belt.

"I know," said Clark with a thin smile. "After four years, though, one would think you'd learn." He pulled out into traffic. "So, Detective Lone Wolf, you must know that running off on your own to hunt a bad ass like Reed isn't a very smart move. How many of the addresses did you scout?"

"I thought I was the Lone Ranger?"

"Note, the definitive word here is lone. How many of the addres...?"

"None."

"None? None of them?"

"Note, the definitive word here is none."

"What the hell have you been doing?"

"I told you, Clark. I had a couple of personal errands to run and--"

"Personal errands?"

"Personal...and it took me longer than I figured it would. Okay? So, did you interview the clerk witness from the drugstore?"

"No."

"No? Why not? You didn't need me to--"

"I spent my time reading up on the Calamity Jane Gang. I thought one of us ought to since we're expected to catch the little dears."

"You're really pissed at me, aren't you."

"I was hoping you'd notice."

"Let's go interview the witness," said Mike, "and, since you went to all that trouble to bone up on the Calamity Janes, you might as well fill me in."

It seemed there wasn't a whole lot more than what Sheffer and Pragg had already given them. Witnesses and surveillance cameras together had given them very little to go on. It was positive they were girls. It was not so positive how old they were, with guesses ranging from thirteen to twenty. The physical descriptions made them not real tall or real short. Nor were they real heavy or real skinny. It was hard to tell under all that Western fringe. Usually only one of them spoke and then just a few words like, 'Stick 'em up!' and 'Put the money in the bag!'. There was no telling if it was the same one who had the speaking role each time. At any rate, no one could recall anything unusual about the voice, such as an accent. They wore fancy gloves with fringe, so that's why we never found fingerprints. No one had recalled seeing an earlier female customer in the store who might have come in to check the layout, though that was almost certainly likely. The girls had never called each other by name. The revolvers were handled by one or two girls. Sometimes two would gather up the loot, while the third kept a gun on whoever was in the store. Until now the best descriptions of the weapons were simply six-guns like in Western movies or television. The bullet recovered from the unlucky Mr. Evers proved that particular gun fit the description. The witnesses said that the girls needed both hands to hang onto the heavy weapons, but they held them steady, arms straight out. Videos from the scenes confirmed that. The third girl had a gun in her holster, but at least two witnesses had the feeling that her gun wasn't real. The girls carried one or two tote bags for collecting the money first and foremost, but they had also been known to take jewelry and cosmetics and cassettes and magazines and cigarettes, and almost always candy. Surprisingly, they had never taken any kind of drugs.

Putting it all together, it offered little that hadn't already been checked and rechecked.

"Well, they have a sweet tooth," noted Mike.

"Right. That narrows down the list of suspects," said Clark.

"We could check dental records."

Clark did not respond to that suggestion.

"What about the jewelry?" asked Mike.

"Costume. Nothing that couldn't be bought in a thousand places and worth nothing to a fence."

Mike sighed. "I can already tell this one is going to be fun."

The drugstore of the latest hit was in a neighborhood of mostly residential apartment houses and buildings. The witness, Cathy Opel, lived on the first floor of one of them, a two-story eight apartment building. According to Pragg's notes, she lived with an Ed Dunson. A barefoot Mr. Dunson answered the door. In his early twenties, with tired eyes and beard stubble, he was in jeans and a Harley-Davidson tee-shirt.

"Don't tell me," he said wearily. "More cops."

"Sergeant Thorn and Detective Brennen, Homicide," said Clark as they showed their ID. "We're sorry to bother Miss Opel, but we're new to the case and would like to hear first-hand her account of what happened."

"It's okay, Eddie," came a female voice from inside. "If it will help catch those terrible girls."

Eddie stood back and waved them into a small, neatly kept living room. The only furniture was a matching green sofa and chair, a coffee table holding a couple of magazines and a newspaper. A forty-inch television hung on a wall.

"Maybe keep it short," Ed said as he closed the door, "She hasn't slept since it happened and--"

"Who can sleep?" remarked the twenty-two-year-old woman.

Her black hair short and curly, Cathy Opel was on the sofa, her legs curled up under her. She was in jeans, with a long-sleeved white blouse. Looking more tired than Dunson, she wore no makeup, and her eyes and nose were red from crying. There was a box of tissues next to her. The young woman looked sadly at the detectives.

"You know, I thought I was dead, too," she said. "It makes me feel kind of guilty...that I was scared for myself when it was poor Arlen who got killed."

"There's no reason you should feel that way, Ms. Opel," said Clark.

"I keep telling her that," said Dunson, sitting down next to her.

"If Arlen had just given them the money, I think it would have been okay," Cathy Opel went on. "I mean, we've all been reading about the Calamity Jane Gang. They'd never hurt anybody. But Arlen got stubborn. He hollered at them, 'I've never been robbed in my life and sure as hell no teenage girls are going to do it now.' He shouldn't have done that. He's...he was almost fifty." She made it sound like fifty was almost a hundred. "And then that awful girl shot him. Just like that. She shot him."

"Could you tell, Ms. Opel, if the girl purposely shot him or if it might have been accidental? Like she didn't mean to pull the trigger? Or maybe her aim...?" asked Clark.

"It didn't look accidental to me," stated Opel. "She had that gun aimed right at him and she pulled the trigger. Bang. Arlen was dead."

"Do you remember how the other girls reacted?" from Mike. "Were they surprised? Maybe scared when she did it?"

The woman wiped at her eyes and blew her nose. "I'm sorry. I just didn't notice anything after the shooting. I'm afraid I went to pieces. I started screaming and covered my eyes. Like I told you, I thought I was dead, too."

"Nobody shouted a name in alarm?" pressed Clark.

"I was screaming. If they did, I didn't hear it."

"Did they take the time to finish what they were doing?" said Mike. "Collecting money and other things?"

"One of them had already gotten what money there was in my cash register. I didn't know until after it was over that they emptied out Arlen's, too."

"But you didn't notice if they took anything else?" said Clark.

"They...the cops...made me look around, but I'm pretty sure they didn't take anything else. When they'd gone...the girls...I ran right to Arlen and then called 911. I think poor Arlen was already dead, though. There was so much blood. God! It was awful! I don't think I can ever go back to work there."

"You didn't see where they ran? If they got in a car?" Mike asked.

"I still had my eyes covered! I didn't see anything more at all."

"And there's nothing that sticks in your mind about the girls? Their appearance or the way they walked or talked or--" pursued the detective with little hope.

"Nothing!"

"Come on! Let her alone!" griped Dunson, wrapping an arm around her. "She's done her best for all you cops."

"Okay, Ms. Opel. We understand it's difficult," said Clark. He took a business card from an inside pocket and laid it on the coffee table. "If you do remember anything…anything at all, please give us a call."

Cathy Opel sniffed and wiped her nose again. "Yes. Of course I will."

Getting back into the car, Clark said, "Sheffer was right. This is a bitch of a case."

"It's bitches we're after," noted Mike. "Dangerous bitches. I don't know if they shot this guy on purpose or not, but it's done and I'm betting they'll be back and maybe meaner than before. I'd sure like to know who's driving the car."

"I don't think it will get any better with the other witnesses. If Sheffer and her people couldn't shake anything loose, there probably isn't anything there to come loose. We're probably going to have to wait until they hit again and hope that somebody sees something helpful, and that nobody else gets shot," said Clark. "Right now, I think we better devote some of our time to Reed. Before he kills again. At least we know who he is and have some places to look for him. Several of them since you didn't get around to--"

"I don't want to hear it, Clark."

If the Calamity Jane girls were bitches, Jason Reed was definitely a bastard. Caucasian, Reed was a husky, big-boned guy, with a personality best described as mean and nasty. He had beaten, trampled, and shot his way through thirty-six years of life. He had been in and out of prison twice. His friends were friends only because they didn't want to be his enemies. His enemies wished mightily that they weren't his enemies. Everyone else tried to stay out of his way.

This past weekend, Reed and one of his buddies had robbed a liquor store where the sixty-year-old male clerk had kept a baseball bat handy for threatening would-be thieves. The idea backfired on him when Reed used it to club the poor guy to death. Fortunately for the police, when the pair had run from the store, they had been seen by two witnesses who later had no trouble picking them out from mug books. One had quickly been apprehended. Reed was still out there and on Sergeant Thorn and Detective Brennen's priority list.

The four addresses on the list of Reed's possible hangouts were three bars and a girlfriend's place.

"Girlfriend? What kind of female would want to be his girlfriend?" wondered Clark.

"One that wanted to stay alive," suggested Mike.

Their first stop was at the nearest of the bars. It was small and dark and it stank. It looked like it hadn't been cleaned since the day it opened, possibly a hundred years ago. At the moment, there was only one customer, who was snoring in one of the two back booths. The bartender was a woman of questionable age who also stank and looked like she hadn't been cleaned since...who knows. She had her nose buried in a paperback Romance novel and only grudgingly took time to look at the mug shot.

"Ain't never seen 'im," she swore.

"Never?" said Clark.

"Never," she repeated gruffly and went back to her book.

Mike approached the customer but then didn't want to touch him for fear of what diseases he might catch. He decided, "He probably wouldn't even recognize a picture of himself if I showed it to hm."

Returning to the car, Clark said, "Isn't the girlfriend's address on this same street?"

"Couple blocks down," said Mike.

"So Let's try there next."

The sergeant started his car and pulled out. Along the street, eyes followed them, cold, suspicious, some even challenging.

"Your car might as well have police painted on it, Clark," said Mike.

"We are police," stated Clark. "Remind me about this girlfriend."

Mike looked at the list and reminded him, "Lana Wayne. Middle twenties, Caucasian, brown and brown. Drugs and prostitution. It should be the building on the corner. We don't really believe he's stupid enough to be there, do we?"

"It's unlikely, but we get paid to make sure."

It was a street of old, brick, tenement buildings that were crumbling from the inside out. Most of them should have been condemned, but then, where would all the residents go?

They parked behind a battered Plymouth, the color of which was no longer apparent. Clark popped the car's trunk and got out to go around to it. He took two pair of latex gloves from a box, handing one of them to Mike.

Mike scowled. "I've got a pair. And what makes you think we're going to need them?"

"It's called being prepared and I'm glad to hear you remembered some for a change." He took up his vest. "And I don't know why you didn't bring your vest."

"Maybe I want to go out in a blaze of gunfire, Clark," said Mike patiently.

His and Clark's idea of when to wear bullet proof vests often differed. Of course, Mike didn't have a wife and kids. And, hell, maybe he did want to go out in a blaze of gunfire.

He glanced up and down the street while Clark got into the vest. They were cops, and people in this type of neighborhood always seemed to be watching. Still, it didn't look like anyone was particularly interested in what they were up to this time. When Clark was ready, they went up the five crumbling cement steps and inside.

No elevators in these old five and six story buildings, so they climbed the stairs. The bouquet of both human and animal waste, and decaying garbage, invaded their noses.

"Don't you love the homey smell of these places?" remarked Mike with disgust.

"Barns definitely smell better," said Clark.

Mike was mildly surprised. "When were you ever in a barn?"

"When I was a kid. My grandparents' place. I hated it. I'm a city boy through and through. But I remember the barn smelled better than this."

"You never told me that your grandparents had a farm. They still got it? I'd love to visit a farm."

"They're dead."

"Shucks."

They left the stairwell on the fourth floor. All was quiet. No televisions or radios or stereos playing. No muffled human voices. Mike put an ear to Apartment 4A but shook his head to Clark. No sounds in there either. They pulled their weapons to stand to either side of the door. Clark reached out and knocked.

Silence.

Clark knocked again and called, "This is the police, Ms. Wayne. Open the door, please."

His politeness did not get them an invitation to enter. Nor did anyone yell at them to go away or shoot through the door. Just silence.

Clark reached carefully to try the door knob. It did not resist. He turned it so it was unlatched, then gave his partner a nod before giving it a shove. It opened with a slight squeak and stopped. There was no response.

"Ms. Wayne?" called Clark.

Nothing. Another nod and the two men went in, guns up.

"Police!" announced Thorn as he went right and Brennen went left.

They were in a medium-sized living room with a small kitchen on the right. No one was there. The only other door was on the left. Probably the bedroom, it stood open. Clark covered it while Mike slid along the wall and took a quick look, and then went in.

Lana Wayne was on the bed, sleeping the forever sleep. She looked like someone had kicked the life out of her. Probably someone named Jason Reed.

"Shit," said Mike.

CHAPTER 10

The detectives made educated guesses as to how long Lana had been lying there.
"Before midnight," said Sergeant Thorn.
"Like last evening," said Detective Brennen.
They eyed each other.
"Somewhere between evening and midnight," said Mike.
"Closer to midnight," said Clark.
He got on his cell to report their sad find and to call in a couple of squads and the Crime Scene Unit and the coroner. Mike put on the gloves that his thoughtful partner had given him and started looking around, careful not to disturb anything. Not that anyone would have noticed the difference. The apartment was pretty much a mess, littered with crumpled and dirty clothes, dirty dishes, beer cans and empty whiskey bottles, fast food containers. some drug paraphernalia but no drugs that he could find. After making the calls, Clark searched with him, but they discovered nothing helpful.

"I really want to find this fucker," grumbled Mike. "Let's give those other two bars a look before Reed gets the word we found the body he left behind."

Clark agreed.

When the backup officers showed up, Sergeant Thorn gave them instructions to watch over the apartment. Once the rest of their people got there, they were to canvas the building and its neighbors. That done, he and Mike left to continue their hunt for Reed.

"Let's try this Black Bull place next," said Mike, looking at the address sheet. "I know that one."

"Social or business?" asked Clark.

"Funny. I went in there looking for another perp once and made an interesting discovery. The place has a handy-dandy escape hatch in case a customer wishes to avoid the usual front and rear exits. Kind of gives you an idea of the clientele they serve."

"Are you able to eye the back door and the secret hatch from one spot?"

"You can."

"Then that's your job. I'll go in the front door and see if I can encourage a bad guy to run out your way."

"Why me? You're the one in a vest!"

"Guess who's fault that is? Besides, you're the young half of this partnership if you have to do any chasing. And you know where the hatch is."

Mike couldn't argue with that. He got out of the car a block from the Black Bull and hoofed it down the alley while Clark drove around to the bar's front entrance. The back door of the building opened onto the alley, a large pile of discarded beer and liquor boxes was to the right of it. To the left an overflowing dumpster. The reek from the empty beer cans, and whiskey and vodka bottles, was enough to make you drunk or sick, or both. Of the neighboring buildings, one was separated from the bar by only a foot or so. The other, however, had a space of almost five feet. Plenty of room for a person to scoot through. There were a lot more of the cardboard boxes piled there. Their purpose, Mike figured, was to camouflage the small escape door. Taking out his gun, the detective positioned himself where he could see both the back door and the buried hatch.

Since this area had been Jason Reed's stomping grounds for a long time, and also because he probably didn't think anyone would find the body of Lana Wayne so quickly, and also because he bragged a lot about how cops never scared him, the stupid bastard had stuck around. Accentuating his stupidity, he had stuck around in his favorite hangout, the Black Bull. So Brennen had been waiting barely a minute when Reed came crashing out through the escape hatch.

"Freeze it, Reed!" ordered the detective sharply, bringing his gun up and ready.

The big killer stopped short, mean eyes snapping around to find his enemy. The man did not have the appearance, however, of someone who would respond well to orders. Especially not a cop's orders.

"I want you on the ground! Now!" Mike's tone was hard, but Mr. Reed's response was simply, "Fuck you!"

Obviously not carrying a gun, the bad guy grabbed a box and threw it at Mike and then turned to run toward the front. Mike tried to dodge the big box, but there wasn't a lot of spare room. It caused him to momentarily lose his balance and fall against the building's brick wall.

"Sonofabitch!"

Mike scrambled to give chase, having to plow through the rest of the boxes to do so. He burst from between buildings just as Clark hurried from the front entrance of the Black Bull.

"Where?" asked the sergeant.

Mike was looking. "There!" Turning left, he took off down the street.

Clark left the running to his younger partner in sneakers and dove for his car.

"Police! Get out of the way!" yelled Mike as he ran past the few pedestrians, trying to keep the fleeing Reed in sight.

When the bad guy went left around a corner, Mike skidded to a stop to give a quick glance around the building before following. Behind him, he heard Clark's siren. So did Reed. The big man sent an anxious look back over his shoulder as he was cutting across a small parking lot. With his head turned, he did not see the pale yellow Chevy Citation that was backing out. The car and Reed collided and he was sent sprawling.

"Yes!" gasped Mike, galloping up to the downed killer.

Reed was already rolling back on his knees, desperately trying to get all the way up. Mike used his own momentum, and his right knee, to knock the man back down.

"Stay there!" hissed the detective.

"Fuckin' cop!" Still unwilling to take orders, Reed made an effort to twist away.

Mike dropped down, putting a knee in the man's back and his gun at the man's head.

"Stay put! Or I'll put a fuckin' hole in your empty head and let the fuckin' air out!"

"What in the world is going on?" demanded a biting female voice. It was the Chevy's driver, who had left the car, leaving the door open, and was approaching indignantly. "What do you think you are doing, running in back of...?"

"Ma'am, please get back in your car!" said Mike. "This is police business."

Clark came squealing into the lot, shutting down the siren. The sergeant was quickly out of the car, gun in hand, and moving to help Mike.

"Please get back, ma'am," said Clark, pulling out his handcuffs.

"You're police? Oh, that's just great! I suppose now I'm really in trou--" She was now almost on top of Mike and his prisoner.

"Lady, will you just get back," grouched Mike, struggling with the fighting Reed.

But she had gotten too close and Jason Reed saw and took advantage of it. His hand snaked out to grab for an ankle. Feeling his hand, the woman jerked her leg back with a loud squeal -- and she lost her balance. Starting to fall, she let out a scream!

Clark instantly turned away from Mike, dropping the handcuffs and reaching out toward the woman in an effort to grab her. She, in turn, twisted around to reach out toward him, but her hand found only air as her body now fell toward Mike and his pinned prisoner. Since his right hand was holding his gun against Reed's head, Mike reacted by trying to bring his left arm around to ward her off. Reed, feeling the weight shift and lighten on his back, rose up like a wild bronco coming out of a bucking chute. When he did, his hard head hit Mike's gun and the detective involuntarily pulled the trigger, the bullet taking off a good-sized piece of Reed's right ear. That understandably enraged the killer even more. He threw Mike off his back and on top of Clark. The two cops, along with the woman, went down in a tangle of arms and legs.

With blood spewing from the right side of his head, Reed scrambled over all of them and into the woman's car, which she had left running. He shifted the Chevy into drive, hit the gas, and the car shot forward, smashing through the low, old and rotten, wooden rail in front of it and across the sidewalk. The pale-yellow Citation then plowed between two cars parked along the curb and clipped a third car that was coming down the street before it sped away.

Jason Reed had exited.

CHAPTER 11

Clark radioed for a squad car and put out an APB on the woman's car and Jason Reed. The irate woman had no idea what her plate number was and he had to get it via her name through Motor Vehicle.

The fortyish female, Donna Woods, was not a happy citizen. Her car had been stolen and she had gotten a nasty scratch on her arm when she fell.

"And you almost shot me!" she declared.

"No ma'am, that wouldn't have…" Clark tried to calm her.

"And you may have broken my arm!"

"I don't think so, ma'am…"

"And my car was stolen! I'm going to sue you for this!"

Mike stood in disbelief, letting Clark handle the interfering bitch. He had lost his prisoner! And he had Reed's blood splattered all over his suit! Blood cost money to get out of a suit, goddamn it, and a new suit was definitely not in his budget.

"Fuck!"

Donna Woods gasped at him.

Mike mustered a, "Sorry, lady."

She gave another annoying squeal.

"I said I was…"

But she was pointing at something on the ground. "What is…that?"

The detectives looked. It was a piece of Reed's ear lying in Reed's blood. Clark moved between it and the woman.

"Don't concern yourself, Ms. Woods," he said, turning her away. "Why don't you sit in my car until the squad gets here. Then they'll take you to the hospital so a doctor can take care of your arm and check to be sure you don't have any further injuries. After that, they'll take you home."

"My purse was in my car!"

"Yes, ma'am. The officers will take all your information."

Mike was eyeing the piece of ear with distaste.

"You better bag that, partner," said his sergeant, who was having difficulty suppressing a grin.

Mike stared at him. "Why do…?"

"It is evidence," allowed Clark.

"Like hell…"

"Needs to be done, partner. Bags are in my trunk."

"Of course they are," muttered Mike.

He went and opened the trunk, reaching in to take an evidence bag. As he slammed the lid, a squad car pulled into the parking lot and two officers got out.

Clark showed his ID. "Sergeant Thorn."

The driver, tall and husky, said, "I'm Desmond. That's Harris. What's happening, detectives?"

"Looks like a bloody mess," said Harris, slim and wiry. He squinted at the piece of ear. "Is that what it looks like?"

"It's a piece of ear!" declared Donna Woods. "I'm lucky it's not a piece of me!"

"You shot somebody's ear off?" asked Desmond, raising an eyebrow.

"That was my partner, Detective Brennen," said Clark. "Unfortunately, the guy belonging to the ear escaped in Ms. Woods' car."

Harris eyed Mike curiously.

"I have to ask," he said. "Does that make you a really good shot or a really bad one?"

Mike gave him a cold eye, his back to the headless ear. "What it makes me, is a really pissed off cop, and no, you don't need to ask. I don't--"

"Oh oh," said Desmond. "If you're collecting that ear, you better--"

Mike turned. A scruffy, reddish-brownish dog had boldly come from between parked cars to sniff at the blood. His nose quickly led him to the piece of ear.

"Hey!" shouted Mike.

The scruffy dog snatched the ear and ran. They all stared after him.

"Well, that's a first for me," said Harris.

"Me, too," said Desmond. "Your report on this one ought to be a beaut."

Donna Woods made a sour face. "It's disgusting."

Clark decided to move things along.

"Gentlemen," he said to Desmond and Harris, "I would like one of you to please take Ms. Woods to the hospital to have her arm looked after and to be sure she didn't sustain any further injuries from this incident. Then I want you to get all her information and take her home. The other should stay here and handle the citizens whose cars were banged up. You can toss a coin."

"You sure you don't want us to track down that dog?" said Harris.

Mike turned back on him with narrowed eyes.

Harris shrugged. "Guess not."

A short laugh escaped Clark, but then he regained control and said, "Come on now, fellas, fun's over. Just see to the lady and the crumpled fenders, please."

Officers Harris and Desmond, wearing unrestrained grins, took the lady to their squad car. Harris helped her in and drove away. Desmond went to the street to look over the damaged cars.

Clark gave Mike a thin smile and said, "Come on, Mike, you've got to admit it's funny. In a weird way."

"I don't have to admit to anything," stated Mike. He stuffed the evidence bag in a pocket and got into the car.

Fighting back a grin, Clark slid behind the wheel and turned off the still flashing red light on his dashboard. Starting the engine, he drove out of the parking lot.

"I am a little curious about how you let Reed get away from you at the Black Bull," said Clark. "I mean, you were watching the escape hatch and you knew he would probably be coming out of that…"

Without looking at his partner, Mike told him gruffly, "He threw a fucking box at me."

"Threw a box? Hell, you should have expected that."

Mike glared at him. "Why would…?"

"Happens all the time on television and in movies. Bad guys throwing stuff at the heroes. That's so there can be a big chase and a fight. Of course, the good guy is supposed to win the fight and take the bad guy off to jail."

"Really? Does the good guy get attacked by a crazy woman who leaves her car door open and car running so the bad guy can get away?"

"Technically, partner, I don't think we can say she actually attacked us and…"

"Technically, I had the goddamned bastard and now we'll have hell trying to find him again! Thanks to that crazy woman!"

"I think it's safe to say that Ms. Woods' day has been pretty much ruined, too," Clark pointed out. "I also think that now would be a good time for you to get word out to the hospitals and clinics that we want to hear about any man who comes in minus a part of his right ear. Maybe you should also let our lieutenant know we ran into a little trouble and Reed got away. You might also mention that a nice lady might be suing the NYPD for…"

Mike was frowning. "You're the sergeant. You should be reporting to our lieutenant."

"You're the one who let that crazy woman help Reed escape."

Mike snarled. "Clark…"

His partner grinned.

Mike took out his cell and put the word out to the medical facilities and then, reluctantly, called Lieutenant Grands.

"You had him and then you let him get away?" complained Grands.

"We didn't let him get away. And he is wounded. I put out word to--"

"He's wounded, but he could drive off in a car?"

"He could still drive, but he was losing blood and--"

"How bad a wound is it? Where did you hit him?"

"I…sort of grazed the side of his head when the lady fell on me."

"I want a detailed report on this entire incident before you go home tonight," rasped Grands.

"Yes, sir," said Mike, gratefully ending the connection. He sighed. "I'm hungry, Clark. Let's eat."

Clark's face twisted in disgust. "You just shot someone's ear off and you're hungry?"

"I didn't have any breakfast! And the damned dog had the ear for his lunch!"

Clark stopped at a hot dog place where Mike ordered two chili dogs and a large fries. Clark ate a bowl of chili. Just as they returned to the car, the sergeant's radio came to life. Donna Woods' car had been found. Abandoned, of course. They drove to the location, less than four blocks from the bloodied parking lot, and took a look. There was quite a bit of blood on the front seat of the car and there would certainly be fingerprints, except they already knew who the fingerprints belonged to. What they needed was a clue to point them in the direction Reed had gone. There was none, nor were there any witnesses to do any pointing. Looking at the banged up, blood-stained Chevy, the detectives knew that Ms. Woods was going to be even more unhappy than she had been earlier.

"At least he left her purse and wallet," said Clark. "That should help her mood a little."

Aware that it was unlikely that Reed would take his wounded ear to an honest doctor, Thorn and Brennen decided to pay calls on a few of the not-so-honest medical practitioners that they knew.

"Gentlemen," slurred William Florid. He sat in a booth in a small, street corner bar. Lifting his empty whiskey glass toward them, he asked hopefully, "Buy a friend a drink?"

The thin, alcohol saturated man, no older than Mike, had struggled through medical school only to lose his first patient on the operating table. Now, during his more sober moments, he was available for patching up the wounds and injuries of those who preferred to avoid the usual places of medical help. At the moment, he was too drunk to help anyone. The detectives left without buying the man a drink.

Next they knocked on the apartment door of one Marvin Holt, who had tried to make his fortune through illegal insurance claims. They were confronted by his caustic wife.

"He ain't here! An' I don't know where he's at!" snapped the abundantly sized, Sylvia Holt on seeing their badges. "An' I don't know why you fuckin' cops don't leave my Marvin alone!"

"Because your Marvin keeps playing doctor when his license has been shredded," said Mike. Then, being the gruff cop, added, "I think we should take a look inside. To be sure."

"I ain't a fool! You need a warrant to do that," she said stubbornly.

"We can go that route if you want, Mrs. Holt," said Clark, being the polite cop, "but it will look a lot better for you, and Marvin, if we can say in our report that you cooperated."

So she grudgingly cooperated, but Marvin Holt wasn't there. Nor were there any suspicious puddles of blood.

Clark politely said, "Thank you," as she slammed the door.

The third and last one they knew about was holding cards in his hand when he opened the door.

"Hi, Russ," said Clark. "You look like you might be busy."

Mike peered around the short, pot-bellied, ex-Army doctor.

Four men sat around a kitchen table that was covered with poker chips, cards, beer, alcohol, and food.

Mike asked them, "Do you gentlemen know if Mr. Widall has had any customers visit him in the last hour or so?'

"Hey! Get the hell out of here!" griped Russ Widall.

"Or has he left to maybe take care of somebody somewhere else?" Mike pursued, ignoring the objections.

"No, I have not! And you have no right sticking your nose in here asking!"

"Only thing he's been doin' is stealin' our money!" piped up one of the players.

"Thank you," said Clark.

Widall slammed the door.

By the end of the day, both detectives were frustrated. Worse, they had to report to their lieutenant that they had nothing to report. Not on Reed. Not on the Calamity Janes.

"And a dog ran off with the ear," said Grands. He didn't look or sound amused. "Not one of your better days, gentlemen. Let's hope tomorrow's an improvement."

"Yes, sir," said Thorn politely.

"Let's," said Brennen gruffly.

"I'd like reports before you leave," said Grands. "Especially your shooting report, Brennen. We want to keep the Shooting Board happy."

"Hell, yes," muttered Mike. "Let's keep the Board happy."

Back at their desks, Clark said, "Don't worry about it, Mike. It shouldn't be a problem. I'll play it down in my report."

"I'd have more confidence in those words of encouragement if you weren't grinning," said Mike.

"You've got to look at it with a smile," insisted Clark. "It will probably be one of the most interesting stories in your career. One to tell your grandchildren."

Mike did not look convinced.

Twenty minutes later, Mike was still struggling with his report when his sergeant tossed his in the lieutenant's basket.

"See you in the morning, Mike," said Clark, making a fruitless effort to cover his amusement.

"You're going home and tell Etta every last detail, aren't you."

"How can I help it?"

He left, Mike scowling after him. A few minutes later, Grands walked out of his office.

"I've got a meeting," said the lieutenant. "I won't be back."

Under his breath, Mike grumbled, "Then why the hell do you need this fuckin' report tonight?"

Being alone in the room didn't speed up the report writing. Worse, as he worked on it, Mike's headache returned with great persistence. Finally he scrounged around his desk for aspirin, remembered he didn't have any, and went to scrounge around Muller's desk. Finding the bottle tucked in a drawer, he took three. They didn't help in finishing the report, either. A report in which the detective kind of skimmed over the ear, and especially the dog.

"Still here, Brennen?"

Mike looked up to see Ben Sharp. The African-American, was one of the night shift detectives.

"I love my job," grouched Mike.

"I hear you shot somebody's ear off."

Mike stared at him. He said, even grouchier, "You heard that already? Where did you hear that already?"

"Hey, something big time like that goes down, the news--"

"I don't want to hear it."

"You asked."

"I really don't want to hear it."

Mike put his sort of finished report in the basket on Grands' desk and left the squad room.

"Night, Brennen. Hope you don't have any bad dreams about ears," Sharp called after him, smiling.

He was ignored.

Downstairs, as Mike walked to the door, one officer whispered loudly to another, "Here comes Detective Brennen. Hang onto your ears."

They were ignored.

CHAPTER 12

Detective Brennen was tired, but he was also hungry again. On the way home, he stopped at a chicken place to buy a carry-out dinner. When ordering it, he told them to include a couple of extra pieces. Rambo would never forgive him if he didn't get his share. When Mike came out of the chicken place, there was a gray Mercedes parked next to his car and Tommy One Bears was sitting in Mike's front seat. Brennen got in, slamming his door harder than necessary.

"I'm really in a pissed off mood, Indian. Go away."

"I did notice it wasn't one of your better days," granted Tommy.

"I've already been told that and, believe it or not, I even noticed it myself. And you're still following me all over the place?"

"Hey, I've got to earn my big bucks."

Mike gave him an if-looks-could-kill look. Tommy wasn't particularly impressed.

"They only want me to touch base with you. In case you might have heard something from the Panelli suspects."

"There's a good chance I'll be hearing from Polinski."

"For shooting somebody's ear off, I presume."

Mike's look turned icy. He said, "Don't start."

"Touchy aren't we. But I suppose shooting off an ear could do that to a man." Tommy had to work at keeping a straight face. "I understand you were interested in my...life. I'm flattered that you cared enough to look."

"Flattering, hell. You know all about me. Fair's fair. Except, you still know a lot more about me than I know about you. We'll have to discuss that sometime. Right now, get out of my car. I want to go home and eat my dinner and go to bed."

"Alone?"

"No! With my cat! As if it's any of your goddamned business who I spend my nights with! Get out of my car!"

Bears shrugged and opened the door to get out.

"Have a good night, Detective. We'll be in touch."

"Go to hell!"

Rambo greeted his roommate with a squeaky hello and then nearly trampled him when he smelled the chicken. Bounding to the counter, the cat literally drooled as Mike took the chicken from the sack. As his human provider was pulling the meat from the bones, Rambo's pawless leg would snake out periodically as though to hurry Mike up. When he had torn the meat into chewable morsels, the detective set the plate on the floor.

"Enjoy," he said.

Rambo devoured his chicken, then proceeded to pester Mike for more while the man set out his dinner and ate. Mike shared his chicken, and his problems, with the black and white feline.

"You wouldn't believe the day I've had, buddy. I've got four lieutenants on my ass...well, maybe not Sheffer...and the Panellis, and some half-breed hired gun...to say nothing of a killer running around without an ear ...and a bunch of teenage--"

His cell buzzed. Mike glowered at where it rested on the counter. Finally he picked it up, and seeing the caller ID, his spirits lifted immediately.

"Mike?" said a female voice when he hit the accept button.

Smiling, he said, "You were maybe expecting Rambo to answer, Betty?"

Betty Warner was his mother's sister. Fifty-one and unmarried, she lived in Boston. She and Mike were the best of friends.

"He's a smart cat. He might," she said with a little laugh. "How's life treating my favorite nephew? You know Grace would want me to check up on you."

"Yeah, she probably would," agreed Mike softly.

Mike's folks, Arthur and Grace Brennen, had been killed in a car accident six years ago. It had devastated Mike. He and his parents had been very close, partly because he was an only child, but mostly because they shared and did so much together. Not the material things -- there had never been much extra money -- but family things. They had always been there for Mike when he needed them, even if it was just to talk something over. Even after he had moved out. They had been so proud when he'd become a police officer. The credit for Mike's honesty and dedication, and determination, was due to his folks.

Then, on a trip to Albany, New York, to visit family, Art and Grace Brennen had been hit head-on by a pickup when the drunk driver crossed the middle line. As so often happened, the drunk survived, but the Brennens died before they could reach the hospital. The long days of preparing the funeral, followed by the sorting and handling of the personal and material items, had been the hardest in Mike's life. His deep sorrow had dragged him down, threatening his work, and his life on the job. His Aunt Betty Warner had pulled him back up.

"So, what's up with you?" asked Mike.

"Maybe I just wanted to call you."

"Uh-huh. What's up?"

"Okay. I just wanted to call you, and I also wanted to give you a reminder not to forget Margo and Donald would like us to come over for Larry's birthday party a week from Saturday."

"I know. He's turning into a teenager. Margo's also been reminding me. Regularly."

Margo Young was his father's much younger sister. She was married to a dentist, Donald, and they had two boys, Larry, turning thirteen, and Frederick, just turned ten. They lived in Albany. Mike said, "I keep telling her I'll be there unless--"

"Unless you can't be there," said Betty.

"That's about right."

"So consider yourself reminded. Now, tell me, what kind of a day did you have?"

"Not such a good one."

"Tell me. You'll feel better."

"Well, I shot somebody's ear off."

"An ear? My goodness, Mike, can't you shoot any better than that?"

"Not you, too!" The detective grinned. "And then a dog grabbed it and ran off with it."

"You're kidding?" Betty started to laugh. "A dog ran off with the ear?"

Mike started to laugh. "A fuckin' dog."

They laughed together.

CHAPTER 13

He was being chased again, and again he was slowed down, this time because he was trying to run in deep sand. And again, whoever was chasing him didn't seem to be having any trouble at all running. He didn't feel that was fair. One of the chasing figures was gaining rapidly. As it got closer, Mike saw it was a grinning man with no ears!

Fuck!

Then he was shocked awake by the buzzing phone again!

"No!"

He picked it up to look at the time as it buzzed a second time.

Two-eighteen!

"No!" he answered.

"Police officers can't say no, Detective Brennen," said a female voice that was definitely not his Aunt Betty.

"Huh?"

"It's Lieutenant Sheffer, Detective. The gun slinging cowgirls have hit again. An all-night grocery store and I understand one of the girls may have been wounded this time." She gave him the address. "I'll see you there."

"Uh-huh," moaned Mike.

He crawled out of bed and stumbled into the bathroom, flipping the light switch. The sight of himself in the mirror was ugly. He splashed cold water on his face and ran his fingers through his hair. Neither half-hearted effort made any improvement to the ugly sight in the mirror.

Mike pulled on a pair of jeans, a green tee-shirt with a growling tiger on it, and put bare feet into the battered old sneakers that were still damp from the rain. The damp clothes he had finally tossed into his dirty clothes basket last night. Except for the damp jacket, which he now pulled on.

Rambo sat on the bed and glared at him with slitted eyes. He was obviously not appreciative of the early hour.

"I don't want to hear about it," Mike told the cat as he put his gun and holster in place and gathered up the rest of his tools of the trade. "You'll just go back to sleep. Probably for the rest of the day."

But the cat wasn't going to let him go without getting his breakfast. With a screech he pounced from the bed to run to the kitchen. Mike followed him and went through the feeding ritual, being extra generous with the crunchies.

"Make that last, ol' buddy, 'cause God only knows when I'll get in tonight. Well, He probably doesn't know either. Don't let any burglars in."

Rambo glared again. Of course he wouldn't. Unless they came in while he was eating.

Brennen was out the door.

The dark neighborhood was quiet. Mike stepped off the curb and walked diagonally down the street toward where he'd parked. He was almost there when he heard a car engine turn over and rev up. He automatically turned his head for a look, wondering absently what other poor soul had to get up at this miserable hour. The car, without its headlights on, was a dark shadow halfway down the block. Suddenly it came rushing down the street right at him.

"Shit!"

No swimmer could have made a quicker dive than Mike made in that split second. He landed on the hood of a parked car and heard the whoosh of the speeding vehicle as it whipped past, mere inches separating the two cars. Rolling off the hood to land on his feet, Mike tried to get a look at the departing shadow and its license plate. He couldn't make out anything that would have helped him to pin the maniac. Even the light over the plate was out.

For almost a minute Mike stood in the street, taking some deep breaths to calm his racing heart and rattled nerves. It was a hell of a way to start the day.

"Damned drunk," he said as he turned back toward his car. He tried to shrug off a strange feeling of uneasiness.

The detective didn't use his siren to get where he was going, though he did turn on his dashboard flasher as he sped through the streets. When he got to the store, he found a busy scene. Two squad cars, red lights flashing, were stopped in the middle of the street. Thorn's and another unmarked were also there, their dashboard lights flashing. An EMT ambulance was just leaving. Considering the early hour, there was a good-sized crowd of spectators. Mike parked, turned off his light, and got out. Exchanging nods with a uniformed officer, Mike ducked under the yellow crime scene tape already strung along the street.

The targeted store was a medium-sized grocery store. It's one, large, plate glass window, had been shattered and scattered inside and outside the store, leaving only jagged shards hanging in the frame. With the help of some sidewalk signs, more crime scene tape had been strung around a section of sidewalk outside the shattered window. Sergeant Thorn and Lieutenant Sheffer could be seen inside talking with a young man in shirt and jeans. The latter was also wearing a white bib apron tied over his clothes. Mike was mildly surprised to see Sheffer in jeans and a plaid shirt and sneakers. Clark was in a suit over an open-necked white shirt. The fact that his partner wasn't wearing a tie was a big concession on Clark's part. Mike had never seen him show up on the job wearing jeans no matter what the hour. The detective nodded a greeting as he joined them.

"You got here fast," remarked Sheffer on seeing him.

"Almost didn't get here at all," said Mike.

"Oh?" said the lieutenant.

"Some drunk tried to use me as bowling pin."

"What?" said Clark.

"Nothing. Forget it. Tell me what's happening."

Sheffer gave a nod and introduced, "Detective Brennen, this is David Patton. He's the one who shot one of the girls. Why don't you go ahead and tell him your story, Mr. Patton."

In his middle twenties and sporting a buzz haircut, David Patton was still pumped up, his long face flushed from the excitement.

"I almost pissed in my pants when I saw 'em come in," he told Mike in a heightened tone of voice. "But they didn't see me. I was at the back of the store. When I saw 'em, I ran into the little office there to call the cops an' to get the gun that Mr. Millner...he owns the store...keeps in the safe there. He always tells us to just hand over the money to any robber, because we don't keep that much cash here at night anyway, but I'd heard those girls killed somebody and I didn't want that to happen here. So I grabbed the gun an' then snuck down that far aisle over there, where they couldn't see me."

They were standing near the two check-out lanes at the front of the store.

"They had poor Barbara...Barbara Yeager is the only check-out clerk at night...scared to death an' one of 'em was cleanin' out the cash register. When the girl doin' that tried to get into the other register, she got mad 'cause it was locked. We keep that one locked at night. Even if she'd got in, there's only like thirty, forty dollars in it...as change to start the next day. Anyway, then Barbara saw me an' cried my name an' they turned an' pointed their guns at me. I took a dive an' they started shootin' up everything, includin' the window Then they were runnin' out an' I jumped up an' saw 'em runnin' to a car and I shot at 'em through the window. I mean, it was already broke, so I just shot through it and kept shootin' 'til the gun was empty. One of 'em screamed and halfway fell, so I know I hit her. They had to help her get in the car."

"He was using this," said Sheffer holding up a plastic bag. In it was a small, five-shot revolver, with a two-inch barrel. "There is blood on the sidewalk, so he did hit somebody. He isn't real sure where he hit her but thinks maybe in the leg."

Patton gave them a sheepish grin. "To be honest, I've never even shot a gun before."

Clark said, "You know, Mr. Patton, your boss gave you the right instructions about not confronting or arguing with thieves. Once you'd called the police, you should have just stayed out of their way. It's unlikely they would have hurt Ms. Yeager, while your inexperience with a gun might have gotten you or someone else injured."

Though the young man's feelings looked hurt, he admitted, "I suppose so, but I really was scared for Barbara. You know, after hearin' how those girls killed somebody just the other night."

"We can understand what it must have been like for you, Mr. Patton," said Mike giving him a brief, encouraging smile. "Do you remember anything about the car?"

"Just that it was dark-colored, and it was a four-door 'cause they put the shot girl in the back seat."

"They've dumped it by now, anyway," said Clark.

"Maybe this time they won't take the time to put it back where they found it," allowed Mike. "We can keep an ear out for stolen car reports later this morning. There's bound to be blood in it and maybe something else that will help." He sent a quick glance around. "What about the check-out girl?"

"The ambulance took her to emergency," Sheffer told him. "She had cuts from the flying glass and she was pretty hysterical. Said she was too scared to remember anything and when the shooting started, she dropped down behind a counter. I'll give her time to calm down and I'll try her again."

"Otherwise it all sounds the same," said Clark. "Bandanas, wigs, hats, the guns."

"But with one of them wounded, we've at least got some places to go look," noted Mike. "We can give our favorite back-room docs another visit. We might be luckier this time."

"You're after another wounded perp?" asked Sheffer.

"Jason Reed," supplied Clark. "Minus an ear."

Mike scowled at his partner. "Was it necessary to bring that up?"

"It's hard not to," said Clark, restraining a grin.

Anita Sheffer raised an eyebrow as she said, "Sounds like an interesting story, gentlemen, and I'd like to hear it sometime, but let's get after these gals. When Sergeant Pragg gets here, he and I will talk to the neighborhood crowd to see if they saw anything and we'll check on the hospitals, emergency clinics, et cetera. And listen for any abandoned cars with blood stains. Since you already know where to start looking for the under-the-table docs, you can start there. Keep in touch."

Mike would have liked to ask the woman if she had learned anything about the Macklin tip, but he couldn't in front of Clark. In turn, Sheffer made no motion or signal to get him alone, which probably meant she didn't have anything to tell him anyway.

As the detectives left the store, Mike strongly suggested to Clark, "My car this time? We don't want to look like cops if there's a chance of spotting our teenage perps."

Clark looked Mike up and down and said, "I don't think you have to worry about looking like a cop tonight."

"Why, thank you, partner," said Mike, and insisted, "My car?"

"Alright," relented Clark, "but I'm not leaving mine sit here. I'll take it home. And just follow me, don't race with me."

"Don't race with you? What's that supposed to mean?"

"I know you."

"Damn," sniffed Mike. "Well, I know you, and you'd be no fun to race with, anyway."

Sergeant Thorn and his family lived in a modest two-story home in a quiet neighborhood. His efficient wife, Etta, was homemaker and mother to their two teenage children. Alex was the youngest, just turning fourteen. Cecily the oldest, sixteen. In the four years Mike and Clark had been partners, the detective had visited the Thorn home many times. Sometimes just for dinner. Sometimes for parties, including a birthday surprise for Mike when he turned thirty. Clark and Etta were good people. Cecily and Alex were good kids, with the normal teenage frustrations and problems. Having no brothers and sisters of his own, Mike didn't mind being big brother to the two youngsters on occasion. More than once they had come to him with problems that they had been reluctant to share with their parents and Brennen had done his best as a mentor. The Thorns were like family to Mike, but on the job, Clark made at least a small effort to maintain his role as sergeant. Which Mike - amused and somewhat frustrated - took in stride.

Clark pulled into his driveway and parked, Mike waiting in the street.

As Clark got in, Mike said, "I was thinking maybe we should try Holt first. He's probably the one they'd most likely know...or know about."

Buckling his seat belt in place, Clark said, "I'll go along with that."

"You're agreeing with me?" said Mike, pulling away.

"It's a sound deduction."

"Really?"

"Mr. Florid didn't look like he was going to dry out any time soon, and if Widall is still playing poker and winning, I don't think his buddies would let him leave."

"Yeah. Right. Sound deduction."

"Exactly. Go to Holt's," said Clark. "And tell me the story about somebody trying to run you over."

"It was a drunk and he missed because I'm youthful and fast on my feet. End of story."

"You kind of sounded like it might have been on purpose."

"No I didn't."

"Sure you did. Who'd want to run you over?"

"I don't know, Clark. Let's talk about something else. What are you getting Etta for her birthday?"

"It's already Etta's birthday again?"

"As her husband, it would be good if you started remembering these sorts of things."

"How come you remember these things?"

"I'm still young. My mind hasn't started to go yet."

"Go to hell."

CHAPTER 14

It was almost 4 a.m. when they slowly cruised past the front of the eight-story tenement and then slowly through the alley. The detectives saw nothing suspicious. Mike parked beside a fire hydrant.

"You want the vest?" he asked Clark.

"I'll skip it this time. Holt wouldn't get caught dead with a gun. But I'll let you go through the door first. Just in case."

"And people say you have no sense of humor," scoffed Mike.

They entered the front of the building cautiously, but there was no one in the dimly lit entrance. With some reservations, Clark took the rumbling elevator in case someone tried to come down in it while they were going up. Mike went along the first-floor hallway and up the back stairwell, figuring if someone didn't want to be seen, that's the way they would come and go. Neither of them saw anyone and they met at the Holts' apartment on the fifth floor. They did pull their weapons and stand to either side before Clark knocked. When there was no response, he knocked harder.

"What the hell is this tonight?" They heard the stormy Sylvia on the other side of the door. "You people think this is the fuckin' Grand Central Station? It's four o'clock in the damned morning! Besides, Marvin ain't back yet and I ain't opening this goddamn door to nobody else!"

"You'll open it for us, Mrs. Holt," said Clark. "This is the police. We were here yesterday."

"What?" The door opened as far as the chain would let it and an eye peered out at them. "What're you doin' here at this hour?"

"We can talk better inside, Mrs. Holt," pressed Clark.

"Marvin ain't here. If you was listenin', I just said that."

"We were listening," said Mike in his gruff manner, "and it sounds to us like Marvin had to make a house call. Who was here to get him and how long ago did he leave?"

The one eye looked a little troubled and Sylvia said, "I don't kn--"

"Yes you do!" said Mike sharply. "We want some answers and we want--"

"Take it easy, Mike," said Clark, again playing the nice guy. "Let's talk inside, Mrs. Holt. We aren't going to go away until you've answered some questions for us."

The eye blinked and the woman muttered under her breath, but the door closed and the chain came off. The detectives went in carefully, taking a look around before putting their guns away. Indignant, Sylvia Holt plopped down on a gray, badly stained, misshapen sofa. A large lamp, wearing a lamp shade too small for it, sat on a table beside the sofa. It's low wattage bulb provided the only light in the living room. Probably a good thing, because Sylvia's night wear would have been hard to adjust to otherwise. In a bright blue bathrobe, fuzzy bright green bedroom slippers, and a bright pink hair net, she was almost nauseating to look at. Not daring to guess what color her night gown might be, Mike tried to concentrate on her chubby face as he asked, "Who came and got Marvin, Mrs. Holt? How long ago?"

"It was maybe half hour ago, but I don't know who it was," Sylvia told him firmly.

"You must have seen them," said Mike.

"I didn't even get out of bed! Marvin answered the door and he didn't say nothin' about where he was goin'."

"Okay," said Clark, "but you had to hear someone. Was it only one person? Man or woman? Young or old?"

"I...well, it was a woman, but how the hell am I supposed to know how old she was."

"And you didn't hear any of what she said? Why she needed him? Where they were going?" said Mike.

"I didn't hear nothin' that they said! I just could tell it was a woman's voice."

"A woman or a young girl?" persisted Clark.

"A woman!"

"And Marvin didn't say where...?"

"Marvin never says what he's gonna do!" Sylvia glared at them furiously.

"Does Marvin have a car, Mrs. Holt?" Clark asked.

"We can't afford no car."

The detectives looked at her quietly for a couple of moments.

"Okay, Mrs. Holt," said Clark. "Thank you for your cooperation."

The woman gave them a "Humph!" and quickly shut the door as they went out.

In the elevator, Mike argued, "It's my car. I should get to sit in it."

"But, as you often remind me, you blend in with the territory so much better than I do. Especially with what you're wearing tonight. Besides, I'm the sergeant."

"As you often remind me," Mike reminded him.

"Yes, I do, because even though you remember my wife's birthday, you don't always remember I'm your sergeant," stated Clark. "I'll give you a call if somebody shows up out front. If it looks like a promising prospect, I'll follow and see where they go. You collar Holt. If you get somebody in the alley, let me know and I'll follow them and you collar Holt. If it's a cab, I'll stop it, and you col--"

"Collar Holt. If you follow somebody, don't be a Lone Ranger. That's my act."

"Let's just keep our fingers crossed that it's who we think it is and that we can get a lead out of it."

"I've sure as hell got my fingers crossed," said Mike. "I'm already tired of the early hours these babes keep."

So Sergeant Thorn sat comfortably in Detective Brennen's car out front, while Detective Brennen took up a more uncomfortable position at the rear of the tenement. Mike hoped they would not have to wait long for the doctor to return.

CHAPTER 15

It was four-forty when Brennen's cell buzzed and he answered, "Yeah?"

Thorn said, "The good doctor just got home. He's yours. I'm after the cab."

"Got it," said Mike.

He had already checked to be sure the back entrance wasn't locked. In this case, couldn't lock because the doorknob and lock were missing. Now he slipped his phone away and pulled his gun to go up the dimly lit stairwell three steps at a time. When the detective reached the fifth floor, he took a quick look into the hallway. He was in time to see Marvin Holt just getting out of the elevator, door key ready in his hand. Not terribly tall, the man was on the bulky side. With a carefully trimmed brown beard and reddish brown hair, he almost looked like a Norman Rockwell hometown kind of doc. Except he had been more interested in money than healing and pulled one too many insurance scams. Though he had seen the inside of a jail a couple of times, he had proven much more useful to law enforcement on the outside.

Mike slid quietly into the hall and, keeping his gun down along his leg for the moment, strode toward Holt.

"Morning, Doc," he greeted. "Already having a busy day, are we?"

The ex-doctor Holt was so startled he dropped his key.

"What? Who...who are you?" he gasped.

"Detective Mike Brennen," said Mike, bringing his gun up. "And my feelings are hurt that you don't remember me from past visits. What I want you to do now is set that little doctor's bag you're carrying on the floor and place your hands on the wall. I believe you know how that's done..."

"I...I..." Flustered, the man's response was slow.

His gun trained steadily on the doctor, Mike stopped some ten feet from him.

"Do it, Marvin!" he ordered. "Bag on the floor, hands on the wall, feet apart."

"Yes...yes," said Holt and did it. Then, as his senses caught up, "If you know me, you should know I never carry any weapons."

Mike patted him down and then kicked the bag down the hall.

"I'll bet you've got a few in there," he noted.

"I mean a gun," stated Marvin, starting to get testy.

"Right. Pick up your key and Let's go inside for a little talk."

"Why should I let you come in?"

"Hey, if you'd rather be handcuffed and taken in for questioning, we can do it that way. I just thought we could do a little question and answer session here and then I could go my way and you could go back to bed. Depending on what kind of answers I get, of course."

"I don't know anything about anything," stated Holt. He hadn't picked up his key yet.

"Now, Doc, I want you to think carefully about this," said Mike. "We have some teenage girls raising hell and the other morning they killed somebody and we want to end their careers really bad before something more happens. You know, before someone else gets hurt or killed. And we want it bad enough that I'd be willing to bet we'd forget about your extracurricular activities tonight. Such as treating and assisting a wanted felon and a killer. What do you say, Dr. Holt?"

Dr. Holt was looking a little worried. "I...well..."

The door suddenly opened and Sylvia Holt looked out at them. Her voice sharp, she said, "Marvin! Did he hurt you? Where's the other one? They keep comin' back and--"

Down the hall, another door opened and a chilling voice came from the darkness within. "If you don't shut the fuck up, I'm comin' out there and rip out your goddamned tongues."

The door slammed shut.

Mike grinned and said to the Holts, "That sounded like a serious threat, lady and gentleman, so how about we go inside."

"My bag," said Marvin.

"Just go inside."

They went in and Mike pushed the door shut behind them. The same table lamp was on and Mike motioned the lady and gentleman to the same misshapen sofa. Sylvia was still an eyesore in her colorful outfit. Marvin wasn't such a shock to the system in a brown, long sleeve shirt, and black pants, and a slightly worn gray sport jacket. Stationing himself in front of the Holts, Mike tucked his gun under his waistband and crossed his arms.

"Let's do this quick and painless, and remember what I just said about aiding and doctoring a killer. I want to know where you went and what you did and who you did it to."

"What's he talkin' about, Marvin? A killer?" babbled Sylvia. "I don't think this is legal, him bargin' in here and you should--"

"Shut up, Sylvia," said Marvin. He eyed Mike cautiously. "I tell you what I can and you'll go away?"

"You tell me what you know, all of it, and I'll go away. If I find out later you forgot some detail, I'll be back and I won't be nearly so sweet."

Holt continued to look at Mike for a few moments, but finally gave a shrug and said, "Why should I give a shit? They didn't even pay me a decent price."

"Gee, Marvin, I feel real bad for you. Tell me about them. How many? What did they look like? Names--"

"There was four of 'em and the only names they used was their first ones. Two of the girls were Teresa and Jill. They were sisters, too, because they called each other 'sis' a couple times. The other young one was Fran and the older one was Margo. Not that she was old, she was just older than the others."

"How much older?"

"It was hard to tell! She was wearing a damned stocking over her head. In her twenties, I think. And the others were probably just in their teens. The way they were dressed, I couldn't tell anything for sure. Honest to God!"

"How were they dressed?"

"You know! They were in them stupid cowgirl outfits and wearing bandanas over their faces, and the wigs and hats. I couldn't see much of anything."

"Margo was the one wearing a stocking?"

"A nylon stocking pulled over her head and a baseball cap on top of that. She had it on right from when she come to get me. I couldn't see her hair and her face was all smooshed and she was in jeans and a Western fringe jacket and Western boots. Okay? There's no way I could ever pick out any of 'em in any kind of a lineup. Honest to God!"

"Swell," said Mike. "You can tell me their sizes, Marvin. Tall, short, fat, skinny...?"

"None of 'em was very tall and none of the young ones was fat, but how could a person tell for sure when they're in those stupid outfits? The older one, Margo, looked like she was kind of on the chubby side. Sort of. At least, compared to the others. And she wasn't much more than maybe five and a half feet tall."

"You're not being a big help here, Marvin."

"I can't tell you stuff I couldn't see! One thing they all were, was bitches! They come to me for help and then threaten me and paid me shit!"

"Well, how much did you get?" Sylvia wanted to know.

Mike gave her a cold look and she went quiet.

"Which one was shot and how bad?" he asked her husband.

"That was Teresa. The bullet took a chunk out of her left calf. It's not a real serious wound, but it had her scared and hurting. It sure as hell didn't keep her from being an ungrateful bitch."

"This one is worth a lot of points, Marvin. Where did she take you?"

"She blindfolded me...."

"Marvin!" Mike growled sharply.

"Honest to God! The minute we got in the van, she put a pillow case or something over my head."

"A van? You came back in a cab."

"She dropped me on Pacific Street and I took a cab from there."

"Tell me about the--"

A light tapping came at the door and Clark's voice came quietly, "Mike. It's me."

Mike let him in.

The sergeant looked the Holts over as he asked, "Is he being much help?"

"Not very."

"I'm telling you all I know! Honest to God!"

"The van, Marvin," said Mike. "Tell us about the van."

"I don't know anything about vans! Well, except this wasn't one of those fancy new kind like you see advertised on television. It was used and just a plain one, with a sliding side door and a couple of seats in the back. And I think one window in the back. On the right side. She didn't let me see much."

"What color was it?" asked Clark.

"It's dark out! And who can tell color in that stupid street light. I think maybe it was a kind of gray. I don't know for sure. Honest to God!"

"Okay, she had to take your hood off so you could take care of the wounded girl. Where were you? A house, an apartment, what...?" said Mike.

"He had a hood on?" Clark frowned unhappily.

"And she didn't take it off until we were inside," whined Holt. "But, it was a basement. An apartment building kind of basement. Like we have here."

"Did you see anything that might help us find the place?" asked Clark

Marvin looked at him blankly. "It looked like a basement. A cement floor, a furnace, water heaters...whatever. What's to see in a basement?"

Mike glared at him and took a deep breath.

Clark said, "So tell me what we have. I got nothing from the cab. Says he picked up Holt on Pacific and came straight here."

"Yeah," said a glum Mike. "Okay, partner, here's our grand total. We've got first names -- Teresa and Jill and Fran and Margo. The first three are teenagers. Margo is in her twenties and is probably the boss lady. Teresa and Jill are possibly sisters and Teresa is the one that got shot. Bullet plowed up her left calf. Margo is the one who came and got Marvin. She was driving a plain, used van, that's maybe gray in color. The girls were still in costume, so we have nothing to add to their description. Margo wore a stocking over her head and a cap, so no description for her except for being kind of plump and maybe five and a half feet tall. They were all bitches and, the worst thing of all, is they wouldn't pay Marvin his goddamned asking price."

Clark ran a hand through his hair and took almost as deep a breath as Mike had.

"I feel real bad for you, Marvin, but I feel worse for us," he said. "You will give us a call if you think of anything else, won't you, Dr. Holt."

"If I think of anything else," said Marvin with a hint of insolence.

"Honest to God," added Mike.

CHAPTER 16

In the car, Mike said, "I guess we're going fishing in juvenile records for sisters, Teresa and Jill."

"Also Frans," said Clark, "and in female records for Margos."

"They've been so goddamned smart about everything, do you think they used their real names in front of Holt?" asked Mike.

"How many perps do you remember that ever worried about their first names?" allowed Clark. "These babes have been smart, but they've been lucky, too. Bluffing their way along without any witnesses noticing anything helpful. The Margo person went to the trouble to not only wear a stocking over her head, but also blindfold Holt, and then took him to a generic basement and they kept their outfits on. So I doubt they cared what Holt might or might not see or hear. Besides, I also believe that bunch was pretty wired after being shot at and one of them being hit. I don't think they even thought about the fact that they were using their first names. Of course, there is the possibility that they don't have records, in which case any kind of name will be useless."

"Hell, Clark, if they're as bitchy and bad as Holt and everybody else says they are, they must have some kind of records. Wouldn't you think?"

"I hope so. If they don't, we're not going to have much to give Grands and Sheffer."

The remark caused Mike's mind to shift gears and he nonchalantly asked, "What do you think of Lieutenant Sheffer?"

Clark looked at him. "As a police officer or as a woman?"

Mike looked back at him. "As a woman lieutenant police officer."

"Please keep your eyes on the road," suggested Clark. "Not that it helps much."

Mike gave him a sour look but returned his eyes to the road.

Clark said, "I haven't worked with Lieutenant Sheffer before, so I don't really have much of an opinion. I've heard she's good at her job and she certainly seems competent. Looking at her as a woman, she's attractive, and I understand she's divorced. Are you interested?"

Mike gave him another sour look. "Give me a break, Clark. I was just curious."

It was about five-thirty when they walked into the precinct.

"Detective Brennen! Two mornings in a row? Be still my heart." said Sergeant Hansen.

"I'll still your heart," grumped Mike.

"Oh, oh. Better be careful, Sarg," said another officer. "Yesterday it was ears, today it might be hearts."

"Damn, Mike," said Clark. "I didn't know you were becoming such a celebrity."

"You'd be surprised how popular I've become," muttered his partner.

Mike was personally glad to find the squad room, and Grands' office, empty. His patience was wearing thin what with Reed and his ear, the elusive Janes, and the Panellis and their suspects.

"Why don't you get started on the juveniles," said Clark, "I'll see how many local Margos we've got and put out a watch-only for a used, plain van, possibly gray in color. Might get lucky."

"That would be a shocking turn of events," said Mike.

In the next hour, the two men came up with an ample number of names. They decided, at least for the time being, to set aside all addresses except those in the general area of the robberies. It was their gut feeling that these girls wouldn't travel all that far from their home neighborhood to borrow cars and rob places. They also excluded African-Americans and Latinos. The descriptions hadn't given them much, but everyone had agreed that the girls were all unmistakably white. The final list included five Margos between the ages of eighteen and thirty. Six Frans, five Teresas, and four Jills, all between thirteen and nineteen. None of these Teresas or Jills were related, but they hoped that only meant that the sister had never been charged with anything. They had just made hard copies of the names and addresses when Lieutenant Grands came in.

He said, "In my office, gentlemen."

The detectives gathered up their lists and went into the office.

"Anita Sheffer called me at home and brought me up to date on the grocery store hit. She also told me that, so far, none of the local hospitals or clinics have had a young girl show up with any kind of a bullet wound," said Grands. "And also so far, no one has found an abandoned car with blood in it."

Clark told him, "They didn't need the ERs because they hi-jacked the ex-Doctor Holt," and went on to report what they had learned from Marvin. Such as it was.

"I think you better pay another visit to the doc sometime today. See if you can't squeeze a little more out of him," Grands said. "And call Sheffer with what you did get, see how she wants to divvy up the names and addresses. If we can latch onto just one of these girls, we'll hopefully be able to track down the others."

When Grands had finished with them, Clark made the call to Lieutenant Sheffer to give her what information they had.

When his partner finished, Mike quipped, "Did she congratulate us on our fine job of digging up all those helpful first names?"

"She could barely contain herself," grunted Clark. "I'm faxing her the Fran and Margo lists. We get to visit the Teresas and Jills."

"She didn't say we couldn't get some breakfast first, did she?"

"And if she did?"

Mike smirked.

"That's what I thought," said Clark. "Your respect for officers diminishes more every day."

"The reason to respect some officers diminishes every day. Never you, though."

"Since when have you ever respected me?"

"You're my idol, Clark. I'm hungry. Let's go."

They stopped for eggs and sausage in a biscuit. Clark ate one, Mike ate two. Then they began tracking down their list, starting with the nearest address, which was a Teresa. They found that the girl had already left for school, but her mother let them know in no uncertain terms that her daughter had not left home at any time in the night and did not have any injuries and had no sister named Jill or any sisters at all! Door slammed!

"Guess we can cross that one off," said Mike.

The next stop was a Jill. She was also on her way out the door for school. This time it was the father who came to the defense of the daughter, telling them that there was no way the girl would ever be able to slip out at night, for any reason!

"Besides," he fumed on, "she was only picked up that once for shoplifting and, believe me, she hasn't done it since and never will again and I'm tired of the cops coming after her every time some teenage girl does something wrong! And her sister, Evelyn, is only eight years old!"

Clark scratched that one off the list.

The next girl was also a Jill. She was home, but when she opened the door the length of the safety chain, they saw she had a terrible cold.

"My folks have gone to work already," she told them on seeing their badges. "I can give you their phone numbers if you want."

"I don't think that will be necessary, Miss Fuller," said Clark.

Mike still asked, "Do you have any sisters?"

The girl shook her head and sneezed.

At the next address, a Teresa, no one was home. At least, no one answered their persistent bell ringing and knocking. They marked it for a return visit. By noon they had finished their list and were discussing whether to try the absent Teresa again or wait until after school hours.

"Let's go see if Doc Holt is up," Clark decided. "Maybe his mind is fresher than it was earlier."

"It's got to be fresher than ours. He's gotten some sleep since then," rumbled Mike.

Marvin was still sleeping and Sylvia, as usual, was reluctant to let them in.

"You know, Mrs. Holt, that we won't go away until we see him," said Clark. "And I have to tell you, my partner is tired and getting more impatient with each minute. The longer you make us wait, the more likely it is that Mike will want to drag him to the station house and question him there. It would really be better all-around if you would let us see him now."

When Mike glowered at him, Clark shrugged and said, "You are tired and you might decide to take him in."

His partner turned to the door and pounded on it.

"I can easily break this door in, Sylvia!" declared Mike in his toughest tone. "And who knows how long it would take to get it fixed."

They heard the chain come off and the lock turn and then Sylvia was once again glaring out at them. She had traded in her bright blue bathrobe for a bright yellow and pink house dress.

"You goddamned cops!" she griped.

Clark smiled. "Would you like to get him out of bed or should I send in Mike--"

She stomped off to the bedroom. The cops stepped into the apartment, closing the door behind them.

"You handled that with your usual expertise," said Clark. "I can always depend on you."

"I'm glad I'm useful once in a while."

It was several minutes before a slow-moving Marvin Holt made an appearance in the same, now rumpled, pants and shirt he'd had on earlier. He gave them an unfriendly scowl and sank onto the sofa. Sylvia did not reappear.

"I don't know anything more," the man said grumpily. "Honest to--"

"We don't want to hear that anymore!" Mike matched his grumpiness.

Clark quickly said, "We were hoping maybe you had a nice dream revealing some new little detail that could help us out...?"

"I didn't dream about nothing. The wigs and hats covered their hair and the bandanas covered their faces and they had gloves--" There was a sudden intake of air and he let loose a loud sneeze. That was immediately followed by two more. "Ahhh, shit! I probably got her goddamned cold, too."

The detectives' eyes narrowed in on him.

"Your wife doesn't have a cold, Marvin," said Mike.

"Not her. That kid from last--" Holt stopped and managed a little smile. "I don't suppose knowing one of them had a cold would help, huh?"

Neither of the detectives were smiling back.

"Which one, Marvin?" asked Sergeant Thorn.

"One of the sisters. Not the one shot. The other one. Jill."

CHAPTER 17

Feeling like they had finally gotten something, Detective Brennen and Sergeant Thorn returned to the car with heightened spirits.

"It was Jill Fuller with the cold," said Mike as Clark picked up the list to check it.

"Right," said his partner as he tried calling Sheffer, but it went to voicemail, so he left a message. He called Grands.

"Excellent," said the lieutenant. "Get some backup and go get her before she gets to thinking too much about your visit and decides to run. I'll take care of getting the warrants."

A squad car met them a block from the apartment building where the Fullers lived. The two uniformed officers were experienced. Beefy Tim Barker was in his eighth year on the force. Slender Barbara Sammoy, her blond hair braided and pinned up, had almost ten years. She and Mike were more than casually acquainted, having dated on and off for a couple of years. They enjoyed the relationship because neither of them was looking for steady commitment. They exchanged knowing smiles.

"If I can have your attention," stated Sergeant Thorn.

"Yes, sir," said Barbara.

"Undivided," said Mike.

Clark told them, "The word used the most to describe these girls, is 'bitches'. They are foul-mouthed and nasty and their guns are real and they've killed. So, it's possible we might have some resistance here. Maybe even a firefight. But keep this in mind -- they could probably kill one of us without exciting the citizenry. But, if we kill a teenage girl, we could be labeled as the bad guys. Let's do our best to avoid that. If you have to shoot, try for arms or legs. If you don't have a choice, then do what you need to do to protect yourselves. We need to back each other up on this. Mike and I will go in the front of the building, you two check and see if you can come up the back. If you can't because it's locked, come back this way and join us. We are meeting at Apartment Number 209, and we'll make entry as a team."

Sammoy and Barker put on their bullet proof vests and slipped down the alley. Mike had only one vest in the trunk of his car.

"Wear it, Clark," he said. "I don't have a wife and kids to take care of. Well, there is Rambo. If anything ever happens to me, you will take Rambo into your family, won't you?"

"On a cold day in hell," said Clark as he took off his suit coat to put on the vest. Pulling his coat back on, he added, "I promise I'll find a home for him. Maybe the zoo would take him."

"You're depressing me, Clark."

"Just don't ever get killed."

The building was similar to the one Mike lived in, though the door to the small foyer was not locked. The detectives ignored the elevator and took the stairs up one flight. Sammoy and Barker were waiting for them.

Pulling their weapons, Mike and Barbara stood to the left of the door while Clark and Tim were on the right. Clark gently tested the doorknob to see if it was locked. It was. He pushed the doorbell. No response. He pushed it again. No response. They knew the girl was there. He knocked loudly. No response. He knocked louder.

"This is the police again, Miss Fuller! Open--"

Two guns exploded, the bullets ventilating the door, spitting splinters into the air. It was definitely a response! Instinctively, all four police officers twisted away from the door, bringing arms up to protect their faces.

"Son of a bitch!" exclaimed Clark.

"Fuck!" agreed all three of his companions.

The explosions stopped.

"I hope they don't know how to reload very fast," said Mike as he stepped in front of the door.

"After you kick, let me go first, Mike. I've got a vest," said Barbara moving up.

Mike wasn't going to argue with that. He gave the bullet riddled door a hard kick and it slammed inward, tearing the safety chain off with it. Clark went in to the left, Tim right behind him. Barbara went right, Mike behind her. They were met with wild screaming and a barrage of unfriendly language.

Jill Fuller had a handful of bullets and was trying desperately to get them into her revolver. When Officer Sammoy came at her, the teenager let out a blood curdling screech and threw the gun at her. Barbara tried to dodge it, but it still glanced off her shoulder. Mike was quick to come around her, only to get Jill's handful of bullets thrown into his face. Worse, Jill then threw herself at him.

Teresa Fuller had managed to get a cartridge into her gun. With Clark bearing down on her, she snapped the cylinder shut and tried to bring the heavy revolver up so she could fire at him. Clark got to her before she did, knocking the gun toward the wall. When she pulled the trigger, the bullet smashed through the glass of a framed picture, putting a hole between the antlers of a white tail buck standing on a mountainside. The detective gave the teenager an angry push, sending her onto a couch behind her. The wounded Teresa squawked as her face twisted in pain.

"You goddamned, fuckin', cop!" she cried.

Clark wasn't feeling any pity. He grabbed her right arm to lift her up and turn her on her face. Planting a hand in her back, he ordered, "Barker, get some cuffs on her!"

Mike wasn't doing as well as his partner. Even with Jill throwing herself at him, he really didn't want to have to shoot her. Even in an arm or a leg. Especially now that she was no longer armed. Especially accidentally, after what had happened to Reed's ear. So he tried to block her with his left arm while trying to keep his right hand, and the gun in it, out of her reach. It didn't work. Filled with a youthful rage, the teenager practically climbed him, and Mike went over backwards with the girl on top. Jill wasted no time in using her advantage to squirm around, reaching with her nails, or from the detective's point of view, her claws. She managed to rake him once, leaving ugly scratches down the left side of his neck. Before she could do any more damage, however, Barbara came to Mike's rescue.

Grabbing the girl's long, bleach blond hair, Barbara pulled the screaming teenager off the struggling Mike. The policewoman then shoved Jill against the wall and ordered, "Stay put, darlin', and cool down!"

Jill wasn't interested in cooling down and it took all of Barbara's strength to keep her in that position. It was Clark, stepping over the fallen Mike, who came to help her. With some effort, Clark got cuffs on Miss Fuller, and Barbara deposited her on the couch next to Teresa.

"Young ladies! Stay put!" ordered the woman.

The young ladies stayed put, but the torrent of ugly words and threats did not lessen.

Clark gave his slightly dazed partner a hand in getting back onto his feet.

"Ouch," Clark said sympathetically when he saw the long, nasty bleeding scratches.

"Ouch doesn't cover it," grumbled Mike, gingerly touching his wounds. Blood was already running down his neck and soaking into his tee-shirt. "Fuck!"

"That might cover it," allowed Tim.

"I don't know," said Barbara. "He really shouldn't use such language in front of these innocent young ladies."

The four cops looked at the seething, far -from-innocent, young ladies.

"Whew," said Clark.

"Fuck," said Mike again.

CHAPTER 18

The Fuller family apartment home was a good size, with living room, dining room, kitchen and three bedrooms. It was on the messy side, but there were two teenage monsters living there. Clark called in to Lieutenant Grands who was on his way with the necessary warrants. Then Clark got ahold of Lieutenant Sheffer who told him 'Good work' and that she would handle Mr. and Mrs. Fuller, which was more than fine with him. If the daughters were this ornery, he didn't want to think about how ornery the parents might be. Or, they could be the opposite, not caring what their offspring were up to. The daughters obviously had no trouble slipping out and robbing people. And shooting them.

Mike hunted up a small towel and was nursing his bleeding scratches as he asked Clark, "So how do you want to do this?"

"I think you and Barbara should take Miss Teresa to the hospital," said his sergeant. "The girl needs attention and so do you. I'll get another squad to come by for Miss Jill, and Tim and I will wait for Grands so we can search this place."

Jill Fuller snarled at Mike. "I hope you get fuckin' infected and die the death of a fuckin' thousand years." She sneezed and coughed.

"I hope you have pneumonia," Mike snarled back.

He and Barbara took Teresa down to his car, the girl limping and complaining about how she was shot and would sue the world. Surprisingly, once she was in the back seat with Barbara, she slumped down and was quiet. The pain from her wound showed in her face and she finally seemed played out. Maybe reality was settling in. When they reached the hospital, Sammoy went into the Emergency Room and brought out a wheelchair. Teresa meekly settled into it.

Barbara, pushing the chair as they walked back in, told Mike, "I'll stay with her. You should probably go get a rabies shot."

"Cute," grunted Mike.

"These are quite nasty," said the elderly, heavy set nurse who took care of him. "Did the young lady you brought in, do this?"

"Her sister did it, but they're peas from the same pod," said Mike, gritting his teeth against the sharp, stinging pain caused by the antiseptic.

When he'd been bandaged and gotten a tetanus shot, but no rabies, he rejoined Sammoy. Teresa Fuller was showing some life again, cussing out the doctor and nurses who were working on her wounded leg. A lot of it was show to hide the tears she was fighting back.

"They told me she's weak from loss of blood," said Barbara with a crooked grin.

"Weak?" said Mike. "I guess we're really lucky that we got the two of them while one was sick with a bad cold and the other was wounded. If they'd been healthy, we'd've been in real trouble."

Lieutenant Grands came in as they were finishing with Teresa and he talked to the doctor before joining Brennen and Sammoy. He told them, "They want the girl to stay in the hospital for a couple days for observation. We'd look bad if some kind of infection set in. Until I've made the arrangements, I want Officer Sammoy to stay with her." He eyed Brennen's neck. "I understand the other Miss Fuller was a little tough on you."

"I think it was a personality thing. We didn't like each other," allowed Mike. "Did they find anything helpful in the apartment?"

"Everything we could ask for. The cowgirl outfits and plenty of loot and, of course, the guns. I left Clark to handle--"

"Afternoon, people," greeted Lieutenant Sheffer as she came up to them. She noticed Mike's bandaged neck. "I wasn't aware that you had been wounded, Detective."

"Just claws," said Mike.

"Maybe just claws," said Barbara, "but I believe the girl was ready to shred him into little pieces."

"Ouch," said Sheffer.

"How did it go with the parents?" asked Grands.

His female counterpart gave them a look of disgust.

"Such wishy-washy people," she said. "They say they had no idea what was going on and I guess I believe them. The father was going to see about getting an attorney and will go to your precinct with whoever he gets. The mother is on her way here to see this daughter. How bad off is the girl?"

"They told us she's weak from loss of blood, but Barbara and I aren't buying it," said Mike.

"They want her to stay a couple days," said Grands. "I'll set it up."

"Well, I'm afraid Sergeant Pragg and I weren't quite so successful. None of the Margos on the list fit the bill. We do think we've got a possible Fran. A gal name of Fran Kott. K-o-t-t. Don and I played innocent and we're hoping the girl will call her boss lady and that Ms. Margo will show up at her place. Don is sitting on her right now." She gave Mike an inquiring look. "Do you think you're up to a stint at surveillance later, Detective?"

Mike gave her a twisted grin and said, "I don't suppose you can promise I won't have to wrestle with another teenage monster?"

Sheffer smiled back. "I wish I could, but with this bunch of toughies, Ms. Margo is likely to be the worst."

Mike winced and said, "Heaven forbid."

Barbara Sammoy laughed. "Maybe you better stay here with little Teresa and I'll do the surveillance."

"Maybe we could both do the surveillance," suggested Mike, cocking an eye at her.

Grands gave them a lieutenant-like scowl, while Sheffer cleared her throat.

"At any rate," pursued the latter, "I've asked Sergeant Thorn to relieve Don at seven this evening and then you relieve Thorn at one A.M. Your orders are to follow Ms. Kott if she leaves or call if Ms. Margo should show up. Either way, call for backup when needed and keep me posted no matter what the time is."

"There is the possibility that one of the Fuller girls will give us Margo's name and address," noted Grands. "Sergeants Thorn and Fells will be ready to question Jill as soon as counsel and the father get there. We'll have to wait a while with Teresa."

Brennen shook his head. "I wouldn't count on any help from Miss Jill. I'd be surprised if she stops bitching long enough to hear the questions."

"Not for you to worry about right now, Mike. You go home and get some rest before your surveillance shift," said Grands. "Now, if you'll excuse us, officer Sammoy and I are going to see to Teresa Fuller's stay in the hospital."

"Of course," said Anita Sheffer.

The moment they were out of ear shot, Mike took advantage of the brief moment of privacy with Sheffer.

"Lieutenant, have you had any chance to check into that tip?"

Sheffer gave a quick glance around to be sure no one could hear them before saying, "I haven't had the time needed to commit to it, Mike. I did make one discreet inquiry, but without results. However, when we get these Calamity Jane girls wrapped up, I'll be able to pursue it more diligently."

"Sure." Mike gave a nod but was thinking there really wasn't much time left to pursue it.

The woman gave him a light smile and said, "Hang in there, Detective. We'll be talking soon."

As she walked away, Mike found himself also wondering if the lady shouldn't be more interested in the possible attempt on Chief Macklin's life as compared to a bunch of bitchy girls in cowgirl outfits. Still, she had been on the Calamity case a long time and now they had killed. It was a more 'real' case and now there was plenty of proof against the girls where there was no proof to back up the Macklin tip. Except for the word of the Panellis.

One of which he discovered waiting in his car outside the hospital. Getting in, Mike closed his eyes and leaned forward to rest his head on the steering wheel and groaned.

"We weren't going to do this car thing again. Remember?" he said.

"Not my favorite spot, either," Joe said, "but you seem to spend a great deal of time in it. Or at the precinct. Would you rather I visited you there?"

"I'd rather you not visit me anywhere."

Joe ignored the remark, inquiring, "You've had a couple of meetings with Lieutenant Sheffer today and we're wondering if you've heard anything we should know about?"

"In case you've forgotten, Mr. Panelli, Lieutenant Sheffer and I are both cops, and we're supposed to be seeing and talking to each other because we're working on--"

"A yes or no would be sufficient. Time is sliding by, however, and in case you've forgotten, we aren't that sure how much time we've got."

"Ask your goddamned source."

"Our source doesn't know. If our source finds out, our source will tell us and then we'll tell you."

"Great. Okay, for what it's worth, I did just ask the lady lieutenant if she'd found out anything. Without any hostility, she said she'd only been able to make one discreet inquiry, with negative results. She did not say who she had been discreet with or what the negative results were. Her sources must be as secret as yours. And not for nothing, detectives do not insist that lieutenants share their sources, discreet or otherwise. As for Polinski and Corry, I've had no reason to be in contact with them. Unless Polinski decides to chew me out for shooting somebody's ear off."

"And letting a dog run off with it," said Joe, with a slight smile.

The comment did not open Mike's eyes or bring his head up off the steering wheel. He said, "My fuckin' life is an open book. And another day like this and there probably won't be any more pages."

"Oh? Why do you say that?"

"You really care?"

"I asked."

"Of course you did, so I'll tell you. This afternoon I was almost blown away by a couple of teenage girls from hell, one of which also tried to tear my head off with her very sharp claws."

"Yes, I did notice the bandage and that your nice tee-shirt was all bloodied," said Joe. "Didn't you also get some blood on your suit yesterday? From the guy's ear? This job seems to be hard on your especially nice wardrobe."

"It's hard on my body, too. And early this morning, some scumbag drunk almost ran me over. If something happens to me, who will you ask to--"

"Somebody tried to run you down?"

Mike finally raised his head from the steering wheel and opened his eyes to look at Joe.

"Why did you say it like that?" asked the detective.

"Like what?"

"Like 'run you down' instead of 'run you over'. It was just a drunk."

"You know, Detective, there is the possibility that you shook somebody up yesterday with your inquiries and they didn't like the idea of you knowing about their plans."

"Shit," said Mike. In spite of the uneasy feeling again, he insisted, "It had to be a drunk. I can't believe I said enough to--"

"Just keep in mind we're dealing with the Rezzoros and they would not like anyone messing things up. Especially after their careful grooming of Captain Nimmer. Just keep your eyes open."

"Gee, I thought that's what you and Bears were for. You remember, to keep my butt from being shot off so I can go ahead and perform my duties as a police officer. Which I will do if you'll get out of my car. And make sure nobody sees you."

As Joe opened the car door, he had to ask, "Are you this crabby with all the citizenry?"

"Only the bad guys," stated Mike.

Once out of the car, Joe turned to lean down and look in at the detective and repeated, "Keep your eyes open."

He closed the door and walked toward the street where Tommy Bears and his Mercedes were undoubtedly waiting. Mike leaned his forehead on the steering wheel again.

"Damn it to hell," he groaned.

CHAPTER 19

When the detective pulled into the precinct parking lot and turned off the engine, he got a glimpse of himself in the rearview mirror. His hair was ramshackle, the left side of his neck covered in bandages, and his tiger tee-shirt, as well as his jacket, were splattered with his blood.

Mike groaned again. "Shit."

When he entered the building, Brennen stopped several steps in to take a deep breath and raise his hands.

"If I may have your attention, officers, I would like to get this out of the way," he announced tiredly. The room fell silent as all eyes turned on him. "Number One, for those who have not yet heard -- and I strongly suspect there are none who haven't -- I had a run-in with, dare I say, a wildcat, who leaped upon me and proceeded to use her claws. Number Two, I was rescued by the efficient Officer Sammoy. Number Three, I have been to the hospital and I'm sure you will be glad to hear that I didn't need a rabies shot and that I am going to live." He paused.

"Thank you for your attention."

With that, Mike continued his journey across to the stairs. He didn't quite make it.

"Guess you're lucky she didn't take your ear off, huh--?"

"I wish the efficient Officer Sammoy would rescue me."

"I have a feeling she'll be Numbers Four, Five and Six, too."

"Maybe we'll hear about that tomor--"

Mike took the steps two at a time.

One man was at his desk in the squad room. The correctly dressed, generic-looking, Gordon Whithers, was their newest, youngest detective. Fresh, honest and dedicated. Eager to learn it all. At times, annoyingly so. Mike briefly wondered why the Panellis hadn't chosen Whithers to go after the suspect lieutenants. The guy could have annoyed the guilty one into confessing.

"Hey. Mike," said Whithers. "Congratulations on nailing those two Calamity Jane girls."

"Thank you, Gordon."

"Thorn said you'd been wounded. I hope it's not too bad."

"I'll be fine. Are Clark and Fells with the Fuller girl?"

"Yeah. Room two. I don't think it's going too well." Whithers smiled a crooked smile. "Sometimes I can hear her yelling and cussing clear in here."

"Oh joy," said Mike.

He went back into the hallway, headed for Interrogation Room Two, and met Fells coming from that direction. Forty-eight-year-old Senior Sergeant Don Fells took his job, and especially his seniority, very seriously. Black hair and mustache neatly trimmed, the all-around medium-sized man did not have a smile or a laugh or even a tiny chuckle in his entire body and soul. Mike was sure of that because, over the last four years, he had tried at least three or four thousand times to tickle the man's funny bone, without success. Mike now considered it a challenge, and he swore that someday he would make the guy laugh, or at least smile.

Not today, though. He was beyond anymore smiles himself today.

"Hi, Sergeant," Mike greeted him. "Any luck with the sweet Miss Fuller?"

"No," stated Fells flatly and marched on past into the squad room. The man considered himself an expert interrogator and he did not take failure well.

Mike continued on toward the room, but the door opened before he got there. A red-faced she-devil, namely Jill Turner, came out with a muscular policewoman holding onto the girl's arm. The detective was relieved to see the girl's hands were cuffed behind her. Coming behind them was Clark and a fortyish, chunky woman Mike recognized as defense attorney, Mrs. Dora Ways. She was looking, understandably, tired and frazzled. And coming last was a deeply depressed-looking man in his forties.

"Please, Jill. Please try to…" the guy was whining.

"Shut the fuck up, Daddy!" screamed Jill Fuller. Then she saw Mike. "You!"

She made an attempt to pull away from the policewoman, but the officer had a tight hold on her and was no slouch at dodging kicks. She steered the girl down the hallway to where the lockup was. Mrs. Ways went past Mike without a word. Mr. Fuller stared after his daughter for a moment and then hurried away to find the nearest exit and escape.

"It doesn't sound like you had much luck," said Mike to his partner.

"Luck?" Clark was almost in a daze. "My God, that girl is…is indescribable. In all my years of interrogating, I have never come across the likes of her."

"Damn, and I missed it," said Mike.

"I'm going to have to use disinfectant to clean out my ears," Clark was going on. "When I get home, the first thing I'm going to do is hug and kiss my daughter and thank God that our worst problems with her are minuscule compared to this monster. I can't believe this kid was ever a cute little baby. She could never--"

"I get the picture, Clark," Mike cut him off. "I've even felt the monster's wrath upon my body."

Clark blinked and shook his head, coming out of his stupor. Seeing the bandages, he asked, "How'd it go for you? And Miss Teresa?"

"I'm fine. She's fine. She's weak from loss of blood."

"Right," snorted Clark.

"She was a lot quieter than her sister, though. Do you know we're doing surveillance tonight?"

"Yeah. I hope we can nab those other two gals and be done with these…" He shook his head. "…nutty females."

"Well, I'm going home to wash off this blood and get some sleep before 1 a.m."

"Just don't be late," said Clark. "It's been a long fuckin' day."

Detective Brennen went back down the stairs, ignored the rain of wisecracks as he crossed the lobby, and was out the front door. Driving home, his only thoughts were of a shower and sleeping. Well, maybe something to eat would be nice, too.

But, the first thing he did was feed Rambo. Then he went in to take a shower, first carefully taking off the bandage and laying it on the bed. His intention to put it back on afterward. Ten refreshing minutes later, Mike came out of the bathroom toweling himself off and found Rambo busy shredding the gauze bandage. The lack of a front set of claws did not slow him down a bit. He had become quite adept at kneading and shredding with his back claws.

"Rambo!"

Like a shot, Rambo retreated to the living room.

Muttering under his breath, Mike tossed the tattered bandage. Looking in his medicine cabinet, he found only a small box of band-aids, none large enough to do his multiple scratches any good. He left his wounds to fend for themselves. Pulling on a clean pair of briefs, the detective took time to gather his bloodied clothes and toss them into the basket. A neighbor lady, Marj Merritt, had a key to his place and came in on occasion to dust and vacuum and would do his laundry. He paid her a small fee, but she and her husband, Vern, were just glad to have a policeman living next door.

Rambo was sitting on the counter when Mike came into the kitchen.

"One of these days," said the man to the cat.

The cat didn't look at all worried.

Tired, but hungry, Mike opened a can of hash, dumping it into a fry pan, followed shortly by three eggs. While that cooked, the detective sniffed at the milk left in his half-gallon carton to see if it was still good. It was and he poured what was left into a glass. Putting the food on a plate, he sat at the dividing counter to eat. Rambo was right there for his share of the hash. When they had finished with their meal, the dirty dishes joined the other dirty dishes already piled in the sink.

Mike scowled at his cat. "You forgot to do these again today. I think it would be a small price to pay for food and shelter."

It was a suggestion he often made. The closest the cat ever came to relenting, was to lick up leftover delicacies from the plates. Fortunately, if the pile of dishes got too high, Marj did those, too.

With his stomach satisfied, Mike set his watch alarm for midnight. He then crashed on the sofa, using the remote to flip through the television channels. Catching the local news, Mike stopped.

"...with the capture of two of the Calamity Jane girls, the police are now concentrating on finding the remaining two. No names are being released as they are juveniles. One of those caught is the girl who was shot early this morning while robbing a grocery store. According to police, neither of the girls is cooperating with the investigation."

"There's an understatement," sniffed Mike. There was no mention of the detective who was wounded in the apprehension.

Mike searched through the channels until he found an old episode of MASH and turned the sound low. He then proceeded to devote several seconds of annoyed thought on the fun-filled Fuller sisters. For another five or six seconds he thought about the now one-eared Jason Reed. He even gave a dozen or so seconds of thought to the Panellis and their suspect lieutenants. His sore scratches intruded on all his thoughts. Then he fell asleep.

CHAPTER 20

Then he woke up. No dreams, no chase, just the goddamned phone alarm going off. And it felt like he'd barely closed his eyes. Mike shut the noise down and struggled to untangle himself from Rambo. It was a tight fit when man and cat both slept on the sofa and Rambo rumbled with annoyance at the interruption of his sleep.

Getting his feet to the floor, the detective sat holding his head for a few moments. Damn but his scratched-up neck was sore and stiff. Standing, he walked through the bedroom into the bathroom and switched on the light. His neck looked awful. The scratches were puffy and that whole side of the neck was red and purple. Maybe he should stop at a drugstore and get something to put on it.

Mike ran the electric shaver over his stubble, brushed his teeth, and combed his hair. Turning on the bedroom light, he wondered if he could get away with jeans for a second day. Decided maybe he better not push it. He put on a long-sleeved white shirt, his navy blue suit pants, and his blue sneakers -- after checking the duct tape in the bottom of the right one. Putting his cop tools in place, he went to the kitchen where Rambo was sitting on the counter. The cat looked at Mike with irritation. It was obvious these crazier than usual hours were not to his liking.

The detective detected the mood and said, "Tough shit."

Irritated or not, Rambo was ready to chow down when his person filled his bowl.

"Make it last," Mike told him. "Who knows what kind of hell I'll get into today. Especially if we get our hands on the other two Calamity Janes."

Grabbing his suit coat and a tie, Brennen shut off the television and lights and was out the door.

It was a chilly spring night, but the detective was too busy being paranoid to give it much notice. He checked all directions before stepping off the curb and double checked the street before jogging to his car. Getting in, he tossed his coat and tie onto the back seat. Slipping the key into the ignition, Mike turned it and thought too late -- bomb! The car did not explode.

"Fuckin' Panellis," griped the detective. "I'll be a nervous wreck before this is over. If it ever gets over. If I'm still alive when it gets over. I'm talking out loud to myself again. I'm already a nervous wreck."

The Garfield jiggled at the end of his elastic cord and continued to grin.

As he drove, Mike found himself glancing into his rear-view mirror all too often. There weren't many headlights at this hour and he couldn't tell if the ones that he saw were following him or not. He didn't dwell on the thought that someone might be following him without their headlights on. He wondered if Mr. Bears was back there somewhere.

Mike didn't see an open drug store, so he set his mind to ignoring his sore neck. He did see a small, all-night cafe, and stopped to pick up a couple of cups of coffee and some donuts. When he got to Fran Kott's building, Mike took time to drive past the front of it. It was a renovated, ten story apartment complex. The foyer was brightly lit, the doors were probably locked, and there was a doorman. The Kotts must be well-to-do to live in a place like this. Which meant it was unlikely Miss Fran was in with the Calamity Janes for money. For that matter, the Fullers hadn't looked all that bad off either.

"Just in it for the kicks," muttered Mike.

Anyway, it was obvious that Miss Margo could not go in the front door to visit Fran Kott. Nor could Miss Fran leave that way unnoticed. Thus the eyes of the law were on the back exit.

Turning left around the corner, Mike turned off his headlights and slowed. When he saw Thorn's car, he stopped in the street. Leaving the motor running, he got out and went to knock on his partner's window. It had been a long, tiring day for Clark and it showed on his face and in his voice.

"Gee, you're here already? Time sure flew by," said Clark, making no effort to squelch a yawn.

"Hey. I'm on time," said Mike.

"And I appreciate it. How are the cat scratches?"

"My cat would never do this to me."

"The two-legged cat scratches then."

"Just know that they hurt as bad as they look and they look like hell. Anything important I should know about?"

"Nothing. My only entertainment has been some poor soul walking their dog at least once an hour. He comes along the sidewalk across the street, from behind. Just so you're aware. I do know that if I had a dog that got me up that often, it would be out the door. For good."

"Your love of animals is endearing to me, Clark."

Ever the sergeant, Clark asked, "Have you got your binoculars or do you need mine?"

"I've got mine, Clark. Go home and go to bed."

When Clark had left, Mike took the same parking place. From that position he could see the building's back exit. A light over it lit up the door and the alley around it. There was also a clear view of the fire escape that zig-zagged down the back of the complex. Getting his small binoculars from the glove compartment, Mike scrutinized the building and its neighbors. Satisfied all was quiet, he laid the glasses down on the seat to grab his sack. Getting out a coffee and donut, he settled in.

In the next hour and a half, the only moving thing Mike saw was the dog walker -- twice. The person was wearing a knee-length, lightweight coat, with the collar turned up, head and shoulders slouched low. The detective couldn't tell if it was a man or a woman. He did find himself having to agree with Clark in that he wasn't sure he'd want a dog that had to piss and/or poop that often either. Through the binoculars, Mike could see it was a small, fuzzy dog, but even if it was daylight, he wouldn't have been able to guess if it was a specific breed. Hell, as a cat person he didn't even know that many cat breeds, except maybe Siamese and long-haired Persians. He had bought a book on cats and cat care when Rambo had moved in to take over his life, but--

The building's back door opened and somebody small slipped out, moving quickly into the darkness. Mike straightened, eyes and binoculars focused on the alley. Shortly, a smallish dark shape crossed the sidewalk to stop in the deep shadow of a tree. There it stayed. Waiting for someone?

"I hope that's you, Miss Fran Kott," said the detective, "and I hope it's your lady boss that you're waiting for."

Mike took the precaution of taking his gun out and laying it on the seat. He expected, and watched for, a grayish van. When Margo showed up, he would call it in and follow her.

Mike caught motion in his rear-view mirror. A quick glance told him it was the person with the dog, now on this side of the street. Absently he wondered if maybe the dog had gotten tired of the trees on the other side. Suddenly a car alarm went off, loud and obnoxious. The racket was coming from behind him.

"Shit!" swore the detective as he twisted around to glance that way. Instantly his rear window disintegrated and there was no mistaking the distinctive sound of gunfire.

"Fuck!"

The binoculars fell from Mike's right hand, instantly replaced by his gun. His left hand had the car door open and he was rolling out onto the street. Lying flat on his stomach, gun in his hands, arms stretched in front of him, Mike fired at the only target he could see. Somebody's legs.

Hoping they didn't belong to the dog walker, Mike did not take any chances. The detective fired three quick rounds and the person dropped to the ground hard. In the same instant, the car alarm stopped to be replaced by a woman's screeching. Mike scrambled to his feet to dodge around the car, wanting to stop his adversary before they could reload, or maybe try to run if his bullets hadn't done the job. He found the dog walker in the short coat trying to raise a good old-fashioned six-shooter toward him. He kicked it out of her hands, sending it under his car. She screamed, partially in pain, partially in rage.

"On your face, lady!" ordered Mike.

"Fuckin' cop! You shot me!"

"I'll shoot you again if you don't roll over!"

"Brennen! Behind you!" warned a familiar man's voice.

Mike's head snapped around. Looking past the back of his car, he saw a dark shape rushing across the street.

Fran Kott yelled impolitely, "You fuckin' sonofabitch! You shot Margo!"

Mike's stomach knotted. Did she have a gun? He couldn't tell in the dim street light and he didn't know if he could shoot a teenage girl if he wasn't sure.

Miss Fran helped him out by firing a shot at him. Fortunately, she was running and her aim was way off. She was having trouble moving and holding the heavy revolver in her hands and pulling the trigger, all at the same time. She got off one more wild shot as the detective threw himself sidewise against his car. By then, the girl's momentum had carried her close enough to Mike so he could reach out and grab her left arm, twisting it. The gun fell out of her hands, but she turned on him, ready for hand-to-nails combat. With the pain of his scratches all too fresh, Mike didn't fool around. He continued to twist her arm and knocked her legs out from under her. She went down, hitting the street with a hard bump.

"Stay there, damn it!" he snapped as he kicked the gun out of her immediate reach. When Miss Fran tried to get up, Mike used a foot to pin the cussing girl down. His voice a whip, he ordered again, "Stay down!"

This time he had her attention. The struggling stopped and the cussing slowed.

The dark figure of a man, holding a gun, came up. He offered, "I can keep them covered for you, officer, if you want to cuff them."

The face was not discernible, but Mike had no trouble recognizing Tommy Bear's voice. Which was slightly amused at the moment.

"I would appreciate, though, if you'd do it quickly," added Bears. "I've called 911 and I'd like to be gone before the men in blue show up."

"No shit," said Mike.

His adrenaline still pumping hard, the detective shoved his gun under his belt and pulled out his cuffs.

"I'm taking my foot off you," he told Fran. "Both of us will be a lot happier if you don't try anything. Besides, this nice citizen might accidentally shoot you if you aren't a good girl."

"Kiss my ass, you fuckin' cop!"

"Maybe I'll just sit on it!"

He removed his foot from her back and replaced it with a knee on her ass.

"You fuc--"

"Put a cork in it and give me your hands!"

Giving the citizen and his gun a look, the girl relented with her hands but seemed to be out of corks.

"Now stay put," he said sharply as he stood up.

The sound of approaching sirens could be heard and people, awakened by both the car alarm and the shooting, were starting to appear.

"If you've got things under control, I'll run along," said Bears.

"So run!"

Tommy went, but he did not run.

Mike pulled his gun back out and returned to the shooter. Since Miss Kott seemed to have recognized the woman's voice, the detective now assumed that this was Margo. The woman was actually crying as she tried to sit up, reaching for her legs.

"I think I told you to roll over, lady!" Mike snapped at her.

"I'm shot! You shot me, you fuckin' cop!" she sobbed.

"Gee whiz. You don't suppose it was because you were trying to blow my head off, do you?" growled Mike with a complete lack of sympathy. "Now roll on your face, goddamnit!"

She complied, but she didn't have any corks for her unlady-like language, either. Mike stooped beside her, his gun pressed into her shoulder so she wouldn't forget he had it.

His voice low and icy, the detective said, "I want to know real bad how you knew this was my car and that I was a cop. I want--"

The sirens closed in and two squads came around the corner to squeal to a stop.

"You think hard about what I'm asking," said Mike, "because I'm part of your life until I have some answers."

He straightened up, then, turning to welcome the boys in blue.

CHAPTER 21

Brennen had one of the officers gather up the girls' guns and bag them. He read Fran Kott her rights, which the girl punctuated with her own lively retort, and put her into the back seat of one of the squads. He made sure an EMT was on the way and, in the beams of a couple of flashlights held by the officers, also made sure Margo's wounds were not life threatening. She had been hit twice. One bullet had gouged her right calf, while another had creased her left ankle.

"From ears to feet," remarked one of the uniforms matter-of-factly. "Is that better or worse shooting?'

Mike's sense of humor was not at its best right now and the look he gave the officer got that point across.

"Put some cuffs on her, hands behind her back," growled the detective.

The cussing, whimpering Margo, immediately protested, "I'm shot! You're gonna handcuff me when I'm shot?"

"You bet your sweet ass," declared Mike and proceeded to read her her rights. Then he called Lieutenant Sheffer. She couldn't miss the barely controlled fury in his tone as he gave her a brief report.

"You're saying you were ambushed, Detective?"

"Not just ambushed, Lieutenant. Set up."

"Set up? Who in the world would do that?"

"That's what I'd like to know."

Another siren announced the arrival of the EMTs.

"I'm going to the hospital with the Margo woman," said Mike. "I want to ask--"

"I want you to wait there at the scene for me, Detective Brennen. Have one of the uniforms go with her. Preferably a woman."

"I'd rather go--"

"I'm on my way," stated Sheffer, ending the call.

Mike muttered some colorful language of his own.

When the paramedics had cared for Margo and loaded her into their ambulance, Mike got his first good look at the woman. The ex-Doctor Holt was right about her being heavier than the younger girls. She was maybe a hundred and forty pounds and no more than five-feet-four in height. Her round face looked kind of smooshed even without a stocking over it. The total appearance didn't exactly fit the image of a leader of violent teenage robbers who had killed. And had now attempted to kill a cop. She did sound vicious enough as she continued to swear and threaten him between gasps of pain.

"I don't suppose you'd like to give me your last name, Miss Margo?" asked the detective, during a brief lull.

"Drogan, you fuck!" she unexpectedly shared. "Don't forget it, 'cause I'm gonna make sure you get yours!"

Mike assigned a woman officer from one of the two squad cars to go with the prisoner. Officer Gale Leeds, her black hair in a short bob, didn't look much older than Margo.

"I don't think she likes you, Detective," noted Leeds.

"The feeling is mutual. Just don't take your eyes off her," said Mike. "I've got some very important questions she needs to answer."

"Yes, sir."

The ambulance left and Mike decided to have a visit with the Kott girl before someone specifically told him he couldn't. He had almost been filled with holes and he was itching to find out why. Opening the back door of the squad, he looked in at her.

"If you tell me how you knew I was a cop on stakeout, I could say you were cooperative," Mike told her.

"Even if I knew, I wouldn't tell you! Go fuck yourself!"

Mike frowned. "You knew! Otherwise how did she know to shoot at me through the back window?"

"I don't know what Margo knew. I didn't know. I was waitin' for her, but I thought she was pickin' me up in the van. When that stupid car alarm went off and the shooting started, I was gonna beat it. Then I heard the scream and knew it was Margo and that's when I figured you had to be a fuckin' cop. It's too fuckin' bad I didn't hit you!"

"You fuckin' tried and you missed! And so did your dragonlady boss," said the frustrated detective and slammed the door. He was mad and confused. "Damn it."

There was another siren and Sheffer arrived. When she got out, she stopped for a look at the remains of Mike's rear window.

"I can see why you're upset, Detective Brennen," she said.

"Upset doesn't cover it. Set up covers it."

The lieutenant sounded a little peeved when she said, "Aren't you being a bit paranoid? We'll be interrogating all the girls and I'm sure there's a simple explanation."

"It can't get much simpler than her shooting at me from behind," said Mike. His tone was more peeved than hers. Probably not the best tone to be talking to a superior officer with, but he was ticked off and didn't particularly care right now. "If a car alarm hadn't gone off, I'd be on my way to the morgue instead of standing here."

"Car alarm?"

"That's what saved me. When I turned to see where it was coming from, Miss Margo's bullets missed me."

Brennen decided not to mention the helpful citizen and hoped Bears' presence would never come up.

"Did you find out where the alarm came from?" asked Sheffer.

"I was busy dodging bullets and fingernails. It stopped and I haven't taken the time to bother with it."

"Look, Mike," said Anita Sheffer, giving him a soft smile. "This has understandably shaken you up. I've got to go and confront the Kott girl's parents. Why don't you go to the precinct and catch your breath and put down on paper exactly what happened here, while it's fresh. Later, we'll talk to all four girls, one by one, and see if we can get the right answers."

Mike also decided that this was not a good time to mention his short conversation with Fran. He wasn't sure if there would be a good time.

He gave in with, "Yeah. Okay."

She nodded. "Good. You see that Miss Kott is booked and I'll get back to you soon."

Signaling one of the uniforms to join her, Sheffer headed for the apartment complex.

Mike turned to the remaining two officers, both men in their middle to late thirties, and said, "Look, the bitch who shot at me was walking a dog. There's no way to tell where it ran off to but keep your eyes open. It was on the small side with fuzzy fur. All the shooting probably scared it to death. I know it almost scared me to death. If you find it, take it to the Humane Society. I'm guessing it's stolen and somebody--"

One of the officers cleared his throat and exchanged a look with his comrade.

"What?" asked Mike with a threatening scowl.

Threat or not, the guy couldn't resist saying, "Well...we can't help wondering if maybe it was the same dog that ran off with the ear."

Now the detective glared at them scornfully.

"You," he said to the one who had spoken, "are to stay here and look for the dog, and also in case Lieutenant Sheffer needs you." To the other one, "You take the Kott girl in and book her." He finished, "I am going to find a drugstore and nurse my painful wounds that I got in the performance of my duty."

Mike got into his wounded car and drove away. But, he did not drive to a drugstore nor did he go to the precinct to catch his breath and write down his evening's escapades. His real destination was the hospital. Although in doing so, he was disobeying his superior's orders. But technically, he could be called a hero, having rounded up the Calamity Jane Gang. Who would discipline a hero?

Besides, he could say he had decided to go to the hospital to get his scratches looked after.

Before heading there, however, there was someone else Mike wanted to have a talk with. He looked into his rear view mirror several times without seeing anything, which frustrated the hell out of him. Finally he just pulled into a deserted parking lot and waited. Shortly, Tommy Bears' Mercedes Benz pulled in to stop beside him. Tommy got out and slid onto Mike's front seat.

"How do you do that?" asked the detective.

"Do what?" said the Indian.

"Follow somebody on deserted streets without being seen?"

"Trade secret."

"Like shit." Then stated, "I was set up, wasn't I?"

"Looked that way to me. Did you learn anything from the enchanting young lady who tried to blow your head off?"

"No, but I'm on my way to try again. I managed to have a short talk with the other little sweetheart. She claims she didn't know I was there. She said that she was just waiting for Margo to show up in her van. My first impression is that she's telling the truth."

"It kind of looks like the lady lieutenant goes to the top of the suspect list. It's her case and if she set up the surveillance, she knew when you would be there. She could have threatened or blackmailed or paid cash to the shooter."

"I know all that. It gives her some black check marks, but I'm not ruling out the other two suspects yet. As lieutenants, they have access to, or know other routes to take, to find out all the same information. I'm going to try and have a private chat with Sheffer later and kind of mention that maybe these attempts on my life are connected to the Macklin tip. To see what sort of a reaction she has."

"Don't make it too private. She might shoot you herself."

"Yeah. It's nice of you to mention that. Now I'm going to go and see if Ms. Margo Drogan has something in her vocabulary besides fuckin' cuss words."

"Good luck." Tommy started to get out.

Hesitantly, Mike started, "I...want to..."

Bears turned his head to look back at him. "Pardon me?"

"I...well, thanks," the cop managed. "Thanks for setting off that alarm. It saved my life."

"You're welcome," said Tommy sincerely.

"And I give you permission to take the rest of the night off. I don't plan on doing anything more tonight that I would need to be saved from."

"Looking at your neck, are you sure about that?"

The detective gave a sniff. "You've got a point, but I still think I'm safe."

Mike went on his way but was unable to tell if the Indian was still following him or not. Which still frustrated him.

CHAPTER 22

They thought he was an accident victim when he walked into the Emergency Room. It might have had something to do with his having rolled around on the pavement, leaving shirt and pants a mess. Also the array of colors and scratches on his neck. Being as they were a different shift than those that had 'waited' on him yesterday, Mike showed his badge and explained he was there to check on Ms. Margo Drogan. He was told she had already been cared for.

"Ms. Drogan's wounds were superficial," said one of the nurses. Her name tag said she was Ann Pilgrim. Where would he be without name tags? Petite, freckle faced with red hair, Ann did not look old enough to be a nurse. "We put her in a room down the hall because she was making such a fuss and using such terrible language. We didn't want her upsetting other patients The woman officer is with her."

"Ms. Drogan does have a personality flaw or two," agreed Mike with a friendly smile.

Ann smiled back. Also friendly.

"Why don't you let me take care of those nasty scratches for you, Detective Brennen," she suggested and ushered him into one of the rooms and sat him down. As she got out bottles and gauze and tape, she said, "I have to inquire how you received these scratches so I know exactly what I am treating. They aren't animal, are they?"

"Human animal," said Mike. "And I've already had them treated once and they gave me a tetanus shot."

"Oh. Not a girlfriend, I hope."

"Not even close. Another friendly female like Ms. Drogan. A prodigy of hers as a matter of fact."

"Oh, dear. What did they do to have police after them?"

"They are the Calamity Janes and calamity is a good name for--" Mike saw Officer Gale Leeds go past the doorway and called, "Officer Leeds!"

She reappeared and stepped into the room. "Detective Brennen. Was it you who asked for me? An orderly said it was a phone call, but--?"

Mike had a sudden, uncomfortable zap in the pit of his stomach.

"Shit! Where's the room?" he demanded, jumping to his feet.

He startled both Leeds and Nurse Pilgrim by pulling his gun.

"Wha--? Oh. This way!" said Leeds.

Running now, the officer led him down the hallway. When she reached the last door on that side, she pushed it open and they both rushed in. And stopped.

Margo Drogan's colorful language, and other personality flaws, had been corrected -- or more correctly -- ended. Her head lolled back on a pillow, glassy eyes seeing nothing, a gaping wound in her neck. Her throat had been expertly slit, the blood spilling down the front of her and running like tiny red rivers across the white coverlet.

"Oh my God!" gasped Leeds.

Mike snapped, "Check the other rooms and the halls! I'm out this way!"

The detective charged through a second door that led into a quiet, shadowy hallway. At the other end, an exit sign glowed red above another door.

"Son of a bitch!"

He was down the hall and out the door in record time, but there was no one around for him to chase further. He heard a car's tires squeal and he looked that way. It was at the end of the parking lot and the noisy culprit was quickly swallowed up by traffic. It was impossible to know if the car had any connection to what had just happened.

The door Mike had run out of had locked on closing so that he couldn't get back in that way. It raised the question of how the killer had gotten in, but Mike knew there were numerous ways it could have been done without causing any suspicions. He walked around to the ER entrance, cussing himself out the whole way. A small group of curious hospital personnel had gathered and they watched the angry cop stomp in and down the hall. A worried Gale Leeds was waiting for him at Drogan's room.

"I couldn't find anyone who didn't belong," she said. "I'm really sorry, Detective Brennen. I had no idea...I didn't know something like this could happen. Why would anyone want to kill her? I mean, she was a prisoner and--?"

"It's not your fault," stated the seething Mike. "You didn't know and I didn't think." He pushed the door open to stare at Drogan's body. Taking a deep breath, he said, "Stay out here by the door. I'm going to call it in."

"Yes, sir." She looked a little white.

"You okay?" Mike asked.

"I...yeah. It's...my first body."

"Put your mind on what that orderly looked like. I may have you look at pictures later."

"Yes, sir."

Closing the door, Mike stared at the deceased dragonlady. "What the hell else is going to happen?" he grumbled out loud and pulled out his phone.

CHAPTER 23

It was almost 5 a.m. and they were in a room across the hall from where Margo Drogan lay dead. Detective Mike Brennen stood before Lieutenant Anita Sheffer, who was sitting in a chair, and Lieutenant Carl Grands, whose back was leaning against the empty bed. Still angry with himself, Mike was also becoming increasingly annoyed with the attitude of his two superiors. They hadn't come right out and said he was in trouble, but their attitude seemed to be that he might be. Mike couldn't understand why he should be in the hot seat. After all, someone had tried to kill him a couple of hours ago. Sure, that someone had been murdered, but that certainly was not his fault. It wasn't Officer Leeds' fault either. Actually, how could it be anyone's fault? There was absolutely no reason why they should have been prepared for a possible hit on Margo Drogan.

Well, Mike knew of one possible reason, but it wasn't one he could offer to his superiors. They wouldn't like it anyway. Why, and who, would kill off Margo just to keep her from talking to Mike? Still, Sheffer was looking a little miffed, and Grands was wearing a sour expression. Not a happy couple. Still, again, Mike didn't feel their attitude was his problem.

"Why are you even here?" asked Sheffer. "My orders were for you to take the Kott girl in."

Mike told her with restraint, "For what it's worth, my scratches were hurting like hell, plus I picked up a couple more scrapes and bruises rolling around in the street trying not to get shot. I decided to come in and get them cleaned and bandaged. I don't see what difference it makes. The Drogan woman would have been killed whether I was here or not."

"Watch your tone, Brennen," warned Grands. "We have a mess here that's going to be hard to explain to the press. Your attitude is--"

"I've been shot at and clawed and ambushed and my collar had her throat cut. You're right. My attitude is a touch on the cranky side. Sir. Ma'am."

Sheffer softened a little. "We understand it's been a couple of rough days, Detective, but Carl is right. When a woman, a prisoner of the police, gets her throat slashed in a hospital, it is a bit of a mess. The press is going to want some explanations. We want some explanations."

"I'd like some myself," said Mike. "We got a guy in a doctor's white coat who sends a cop on a wild goose errand. Said guy then walks right into the now unguarded room where a woman is helplessly handcuffed to a bed and has no way to run. Wearing the white coat, the guy is able to walk right up to her and cold-bloodedly slit her throat so fast she doesn't have time to scream. And believe me, if she'd had a chance, she'd have brought the roof down. Then the guy is out of there so fast that he's gone when we walk in moments later. In and out and gone, in a matter of seconds. Sound like a hit to you? Sounds like one to me."

"You're saying it was a professional killer, Detective?" asked Sheffer with raised eyebrows.

"That's exactly what I'm saying," said Mike. "It was way too slick to be just some off the street thug. And a vehicle was waiting for the guy right outside the door. Gone before I could even get out there."

Grands found it hard to swallow, too. "Margo Drogan was not some high profile target, Brennen. Why would anyone send in a professional to kill her?"

Mike said, "That's one of the questions I'd have liked to have asked Ms. Drogan. Just who put her up to it. And don't you find it peculiar that she was out walking a dog, which was probably stolen, around the neighborhood in the middle of the night? And just happens to come up behind me and tries to blow my head off? Last time I looked, I didn't have a bumper sticker that said, 'Cop on board'."

"I admit it's strange," allowed Sheffer, "but not out of the realm of possibility. She could have found out that the Fuller sisters had been picked up and was being extra cautious, checking the streets around Kott's building before she made contact. And saw you sitting in the car--"

"She was walking around when Clark was there and must have seen him, but didn't shoot at him," declared Mike. "I'd like somebody to explain that to me."

With some sharpness, Grands said, "What we need to do is talk to the other three girls. They may have the necessary answers to clear this up. For now, Brennen, I want you and Officer Leeds, to go back to your respective precincts. She needs to make her report and to look at mug shots to see if she can spot this mysterious orderly. You have a couple of dandy reports to write up. And stick to the facts. I don't want you throwing in these stories about professional hitmen and being set up"

His jaw clenched in frustration, Mike grunted, "Yes, sir."

"Whatever happened, we still owe you congratulations on putting an end to the Calamity Jane Gang, Detective Brennen," said Sheffer. "They are a mean bunch and it's good to get them off the streets."

"Of course," Grands agreed, though with less enthusiasm than the lady lieutenant. He did add, "You do have a knack for getting the job done."

Mike's, "Thanks," wasn't exactly enthusiastic, either.

In the hallway, there seemed to be a platoon of cops wandering around. The Crime Scene Unit had taken over the murder room, but Mike wasn't too optimistic that they would find anything useful to follow up on. He found Officer Leeds and motioned her aside.

"You're going to be sent back to your station house to write a report and look at mug shots," he told her. "I would like you to concentrate on locals with reputations as hitters. Also try crime syndicate wise guys. And I would like you to call me personally if you find any possibles. Please."

She nodded. "I'll give it my best shot, Detective Brennen, but I didn't see him very well. I've gone over it a hundred times in my mind and all I can remember is that he did a good job hiding his face. I'm afraid he was just somebody telling me I had a phone call."

"Do your best. And thanks."

Driving to his precinct, Mike was hardest on himself, cussing his lack of caution. And, again, he hadn't gotten a chance to talk to Sheffer alone, so he cussed himself out for that, too. When he pulled into the parking lot, he realized he had never gotten a new bandage on his scratches and did some more cussing. Getting out, he glared at his car's shattered rear window and cussed at that. Retrieving his suit coat and tie from the back seat, Mike had to shake glass from the both of them. Even so, he could see tiny, glistening shards still clung to them. He cussed them out. When he got to the precinct door, the detective stopped and gave his watch a glance. It was just shy of 6 a.m. He was showing up early for the third morning in a row. He cussed at the time and went in.

"Hey! I win!" declared one of the uniformed officers.

"Shit," said another. "I didn't think there was a chance in hell that he'd do it for three days in a row."

"I still think it's a clone," grunted a third.

Sergeant Hansen smiled. "You make us proud, Detective Brennen."

"Sounds to me like I'm making somebody some money," sniffed Mike. "Cops gambling right in their own precinct. I'm ashamed."

No one was in the detective's squad room to give him a hard time.

The first thing he did was sit at a computer and key in Margo Drogan's name. Thorn had hunted up the list of Margos and Mike had barely glanced at it. Sheffer had said the young woman hadn't been on that list. And she was right. There was no Margo Drogan to be found. Mike cussed some more and reluctantly turned his mind to writing the report. He was still struggling when Lieutenant Grands came in about forty minutes later.

"Brennen," said the man and motioned at him as he walked to his office.

Mike's head drooped and he took a deep breath. Then he stood up and went into the office.

"Brennen, I do not condone your attitude at the hospital, but, after thinking about it, I guess if anyone had a right to have an attitude at the time, you did," said Grands.

Mike blinked in surprise and started to open his mouth with a reply, but the lieutenant was going on.

"The Drogan woman's murder, however, belongs to you and Clark. Lieutenant Sheffer and I could not come up with any reasonable suggestions as to why she was killed, especially in that fashion. It doesn't look like the lab picked up anything helpful, either. As you pointed out, the perp was in and out and gone and left nothing behind. The two of you give it your best shot and try to stay out of the way of the press. They really want to know why a woman in our custody was killed at the hospital."

"Yes, sir," said Mike. "If it's okay, I would like to run home and clean up."

"How's the report look?"

"Almost done."

"Finish then go."

"Yes, sir."

CHAPTER 24

Rambo had dug himself a comfy cave in the bed covers. He gave Brennen an annoyed glare with the one eye that was visible inside the darkness.

"I don't want to hear one screech," said Mike.

The detective pulled off his clothes and threw everything into the clothes basket. If his neighbor lady couldn't wash what he threw into his laundry collection, she took it to a drycleaner down the street. His drycleaning bill would be a dandy this month.

Mike took a fast shower and then stood and stared into the closet.

"Blood, glass, rain, cat hairs...I'm running out of clothes."

He decided to compromise, putting on a newer pair of jeans, a long-sleeved light tan shirt, a brown tie and brown sport coat. After double-checking the duct tape, he finished the outfit with his brown sneakers.

"If somebody doesn't like what I have on, they can screw themselves. Or fire me. Or both. Right now, I don't care."

By now, Rambo had emerged from his hidey-hole. Since Mike had disturbed his rest, the cat decided he might as well have a second breakfast. The best he got, though, was his person pouring more crunchies into the bowl. No second helping of Fancy Feast. A loud, complaining screech followed Brennen out the door.

Mike stopped at a drive-thru, picking up a sausage and egg biscuit breakfast, but it did little to satisfy him. It was eight-thirty when he got back to the precinct.

"You're running late this morning, Detective," remarked Jan Murphy, the day watch Duty Sergeant.

"God save me from Duty Sergeants," muttered Mike going up the stairs.

Clark Thorn and Harry Muller were in the detective's squad room. When Clark saw Mike, the sergeant slowly shook his head. "I leave you alone on a simple stake out and you turn it into a war zone, to say nothing of a mysterious murder."

"Don't beat me to death on this one, Clark," pleaded Mike. "None of it was my doing. I'm beginning to think I've got a black cloud over my head."

"Well, maybe not black, but it is a dismal gray."

"Thank you."

"Tell me, Mike," said Muller, "was the dog last night the same one that--"

"Don't say it, Harry!"

Harry grinned.

"Speaking of the dog," said Clark, "one of our guys at the Kott place called in to leave you a message that they'd found the fuzzy dog and returned it to its owner. Had name and address tags on its collar. I guess the Margo woman took it right out of someone's fenced yard."

"Wow. Finally, a happy ending," said Mike.

"Let's get over to juvie and--"

"I want to call Leeds first and see if she's had any luck with pictures."

He did that and Officer Leeds had no good news, telling him, "I'm sorry, Detective, but so far I haven't recognized anyone from the mug books. Like I said, I didn't get a very good look at him and--"

"Please keep trying and call me if you get lucky," urged Mike in frustration.

"Damn it," griped Mike after the call. "If I'd just gone right to the hospital room and asked Drogan those questions instead of..." He cussed himself out. Again.

"Life is full of ifs, Mike," said his partner. "Especially a cop's life. You don't want me to beat you to death on this, then don't beat yourself to death on it. Let's get over to juvie and see how Miss Kott and Miss Fuller are this morning. Maybe they've calmed down some and can give us some ideas on who would want to kill their 'lusterless' leader."

"I can't believe they'll ever talk to us and if they do, I doubt they'll tell us anything we want to hear," said Mike. "If anything, they'll teach us some new cuss words."

As the two detectives walked out, Clark pointed out in open relief, "Since your car got shot up, we'll have to use mine."

"Yeah, yeah, but I want to drop mine off at the police garage so they look for bullets and take plenty of pictures of my missing window. Dear Ms. Drogan may be dead, but when somebody comes asking me why I had to shoot at her, I want plenty of proof that she came after me first."

"It was a righteous shoot, Mike, and I think you have a complex when it comes to shooting boards and IAD," said Clark.

"You got that right."

Clark followed Mike to the garage and picked him up.

As they headed for Juvenile Detention, Clark said, "Tell me, partner, why do you think someone is trying to kill you?"

"Gee, Clark, I wish I knew," said Mike, wishing he could tell him. "It's just that after almost being flattened by a car and then being shot at through the rear window of my car, it feels kind of fishy to me."

"I guess you could look at it that way, but the two incidents really have nothing in common. The car could have been a drunk. The shooting could have been a lucky guess by a cop hating female who was feeling vengeful that you broke up her girl gang. Unless, of course, you could also place the vengeful woman in the car that almost ran you over and that seems pretty far-fetched to me," said his sergeant. "I do agree that it's been a couple of exciting days for you, but it could just come down to that little gray cloud over your head."

"Thanks so much, Clark," said a sullen Mike. "Please let me know when the cloud goes away, will you."

At the Juvenile Detention Center Ed Fuller was waiting for them, not looking any stronger or in charge than he had the first time they had seen him. The mother, Janet Fuller, was at the hospital with the wounded sixteen-year-old Teresa they learned from Mr. Fuller. Mrs. Dora Ways, their attorney, was with Mr. Fuller. Adequate at her job, Mrs. Ways wasn't part of any big-name law firms but was the middle-class man's attorney. Probably remembering the previous day, Mrs. Ways didn't look like she was happy to be there. Since the father and the lawyer were present, Clark asked that they bring Jill Fuller first.

They waited in a small interview room where the only furniture was a three-foot square wooden table and two straight-backed metal chairs. Mrs. Ways sat in one of the chairs, a notebook and pen in front of her on the table. Mr. Fuller and the detectives stood. A husky woman guard brought Jill into the room. Her hands cuffed in front of her, Jill's appearance was on the repulsive side. Her long, bleach-blond hair resembled a nest most rats would avoid. Her roundish face was unwashed, while her nose and eyes were unusually red due to her cold. Mike doubted any of the redness was due to crying. He doubted the girl had enough emotion to produce tears. She did send her father a glance that was a long way from being respectful. The father stood with his eyes on the floor.

"Is it really necessary that she wear handcu--" started Mrs. Ways.

Just then Jill recognized Mike.

"You! You fuckin' cop!" she screeched and made a dive for him, nails reaching for his face.

Mike side-stepped, right hand grabbing the cuffs, left hand coming down on the girl's shoulder. Twisting both himself and Jill around, he easily propelled her into the second chair, sitting her down with a thump. The guard immediately took a position behind her, placing strong hands on the girl's shoulders. Still holding her cuffed hands, Mike leaned over into the girl's face.

He hissed, "Listen to me, you juvenile bad ass. You ever come at me like that again, I won't care if you're fifteen or a hundred and fifteen. I will squash you like I would any other bad ass. Is that clear enough for your fucking pea sized brain?"

While Jill's defiant expression did not change, the detective's icy threat did take some of the smolder out of her.

Still looking startled, Dora Ways said, "I understand the situation, Detective Brennen, but I think you could better control yourself and your language."

Detective Brennen completely ignored her, holding his position in Jill's face for several more seconds. Finally he let go of the cuffs and stepped back, his eyes never leaving the girl.

Mrs. Ways cleared her throat and said, "Miss Fuller, scenes like this are not in your best interest. I must ask you to--"

"Shut up, bitch!" stated Jill.

Ways scowled and made a futile attempt to look like she was in control.

"Jill, honey," Ed Fuller tried, "please try to--"

"You can shut up, too, you fuckin' clown!"

Clark gave an audible sigh and said to no one in particular, "This interview is going well, don't you think?"

Without further preamble, Mike said, "Did you know that the leader of your little gang is dead, Miss Fuller?"

He knew she couldn't have known it, but he was curious to see her reaction. The news actually took some of the defiance out of her sails,

"What?" she said. Then her sails puffed up again. "You son of a bitch! You killed her!"

"I slowed her down when she tried to kill me, but later at the hospital, somebody paid her a visit...and they slit her throat."

The bluntness brought small gasps from Ed and Dora and even Jill was a little startled. Mike paid no attention to the former two, but eyed Jill as he said, "Who do you know who would want to do that to your boss lady, Miss Fuller?"

The girl was actually staring at him. "Somebody cut her throat? No shit?"

"No shit. Who would do that? You know any candidates?"

"Hell no," said Jill, but added with contempt, "Except for the cops. Prob'ly you."

In the next half hour, that was the best they got out of her on that subject. Or any subject. Like, who had pulled the trigger on the man at the drugstore?

"What man? What drug store? I don't have any fuckin' idea what the fuck you're talkin' about."

The girl had little to say to her lawyer, and what she did say, often turned Mrs. Ways ears red. The teenager's father offered no help. For the most part, he stood in a corner looking ill. Brennen finally tired of it all and walked out. Clark joined him shortly and Jill Fuller was taken back to her cell. Fuller and Ways left without a word to either of them.

"She," said Clark, "is a piece of work. I know bad guys who couldn't keep up with her. And I was especially impressed with the manner in which you got Miss Fuller's attention there at the beginning. Very professional."

"It felt damned good," declared Mike sourly, "and I didn't see where professional was getting us anywhere at all. And as far as I'm concerned, it will be a waste of time even talking to Fran Kott. When I asked her last night, it sounded like Drogan hadn't even told her a cop was watching the place. Her story was that Drogan was coming by to pick her up in the van. And it's very unlikely she has anymore idea who would have killed the dragon lady than Jill Fuller did."

"Well, Miss Fuller did think you were a pretty good suspect," noted Clark. "And the other two would probably agree with her."

"If I'd done it, I'd be bragging. I wouldn't--" His phone buzzed. He answered with a sharp, "Yeah?"

It was Sergeant Fells. "I don't care for your tone, Brennen."

"Sorry, Don," Mike managed. "What do you...?"

"And I don't enjoy taking messages for you."

"Why didn't they call my...?"

"That's a good question."

"What's the message, Don?"

"Somebody named Billy wants to see you," stated the man crisply. "He said it was very important and you'd know where to come."

"Billy?" Mike frowned.

"You don't know who...?"

"Yeah, but...he say what--?"

"Message delivered." Sergeant Fells hung up.

Mike glared at his phone. "Clark, how come you seem to be the only sergeant that understands and appreciates me?"

"Understands you? Appreciates you? Me?" Then, "What was the message? Maybe something more productive than listening to Miss Kott cuss us out?"

"Billy wants to see me. Very important."

"Is this a person I should know?"

"I don't think you've had the pleasure. He's probably the only snitch I've ever had that has never told me one piece of useful info. He's the very description of a scumbag asshole and I'm real surprised to hear from him."

Clark scowled. "I can't wait to make his acquaintance. What kind of info would he consider very important?"

"That he doesn't have a nickel left in his pocket," said Mike. "Let's go."

Clark's scowl did not change. "But, if he never has anything useful, why are we going?"

"So we don't have to listen to Miss Kott cuss us out. Also because I'm hungry."

Clark gave it a moment's thought and then nodded. "Good enough reasons."

CHAPTER 25

They stopped at a small restaurant. Clark had eaten breakfast and it was too early for lunch as far as he was concerned, so he drank some coffee and watched Mike devour pancakes, eggs, and bacon. A couple of times Clark slowly shook his head. Mike refused to acknowledge the movement.

When they got back in the car, Clark asked, "You want to meet this Billy person or not?"

"Might as well. You never know, someday he might actually have a tip worthwhile." And Mike gave him a street name.

"Ah. One of our more colorful areas. Why am I not surprised?"

It was an area that offered prostitutes, gambling, drugs, all the low-end entertainment. It was an avenue of the illegal, money making businesses. It was also a melting pot of most every color and shape and size of human being – all at their worst. It kept the vice cops busy and all cops on their toes.

"We should be in my car," commented Mike as Clark drove slowly along the street. "Everybody's looking at us like we were cops."

"I say again. We are cops. Also your car has a hole in it," said Clark. "What am I looking for here? Scumbag asshole is a pretty general description for this area."

"A skeleton kind of guy with hair the color of manure, and he usually has braids. He should be hanging out in one of these allies."

"Kind of like this guy over here?"

Mike looked. Standing in the mouth of an alley was a skeleton kind of guy with manure colored hair in frizzled braids. He wore a threadbare sweater with a threadbare shirt and threadbare pants, the color of all of them questionable. The loafer type moccasins on his feet were hanging together through the grace of somebody's god.

"Yep. That's our Billy."

"Not ours, if you don't mind. Yours," corrected Clark.

"He is looking a little more desperate than usual. Swing around the block and drive up the alley."

Clark drove around the block and up the filthy, trash-filled alley. He stopped about thirty feet behind Billy and shifted into Park before giving the horn a quick toot. Billy almost jumped out of his skin as he whirled around. Mike opened his window and poked his head out so the man could see who he was. After a nervous glance around, Billy shuffled over to Brennen's side of the car. It was obvious by the scumbag's fragrant aroma that the man hadn't been acquainted with soap and water for a long time. His skeletal face and yellow rotting teeth were painful to look at. Whatever his age, his body was old and used up.

"Hey there, Billy. Haven't seen you for a while," said Mike, now wishing it had been longer. "You look like death warmed over -- two or three times. What the hell you been doing with yourself?"

"Ya took yer sweet fuckin' time gettin' here," grumbled Billy in a tone that was almost as lifeless as the rest of him. Lifeless and frightened.

"Some of us have to work, Billy. Not everybody can live a life of leisure like you."

Billy gave Clark a suspicious look. "Who's he?"

"He's my partner, and a pretty good one. You'll like him once you get to know him. You want to shake hands?"

It was hard to tell who disliked the idea of hand shaking more, Clark or Billy. Neither made any effort to raise a hand.

"Tell me," Mike went on, "what kind of urgent information do you have that was worth calling the precinct for? I know you, Billy, and it's hard to believe--"

"I heard ya was lookin' for a guy name a Reed. Maybe...I think I can he'p ya." The man continued to glance around, jumpy.

Mike eyed him curiously. "You can help us? That's kind of interesting. What kind of crowd are you hanging with now? It seems unlikely a tidbit like that would be floating around, and I doubt Reed would be happy to share his whereabouts with you."

"Ya wanna know or not? I don't like standin' here talkin' to a fuckin' cop car!"

"Now, now, William. Far be it from me to discourage a helpful citizen. You got a possible location on Mr. Reed, we'll be glad to hear it. Won't we, Clark."

"Thrilled," muttered Clark. He had opened his window in an attempt to escape the disagreeable odor emanating from William despite his being outside the car. It hadn't been much help. The alley had a distinctive odor all its own.

"Ya know that ol' school near here? There's some ol' houses 'cross the playground? He's 'spose to be in the ol' brown 'un."

Mike cocked his head. "He is, huh. The ol' brown 'un. Give me a break here, Billy. Who the hell did you hear this from?"

"I ain't tellin' ya that, Brennen," protested the scumbag. "Ya know I won't tell ya that."

"And you know that I don't count you among my more reliable sources, William. You can't expect to get paid much for something like this until we check it out."

Billy pouted and whined, "I been standin' around here all mornin'. I got things I could'a been doin'--"

"Hell, yes," spoke up Clark. "He's probably missed the morning's board meeting over at Gooden's Pool Hall."

"Calm down, little man," Mike told the street bum. "I didn't say I wouldn't give you anything." He held out his hand to his partner and said, "Give me a five, will you, Clark."

"He's your snitch," griped Clark, but he pulled out his wallet and passed him a five.

Mike held it out.

"Only a five?" said Billy, but the snitch didn't waste any time snatching it.

"If we find Mr. Reed at the old brown house by the old school, Billy, we'll be glad to come by and give you some more. That's the way we play the game."

William gave them a disappointed grunt and a sour look, then turned and shuffled away.

"You're welcome!" Mike called after the man.

Billy disappeared around a building.

"I can't wait to tell Grands about this big-time tip," remarked Clark, shifting into drive. "A penny's worth of shit from a pile of walking garbage. And I want an I.O.U. from you for five bucks."

"Yes sir," said Mike. "Make a left on the street."

"We should go right."

"School's to the left."

"What? You really think that little worm would know where to find a bad-ass like Reed?"

"You want to get your five dollars' worth, don't you?" allowed Mike. "We can at least give it a look."

"It's a waste of time. And I'll get my five dollars' worth back from you."

"Then I want my five dollars' worth."

Clark gave him an irritated glare.

"Look, Clark," Mike appealed to him. "Billy has manure for brains. That's probably why his hair is that color. He does not have an imagination. He doesn't even know what it is. He must have heard something, somewhere, that triggered that one cell mind of his. If only briefly. People talk around him because he's a nobody...the kind of character that no one notices."

"How could anyone not notice that delightful odor?" said Clark and turned left.

CHAPTER 26

It had been a pleasant, middle-class neighborhood at one time, with the three-story grade school built to serve the family-oriented area. But it had gone downhill a long time ago and now most of the houses were sad relics, while the school had been abandoned for years. Clark drove past the front of the old, two story, brown house for a look. There was little of the brown paint left on its neglected, rotting frame. The front porch was partially collapsed. The curtainless windows were dark empty eyes. Like its neighbors, it looked deserted and uninviting. No spring rains would help the small front yards filled with discolored weeds and patches of bare earth. Clark drove on around the block and passed the desolate school. The only young people who attended it now were the truants and the expelled kids from other schools. They could see a few kids slinking around in the shadows of the breezeways between classroom buildings. A few more were shooting a basketball at an old netless hoop.

"Cheerful neighborhood," remarked Clark.

"I grew up in a neighborhood just like this," said Mike, feeling memories wash over him. "Same kind of school."

Parking a block away in the shadow of the school, the detectives took turns looking through binoculars at the back of the brown house and its neighbors.

Each place had a sagging, narrow, one car garage. Pieces of picket fence poked through the weeds here and there. Piles of trash and junk, including some rusted hulks of ancient cars, filled most of the back yards. They were even less inviting than the fronts. They saw no movement.

"So, how do we want to handle this?" asked Mike.

Clark's eyebrows went up. "You're actually asking me?"

"Hey, you're my sergeant."

"Since when has that made any difference to anything?"

"Let me make a suggestion," Mike decided. "Why don't you drive around to the front and go in that way and I'll go in the back?"

"Or, you could drive around to the front and I could take the back."

"Clark, as I have mentioned one hundred thousand times before, you and your car look like cops who would go in the front. I, on the other hand, can ditch the coat and tie and fit in much better in my shirttails and jeans and sneakers for slipping into the back."

Clark sighed. "In that case, I guess I'll take the front and you can take the back."

"I knew we could work this out. And I think maybe you should put your vest on."

"A vest?" said his partner. "You don't really expect Mr. Reed to be there do you?"

"No, not really, but maybe, so put your vest on."

"You didn't bring yours."

"Even if I had it, it would have ruined my back door disguise."

Clark punched the button to open the trunk and got out. Mike got out to pull off his coat and tie, tossing them into the back seat. Then he pulled his shirt out to cover gun and badge and handcuffs and rolled up his sleeves a couple of turns. Clark had his coat off and was putting on the bullet proof vest. He watched his partner in disdain.

"Are you sure this isn't just another excuse for you to remove your civilized clothing?" he asked.

"Damn. I was afraid you'd catch on."

Clark put his coat back on and got into the car, saying, "I'll tell dispatch where we are and have them alert a squad. Just in case. Let's not drag our feet on this. I don't think Grands would want us to waste much time on the word of sweet-smelling William."

"I'm off and running. I'll give you a call when I get into position."

With that, Mike put on a who-the-hell-gives-a-damn slouch and strolled off across the school yard on the sunny, mild spring day. He did not run. He did have to do some sidestepping to avoid an over abundant amount of litter. Fast food sacks and wrappers and plastic cups, soda cans, snack bags, candy wrappers and, mixed among it, discarded scrapes of food covered with busy ants and such. Mike's breakfast felt a little heavy at the repugnant sight. Sadly, there was also plenty of unschool-like litter. Lots of cigarette butts and even cigar butts, beer cans, shattered liquor bottles, bent and rusty hypo-needles. Scattered among it all was glass from the school's broken windows.

Hands in pockets, the detective weaved across the yard, letting his head loll, but his eyes were busy. His goal was the garage next to the brown house. When he reached the decrepit little building, its doors long gone, he paused for a glance around and then slipped inside. Which wasn't easy. Mike had never seen such an array of rusted and discarded junk in one small area. Pieces of cars, bicycles, furniture, toys, tools, just about anything and everything, including the kitchen sink. When he bumped into one of the pieces, the rest of the stuff shifted and Mike heard the scurry of small creatures

He grimaced. "Shit."

Watching where he put his feet, he made his way to a one-by-two foot window, its glass, no surprise, missing. He pulled out his cell.

"Clark."

"I'm here."

"I'm looking at the house from the neighboring garage. I don't see anything moving over there, but there are things running around in here."

"Where's your cat when you need him?"

"Cute. I'm going over to the garage behind the brown house now. I'm leaving my phone open."

"Don't step on any things."

Again, Mike checked out the surrounding scene and then leisurely moved to the next garage. It still had one door, but it hung from antique hinges that no longer looked reliable. Inside, among another pile of junk, was the rusted shell of a car sitting on cement blocks. Mike tried hard to ignore the scurrying sounds. Going to the doorless doorway in the side of the building, he pulled his gun with his right hand and held his phone in his left. Crouching, he studied the back of the house.

"Clark."

"Yeah."

"I can see the back door and most of the windows and nobody's looking back at me. Are you ready to go in?"

"Can't wait."

"Give me thirty seconds."

"I'm counting."

Mike slipped his phone into a pocket and took his gun in both hands. Leaving the garage, he took a quick peek around the corner. All clear. His eyes moved over the house's windows again. They looked all clear. Dodging a jungle of weeds and trash, he crossed the yard swiftly to jump to a small porch. Staying to one side of the door, he tried the doorknob. It responded with a squeak that brought a wince from the detective but didn't seem to alarm anyone else. Mike moved in front of the door and, gun ready, kicked it in.

Clark came through the front door, snapping, "Police!" That didn't seem to alarm anyone, either. The smell was of dust and decay. Lots of dust, with tiny footprints left by four-legged scurrying things. Under the windows that were broken, were small piles of dirt and leaves.

Mike had come into the kitchen. A mound of trash filled its' sinks and flowed over onto the counters and floor. Some cupboard doors were open, others missing. A number of broken dishes were scattered around.

Clark had come into the living room. There was also a scattering of trash there and in the connecting small dining room. None of it was fresh trash, though, and nowhere did they see any footprints left by two-legged things, including on the stairs. Mike still went up them for a look and found nothing. When he came back down, his partner was looking into a closet near the front door.

"No skeletons," said Clark.

"No ghosts," said Mike.

He stuck his Glock under the front of his belt and placed his hands on his hips. Clark holstered his thirty-eight.

"I hope you got my five dollars' worth," said the latter.

"I think we should look in the neighboring houses," said the former.

"What?" Clark looked at him in frustration. "And then I suppose we could go through the school, too. And the houses on the other side of the school. And the houses down the street and around the corner."

"Well, if you want to--"

"Ah, come on, Mike. The little worm was pulling your chain. You keep telling me that smelly Billy is full of manure and that he's never given you any useful tips. So he needed some cash today and heard on the street we were after Reed. Imagination or not, even he can send us to an empty old brown house. Why are we listening to him?"

Mike sighed, and shrugged, and said, "Beats me."

"Good. Let's go get some lunch."

"Lunch? I just ate breakfast."

"Not my fault."

As they went out the front door, Brennen told his sergeant, "Now this is how an officer can lose the respect of his underlings."

The detectives started across the porch, carefully avoiding the collapsed side on their left. That's when Mike caught movement in his peripheral vision.

CHAPTER 27

Mike Brennen's head snapped around, a sudden knot grabbing at his gut. Two men, one white and one black, were coming around the house from the right. More movement came from the left. It was another white guy, this one with a big bandage where his right ear should have been.

"Clark!" Mike gave a sharp warning as he grabbed for his gun.

Hearing him, Clark's head started to come around, his hand moving toward his weapon. Mike, shifting into high gear, gave Clark a shove with his left hand, hoping to push him out of harm's way long enough so his partner could get his gun out. Mike's right hand had gotten ahold of his Glock, but the bad guys already had their guns ready. Worse, they didn't waste any time in pulling the triggers. Even as Mike brought his weapon around toward Jason Reed, he saw the flash from the barrel of the man's automatic. Instantly, he felt a powerful blow to his left side and he was knocked back against the house. Then he was sliding down the wall, taking what was left of the peeling brown paint with him. More shooting in the background echoed painfully in the detective's head. When his butt bumped onto the porch, Mike tried to bring his gun up. It didn't happen. Reed had put his foot on it, and on the cop's hand, grinding it in. Then the bad guy's smirking face was in Mike's face and the detective very much wanted to put a bullet up the fucking bastard's nose. Bitterly, he knew it was going to be the other way around.

"Nice ta see ya again, Detective Brennen," said the man with a Hollywood sneer.

The man's teeth and breath, Mike ridiculously thought, were almost as yellow and rotten smelling as Billy's. Which led him to his next thought -- that fucking little piss ant had set them up!

Jason Reed got his attention back by pressing the barrel of his gun hard against Mike's left ear.

"First, Mister Fuckin' Detective, I'm gonna blow your fuckin' ears off," said the man, this time with a Hollywood snarl. "First the left one, and then the right one. An' then I'm gonna put a fuckin' bullet right between your eyes. An' you wanna know the fuckin' best part? I'm gettin' paid to do it! I mean, I'da done it just for the fuckin' hell of it, but somebody came along an' fuckin' said they'd pay me to do it. Can you believe that, Mr. Cop?"

While Reed was enjoying himself, Mike was beginning to feel a lot of pain, which was bringing on a lot of nausea. The stink of Reed's breath wasn't helping any. Mike suddenly leaned forward and upchucked his pancakes and eggs and bacon. Down on one knee, up close to the detective, Mr. Reed got a good share of it on his clothes.

"Sonofabitch!" declared the man with a total lack of sympathy. "You fuckin' cop! Here goes ear number one!"

Reed grabbed a handful of Mike's hair and yanked his head back, slamming it into the house. Even with dulling senses and blurring eyesight, the detective felt the barrel of the gun and could only wait for his ear to disintegrate. When the boom of the gun came, along with several other shots, the sound reverberated in his head but didn't seem to have any particular effect on his ear. On the other hand, there seemed to be a lot of red stuff coming out of Reed's left ear. At least, where his left ear used to be. Left? Hadn't he shot off the guy's right ear? Why was the left one bleeding?

A foot kicked the dead Jason Reed away from Mike Brennen. A new face appeared in front of him and a hand gave him a not-so-gentle slap in the face.

"Brennen!" said someone too sharply.

"Ahhh...don't." Mike wanted to go someplace where his increasing pain would stop. Instead, he was staring into another disagreeable face. In disbelief, he managed, "Panelli?"

"Good, you know me. Now I want you to forget me."

"I'm shot," said Mike.

"No shit," said Joe. "You got that fucking right."

The ambush came rushing back into Mike's conscious.

"Clark? How's Clark?" he asked and made an effort to get up. Pain washed over him and he lost what was left of his breakfast. He almost lost consciousness along with it.

"No you don't! Listen to me! This was a goddamned setup and--"

"That fuckin' Billy," moaned Mike.

"Listen to me!" Joe placed his hands on each side of Mike's head to stop its wobbling and looked into the detective's hazy eyes. "Your partner is hit and he's out, but I don't think it's too bad."

"Think?"

There were sirens in the distance now.

"I'm not a goddamned doctor!" snapped Joe. "Now pay attention."

"Quit your goddamned yelling!" Mike snapped back and immediately hated himself. There was another crazy drummer beating on the inside of his skull.

Joe went on, "We don't want you babbling things. You can't mention anything about the Macklin business or about our lieutenant suspects. And for God's sake, don't mention the Panellis. You hear me?"

"I hear you...I hear you...and it's your suspects, not ours."

"What? Christ," groaned Joe.

The sirens were rapidly drawing closer.

"How bad am I?" asked Mike.

"Not too bad, I think."

"I think? Fuck you. I could be dying."

"Not this time. I'm going. Keep your mouth shut. I'll see you later."

"Later?"

But Joe Panelli was gone and the sirens came screaming and Mike Brennen groaned some more. His pain turned mean and the drummer beat faster. A black haziness surrounded him and, desperately wanting some peace and quiet, Mike let it close in.

CHAPTER 28

Mike Brennen dragged open heavy eyelids to a hazy, dim light. He waited for his brain to catch up to his eyes, but even then he wasn't sure where he was. Not wanting to make any wild guesses, the detective spent several minutes sorting out sight and sound. Not that there was much of either one. The only sound that registered was a soft...snoring? As for sight, he finally realized that the hazy problem belonged to his eyes, whereas the dimly lit part belonged to the room. What room? Where? He could see a television on the wall opposite the bed. So, definitely not his bed. Not his room. It reminded him of a hospital room.

Hospital?

Memories began to stumble back. An old school...a garage filled with junk, and things...an old house filled with trash and dirt. Then a sneering Jason Reed in his face! He'd been shot! And then someone else in his face--

"Shit! Panelli!" Then "Clark! How's Clark?"

The snoring stopped abruptly.

"Well," said a sleepy voice, "welcome back, Detective Brennen."

Mike started to turn his head toward the voice and the drummer began to bump and boom in his skull again. Not as bad as earlier, but it definitely got his attention. So he stopped his head and just used his eyes and saw that the voice belonged to Detective Ben Sharp, from night shift.

"How's Clark?" repeated Mike anxiously.

"He's in intensive care. His vest saved his life, but he still took two hits. The doctors are saying he should be okay, though," Ben assured him. "You were luckier. Bullet put a short tunnel through your left side. Not so bad."

"Lucky? A tunnel in my side?" Mike groaned and grumbled, "I got fuckin' shot and it hurts like hell."

Sharp grinned.

"You sound like your normal, feisty self, to me," he said. "But you better save some of that energy. The brass is going to be after you, and Clark, with some real interesting questions. Shit, you got all of us curious as hell. That's part of why I'm sitting here. Clark will be out for a while, but in case you said something helpful in your sleep or when you woke up, they wanted someone sitting here to hear it."

Mike was suddenly worried. Had he said Panelli's name out loud?

He cautiously asked, "Did I say anything?"

Ben gave him a sheepish look. "Well, I guess I fell asleep for a little while."

"I won't tell if you won't," said Mike with relief. "You said that was part of why your here? Is there another part?"

"Oh. Well, Grands finally decided that maybe somebody is trying to pop you. You know, somebody tried to flatten you with a car, and then that Drogan woman ambushed you and now this Reed business, which was for sure another ambush. The lieutenant didn't want anybody to try again here in the hospital." Sharp gave him another grin. "None of us want anything to happen to our favorite cop."

"Good God, no. You wouldn't have anybody to pick on."

"Well, Grands may have accepted the fact that someone is trying to kill you, but he wants to know who and why. And he wants to know who took out the three shooters that--"

"Three of them?" Mike was still having some trouble with details. "Yeah. Okay. There was a black guy and a white guy and Reed. Reed's the one who shot me."

"Yeah, Reed got you. The other assholes got Thorn. But who the hell got Reed and the assholes? They were all dead'r than door nails when the first squad got there. Reed had a fuckin' tunnel blasted through his rock hard head." He smiled crookedly. "Oh, you might be interested to know that it pretty much took off his left ear. The one you missed in your earlier dust up. But we know you didn't do it. Your gun was out but it hadn't been fired and Clark's gun was still in its holster. So who was the cavalry that saved you? And who the hell's behind the ambushing? Sure as hell not Reed...or Drogan. They were the triggers, but there's no connection between--"

"Ben!" said Mike and then wished he hadn't said it so loud. "Ben, you're giving my drummer a headache. And much as I hate to disappoint you and the brass, I can't answer any of those questions." On the grounds that it would get him in deep shit. "I can barely remember the getting shot part."

"The Lieutenant's going to want more than that. Nobody's crying over those dead bad asses, but they are dead and the--"

The door opened and a nurse poked her head in.

"Detective Sharp," she said quietly. "You have a call at the station out here."

The man frowned at her. "Can't I take it in here?"

"Not at this hour," she stated and was gone.

"Well, shit, why didn't they call me on my cell?" griped Ben.

"Maybe they didn't want to wake me," suggested Mike. "Or you."

"Funny. I'll be back." And he left.

"This hour? What is the hour?" muttered Mike. The blinds on the window were partially open. It was dark. Was he having another fucking nightmare?

The door opened again and Joe Panelli came in. He was carrying a bundle under his left arm.

Mike stared. "It is a fucking nightmare."

"I can't deny that," said Joe, "but we have to wake up and--"

He was pulling the coverlet off Mike as he spoke. Mike grabbed it back and the move sharply reminded him of his wound. His pain and anger were more than apparent in his tone of voice as he griped, "What the hell are you doing? I'm in a goddamned hospital and it's the middle of the night, I think, and I've been fucking shot!"

"You got that all right, but we don't have time to discuss it right now," Joe rasped in quiet urgency. "We got word that the hit on Macklin is tomorrow...make that today...this morning. We've got to find out which of those cops has to be stopped."

Mike Brennen glared daggers at Joe Panelli.

"I can't do this." The detective's low growl held menace. "My body hurts. My head hurts. And I still don't see any real proof that--"

"Proof?" Joe glared daggers back, not in the least affected by Mike's menacing growl. "Goddamn it, Brennen! People have tried to run you down and put holes in you! One of those lieutenants is working overtime trying to shut you down before you screw things up. I'll lay you odds that you're the reason they decided to hit Macklin right now, before their plans get so muddied up they won't work. Or maybe you want to wait until you're dead to believe it?"

They glared at each other for several long seconds.

Finally, quietly, Mike said, "I doubt I have any clothes here. Crime Scene would have taken them and…" He stopped. "Wait a minute. What happened to Ben? The cop that was in here with me."

"He's been taken care of, and I brought you some of my clothes to wear," said Joe.

He tossed the bundle he was carrying onto the bed. A jacket, jeans, shirt, and under shorts.

But Mike was scowling, not happy with the answer he'd gotten about his colleague. "He's been taken care of? What the hell does that mean?"

"Christ! Do you have to be a fucking cop all the time," griped Joe. "The call told him to meet your Lieutenant Grands in the hospital lobby. If you quit fooling around, we should be able to get out of here before he starts getting suspicious."

"Shit," said Mike. "So what happens to my honest, dedicated career when they find me gone?"

"Save the police chief's life and they'll give you a medal."

"Sure they will." The detective sighed. Reluctantly, he said, "I'm going to need some help here."

Reluctantly, Joe agreed, "I know."

Mike grit his teeth as Joe got him sitting up on the edge of the bed. The pain in Mike's side was ugly, but manageable. It was the second drummer joining the first drummer in his head that made him wish for peace. Joe had to do the bending to pull the shorts and jeans up to where Mike was able to get them on the rest of the way.

"You could have brought me one of your thousand dollar suits," muttered the detective.

"I don't have any thousand dollar suits. The cheapest would be around three thousand and I sure wouldn't want any cop blood on it. Besides, these jeans cost over five hundred."

In the process of slipping into the long-sleeved, light blue shirt, Mike stopped to stare. "You're shittin' me. Five hundred dollar jeans?"

"And this shirt was probably a couple hundred and the jacket is real leather and cost--"

"I don't want to know."

"You asked."

"No I didn't."

"If you can handle the buttons, I'll see if I they left those stylish sneakers of yours."

Moving his left arm as little as possible, Mike managed the buttons.

The sneakers were sitting alone in the closet.

"The way things are going, my wardrobe will be shot to hell," said Mike. "Literally."

"Now there's a loss," said Joe. As he handed Mike the shoes, he saw the duct tape. "What's this? Duct tape to patch your sneakers?"

"You don't need to pick on my footwear." Mike looked at his feet and right now they were looking a long way off. "I don't think I can--"

"Yeah, yeah."

So Joseph Panelli stooped to put sneakers on the bare feet of the two-bit, mouthy, albeit honest cop. The two-bit cop showed wisdom by not being mouthy at this tender gesture.

When he finished, Joe picked up the jacket to help Mike into it.

"Now Let's get the hell out of here."

"Where's my gun and badge and wallet and stuff?"

"I think it's unlikely that they would leave those sorts of things lying around in a hospital room. You won't need them anyway."

"With people trying to kill me, I at least need a gun."

"I'll protect you. I'm getting good at it."

"Fuck you. Just remember whose fault it is that I need protecting."

"Can we please get out of here before your babysitter comes back? Or do you want to explain to him why I'm here?"

"Let's get out of here."

CHAPTER 29

After making sure the nurse wasn't looking their way, Joe loaned Mike a shoulder to lean on for their journey down a back stairwell and along a couple of desolate, narrow hallways. Panelli overcame a couple of locked doors with a key card.

"You've got a card for getting around the hospital?" fussed Mike, but then added, "By now, why am I surprised about anything?"

"Good question," said Joe.

They exited through a 'Doctor's Only' door. It was a clear, breezy, spring night, but Brennen wasn't noticing the weather. He did notice that one of the cars in the doctor's private parking lot was Tommy Bears' Mercedes Benz. At the moment, though, Bears was leaning against a deep blue Acura sedan. On seeing Brennen and Panelli, Tommy opened the passenger's door of the Acura.

"Mr. One Bears. No surprise there either," said Mike as he gratefully sank onto the front seat. He asked, "Out of curiosity, which one of you let the air out of Jason Reed's empty head?"

Tommy raised an eyebrow. "Jason Reed? Can't say as the name is familiar to me. Ring any bells for you, Mr. Panelli?"

"I've never been good with names," said Mr. Panelli. "Let's go before somebody comes looking."

Joe drove the Acura out of the lot with Tommy right behind them in his Mercedes. A few blocks later, on a dark and quiet street, Joe pulled over and parked. A few moments later, Tommy joined them, getting into the Acura's back seat. Joe turned a dashboard light to its dimmest setting.

"Is this one of those clandestine type of meetings?" remarked Mike.

"I'm glad getting shot didn't dull your sense of humor," said Tommy. "I'd have missed it."

"I wouldn't," said Joe. Then, "We need another plan, Detective Brennen. Admittedly, your first one worked well. Almost too well considering there have been three attempts on your life. The problem is, we still don't know which of the lieutenants is our assassin and our source says we're out of time."

"I don't understand why your source can sniff out the victim and the time, but can't sniff out the guilty lieutenant?"

"The source can't," stated Joe. "Leave it at that."

"Leave it at that." Mike gave a disgusted snort. "You know, if there wasn't a hole in Reed's head, maybe we could have asked him who it is that wants to put an end to my brilliant career."

"If he didn't have a hole in his head, there would be a hole in your head," Tommy pointed out. "Options were limited when it came to saving your life and your partner's life. Whoever did that had to act fast because bullets were already flying and sirens were coming."

"Yeah. If I ever run into whoever did that, I'll thank them."

"I'm sure they were glad to help out."

"It's becoming a daily chore," remarked Joe.

"I said thanks," groused Mike. "And it's not my fault--"

"And you can't really believe that that stupid bastard, Reed, would actually have known who was paying him." Joe shook his head.

"No," admitted Mike sourly. "But I bet I can shake some kind of a name out of that little piss ant, Billy."

"The street trash?" said Tommy. "Well, you might have a small problem there, too."

"What? Why'd you kill him? I was looking forward to wringing his scrawny little neck my--"

"It wasn't us, damn it," said Joe gruffly. "When we left you at that house, we backtracked to get the little prick. What we found was a cop car sitting in the same alley where you talked to him, only he wasn't talking to anybody anymore. Would you care to bet that even if Reed and his bozos had done the job right, that they wouldn't be dead in some alley, too?"

Again, Mike admitted angrily, "No. Damn it."

"So, is there anyone left that we can ask?" said Tommy. "Or are we up the proverbial tree with three lieutenants?"

"After the last three days, there must be--" started Joe.

"Why don't we just ask the lieutenants," said Mike.

"What?" said Joe.

"Excuse me?" said Tommy.

"I'll just call them up and ask them. More or less," said Mike. "Can the Panelli spy network come up with the phone numbers and addresses on their suspects?"

Joe gave him a half smile. "It's already done. We just have to call my brother to get them."

"Gee," said Mike. "I feel bad having to get Thomas out of bed at this hour."

Joe took out his cell phone, punching a button. "For your information, Thomas and my father aren't getting anymore sleep than we are. If you want, though, I can tell him you're concerned. The news might cheer him up."

"Somehow I doubt any news from me would cheer him up. For that matter, I'm not so sure I want to cheer him up."

Joe turned his attention to the phone as it was answered.

"Thomas. I need you to send me a text with the phone numbers and addresses for our suspects. They should be on your desk." He paused. "Yeah, he's here." Pause. "No, he's not in the best of shape, but he was worried about waking you up." He smiled. Then, "Thank you." He ended the call.

"He really asked how I was?" asked Mike. "And what's that smile about?"

"He really did. He wanted to know if the two-bit, smart-mouthed cop would survive long enough to ferret out the bad guy - or girl - lieutenant. His words."

"I'm touched."

Tommy asked Mike, "How is your side?"

"It's not happy, so I would prefer no one ask me to run any foot races or dodge anymore bullets."

"Your dodging wasn't so hot yesterday when you were still in one piece," noted the Indian.

"It was an ambush!"

Joe's phone announced the arrival of a text. As he opened it, he asked Mike, "So tell us what it is you've got in mind with these calls. You got a favorite in mind?"

"Not necessarily. Like I told Tommy yesterday...was that yesterday? Whatever. Anyway, it's no secret in police circles that I was on the Calamity Jane case or that I was after Reed."

"Especially since you separated him from one of his ears," Tommy couldn't resist, but he did refrain from grinning. Barely.

"Anyway..." said Mike again, gruffly, "...as lieutenants, any of them could have gotten the information needed to set me up. Or they could even have gotten it with help from Captain Nimmer. But if I were picking, I'd still be picking Corry. He stopped being a good cop a long time ago. While on the other hand, working with Sheffer the last couple of days, I haven't seen even a flicker of guilt. I suppose she could be a good actress, but hell, I find it hard to believe you could be doing your duty as usual when you were planning to assassinate the police chief. That's hard for me to swallow.

"As for Polinski, he might be having a lot of personal problems, but the man's been tracking down bad cops a long time. I find it hard to believe he'd dirty himself by becoming one."

"But you'll give them all a buzz?" said Joe.

"Yeah, and it wouldn't hurt to be ready to follow them. If the hit's this morning, I can't see them getting any sleep. Maybe I can stir up the right one and send them running to the Rezzoros."

Tommy suggested, "We've got two cars, so why don't we check out two of the birds at once. Maybe the male birds first?"

"I'll agree to that," said Mike. "But we should pick up a burner phone. You don't want them seeing your ID when--"

"I already have a burner," said Joe. "I keep one or two handy in the car. For emergencies...like calling lieutenants."

"Of course you do," sniffed Mike.

"I'll take Corry," said Tommy. "You can put your eyes on Polinski."

"Good," said Joe and read off Corry's address to Bears, who didn't bother to write it down.

"Can't remember Reed but you can remember an address," remarked Mike.

"Addresses are easier."

"Yeah. Right. Just let us know if Mr. Corry gets upset."

Tommy smiled. "I'll be in touch."

Tommy One Bears slid out to return to his Mercedes, driving away.

"Shall we pay Lieutenant Polinski a visit?" said Joe.

"My favorite lieutenant," replied Mike.

Joe glanced at the address and took off.

CHAPTER 30

Financial woes or not, Lieutenant Marvin Polinski had so far managed to hold onto his modest home in a middle-class neighborhood. It was a quiet tree-lined street of older two-story houses, with porches and small front yards. With headlights off, Joe coasted the Acura to a stop a couple of houses away from the dark Polinski home.

"Well, it doesn't look like he's up pacing the floor," noted Mike.

"Might be he's at the Rezzoros," Joe pointed out.

"Let's find out," said Mike and punched the number into the burner.

It had to ring only twice.

"Polinski," said the lieutenant in the resigned tone of someone who had to be available twenty-four hours a day. He did not sound like someone who was about to go out and assassinate a police chief.

"Maybe you should think about what you are about to do," said Mike, keeping his voice low and gruff. He sure as hell didn't want the IAD officer to recognize him.

"What? Who is this?" said Polinski, on the snippy side.

"Somebody who knows--"

"You listen to me, buster! I'm a cop and you sure as hell don't want to fool around with me!"

The line went dead.

"Ouch," winced Mike. "That was short and not so sweet."

"How did he sound?" asked Joe.

"Pissed as hell, but I'm pretty sure he didn't know what I was talking about. Or that it was me. Shit, if he'd known it was me, he'd have come through the phone and strangled me right here and now."

"He really likes you that much, huh?"

"Like the plague. Let's see if he does anything, but he sure didn't sound like he was getting ready to go out and kill a police chief."

"Maybe he'll just call the Rezzoros."

"It just didn't feel that way. I'm betting it's not him."

No lights came on in the lieutenant's house or the garage and no car hurriedly drove away. It remained dark and quiet.

Joe's phone buzzed and Mike answered it. "Yeah."

"Any luck?" asked Tommy Bears.

"I believe it's safe to cross Polinski off the list," said Mike.

"I'm outside Corry's apartment building if you want to go ahead and give his cage a rattle."

"Right." Mike laid Joe's phone aside and punched in the number into the burner. The phone was snatched up halfway through the first ring.

"I told you I would be there so fuck off!" Corry's voice was sharp, but it was also slurred. The Vice Lieutenant was evidently building up his nerve with some bottled help.

Hearing the man's remark and tone, Mike was immediately confident that Corry was the one they wanted. The detective made no attempt to disguise his voice as he said, "Sounds like you're already having a bad day, Lieutenant. Are the Rezzoros giving you a--"

Corry knew him immediately. "Brennen! You sonofabitch! You're a fuckin' dead man!"

"You tried that already. It was you in the car, right? Did you also handle the arrangements with the Drogan woman and Reed? And how much did you pay that poor slob Billy to give me that little tip? You don't really believe the Rezzoros will keep any promises they've made, do you? You can't be--"

"You stupid asshole!" declared the lieutenant. Mike could almost smell the liquor. "How the hell did you ever get mixed up in this? You think you can get in the way of the fuckin' Rezzoros? You--"

"I am in their way, and I'm in your way, and I'm not moving. As of now, this deal is dead," stated Mike. Then he piled on the disgust and loathing as he said, "You're into some bad shit, Corry. A cop killing a cop. That's as--"

"You're fucked," Dick Corry rasped. "The Rezzoros will squash you like a bug."

"You're the bug, Corry. And you're a lot closer to being squashed than --"

The line went dead.

Mike winced again. "I think we've solved the mystery."

Joe said, "From listening to this end of the conversation, it sounds like you were right about Lieutenant Corry."

"I didn't want to be right about him," said Mike. The disgust and loathing were still there, along with a generous addition of anger. "I didn't want it to be any of them, damn it. A fucking dirty cop who is going to kill a cop!"

"So, now we know. Who do you want to take it to?"

"Somebody who can take the right steps, as quick as possible, to make sure it doesn't happen."

"Let me guess. The lady lieutenant."

"She's the perfect choice. She already knows about it, more or less. More important, Sheffer is respected and the brass will listen to her where they're unlikely to listen to me."

"That's a flaw we overlooked when choosing you," mused Joe. "Nobody listens to you."

"Hey, I tried to tell you that I wasn't the--"

Tommy's voice came over Joe's phone. "You there?"

Mike grabbed it up. "Yeah!"

"Ouch. You sound testy," said the Indian.

"Very!" grumped the detective.

"Well, your lieutenant is running like a rabbit. I'm on his furry tail. I'll let you know if he takes me to the wolf's den."

"Thank you so much. We're going over to Sheffer's place. I'm dumping it all in her lap now."

"Good luck," said Tommy.

Joe started the car but left the headlights off until they turned onto a major street. He said, "Don't use my cell to call her."

"Yeah, yeah. If I had my phone, I had her number in that." He checked the text and punched it into the burner.

Anita Sheffer answered on the third ring. She didn't seem quite as resigned to nighttime interruptions as Polinski had. "Yes?"

"Lieutenant Sheffer, Mike Brennen."

"Oh? It's very early in the morning, Detective Brennen, and no caller ID?" she said with more surprise than annoyance.

"I'm afraid they took my phone and everything else when I ended up in the hospital. Had to grab a burner."

"I heard you were shot. I hope it's not too serious. Are you calling from the hospital, then? What's happening?"

"I think I'll survive, thank you," said Mike, but purposely avoided saying where he was calling from. "What's happened, Lieutenant, is that I had the chance to knock the lid off the assassination thing. I got word that the hit on Chief Macklin was going to go down this morning sometime and it helped me sniff out the shooter. But now I've reached the point where I need to pass it on to someone who can get people moving on it."

"Such as me?"

"Such as you, Lieutenant. I've already told you about it which saves me a lot of time and trouble trying to explain it to, say, Lieutenant Grands."

"Please know I want to believe you on this, Mike. You say you got word. Can't you share your source with me now? I could move people a lot faster if I could tell them where the information was coming from."

"I'm sort of hoping the name of the shooter will motivate them," said Mike. "Though it's someone they're not going to like."

"Really?" said Sheffer. "Who is it?"

"It's a cop. A lieutenant in Vice at my own precinct. Dick Corry."

A couple moments of silence. "That is tough news, Mike. You're sure? We don't want to accuse a lieutenant without plenty of proof."

"I talked to him on the phone just a few minutes ago and he all but admitted it, plus he's falling apart drunk. And in the next half hour or so, I should be getting more substantial information for proof."

"That sounds promising," said the lady lieutenant. "Look, Mike, you're not sounding like you're in the hospital. Wherever you are, why don't you come over here to my place. You can give me a complete rundown of everything you've got. I'd really like to know all of it before we call it into Macklin. We both know there will be a lot of questions and I want to be able to answer them." Her voice smiled. "I'll fix us a fresh pot of coffee."

"That works for me," said Mike. "And I admit, the coffee part sure sounds good."

"Very good. Do you need my address?"

He didn't, but he didn't want her to know that. He said, "Yes, please."

She gave it to him and said, "See you soon, then."

As Mike disconnected, Joe said, "Sounds like your mood is on the upswing."

"About time," said the detective. "I'm going to enjoy dumping this goddamned nightmare into somebody else's lap. Maybe I can finally get rid of this fuckin' headache."

CHAPTER 31

Mike Brennen gingerly stepped out of the car, tucking the burner phone into the jacket pocket. When Tommy called about Corry, he wanted to be able to share it with Sheffer. The detective took a slow breath. Where he was well aware of his pain, he had not realized how drained he felt.

"Are you going to make it?" asked Joe with honest concern. "You look like shit."

"Gee, maybe that's why I was in the hospital," grumbled Mike.

"Her place is across the street, third house to your right. Can you make it or not?"

"So long as nobody chases me. Or ambushes me."

"You should have her call you an ambulance, or at least a squad car to take you back to the hospital," said Joe. "I'll kind of drive around here for a little while. Just for the hell of it."

"It's been fun working with you," said Mike. "Bye."

He closed the door and started his none-to-steady journey.

It was a neighborhood not quite as nice as Lieutenant Polinski's. The houses were older and smaller, but it was a clean neighborhood where people cared about their streets and yards. The third house was a small, two-story, with a black, wrought iron railing on a small, cement stoop at the front door. An outside light was on, illuminating the house number. When Mike turned up the front walk, Joe drove slowly off.

Gripping at the railing, Mike mounted the two steps of the stoop and rang the doorbell. In a moment, Anita Sheffer opened the inside door and looked at him through the glass of the storm door. Smiling, she unlatched it and opened it for him.

"An early good morning to you, Detective Brennen," she greeted. "Welcome to my simple abode."

Mike stepped up into the house as the lieutenant glanced up and down the street. Closing the doors, she asked, "However did you get here? You certainly don't look as though you could walk very far."

"A cab," Mike lied with reluctance. "He got another call, so he took off in a hurry."

"Well, come into the kitchen. You can sit and have some coffee."

She led him through a dark living room that was barely larger than his own and into the lighted kitchen. Only then did Mike see that the woman was obviously braless in a tight-fitting tee-shirt with the words I AM WOMAN on it in red letters. The jeans she had on were also tight, accentuating her trim figure. This was a new picture of Anita Sheffer, and Mike realized no cop should be looking at a lieutenant the way he was looking at her. If Sheffer felt embarrassed by his attraction, she ignored it. She waved him to a breakfast nook in a kitchen too small for a table and chairs.

"Have a seat," she said. Getting a better look at her visitor, her eyebrows went up. "Good heavens, Brennen, you're white as a ghost. Surely, they didn't let you walk out of the hospital looking like that?"

Mike slid onto one of the nook's padded benches with relief.

"Actually, it was more like I crawled out," he said with a half-smile, but didn't elaborate. "Coffee sure smells great…"

"Oh, forgive my manners." The lieutenant turned to the counter and coffee maker, pouring him some of the steaming black liquid into a sunflower decorated mug. Packets of sugar and a small carton of Half & Half along with white napkins in a yellow napkin holder, were already on the nook's table.

Setting the mug in front of Mike, Sheffer said, "From the story I heard, you were almighty lucky to survive that shoot out with Reed. I find myself as curious as everyone else about how all three shooters were found dead and neither you nor your partner had fired a shot." She cocked her head. "How did you manage to pull that off?"

Mike took a grateful sip of coffee before saying, "That's the prize-winning question, all right, but I don't have the answer. I vaguely remember being hit and going down. After that, my most vivid memory is of Reed putting his ugly face in my face. He took the time to brag about how he was getting paid to kill me when he would have been glad to do it for free. After that, I'm a blank."

Sheffer raised a solitary eyebrow. "You're talking about being set up again?"

"No doubt about it. And I'm sure now that the Drogan woman was paid to do the same thing. I believe Corry must have arranged them both. And I'm pretty sure he even tried it himself when he tried to run me down with a car the other morning. Even Lieutenant Grands has finally accepted that someone is trying to do away with me, he just doesn't know why."

"Whew. This has become quite the scenario," said the lieutenant as she poured herself a cup of coffee. Sliding onto the seat opposite Mike, she stirred in some of the Half & Half. "This Corry has been a very busy man. Tell me how you first got on to him. Was it through the same source that told you about the Rezzoro's plan?"

In the midst of taking another drink of coffee, Mike stopped. He was sure that, so far, he had not told Sheffer about the Rezzoros being involved. Suddenly things looked like they were about to drop out from under him.

Slowly setting his cup down, Mike said, "You seem to have dug up some information on your own, Lieutenant."

Anita Sheffer's green eyes lost all semblance of friendliness and her smile became thin and empty.

"Oops. Guess I made a little slip there didn't I, Detective Brennen?"

Detective Brennen leaned back, giving her a look of contempt. "I'd say it was more like a giant slip. Like all the way down from a highly recognized lieutenant to a low-life Rezzoro puppet. You really know how to hurt a guy."

"We didn't invite you into this," said the transformed Anita Sheffer. "And to set the record straight, I'm nobody's puppet. Mine is more of an… intimate connection."

Movement in the corner of his eye brought Mike's head around, his hand instinctively reaching toward his back for his gun. Except, there was no gun.

"Fuck," he said.

The man who had come into the kitchen was Nicholas Rezzoro and he did have a gun. It was pointing at Mike.

One of the first things Mike noticed about the middle brother of the Rezzoro family was that he wasn't nearly as good looking in a tee-shirt and jeans as Sheffer was. Short of six feet by a couple of inches, he was heavy built, his black hair beginning to recede. His black eyes looked out from under heavy black eyebrows, and over a slender nose that didn't match his square-jawed, tough-guy face. At the moment, the man was wearing a twisted, highly amused smile.

With no small amount of relish, Anita Sheffer introduced, "Detective Brennen, I'd like you to meet my fiancé, Nicholas Rezzoro."

Mike stared. "Fiancé? Shit." This was definitely an unexpected development. "That's a hell of a shocker, Lieutenant. A smart, good-looking lady like you, couldn't do better than a syndicate bad ass like Nicky? Well, considering the turn of events, not so sure you are all that smart anymore."

"Don't you fret, Detective. It's the smartest move I've ever made. A chance to get out of a thankless job that's dominated by wise-ass men," said Sheffer. "If you knew Nick at all, you would know what a lucky lady I am."

Mike sniffed. "I know Nicky much better than I care to."

"Oh?" said a surprised Sheffer.

"You mean, with all the ruckus going on over the last couple of days, he didn't mention what good buddies we are?"

"Watch your mouth, Brennen," warned Rezzoro in a gruff voice that matched the rest of his description. With the possible exception of the nose. "Just put your hands flat on the table while I make sure you don't have a gun."

That was when the burner gave a jingle. Tommy was calling.

"Is that the further proof against Corry--?" started Sheffer.

Mike couldn't let them answer it. Without hesitation, he quickly pulled it from the jacket pocket and gave it a hefty throw. It smashed into the wall above the sink and broke up.

"You bastard!" cried the woman. "Who was that?"

"Nobody."

Rezzoro moved, pistol whipping Mike across his head. The blow sent him against the back wall of the nook. Nick ordered, "Hands on the fucking table!"

Head dizzy, Mike sullenly complied. Nick placed the barrel of his automatic against the detective's head while he checked the jacket and under his shirt.

Anita wanted to know, "Nick, how were you mixed up with Brennen?"

"I'm a shark, and he's a smart-ass fisherman. Shit happens." Rezzoro backed away from the table. "Show me your ankles, too."

Mike slowly twisted to bring his legs into view and pulled up the legs of the five-hundred-dollar jeans a couple of inches to prove there was no backup gun.

"But, I'm a homicide smart-ass fisherman," he said, "and Nicky was a juicy shark suspect in the brutal murder of a--"

"Just shut your mouth!" snapped Rezzoro, giving him another rap on the head with his gun. "Anita doesn't give a fuck about our past history."

"Ouch," griped Mike, gently touching his pounding head. Then went right on looking for more trouble with, "But it's such interesting history, except for the lousy ending. It was about a year ago when a seventeen-year-old girl was beaten to death after being picked up and used like a whore. We had the privilege of bringing in slimeball Nicky as the prime suspect. The poor girl didn't stand a chance--"

Mike was expecting, and was preparing for, another move from Rezzoro. He wasn't expecting it to come from Sheffer, and she was very quick! The woman's right hand struck out like a snake, backhanding him hard on the right side of his face. The blow knocked his battle-weary head back against the wall again and turned his cheek bright red.

More than a little pissed, Mike snarled, "You can't be surprised. A smart bitch like you has to know that you aren't the first trick to jump in bed with Nicky. He--"

Having enticed her with his words, Mike was ready for her move this time. When she lashed out, he blocked her right-handed swing with his right arm and slapped her with his left hand, making no effort to be gentle about it. His wounded left side did pay the price, however.

Sheffer squawked and blood spurted from her nose.

"Sonofabitch!" exclaimed Rezzoro, his gun moving toward Mike's head again.

Brennen moved to block that, too, his plan to make a grab for the weapon, Nick was smart enough to realize it in time and checked himself, again backing away.

"You fuckin' cop!" declared the man. "You try something like that again, I'll pop you right here and now!"

Anita was pulling napkins from the napkin holder to hold over her nose. Her green eyes blazed.

"You goddamned sonofabitch!" she spit out. "I should have shot you when you first walked into my office!"

Mike's eyes were on the gun, but now he switched them back to the woman and sourly admitted, "You were good. You had me convinced that you were the dedicated cop I'd heard about. It's a bitter disappointment to find out you come from the same pile of shit that the Rezzoros--"

Sheffer made another quick move. Still holding the napkins to her nose with her left hand, she leaned across the table and grabbed a handful of his hair with her right hand. Giving it a nasty tug, she hissed, "I'll give you a goddamn headache like you've never had!"

Considering the headaches he'd been having the last few days, it might take some doing, but Mike did not doubt she was capable of it. When he started to reach for her arm, Nicholas joined in the fun by jamming his gun into the detective's side. The left side. Where a bullet had left its mark not so many hours ago. Mike grunted at the pain and would have doubled over if the ex-nice lady lieutenant hadn't been trying to pull his hair out by the roots.

This day was decidedly not going to be better than yesterday.

"No more fucking around!" Anita rasped. "Tell us who your magical source of information is, Brennen! And who was it on that phone, damn it?"

"And who the hell saved your ass from Reed?" demanded Rezzoro.

"Was it the same heroic citizen who warned you about Drogan?" came back Sheffer.

"Christ! You guys do stereo real good," griped Mike. "And, hey, I got questions, too. Like who killed Drogan? And how'd you even find her if she wasn't on our list?"

Anita smirked, letting go of his hair. Mike fell back in relief as the woman said, "She was on the list, you dumb ass detective. As Margo Arnett, her maiden name. She's divorced now, but kept the name Drogan. When I offered her money to kill a cop, she was glad to help out."

"And when she missed, you didn't want me asking her questions. That's why you wanted me to stay away from the hospital. Was she going to be dead, anyway?" allowed Mike. "Who'd you send to slit her throat? One of your boyfriend's sick bastard--?"

Sheffer gave him a hard glare. "You answer our questions, not--"

A soft knock came at the kitchen's back door and a voice softly said, "Hey, Nick? It's Fred and Steve. And do we have a surprise for you."

Anita and Nick exchanged glances and she went to open the door.

CHAPTER 32

Rezzoro moved to the middle of the kitchen as Sheffer opened the door. Mike wasn't sure he could handle any more surprises and watched worriedly. He definitely wasn't ready for the surprise that came in the door.

The men named Fred and Steve entered -- shoving an enraged Joseph Panelli ahead of them. Sheffer and Rezzoro were more astonished than surprised.

"Panelli? What the hell?" exclaimed Nick.

Thinking things couldn't get any worse, Mike stared as they got worse. A moan escaped him. "No."

"Fred?" queried Rezzoro.

Fred, in his middle twenties, was roughly handsome with the build of a lightweight boxer. A sharp dresser in an expensive gray suit, white silk shirt, and a black tie, the hood was full of himself.

"We spotted this car with its headlights off, cruising around the block," he explained. "When we checked it out, this is who we found."

His partner, Steve, was not so brash. Dressed more casually in a dark brown polo shirt and slacks with a light brown sport jacket, he was older and had enough battle scars to make him a careful man. He said, "I don't know who was more surprised, him or us."

"Was easy takin' him," said Fred with a grin. "I used the ol' Freddy lure. It never fails."

Mike gave Joe a depressed look. "How the hell did you let this happen?"

Joe's return glare was one of anger. "I wasn't exactly watching for the fucking Rezzoro clan, Detective Brennen. You're the one that had such great things to say about the lady lieutenant."

Mike clenched his jaw and gave him an ugly look. Then gave a painful shrug and said, "I was wrong. She's a goddamned bitch. And, are you ready for this, she's also Nicky's fuckin' fiancé."

Now it was Joe's turn to be astonished. "Nick Rezzoro and the lady lieutenant? You've got to be kidding."

"Who could kid about something like that? And now that I've gotten to know the real her, I think they make a perfect pair."

Joe couldn't miss the lady's bloody nose and asked, "Run into a door, Lieutenant?"

"A door named Mike," boasted Mike. "One of my better--"

"Shut up!" spit out Sheffer, throwing her bloodied napkins into the sink. The bleeding had slowed to a trickle. "I can't believe this! Panelli and Brennen?" She gave Mike a hard look. "Panelli is your fucking source?"

"Wise ass and bad ass," said Rezzoro. "This sure as hell is one for the books."

"Not as strange a book as the two of you in bed together," remarked Joe. "Actually, I'm surprised there was room in your bed for her, Nick. Stories I've heard, they come and go pretty regular."

Mike winced. "Careful, Joe. The lieutenant is kind of touchy on that subject."

The angry Anita started, "Nick and I are--"

"You don't need to explain anything to them, Anita," said Nicholas. He turned on Mike. "So now we know Panelli is your fucking source."

"Your deductive powers would scare Sherlock Holmes," grunted Mike.

"That's how you survived that clown, Reed," snorted Nick. "You had Panelli back up."

"And Drogan? Panelli was the helpful citizen?" asked Sheffer.

"More or less," acknowledged Mike.

Rezzoro said to Joe, "I have to ask why it is that the Panellis own a two-bit, nobody cop like Brennen? That's the best you could do?"

"Two-bits seems to be my going rate," put in Mike with resignation, "but it's an honest two-bits. Nobody owns me, thank you very much."

He was ignored.

"I don't know, Nick," said Joe. "Your lady lieutenant doesn't seem to be doing all that well. Do you really plan to marry her or is that just a tease to getting the most from her?"

"A tease?" said Mike. "I'd say it was more like a threat."

"You bastards," Sheffer hissed.

"Want us to shut their mouths, Mr. Rezzoro?" asked Fred eagerly.

"Soon," said Mr. Rezzoro.

Anita turned on her fiancé.

"We should be asking who Panelli's source is, Nicholas," she pointed out icily. "You've obviously got a fuckin' mole in your happy family that's passing information along to outsiders. The Panellis no less."

Nick's eyes narrowed on Joe as he said, "I don't suppose you'd like to share the name of that source with us...Mr. Panelli."

"I wouldn't share my grave with you."

Mike cringed. "Bad choice of words there, Mr. Panelli."

"Doesn't matter," said Rezzoro. "Now that we know, it won't be hard to dig the worm out."

"But what if they know this morning's plan?" Anita persisted.

"They can't know that," stated Nick.

"Sure we do," lied Mike. "Corry told me when I--"

Rezzoro didn't look worried. "Like hell he did. All he knows for sure is that it's this morning."

"Does he know he's a dead man as soon as he's killed the Chief?" said Mike.

"What he knows, is that his family will be well taken care of for the rest of their lives," Sheffer told him and then gave in to a wicked smile. "You might be interested to know that I'm going to be the heroine who tries to save the chief's life. I shoot Corry, but I'm just a little too late to stop him from killing Macklin. Hell, maybe I'll get a medal for my efforts."

"Not worried about witnesses?" said Joe.

"There won't be any at five thirty in the morning," said Anita.

"A heroine?" Mike scowled. "That's a stretch even for your acting abilities. It'll never happen. I--"

"Why don't you shut the fuck up!" snapped Sheffer.

She unexpectedly moved on him, lifting her right leg and dropping her foot on his left foot. She only wore sandals, but she put a lot of power in it. The hard-souled sandal stomped down on Mike's tennis shoe with rage and the detective felt the explosion of pain all the way up his leg. Mike's anguished cry filled the house.

"Son of a bitch!" exclaimed Joe and grabbed for Mike as the detective collapsed to the floor to grab a hold of the tortured foot. Anita lifted a leg ready to kick the cop.

Nick stopped her. "Enough, Anita! Let's just figure out what we're going to do with these two."

Enjoying the cop's misery, Fred suggested with a little too much enthusiasm, "A couple of bangs in the head, Boss? I could use Panelli's own gun."

Again dabbing at her nose, the furious Anita complained, "Too damned quick. I want them to feel it coming."

Stooped beside Mike, Joe told him, "I think your lady lieutenant sucks."

"No shit," gasped Mike, eyes shut against the pain.

Nick said, "I think an early morning swim would be nice. Steve, do you think you can find a nice quiet place to take our guests, and their car, for a refreshing plunge?"

"I know just the spot," said Steve.

"That's a great fuckin' idea," said Fred, grinning.

In spite of his current suffering, Mike's eyes came open. He thought it was a fuckin' bad idea. "No swimming. My foot hurts!"

"The water is the best cure. You won't feel it anymore." snarled Sheffer. "And I think that since they're in this together, they should stay together. I'll be right back."

She went off down a short hallway and up some stairs.

Joe looked up at Rezzoro and shook his head. "She's your fiancé? How the hell did you pull that off?"

Asshole Nick's smile was crooked as he answered, "Believe it or not, she came to me. She needed some financial help for her son Randy. Said she liked what she'd read and heard about me."

"How romantic," said Joe.

"She liked what she read and heard? That's sick," moaned Mike, nursing his throbbing foot. "You gonna send wedding invitations to the cops?"

"Not to you for sure," said Nick. To Joe, "I just can't believe you and Brennen are working together. Why the hell did you pick him?"

"Because he gets the job done. Or haven't you noticed that, thanks to Detective Brennen, your plans are screwed."

Mike Brennen looked startled. "Was that an actual compliment?"

"Our plans are in great shape," stated Rezzoro. "All he's done for you is get you killed."

Sheffer returned carrying a pair of handcuffs.

Nick looked impressed. "Nice touch, Anita."

"Thank you, Nick," she smiled. Then ordered, "Get him on his feet!"

Joe and Fred lifted Mike up and the detective leaned against Joe while taking his weight on his right foot.

"Ah, shit," he groaned as Sheffer locked his left wrist to Joe's right.

Fred grinned, again. "We ought to get a picture of this. A Panelli handcuffed to a cop."

Rezzoro laughed and started, "I like--"

Joe, his own rage reaching a breaking point, suddenly planted his left fist in Nick's face. It was a dandy blow, knocking the unprepared Rezzoro back against the kitchen counter. It also gave the man a bloody nose to match his fiancé's. For his effort, Joe got a hard fist in his lower back from Steve. It sent him to his knees, jerking Mike down and off balance, putting weight on his bad foot.

"Shit!" griped Mike.

But when he saw Anita aiming a foot to kick Joe, Mike ignored his pain to grab her leg and quickly lifted it upward. Lieutenant Sheffer fell back and hit the floor with a good thump.

Steve moved, putting his gun in Mike's face. "Stop! Or I'll put a bullet in your other foot and you can die a cripple!"

Mike stopped, breathing hard. Joe pulled himself up and helped the detective up again. Nick turned to help his lovely Anita onto her feet.

She glared at their prisoners. "Goddamnit, maybe we should shoot them right now," she rasped.

"Just get them the fuck out of here!" Rezzoro ordered his henchmen. "I'll follow you in my car and give you a ride back."

Fred and Steve grabbed jacket collars to shove Mike and Joe toward the door, Mike struggling to keep weight off his bad foot. Sheffer stepped up to him and he winced.

But she just smirked and said, "It was a pleasure working with you, Detective. Too bad you had to be so damned good at your job."

Mike blinked. "Damn. Two compliments in one night. I can hardly stand it."

CHAPTER 33

Gritting against his pain, the disgruntled Mike had to ask Joe, "Tell me what the hell the infallible Freddy's lure is?"

They were in the back seat of Joe's car. Steve was driving, Fred was riding shotgun, his gun on the two prisoners. Following behind them was Nick Rezzoro in his white Cadillac.

Fred grinned. "Yeah, Panelli. Tell him what the Freddy lure is."

Joe glowered at the young henchman and said, "The disgusting idiot pissed in the middle of the street."

"Huh?" said Mike.

"That's the Freddy lure," said Fred. "Gets their attention every time."

Mike glared at the idiot and said sourly, "That is disgusting. It's also illegal and you're under arrest."

Fred laughed. "That's a good one, cop."

Mike said to Joe, "That's really how they got you?"

Joe rumbled, "He acted like a drunk crossing the street. When he stopped in front of me to piss, I braked. What the fuck would you have done? Run him over?"

Mike had to shrug at that, wincing at all the different pains it caused. He did admit to himself that he would probably have stopped, too. If only to arrest the guy.

"If I'd known he was a Rezzoro scumbag, I would have run him down, but I didn't know that until his buddy had a gun aimed at my head," said Joe. "What Mr. Fred and Mr. Steve don't realize, is that they're both fucked, and their hours are numbered."

"Never gonna happen," said Fred. "When our police chief takes over, the Panellis will be toast no matter how legit they think they are. It's just too bad the two of you won't be here to see it."

"We'd be glad to stick around," Mike offered.

"Another good one." said the jolly Fred with an ugly laugh. "I love a cop with a sense of humor. Even a broke foot don't slow him down." And he turned his back on them.

"How come everybody likes my sense of humor but you?" Mike asked Joe.

"Everybody but me? Was Sheffer laughing?"

"Well, I suppose..."

"How about Polinski? Or Cor--"

"Forget it."

Joe leaned closer to Mike and fumed in a harsh whisper, "So maybe I stop for pissing assholes, but what about you? You walked right into that bitch's arms. How the hell...?"

Mike fumed back in a harsher whisper, "Oh, sure, blame Detective Brennen. No matter that the Panellis told me there was one assassin, not two."

Joe gave him a sour glare, then sighed. "How's the foot?"

"Hurts like hell...but I've got an even bigger problem."

Joe gave him a snort. "No shit. Now there's a news bulletin."

Mike whispered self-consciously, "I can't swim."

Joe stared. "What?"

"I don't know how to--"

"I heard you. Is this some more of your terrific sense of humor?"

"It's a real fuckin' problem. I can't swim."

"Brennen," hissed Joe, "what difference does it make? Nobody can swim when they're wearing handcuffs and shut up in a car filling with water. Except for maybe fucking Houdini."

"Hooray for Houdini," muttered Mike. Then, voice even lower, "Look, I can get us out of the handcuffs, but I obviously can't do it while these two pricks are in the car with us. That means I have to wait until we're in the water to get them off. So can you keep me from drowning?"

Joe almost cracked a smile. He said, "You get the cuffs off, Detective, I'll do my best to save your battered, humorous hide."

"Thank you."

Fred's head turned. "What the hell are you two muttering about? Planning your escape?"

"Yes. We're discussing how Houdini would've handled this," grouched Mike.

Fred laughed some more. "That's great! I love it!"

"I really hate you," snarled Mike.

Too soon they reached the warehouses and wharves that lined the river. There was some activity even at that early hour, but Steve drove past the busy areas until he reached a deserted, isolated wharf. Only one light pole made a weak attempt to cut into the darkness surrounding the deteriorating old warehouse and its parking lot. A seven-foot, chain-link fence and gate blocked the way, with a rusted metal sign warning NO TRESPASSING. The gate was chained shut, but Fred got out of the car and made short work of the padlock with a tool he took from an inside pocket. Then he swung the gate wide and Steve drove in, Nick Rezzoro coming right behind him in the Caddy. Fred followed after them on foot. Steve stopped about thirty feet from the wharfs edge and the dark water below, shifting into park.

"Sorry, but this is where we part company," he said as he popped the trunk lid and then lowered the front windows.

"He doesn't sound sorry," muttered Mike.

Fred could be heard rummaging around in the trunk. Steve got out and Rezzoro poked his head in.

"It's going to give me great pleasure telling Anthony Panelli he's less one son," said Nick. "He won't even be able to have a big, fancy funeral to bury you, because he won't know where your water-soaked body is."

"It won't be a problem, Nicky," growled Joe. "My family will make up for it by attending your fucking funeral."

"Keep dreaming, Panelli," snarled Nicky. Switching his attention to Mike, he said, "I'm going to miss you sniffing at my heels, Brennen. When you get to wherever it is you're going and you see that little gal I messed around with, tell her 'Hi'. She was one sweet little piece of ass."

"Is that finally a confession, Nick? And Joe here is a witness."

"Funny to the end, cop. Happy drowning."

Rezzoro pulled his head out and Mike hissed, "I really hate him, too."

The trunk lid was slammed shut and Fred came around the car carrying the jack handle. He grinned in at the prisoners, saying, "Sure wish we could enjoy the show you two will be putting on trying to get out of there."

"You're welcome to come along and join the fun," invited Mike.

Fred's grin turned into a sneer. "You fuckin' cop. Open that wise ass mouth under water and you'll just drown faster."

With that, he leaned in to jam the jack handle between the gas pedal and the seat. The car's motor revved up and Fred slammed the door.

"I hope you two have a pleasant trip," hissed Rezzoro. Then, "Do it, Fred!"

Fred reached in the open window, his grin back.

"Take a deep breath, boys," he said and shifted the lever to drive, quickly jumping back.

With a roar, the Acura shot forward.

"Oh fuck," moaned Mike Brennen. "This is not how I want to die."

"Brace yourself!" snapped Panelli. "And we are not going to die!"

The car hit the water with a jolt. Immediately, Joe leaned across the front seat, using his left hand to hit the unlock button for the doors. As he fell back onto the seat, the cold, dark water began rushing in through the open front windows. Grasping the door handle, Joe got the door unlatched. Then quickly discovered that with only one hand to use, he could not get the door open any further against the increasing pressure of the water.

"Step on it, Houdini," he said urgently.

Mike was struggling against terror and pain. The former caused by the water rushing in. The latter caused by his tortured foot and wounded side. Desperately he bent down to get at his right sneaker. When he had it off, he had to bring the shoe up to where his cuffed left hand could get at the tape that held the key inside it.

He hollered, louder than necessary, "Hold still! I need two hands!"

Almost complete darkness engulfed them and the water started to come over the front seats like a river over a dam. It was freezing cold and both men grit their teeth as it splashed into their laps and rose up their legs. Mike frantically felt for the duct tape with his left fingers. Joe had managed to get his left leg in place to keep the door from latching. His right arm and hand were twisted around in an awkward position so Mike was able to use both of his hands.

"Brennen!" said Joe with a clenched jaw.

"I've got it! I've got it!" declared the detective as he ripped out the tape and separated the key from it.

"Christ! Don't drop it!" cried Joe. "It's gonna work on these cuffs?"

"It should! They're pretty universal!" Mike's teeth chattered.

"It should?"

"Just hold 'em up! I can't see worth a shit!"

In desperation, the men held their wrists above the water that was climbing swiftly up their chests. Mike's fingers searched out the key hole and he went to work.

Joe, worried. "Shit! I thought cops were fast at this sort of thing!"

Mike, terrified. "Shut the fuck up! It's goddamned dark! And the fucking water's coming in fast!"

Water closed over their shoulders and started up their necks. Finally the detective freed Joe's wrist, leaving the cuffs to dangle from his own

"Get me the hell out of here!" pleaded Mike.

"Take a deep breath and get a tight hold on my shirt!" ordered Joe.

Now able to get both legs against the door, Joe braced against Mike and pushed. It opened and water covered them.

CHAPTER 34

Brennen clung to Panelli like an anchor. Eyes tight shut, the detective was sure he was going to die in this cold, watery, black hell. Ignorant in the skill of slowly exhaling when underwater, Mike's lungs felt like giant balloons ready to explode. He was as close to panic as he'd ever been. Give him dry land and a half dozen Jason Reeds and he'd have been a much happier man. Fortunately for both of them, Joe was a strong and skilled swimmer. Though it felt like forever to Mike, once they were free of the car, it was only a few seconds before they broke the surface. The detective opened his mouth to suck in air for a brief moment, then was sucking in water as he sank beneath the surface again. Panic started to rush back, but Joe got a hold of him and hauled him back up.

"Help me, Brennen! Kick your fucking feet," gasped Joe.

On Mike's part, it was a weak effort at best, but together they managed to keep their heads above water. Fortunately, they had come up underneath the pier where eyes could not see them. Listening ears were another matter as Mike choked and coughed uncontrollably.

"Cover it," urged Joe urgently, trying to keep his own ragged breathing quiet.

Mike struggled to breathe without coughing, and without swallowing anymore water. He bumped into a piling and let go of Joe to grab it. It turned out to be slippery and gave Mike little confidence that he was safe. He began to shiver and his teeth started chattering. And it was so damned cold and dark. Where the hell had Panelli gone?

"Where'd you...go?" his teeth chattered into the darkness. He got no answer. "Shit. Panelli...where--"

There was a little splash of water.

"Here," said Joe, shivering, teeth chattering. "I found a ... ladder. Give me a hand. It's just a ... few feet."

As unhappy as he was with the slippery, wooden piling, Mike was almost reluctant to let it go. Joe made the decision for him by grabbing an arm and giving it a good pull. Before he even had time to think about it, Mike bumped into the ladder. The two men thankfully wrapped their arms through it, one on each side, and took time to breathe life back into their bodies.

"Air never ... tasted ... so good," said Mike, trying to keep his voice low and the chattering to a minimum. "Do you ... think they're still ... up there?"

"They didn't ... sound like they ... were gonna ... stick around long," breathed Joe. "Besides, the noise we've made ... I think we would have heard from them by now."

"I don't think we ... can wait long. We've got to get out ... of this freezing water."

"Will you be able to climb with that wound? Your foot?"

"What wound? What foot? I can't feel anything."

"Let's hope there isn't something sitting ... on the trap door."

"Thank you so much ... for that happy thought."

"I'll go up to see how it looks." said Joe.

Mike felt the man brush past his arms and start up the ladder. Then he pulled himself around to where he could get his right foot on a rung. Unfortunately, the moment he tried to use the left foot, he was quickly reminded of his pain. On top of that, his wound made itself known again, too. Mike gritted his teeth, which at least stopped the chattering, but he had a feeling it was going to be a long way up.

"I'm at the top," said Joe from the darkness above. Too far above. "This trap door isn't giving. I'm going to have to put my shoulders to it."

Mike was still gritting his teeth and could only respond with a groaning grunt.

"You okay?" asked Joe.

"No. Just get the ... damn door open."

Now Joe grunted as he pushed. Finally the encouraging sound of scrunching and squeaking came. If Rezzoro and his boys were still there, they'd find out in a hurry.

"Hey!" exclaimed Joe suddenly as the door was pulled unexpectedly open. "Fuck!"

"It's me!" said someone else.

The door was dropped with a thump on the pier. Mike looked up to see black shapes against the square of muted yard light.

"Give me your hand," said the new voice and Joe was almost bodily lifted up. "Is Brennen down there?"

"He was when I left," said Joe.

"Damn right I'm here," grumbled Mike. "Not sure I can get up this fucking ladder, though."

"The lady lieutenant stomped on his foot," said Joe. "Kind of cramped his style."

A large form started down the ladder, and Tommy Bears said, "Your lady cop turned out to be a--"

"A first-class bitch," said Mike.

Tommy stopped beside him on the ladder. "Want me to do this fireman style or can you hop?"

"I'll hop, just don't let me fall back into the water. Please."

It was a painful struggle, but with Tommy's help, Mike finally made it to the top. Once there, Joe helped him get clear and Mike rolled onto his back to sprawl on the wharf.

"That's some interesting jewelry you're wearing," commented Tommy on seeing the dangling handcuffs on Mike's wrist. "Guess they were serious went they sent you into the water."

"Pretty sure they wanted us to stay down there," said Joe. He had sunk down cross-legged, still catching his breath.

"Thank you, Joe," mustered Mike quietly. "For getting me out of that car and the fucking water."

"Thank you for your Houdini magical key," said Joe.

Tommy eyed them. "Magical key?"

"Later. We need to get out of here," urged Joe. "To the Panelli home."

"I'll get my car," said Tommy.

"Rezzoro and his goons?" asked Mike.

"They took off right away," said Tommy. "They obviously didn't know about any magical keys." He went for his car.

Mike and Joe slowly took in air, shivering in the cool, early spring morning. Then the former quietly said, "I meant it...Joe. Thanks. Drowning is definitely not how I want to die."

Joe smiled into the darkness. "You're welcome." Then, "Tell me, how long have you been taping a key inside your shoe?"

Mike sighed. "A while. Couple of years I guess."

"And...you going to tell me why?"

Mike had a coughing spell before he could answer. "In case somebody handcuffed me to a Panelli and tried to drown me."

"Wise ass."

The detective silently looked up into the night as an ugly memory came back all too clear. Teeth chattering periodically, Mike told him, "Some bad guys grabbed a cop I knew. It was a revenge thing. They beat him up bad and then handcuffed him to a pipe in the basement of an abandoned building. They took his key and left him. If anybody heard his cries for help, they ignored them. By the time he was found, it was way too late." Mike paused before adding, "That wasn't a good way to die, either....so, call me paranoid, I started carrying the extra key. Easy enough in tennis shoes."

Joe was quiet for a few moments. Then, "It would be worse than drowning, and well worth carrying a key taped in your shoe."

The Mercedes Benz arrived with a rush, stopping next to the two exhausted men. Tommy got out, leaving the motor running, and opened the back door.

"Tell me, Brennen, how come you're always wet when I invite you into my car?" asked the Indian as he started to help the detective up.

"Oh oh," said Mike before they got far. "I don't feel so good."

With Tommy hanging onto him, Mike proceeded to throw up more water.

"Goddamn!" said Tommy.

Mike coughed. "I think I'm good now."

"Shit, yeah," sniffed Tommy.

Joe had gotten to his feet and wore a crooked smile. "Better let me help you get the crippled cop into the car."

Together they hobbled Mike over and slid him inside. Joe went around to get in from the other side as Tommy closed the door.

Getting behind the wheel, he asked with some amusement, "Want some heat?"

"Heat would be wonderful, Mr. Bears," said Mike. "I don't suppose you have something to heat up our insides?"

"As a matter of fact, I do, but only if you promise you won't toss it back up after you drink it."

"I promise," said Mike.

"Sure," said Tommy with doubt.

"And could I get you to make me a promise...?"

"What?"

"Please be careful you don't drive off into the water. Once in a lifetime is more than I ever want to do that."

Tommy smirked. "I promise." He made a tight turn and drove off the wharf without going into the water.

Joe was pulling open a section of the back seat, revealing a couple of bottles of liquor and glasses. He poured two stiff drinks.

Mike took his and downed it in one swallow Joe did his in two.

"Wow," choked Mike. "I think maybe I'll live now."

"How the hell did you find us, Indian?" Joe wanted to know.

"Corry. When he ran, he didn't run to the Rezzoro stronghold. He led me to some quaint little neighborhood. Must have been Sheffer's...right?"

"Sheffer's," Joe confirmed. "And Rezzoro's men surprised me. Brennen and I both ended up in the witch's pot."

"The lady is in it with Rezzoro, too?" Tommy was surprised.

"The lady is in Nick Rezzoro's bed," said Mike.

"What?" said a surprised Tommy.

But Joe wanted to know, "So you saw us there? At Sheffer's?"

"Saw your car coming out of the alley, followed by a white Caddy. A street light gave me a glimpse of Rezzoro in the Caddy and I recognized one of his goons behind the wheel in your car. I decided it might be a good idea to follow."

"You followed us?" said Mike. "You followed us!? And you didn't stop them from sending us into the water!?"

"I didn't think an all-out gun battle with three men was a good move at the time."

"And after they left? You could have jumped in and--"

"--and got all wet. I knew you'd make it out."

"What? You knew we'd make it out? How could you know that?" the detective fussed. "We might have been unconscious. And we were wearing handcuffs!"

"I saw your heads bobbing around in the back seat, so I knew you were alive and well at the time. I admit I didn't think about handcuffs, but, you're survivors. I wasn't worried."

"There is one small detail you didn't know when making that deduction," said Joe.

"Oh?"

"Our honest, dedicated detective can't swim."

"You're kidding."

Mike scowled. "Why would he be kidding? Lots of people can't swim."

"I don't know any," said Tommy.

"Well, now you know one. Where the hell was I supposed to learn to swim? In a rainstorm? Our neighborhood did not have a swimming pool. The closest we got was when they opened a fire hydrant."

Tommy shrugged. "I would think that a cop should know how to--"

"Son of a bitch my foot hurts." bitched Mike. "And my side."

He pulled the soggy bandage off and dropped it on the floor. Putting a hand to the wound, it felt warm and sticky. "Great. I'm bleeding."

"Not in my car!" declared Tommy.

"I only promised I wouldn't throw up."

CHAPTER 35

Joe called ahead to make sure the Panelli's back gate would be open for them.

"I'll tell you what's happening when we get there," Joe said into Bears' cell phone. That didn't seem to satisfy the party on the other end because he repeated more firmly, "When I get there."

"What exactly is happening?" asked Tommy as Joe handed him back the phone. "Why do the Rezzoros need two assassins? And you said Nick and the lady lieutenant are a thing?"

"They are," said Joe.

"Engaged things," added Mike.

"No shit? Engaged?" That got Tommy's attention. "So she's the one who kept trying to end the career of our dedicated detective?"

"She confessed all. She set me up with Drogan and Reed," said Mike. "I figured it was Corry, but if I'd thought about it a little harder, I'd've known he was too screwed up to handle something like that. The man's not thinking anymore, let alone able to set up hits. And I'd bet a million it was a Rezzoro man who killed the dragon lady in the hospital."

"Like Fred or Steve?" suggested Joe.

"More like Steve. Fred didn't seem clever enough," sniffed Mike. "It didn't come up in the conversation, but I'm also pretty sure it was Sheffer who sent Corry to make that run at me with a car. When the Calamity Janes pulled their early morning job on that store, the lieutenant saw an opportunity and took it. She probably called Corry and set it up before she even called me. He could have stolen a car on the way to my place and then dumped it when he picked his own back up. I was right about it being a drunk. A drunk cop out to kill me. The bastard."

"So I ask again," said Tommy. "What's happening?"

Joe said, "Piecing together what we picked up from the happy couple, Lieutenant Corry is going to hit Police Chief Macklin at five thirty this morning. They didn't say where, so we'll--"

"At that hour, where else but at his condo building," said Mike.

Joe nodded. "Okay. You know where that is?"

"I do. Never been to his place, but I've seen the building. High-end condos where getting in could be tricky, but the parking ramp would be the perfect place for a hit. There'd be slim chance for witnesses at that hour and Sheffer would be able to play her role as heroine without contradiction."

"What about cameras?" asked Joe.

"Easy enough for a cop to handle that." reasoned Mike. "Those cameras won't see a thing."

"What kind of excuse is she going to have for being at the ramp at that hour of the morning?" Joe wanted to know. "She doesn't exactly live in the neighborhood."

"I can't guess what her plan might have been, but I think when I started poking my nose into it, it gave her a dandy idea. And when a Panelli came through her door, it got even dandier," said Mike. He went on, "Good ol' dedicated Detective Brennen walks into her office one morning claiming he's picked up a tip that there's a threat on Macklin's life. Then when Detective Brennen suddenly disappears a couple of days later, she suspects foul play and takes it on herself to investigate further. What the sharp lieutenant discovers is that the Panelli family actually does have such a plot. She hurries to warn Macklin, only, sad to say, she's a little too late. She can't save the chief, but she does kill the assassin, Lieutenant Corry."

"For icing on the cake, I wouldn't put it past her to arrange for an anonymous phone call to say where a certain car could be found. They find my body in Joe Panelli's car, it strengthens the case against the Panellis."

Joseph Panelli wasn't looking too pleased with the detective's plot line.

"What about my body being handcuffed to your body in my car?" he said. "In the back seat."

"I'm not sure how she would have handled that, but you can be sure that whatever she came up with, it would have sounded completely believable coming out of that lady's mouth. She should have been a fuckin' actress. Bitch."

"Ouch," said Tommy. "Such language aimed at a superior, Detective Brennen."

"Superior, my ass. Three times she set me up! Three fuckin' times!" He took a breath. "And…I owe the two of you for saving my neck two of those times. And Joe again, for my early morning swimming lesson." Mike shook his head. "This is a hell of a position to be in … a cop thanking the Panellis. More than once."

A smile touched Joe's mouth. "It will be our secret. And, as you've pointed out a couple of times, if you hadn't been helping us out, you wouldn't have been in such perilous positions. As for the swimming lesson, I think we came out even on that one. After all, you gave me a lesson on how to unlock handcuffs in the dark, under water. Houdini would have been proud."

"That the magical key you mentioned?" asked Tommy.

"Keeps one taped in his shoe if you can believe it," said Joe. "He can tell you the story that goes with it sometime."

"Can't wait. But it sounds like we don't have a lot of time for planning. Just how do you intend to change the ending to this Rezzoro-Sheffer plot?"

"What the hell time is it, anyway?" Mike wondered suddenly.

"Three-forty-six," answered the Indian.

"Enough time for us to get some dry clothes," said Joe.

"And shoes," said Mike, holding up his bare right foot, and then winced at the pain the movement caused both the left foot and his wound. He added with a grimace, "Well, one shoe."

Joe smirked. "We'll see that wound gets a fresh Band-Aid, too, and--"

Mike scowled back and got cranky. "A Band-Aid? I've been shot and dragged out of my hospital bed and thumped on the head, had the shit stomped out of my foot, and practically drowned. On top of that, every disease known to mankind is in that cruddy water and I've been drinking it, to say nothing about what kind of things are probably crawling around in my wound now…and my scratches. I need more than a Band-Aid, thank you very much."

"Kind of grumpy," noted Tommy.

"We have a lady that will do you up professionally, Mike," Joe assured him. "So relax."

"A lady?"

"We can't go to an ER," Joe pointed out. "Even if we had time. Our Anna is excellent at caring for nasty problems. You'll be fine."

"Relax. I'll be fine. Right."

The back gate was open and Tommy parked at the same door that Mike had been taken to just a few days earlier. At the moment, he couldn't remember exactly how many years ago that had been.

It took both Tommy and Joe to get him out of the car and into the house. Thomas opened the door for them and gave Mike a hard look as they came in. Anthony was also there and both men were fully dressed.

"What's wrong with him now?" griped Thomas and then took note of their soggy appearance. "You're both soaking wet! What the hell happened?" There was a definite lack of sympathy in man's tone.

Anthony Panelli eyed the handcuffs dangling from Mike's wrist. And the bare foot.

"I don't care for the looks of this, Joseph," he said.

"It's nice he noticed our looks," rumbled Mike. "Though it's looking a lot better than it did an hour ago."

"It's been a particularly busy night, Father," said Joe. "We have--"

"I suppose the cop screwed up again," griped Thomas. "I don't believe--"

"Shut up, Thomas!" snapped Joe.

Thomas' mouth went shut, but he gave his younger brother an angry glare. Mike helped the situation out by giving Thomas a nasty smirk.

Collecting himself, Joe went on, "Tommy and I will come to the study as soon as we get Brennen to my room, Father. Thomas, please have Anna to put her first aid kit together. Tell her to include elastic wraps." To Tommy, "We'll take the elevator up."

Mike's eyebrows went up. "You have an elevator? And my foot is grateful."

They went to a door in the hallway where Joe punched a small button beside it. The door slid open sideways, and the three men got in. It was a smooth, short ride, and it opened onto another carpeted hallway. Low lights in stylish wall fixtures provided the lighting. Four large, elegantly framed paintings hung along the walls, each with their own small spotlight. Undoubtedly originals by famous artists, all of them scenic with mountains and lakes and wild animals. Under other circumstances, Mike would have been more impressed. Right now all his attention was on his pain.

There were four closed doors off the wide hallway as well as an opening to a narrower hall. Joe took them to one of the doors and opened it, he and Tommy taking Mike through it.

Mike blinked and quipped, "Wow. This is bigger than mine."

The large bedroom was done in brown and gold. Expectedly, there was a king-sized bed with a quilted bedspread in two shades of brown. Two giant, maple, chests-of-drawers sat side-by-side on one wall. In the wall across from them were a set of double doors that probably led to a walk-in closet. Across from the foot of the bed was a large screen television on a long heavy wooden table. The carpet, a mixture of rich, deep brown and gold, felt inches deep.

"Hell," muttered Mike, "it's bigger than my whole apartment."

His comments were ignored. They guided him over to the bed and sat him down. Joe went to a door next to his bed and opened it to turn on the light. It was the bathroom. He then opened the closet doors and ducked in to return in a moment with a crutch.

"This is a leftover from a broken leg. Do you think you can get out of those clothes and maybe take a shower using this? If not, one of us can…"

"I'll manage." Mike held up the wrist with the dangling handcuffs. "It would be nice to get rid of the jewelry, though."

Tommy reached into an inside pocket of his jacket and pulled out a small leather case. Unzipping it, he took out a small tool.

"Mr. Tommy One Bears, a man of all trades," said Mike as the man rescued him from the cuffs.

"Tommy and I are going to talk to my father and brother. You've got time for a shower if you don't dawdle. It would be the best way to get that wound cleaned good. I'll get you some clothes when we get back." Then added, "Don't fall down."

"Maybe I should be there to hear what you're going to tell them," the detective lightly protested. Then again, why would he want to be in on a Panelli powwow? Especially with Thomas there.

But Joe pointed out, "You already know what's happened. It's more important that you get cleaned up."

That was very true. Mike agreed, "Right."

The two men left the cop sitting on the king-sized bed.

"Don't dawdle…?" said Mike.

CHAPTER 36

Brennen took a minute to close his eyes and take some deep breaths, relishing the fact that he was still alive. In spite of the four attempts to change that status. Now, with luck, the entire mess would be over in a couple of hours. Hopefully with the good guys winning. Except, no one would ever know the Panellis were the good guys. Maybe it would only be the two-bit cop stumbling into that role.

Dragging his eyes open, Mike pushed the thoughts away and gathered his energy. Carefully he took hold of the crutch and pushed to his good foot. Slowly he hobbled into the bathroom and stopped - and stared. At a guess, he figured his bathroom would probably fit into this bathroom about half a dozen times. Maybe more. Done in the same brown and gold as the bedroom, it had all the bathroom necessities, including a television and a tub large enough for a pool party.

"So this is what a bathroom is supposed to look like," he said. "I'm going to have to have a talk with my landlord."

Mike played with the switches and was glad to find that one of them turned on a ceiling heat lamp. Next came the chore of removing the cold, wet clothes, from his cold, wet body. Not an easy chore leaning on a crutch. He did note that there was blood on Joe's shirt and jeans and even the leather jacket.

He said, "Darn."

Unable to avoid seeing himself in a multitude of mirrors, Mike noted his body looked puckered and goose-bumpy from top to bottom. His wound was puffy and raw, the entire left side turning multi-colored, though at least the bleeding had pretty much stopped. His scratches were also puffy, his neck even more colorful than his side. He was not a handsome sight. And all of it hurt.

He indulged in a groan as he sank onto the toilet seat and went to work getting off his left tennis shoe. That was hard! The foot had swollen and did not take well to the removal. There were several more groans involved before the shoe and sock fell to the floor. And he stared at his vividly colored, swollen foot.

"Ah, shit. What the hell else can happen?" he moaned. Then regretfully said, "Forget I asked that!"

Back on the crutch, Mike pulled open the shower door to hobble into the roomy stall. Turning on the water, he adjusted the temperature to mostly hot and luxuriated in the pulsating stream of hot needles. Maybe he would dawdle.

He didn't. Mike, using one hand, carefully cleaned out his wounded side and the scratches, gritting his teeth against the pain. Much as he would have liked to scrub his whole body, it was impossible standing on a crutch. He did what he could before stepping out to take one of the several big, fluffy, brown towels hanging on a wall rack. Again carefully, he dried off the best he good before returning to sink gratefully back onto the bed. Using his right hand, he raised the towel to begin rubbing at his wet hair. It was at that moment that the Panelli brothers and Tommy Bears came in. So did a sixty-plus-year-old woman wearing a light blue bathrobe and blue slippers. She carried a tray loaded with a little tub, numerous bottles of whatever, and tape and bandages.

Mike quickly pulled the towel off his head to cover his lower extremities.

"Hey!" he exclaimed. "I'm naked here!"

"You're not her type," said Joe.

"And you're sure as hell not ours," snipped Thomas.

Tommy remained prudently silent, but there was amusement in his eyes.

"You could've at least knocked or something," muttered Mike.

Impatiently Joe told him, "Anna's got kids your age. Just let her get you cleaned up and bandaged so we can get going." He did take notice of the glorious left foot. "That is nasty." With a small, twisted smile, he added, "Probably need to see a doctor and get that x-rayed first chance you--"

"You think?" griped Mike.

Anna prepared her doctoring tools. Joe hurried into the closet returning in moments with jeans and shirts. From one of the chests-of-drawers, he pulled out underwear and socks. Tossing some of the clothing on the bed, he headed for the bathroom.

"It would be nice if you didn't bleed on those," he tossed over his shoulder. "I'm grabbing a shower."

The bathroom door shut.

Anna had poured solution into the tub and now dipped a clean cloth into it. When she laid it onto the wounded side, Mike squawked and jumped.

"Don't tell me a tough two-bit cop can't handle a little pain," smirked Thomas.

His temper short, Mike rasped, "Take a good look at my side, you bastard! Look at my goddamned foot! The Panellis sit here in this fucking house while I'm running around being their two-bit errand boy solving their fucking problem and getting shot at and beat up and--!"

Anna had stopped, gaping with wide eyes at the erupting Mike. Tommy winced. Thomas Panelli glared in anger.

"You screw-up!" Thomas erupted back. "You're a pain in the ass and--!"

Now Tommy flinched and started, "Thomas, maybe--"

It was too late. The tough two-bit cop unexpectedly stood up on his one foot and hit Thomas Panelli. With a fist. In the face. Fortunately, Detective Mike Brennen was not up to strength, nor in the best of shape, so the blow was mediocre. It did cause Mr. Panelli to lose his equilibrium and go down, landing on his ass in the thick, brown and gold carpeting.

Anna's eyes went even wider as she gasped and exclaimed, "Oh!" and took a step back.

This time Tommy cringed.

Forgetting his bad foot in the heat of the moment, Mike accidentally touched it to the floor. With a painful gasp, he fell back in a sprawl on the bed. Startled, Thomas stared at the cop. Then, as his senses came back online, he put a hand to his stinging face as rage took over. The man came off the floor fast, with negative intentions. Tommy One Bears moved fast, too, stepping between Thomas and the bed and Mike.

"I don't think this is going to help the situation, Thomas," he said. "Besides the fact that we don't have time for a brawl."

"Get the hell out of my way, Indian!" rasped Thomas. "No goddamned cop is going to hit me and--"

"What the hell's going on?" Joe had opened the bathroom door and stood there dripping, one of the brown towels wrapped around his waist.

Thomas started to answer him with, "This fucking cop--"

"Never mind! Get out of here, Thomas," the younger brother ordered the older brother. "Wait in the study."

His face red with fury, eyes ablaze, Thomas sent the cop a menacing glare. Mike was at least as furious as he shot daggers back at Thomas from his prone position. The Indian was not in an enviable position.

"I won't forget this," rasped Thomas.

"Neither will I," fumed Mike. "It's the most fun I've had in the last few days."

Thomas Panelli turned and strode brusquely from the room.

"Can I get dressed now? Or maybe you want to take on Bears next...or Anna?!" declared a pissed Joseph Panelli, but he didn't wait for any reply. He stepped back into the bathroom and shut the door, with purpose.

Anna was still staring at Mike with no small amount of astonishment, and it didn't seem likely that it was because the cop's towel had fallen to the floor. Tommy reached down to grab the towel and hand it to him. Mike snatched it and sat up, again draping it over his private parts. He grimaced as body complained in many places.

"Shit," he gasped. Then saw Anna staring at him and managed a weak smile. "Sorry. I..."

Anna blinked and carefully returned to her job, but she continued to send him glances. Tommy was wearing a thin smile.

"What?" scowled Mike quietly and added in a whisper, "And what's with her...?"

Tommy leaned to speak softly into his right ear. "You hit a Panelli."

"Yeah, I did, and I enjoyed it. So...?"

"It's not something you do to a Panelli."

"Like hell..."

Tommy shrugged and raised his hands in surrender. "Hey, I'm not about to tell a tough cop what he should or should not do."

"Good," said Mike.

Anna finished bandaging the bullet wound and quickly cleaned the scratches, Mike clenching his jaws tight as she did. She was taping a bandage to the neck when Joe, dressed except for shoes, came out of the bathroom.

"How you doing, Anna?" he asked.

"You need me to bandage foot, Mr. Joseph?" she answered, giving him a brief smile.

"I'll take care of that, Anna. Thank you."

"Do you have anything I should take care of?"

"I'm fine. Thank you. You may go."

"Thanks a lot...Ms. Anna," said Mike sincerely

"You're welcome," said Anna and quickly gathered up her things. She gave Brennen one more glance as she hurried from the room.

Joe Panelli eyed the detective coolly. "You know, you're not making an endearing friendship with my brother."

"Well, that breaks my fucking heart," said Mike. "I didn't know being friends was one of the rules in this nutty game we're playing."

Joe stooped, taking one of the elastic bandages Anna had left on the bed. "This will hurt."

"No shit."

As Joe carefully wrapped the foot, Mike held his tongue. When it was done, Joe went to the closet again and came back with one black loafer and a pair of sneakers for himself.

"That will be easier for you to get into," he said dropping the one shoe. "You need help dressing?"

"No...!" Mike stopped, rethinking. "Probably. Some of it. Please."

"I can handle that," said Tommy. "You better go join Anthony and Thomas."

Joe nodded. "Time's short." And he went out the door still carrying his sneakers.

Tommy took up the undershorts and stooped to hold them for Mike.

"Thank you," said the cop.

"You're hurt, Mike. There's no shame in needing help."

"But you're never going to let me forget it."

"Probably not, but I promise not to remind you too often."

The Indian gave him one of his small smiles.

"You know," he said as he helped Mike into the shorts and jeans, "I guess I can understand a cop's attitude toward the Panelli family considering their past history, if they insist on ignoring their current honest, hardworking present life. Maybe even your attitude toward someone such as myself, though I think 'hired gun' is kind of a hard description. However, we've been helping each other out for several days now and your growing crankiness--"

"--is maybe starting to piss you off?"

"You could say that."

"I guess I can see that, but I haven't been sleeping well, or much, and people have been trying to kill me. And they are hurting me in the process. Plus, I'm also having to put up with my superiors and fellow cops and their attitudes toward me. Even you have to agree that things like that could make a person a bear to live with. No offense."

"None taken. And I do agree the world has been pretty rough on you of late."

Mike stood so they could get the jeans in place and zippered up. He sat again so they could get the shirt on.

"On the other hand," said Mike, "I realize I do have a cop thing with the Panellis and I have been kind of cranky about it. They have gotten me into some hot water, you know, but you and Joe have also gotten me out of hot water. And very cold river water. So, I suppose I could try to smile a little more. If Thomas keeps his fucking mouth shut."

Tommy winced as they finished buttoning the shirt. "Maybe just ignore Thomas."

"I'll think about it."

Mike slipped into the one shoe and got hold of the crutch.

"Guess we can go try out my new attitude."

"Any effort would be appreciated."

"Race you to the elevator?"

CHAPTER 37

When they stepped off the elevator, Tommy steered Mike to the right. This wide, carpeted hallway also held the spotlighted, elegantly framed oil paintings on the walls. More of the majestic mountains and meadows, but again Mike's mind was a long way from flowers and meadows. His mind was worrying about the problem that faced them. Would they be on time and in the right place to save New York's police chief? He shuddered inwardly.

Tommy stopped him at a double set of doors and knocked. One of the doors was opened instantly by Joe Panelli, who also closed it once the two men were inside. Anthony Panelli was sitting behind his desk, hands folded on top of it. Thomas Panelli, already showing some color and puffiness on the left side of his face, was standing beside the fireplace. The angry heat still in his eyes might possibly have gotten a toasty fire going in the fireplace.

Joe said, "Please sit down, Brennen."

Mike gratefully sat, trying to keep the injured foot out of harm's way. He rested the crutch against the ornate desk. Joe went to a cabinet in the corner of the room and opened it to reveal a generous array of liquor choices.

Anthony Panelli spoke, his tone somewhat on the frosty side. "It seems, Detective Brennen, that you did what we asked of you in ferreting out the Rezzoro assassin." Was the father annoyed because his eldest son had been bounced by a cop? Or was he just in a frosty mood? "It has gotten messier than we would have liked, however."

Joe, looking hard and solemn, had poured a shot of some very expensive whiskey. Now he handed it to Mike, who took it with a smile and even said, "Thank you."

Joe did not return the smile. Touchy family.

Mike swallowed the whiskey. Damn, that was good stuff and it seemed to warm all his insides. He handed the glass back to Joe, resisting the urge to order a refill. Probably not a good idea considering what was ahead of them. Especially on his very empty stomach.

He put his attention on Anthony, responding to the man's remark with, "Messy does describe it, but it's not like I had any control over the circumstances. In spite of what Thomas may think, Sheffer's the one that tossed in the monkey wrench. Too bad your source didn't come up with the little tidbit about Nicky and lieutenant being in bed together."

So much for his smiley attitude.

"Our source couldn't have--" Anthony actually started what sounded like an apology but caught himself. His patriarch attitude would never condone that. He said, "However way we look at it, it is not finished."

"Nope, it isn't. That's because, as your eldest son keeps reminding me, you picked a nobody like me. A nobody with no tangible proof and no time to convince anyone that the renowned Lieutenant Sheffer and longtime cop, Lieutenant Corry, are out to do away with Police Chief Macklin. With the backing of the Rezzoros. That's a hell of a story to tell, no matter how you look at it."

Anthony suggested, "We could phone Macklin. Tell him his life is in danger and that it would be best if he stayed home until the situation is resolved."

"Sure," said Mike. "I'll give him a ring. 'Chief Macklin, sir, I'm a two-bit cop you've never heard of, but I have to tell you that the highly respected Lieutenant Sheffer is in a plot with Nicholas Rezzoro to...'"

"Why not just call 911 and tell them Macklin's life is in danger and to send squads to his place?" snipped Thomas.

"That might put an end to Corry, but then you're back to the two-bit nobody detective telling the police chief that the well-regarded Lieutenant Sheffer is a bad guy-- girl. She could still make herself out as a heroine and I'd probably get the ax for accusing her of being a bad apple. Polinski would love that."

"All right then, tell us what kind of a solution you have in mind," said Anthony, his frostiness dipping another degree or two.

"Go and confront Macklin in person. Considering I don't have my badge or ID, he might not be too receptive, but at least he'll be forewarned. When Corry and Sheffer pop up, I won't have to introduce them at the last second."

"And you think you'll be able to prevent him from being killed?" said Thomas, still snippy.

Anthony sent his oldest son a sharp-edged glare.

His friendly attitude losing ground, Mike said, "With Tommy and Joe backing me up, it shouldn't be a problem."

Tommy closed his eyes and sighed.

"It could still be a dangerous situation," said Anthony, "and you're looking a little worse for wear, Detective. You're down to, literally, one foot to stand on. Are you sure you can handle it?"

"Maybe not with bells on, but Ms. Sheffer made me a very angry man and I want to stop her," said Mike. He conjured up a smile to add, "And it's nice of you to be concerned for me."

It was obviously a strain, but the senior Panelli said, "I should say thank you for saving Joseph's life tonight."

He did not actually say thank you.

"It was a joint effort," said Mike. "Including the cavalry showing up to pull us out."

Tommy One Bears cleared his throat. "Excuse me. It was the Indians that showed up to pull you out."

Mike sent him an amused glance and said, "I stand corrected, Mr. Bears."

Anthony went on, "Perhaps I should also touch on Thomas's, shall we say, negative attitude. His dealings with police officials have sometimes led to some...resentment. He, and Joe, worked very hard to turn our family around and away from the...old life. He tends to resent the attitude, and often disrespect, of the police toward our new life. Of course, we admittedly are the ones who invited you here, though as a police officer, Thomas instinctively looks on you as...hostile. It's not really anything...personal."

Mike smiled.

"I'm glad you touched on that," he said, "because I was wondering why he had such a hostile attitude. But, hey, I understand perfectly. As a police officer, I admittedly haven't forgotten the Panellis' old life. Nothing personal."

Behind him, Bears sighed again.

Anthony Panelli's frostiness dipped a little more.

Thomas Panelli clenched his jaw, fighting off his instinct.

Joseph Panelli closed his eyes for a couple of seconds, possibly counting to ten. Or twenty if he was a fast counter. When he opened them, Joe went to the table with the bronze eagle on it. Setting down the glass he still held, he picked up another object and returned to Mike. He held out a Browning automatic and one extra clip. The detective started to frown.

"You don't want to go into this unarmed, do you?" Joe cut off any remark.

No, he certainly did not. Mike took the weapon. Slipping the spare clip into a pocket, he gave the gun a professional once over and then started to put it at the small of his back. His wounded side protested, and Mike grimaced. He stuck the gun under his front waistline instead.

Anthony didn't miss the sign of discomfort. To his son, he said, "Are you sure you don't want a couple more men, Joseph? Detective Brennen is obviously not--"

"No," Mike stated firmly. "I don't want any more Panelli help getting underfoot. I'll be fine, and I have complete confidence in Joseph and Mr. Bears."

Joe still said, "Put Dollen and Webber on standby."

Mike scowled. "I--"

Tommy moved up to tap his shoulder and said, "No more time, Detective. We've got to go."

Mike didn't scowl but was unable to come up with anymore smiles as he said, "Yeah. Right."

The detective took hold of the crutch and got carefully to his feet.

"Good luck, Detective Brennen," said Anthony Panelli. "We...appreciate your assistance in this difficult matter. It was important and you...came through for us."

Now a crooked smile did appear and Mike told him, "Maybe next time call 911."

"I'm hoping there won't be any next times...Mike," said the old man.

The smile remained as Mike just nodded. He avoided giving Thomas a goodbye glance.

CHAPTER 38

Brennen and his crutch rode in the front of the Mercedes Benz with Tommy Bears. Joe Panelli was in back. Mike did not care to know where the backups Dollen and Webber were. He was hoping he would never see them at all. The time was about quarter after five and traffic was light, many signal lights were still flashing yellow. Not that it mattered. Tommy Bears was not yielding to any light -- yellow or red -- as his powerful Mercedes reached sixty-plus on the city's streets. Mike held his tongue. They were in a hurry, after all. Still, he mentally hoped that all police officers in their path were at breakfast. He had no badge or ID with him and the prospect of explaining his position did not appeal to him.

The three men said little during the journey. What plans could be made, were made. Mike was going directly to the chief's condo in hopes of catching him there. Joe and Tommy were going to scout the connected, four-story parking garage. Their hopes were that at least one of them would turn up at the right place at the right time.

It was five-seventeen when Tommy pulled to a stop in front of Macklin's twenty-floor, upscale condo complex. Joe was quickly out and gave Mike a hand in struggling with the crutch and getting on his feet...foot.

"You're not going to cave on us, are you, Brennen?" asked Joe cautiously.

"And miss all this fun? Hell, no. Just try to be there if I need you."

"We'll do our best." With a glance at the lighted lobby of the building, Joe added, "Good luck."

Mike snorted. "Good luck to all of us."

Joe gave him a curt nod, slipped into the front seat, and Tommy took off.

Mike turned his tired and hurting body toward the building. His adrenaline on high, he hoped it would carry him through. Hobbling to the glass doors, he looked in to where there was a small desk. A large doorman sat there reading a book. Rather, doorperson, because in this case it was a woman. The lady was probably in her forties and was wearing a tailored, two-tone, brown uniform. Her brown hair was cut short in a masculine style. Every inch of her was neat and efficient looking.

Gripping the door handle, Mike gave it a pull. It was, as expected, locked. The doorwoman was getting to her feet, giving the detective an uninviting once over. Mike scrounged up a smile for the over six foot, stoutly build woman as she came to the door.

"You don't live here," she stated firmly through the glass.

Mike couldn't help but be amazed. "You know that? Out of all the hundreds of people who live here?"

"I'm positive of that."

"Look..." He checked the name tag pinned to her uniform. "...Betty, I'm Detective Mike Brennen and it's very urgent that I see Police Chief Macklin."

"You don't look like a detective. Let me see your badge and ID."

Mike tried to look more like a detective as he admitted, "I don't have my badge and ID with me. If you--"

"Show me some kind of ID."

"Shit," muttered Mike. "Look, Betty, there's no time for this. It's really a matter of--"

"You come banging on the door at this hour of the morning, looking like some kind of street bum, and you want me to--"

"Street bum? I'll have you know these are first class clothes. And I am not banging on the door. Lady, the chief's life is in--"

"No ID, no--"

Mike pulled out the gun, more or less just showing it to her without pointing it.

"This is my ID. And I am ordering you to open this door immediately. The chief's life is in danger!"

With widening eyes, Betty took a step back.

"I'll call the chief and report you!" she threatened.

"Great! You should do that! Call Chief Macklin and tell him that Detective Mike Brennen is here to warn him that his life is in serious danger." Mike leaned on the crutch and pulled up his shirt to show his bandaged side. "Look, I've been shot, and the guys who shot me are going after Macklin now, and you can bet that they going to shoot him dead'r than I am!"

Betty made a command decision by backing up to the desk and picking up the phone to punch in a number. She waited for what seemed an eternity before she spoke briefly into the mouthpiece and then hung up.

Staying where she was, Betty said, "His answering service is already connected. It doesn't mean he's left, it just means he doesn't want to be bothered. They said to call him at his office in--"

"Lady! He's not going to make it to his office! Bad guys are going to shoot him! Open the goddamned door or I'll be forced to shoot it into little pieces!"

Still hesitation. "I'll call the police!"

"Just open the fucking door and then you can call in the cops and the fucking FBI and even the Marines if you want! But you've got to let me in!"

At last Betty moved. Pulling a card key from her pocket she went behind the desk to run it through a locking mechanism there. The doors clicked and Mike quickly came in to hobble over to the elevator.

"Do your thing with the card," he told her sharply.

She used the card on the elevator and Mike was relieved when they opened.

"I will call the police," said the doorwoman determinedly.

Getting in, Mike declared, "Go for it, Betty!" The doors slid shut.

Gun still in hand, Mike unconsciously held his breath as he rode up to Macklin's place on the eighth floor. When the doors opened, Mike stayed to the side and cautiously peered around the corner in case trouble waited for him. There was none in the small, well-lit, empty lobby. But at the other end, another elevator door was closing and Mike got a brief glimpse of someone in uniform. Almost certainly Chief Macklin.

"Shit!" said Mike and hobbled that way as fast as he could.

This elevator was labeled TO

RAMP. Mike stabbed the button. To the left of the elevator there was a stairwell also marked TO PARKING RAMP. Mike closed his eyes. That simply was not an option. He would have to wait for the elevator. He watched it stop at Level Two. At least he knew where he was going and fortunately the elevator started coming right back up. He cursed himself for destroying his burner phone. Now he had no way to let Tommy and Joe know what level.

When the elevator dinged to a stop, Mike again kept to one side just in case it was returning with trouble. It was empty and he got on, punching number two. Silently, and with little motion, the elevator started down again. Mike almost held his breath, hoping he wouldn't hear any shots telling him he was too late. The detective wasn't at all sure what exactly he would be facing or how he would be handling it with a crutch in one hand his gun in the other. He wouldn't be able to make any fast moves. He would be an easier target than Macklin for Corry's or Sheffer's gun. He did feel some relief when the elevator gently bumped to a stop and no shooting had disrupted the quiet.

As the doors slid open, Mike again stayed to one side and took a quick look out. What he glimpsed was the back of the broad shouldered Police Chief Macklin some ten feet away. Another ten to fifteen feet further was Lieutenant Dick Corry. He was facing the chief, gun in hand. Mike pulled back. He hadn't been able to see if anyone else was nearby, but time for being careful had run out. So he hobbled out, raising his gun to cover Corry.

The would-be assassin and his mark were standing under one of the florescent lights. The lieutenant in a crumpled brown suit. The fifty-two-year-old chief in his perfectly pressed uniform. Dick Corry, so drunk he had to spread his feet to keep from falling, was a crushed soul.

"Don't do it, Corry," warned Mike sharply to get his attention. "This is a bad move and it's not going to work. You don't have to die this way. Sure as hell not for the Rezzoros."

At the sound of the voice, Corry's head bobbed in confusion. Drooping, expressionless eyes tried to focus on the speaking intruder. Macklin's head moved slightly, now concerned as to who was behind him. His main attention remained on Corry and the gun aimed at him.

The confused man did ask Mike, "Who are you? What the hell is happening here?"

Mike moved slightly forward, trying to keep his gun steady as he handled the crutch. "I'm Detective Mike Brennen, sir, and you need to--"

"Brenneth? You sonthabith," slurred Corry. "They saith you wath death. You keep gettin' in the way…"

"Chief Macklin, please move back to the elevator," urged Mike. "You have to get out of--"

"Chief Macklin, let me clear things up for you."

Anita Sheffer stepped from the deep shadow of a cement support beam some twenty feet on the other side of the pair of men. The woman had changed into a smart-looking, dark blue pant suit. As usual, she was looking the professional, always-in-charge police lieutenant. Another confusing player to Macklin, but at least one he recognized -- and trusted.

"Lieutenant Sheffer. For God's sake, what's this about?" Macklin sounded confused and impatient.

Mike had stopped about six feet from Corry. Anita Sheffer was some twenty feet off to his left. He couldn't cover both of them.

"Chief Macklin, you can't trust her. She's not what she seems and is--" Mike tried to warn, his voice hard.

Anita Sheffer sent him one of those looks that could kill.

"You're supposed to be under thirty feet of water, Brennen," she declared icily. "I'd be interested to hear why you're not, but it's time to finish this."

"Finish what, damn it!?" demanded the chief.

"Sorry, Chief, sir," mocked Sheffer acidly as she brought her gun up. "You're about to be assassinated by a drunk cop and I got here a little too late to save you." Then, with heated venom, "Corry! Shoot him, damn it! What are you waiting for!?"

"Get down, sir!" Mike shouted at Macklin.

But the chief had not been deaf to the hatred in Sheffer's tone and the words she spoke and he was no fool. He was already diving behind the nearest car.

Dick Corry was too drunk to react to any of it. Too drunk to notice Anita Sheffer turn her Glock on him. Too drunk to feel the three slugs that banged into his chest. His body stumbled toward Mike who was unable to easily get out of his way. Or out of Sheffer's as she turned her gun on him. He managed to squeeze off a couple of shots, but his aim was less than steady under the circumstances. One shot clipped her arm, the other missed completely. Then Corry's body was falling into him and he had to twist away to avoid being bowled over. Pain instantly zapped through his body and in the long seconds it seemed to take him to bring his weapon back on Sheffer, the lady lieutenant had him in her sights and she was wearing that icy smile.

Deja vu. Someone had a gun pointed right at him. Deja vu, he heard two shots but again felt nothing. Anita Sheffer, on the other hand, went suddenly backwards onto the trunk of a car and from there she half-rolled, half-slid onto the ramp's cold floor. No more icy smiles. Ever.

"Anita!"

There was actually emotion in Nicholas Rezzoro's voice as he came charging from somewhere, ducking down beside his fallen fiancé. He then sent a crazed look at Mike.

"Goddamn you, Brennen! You're fuckin' dead!"

Struggling with his pain and the crutch, Mike found himself wondering why it was that so many people seemed to want him dead.

"Nicky! Over here!" came Joe Panelli's familiar voice.

Nicky's head snapped around. His arch enemy was coming from between cars about fifteen feet away. Filled with rage, Rezzoro straightened, bringing his automatic up. Like two gunfighters, Joe and Nick fired at each other. Joe was by far the more skilled. He put one bullet into Nicky's heart, followed by a quick second one into the man's forehead. Rezzoro also fired twice, one while he was still alive, the other by his dead finger. Neither one hit Panelli, but an unexpected shot from somewhere else, did.

Joe gave a short cry as the blow turned him around and sat him on the floor.

Mike, his right arm still holding his gun out zombie-like, was having trouble keeping up with the action. He did see a shape come from the same direction Rezzoro had appeared from and even put a name to it. Steve, Nicky's friendly henchman. With effort, Mike swung his gun to cover the man and fired off a shot. As before, his aim wasn't anything to brag about. He hit Steve in the shoulder but it wouldn't have stopped him from finishing off Panelli.

Which didn't turn out to be a problem as Tommy Bears was suddenly there to take care of it. The Indian's shooting was just fine. One bullet in Steve's moving head.

At the same time, Tommy glanced Mike's way and sharply barked, "Brennen! Your left!"

It was a good thing he said it sharply, because it had to penetrate Detective Brennen's thickening haze. Mike responded, unfortunately, by turning left again. This time the pain caused him to drop the crutch and he went down to hit the cement hard. The hazy blackness swirled around, threatening to engulf him. Suddenly, through the haze, he saw a grinning face.

"You're hard to kill for a two-bit fuckin' cop," said Fred, leaning over the detective. "But this time your ass is--"

Fred shouldn't have wasted those seconds mouthing off, because the cop put the time to good use. Teeth clenched against the pain and haze, Mike shoved his gun into Fred's ribs.

"I'm really tired--" A bullet exploded, tearing into the bad guy. "...of being called--" Another bullet exploded. "...a two-bit fuckin' cop!" Another bullet exploded. "You can go to fuckin' hell!"

Fred's dead body collapsed on top of Mike. No more grins.

Tommy appeared above them and, grabbing a handful of Fred's jacket collar, pulled the body off the detective.

"You okay?" asked the Indian.

"I'm miserable," answered the cop.

"Did you get shot again?"

"No ... I don't think so."

Sirens could be heard.

"I've got to get Joe out of here." Tommy took the gun from Mike and the extra clip from his pocket. "These are ours. Don't use our names when you explain about the dead bodies."

"What? Wait." Tommy vanished from his hazy vision. "But...you can't leave me with this mess."

Mike tried to get up. The best he could do was roll onto his right side. From there he got only a brief glimpse of Bears helping Panelli up and then the two men were gone.

"Fuck," groaned the detective.

He was covered with Fred's warm, sticky blood. That, and the increasing pain, brought on a spell of nausea and Mike lost the Jack Daniels. It was the only thing he had to lose.

Police Chief Macklin appeared in Mike's fuzzy vision, a gun aimed at the detective.

"You'll forgive me if I ask whose side you're on...?" said the confused chief. "Is it Bremmen..?..Brenneff..?"

Mike rolled to lie on his back again, letting exhaustion claim him.

"Detective Brennen. I'm on your side," he said weakly.

"You're a hell of a mess. How much of this blood is yours?"

"I don't know."

"Were you shot or not?"

"Not. This time. I don't think."

"I didn't get a good look at those other two men. Who were they?"

Mike closed his eyes and sighed. "What other two men?" And darkness took him.

CHAPTER 39

Mike Brennen had only a vague memory of the ambulance ride and his arrival at the hospital. He remembered them cutting off the shirt and jeans, looking for a new wound under all the blood. His conscience suggested he should feel some remorse over the loss of still more of Joe Panelli's clothes. Mike thought he did well not to smile.

After that, the detective drifted in and out of the world. It didn't take him long to discover he much preferred being out than in. When he was in, there was a constant buzzing around him. Like gnats. Big gnats. Like Macklin and Grands and probably some others he should have known but didn't recognize in his shadowy state of mind. Mike vaguely remembered giving them a brief story about the planned hit and Sheffer and Corry and the Rezzoros -- and Captain Nimmer, which brought on considerably more buzzing. They never seemed to be satisfied, though, and continued to ask repetitive, annoying questions.

Who had given him the assassination tip? Who had told him about Corry? Who told him about Sheffer and Nicholas Rezzoro? Who says that Captain Nimmer is a Rezzoro man? Who were the shooters that did in

Jason Reed and company? Who killed Margo Drogan? Who sent Detective Sharp on a wild goose chase so they could get Mike out of the hospital? Who killed Nick Rezzoro? Who killed Steve? Who took the gun that Mike had shot Fred with? Who were the two men who left the scene? Who...who...who...??

Mike felt like his head had become an anvil and everyone was pounding on it with iron hammers. Being out was definitely the place to be. Eventually they gave up and left him alone to fade into oblivion.

A giant, black and white cat was chasing him this time. They were running through the woods. Mike was stumbling into trees and over roots, but the cat was gaining in leaps and bounds. Suddenly it pounced!

"Rambo!"

He woke with a start, eyes popping open.

"Oh! Mr. Brennen. Are you okay?" said a startled, female voice.

Mike turned his head, carefully, without lifting it from the pillow. You end up in a hospital often enough, you finally learn not to make sudden moves. The nurse had evidently been checking the bags of blood and clear liquid that were dripping into the detective's arm.

"My cat. Rambo." His voice was scratchy, his mouth and tongue and throat felt like scour pads. "He's probably eating the furniture by now. Whenever now is. I should call my neighbor. To ask her to feed him. The cat."

The short, fiftyish nurse gave him friendly smile.

"Now, is Friday..." She glanced at the clock. "...at four-thirty in the afternoon, and I'd be glad to make the call for you, if you'd like." She took a moment to pour water from a covered pitcher into a plastic cup. Dropping a straw into it, she offered it to her patient. "You sound like you could use some of this."

Gratefully, Mike took it, sipping in the wonderfully cold water. He drained the cup and handed it back to her, noticing her helpful name tag. Sharon Jove.

"Thanks, Sharon," he said.

"You're welcome," she said. "What was the cat's name...Ramble?"

"Rambo. He's a tough guy."

Sharon looked puzzled.

"You know, Sylvester Stallone. Rambo."

Continued puzzlement. Mike dropped it.

"My neighbors are Marj and Vern Merritt. They take care of Ram...the cat for me when I'm gone or can't get home." He gave her their phone number. "You want to write it down?"

"That's fine. I have a good memory for numbers."

Another good memory. He said, "Well, thanks very much. My cat will be very grateful."

"I'm happy to do it for you and your cat." Then, curiously, "I understand you're a hero."

"Huh? Me?"

"You saved the police chief's life."

"Really?"

"You don't remember?"

"It was a long night," allowed Mike.

A long fucking night.

"I guess I didn't think anybody had actually noticed," he added with a shrug and was immediately reminded of his wound. And now he noticed his left foot was wrapped in bandages and resting on a pillow.

"Oh, I think they did," said Sharon with another smile. "They've even put an officer outside your door. Would you like to see him about anything?"

"No!" exclaimed Mike, then quickly gave the nurse a crooked smile. "I'd just as soon he didn't know I was awake yet."

"No problem," said the nurse and actually gave him a wink. "Would you like help in going to the bathroom before I leave?"

The question was unexpected and Mike must have looked embarrassed to Ms. Jove.

"With your injured foot, you really can't go to the bathroom by yourself yet," she told him. "Tell you what…"

Going into the bathroom, Sharon came back shortly with a urine bottle. Laying it on the bed within his reach, she said, "Just in case. This will be easier for you."

Mike gave her another crooked smile. "Thanks."

With a parting smile, Sharon headed for the door. "Supper will be around in about an hour. Push the button if you need something."

When she was gone, Mike gave the clock a look. Four-thirty. And still Friday. Not even twelve hours since the parking ramp. Why did it seem like days ago?

The door started to open and Mike quickly closed his eyes. Maybe whoever it was would go away if they thought he was sleeping. He sensed whoever it was come right up to his bed. It was a man because he smelled aftershave.

"Detective Brennen."

Mike winced inwardly, hoping it wasn't who it sounded like. But he knew it was.

"You're not asleep are you?" said Ichabod Crane, alias Lieutenant Marvin Polinski. "The nurse just left."

Mike opened his eyes. "I'd just like to be asleep, Lieutenant. I haven't had much of it lately."

"So I understand. I also understand that your far-fetched tip about an attempt on Police Chief Macklin wasn't so far-fetched," noted Polinski flatly. "You're practically a hero."

"Yeah. Lucky me. I practically got killed. Four times. Five if you count the parking garage."

"I've also heard that you still aren't revealing your source of information. For that matter, not much information of any kind."

"It's over. Macklin's alive."

"Five other people aren't. That parking ramp was like a war zone. Sheffer killed Corry. Macklin killed Sheffer. You killed--"

"Macklin killed Sheffer?" Mike was surprised.

"You didn't know that?"

"I was busy."

"Yeah. You were pumping four bullets into a bad ass named Fred Dorn. With an invisible gun. Another Rezzoro wise ass named Steve Packard was killed by still another gun. And Nick Rezzoro was killed by still another gun. All those guns and none were at the scene. Want to know another interesting fact?"

"Not particularly."

"Two of those same guns also put holes in Jason Reed and his two scumbags."

"That is interesting."

"Yes."

Mike sighed, and said, "Look, Lieutenant, if you've come here for a reason, could you please get done with it. Otherwise, I really would like to sleep."

"Tell me about Captain Nimmer."

Mike screwed up his face. "I guess I mentioned him, too, huh?"

"One of a few new facts you shared. You said that your mysterious source told you that the Rezzoros' plan was to kill Macklin so Nimmer could take his place."

"Yeah. My source did say that, and that's absolutely all I know about Nimmer,"

"If a captain is rubbing elbows with the Rezzoros, that's IAD business. Technically, Corry and Sheffer were IAD business."

"Gee. You don't suppose that's why I came to you in the first place, do you?" Mike couldn't resist turning his initial visit in his favor. What the hell.

Polinski didn't attempt to answer the remark. He said, "It's been difficult accepting that Lieutenant Sheffer was so deeply involved. She was...had been...a fine officer."

"I agree, but once she starts trying to kill you, she's less attractive."

"And there's no initial proof that Captain Nimmer is involved in this matter or with the Rezzoros."

"Then it looks like you've got your work cut out for you."

Polinski looked down at him, jaws clenched, eyes -- apprehensive?

He finally said, "Have you mentioned to anyone that you did come to me?"

Resisting a grin was hard, but Mike managed it.

"I don't think so. Like I said, there's been a hell of a lot of questions and I haven't been too sharp, but I'm pretty sure that your name didn't come up."

"I'm gla--" Marvin Polinski stopped, clearing his throat. "Then I don't see how it would serve any purpose to...mention it. It could even hinder my own... investigation. "

"Forget it, Lieutenant. I don't see any reason to bring it up either."

The man gave a nod, but it didn't look like the word 'thanks' was in his vocabulary any more than it was in Anthony Panelli's. He said, "There will still be a lot of questions."

"Yeah, I'm sure there will be, but it will be a waste of everyone's time. My fellow officers will just have to take my word for it that answers won't change anything. Drogan, and you could say Corry, were the only ones actually murdered. We know Sheffer did in Corry, and if you show pictures of Fred and Steve to Officer Leeds, I bet she picks out one of them for Drogan. I think it sounds like something up Steve's alley. I also think Drogan would have been dead even if she had killed me. She just happened to be a handy way to take me out of the picture without raising questions. Ditto Reed."

"It looks that way," said Polinski, actually agreeing with him. "It will all have to be written down, of course."

"Of course," said Mike.

"But...there's time for that later. You, ah...get some rest now."

"Thank you, Lieutenant," Mike laid it on.

Polinski gave him a curt nod and left. When the door had closed, the detective allowed himself a grin.

CHAPTER 40

Mike's supper consisted of some kind of meat mixed with some kind of noodles. A small forkful proved it was all tasteless. He was frowning at it when Lieutenant Grands came in.

"Something wrong with the food?" smirked Grands.

"Is that what this is? I was wondering," said Mike. "I don't remember the last time I ate, but I'm not quite desperate enough to eat this. You don't have a cheeseburger in your pocket, do you?"

"'Fraid not. Just stopped in to see if you were going to live."

"Not if I eat this."

The lieutenant took note of the almost empty pint of blood which was dripping into Mike's arm.

"Maybe you can talk them into another bottle of the red stuff," he suggested. "I was told you lost a fair amount of yours while you were chasing about."

"It was a rough night. I'm just glad I didn't lose all of it."

"We're glad you didn't either."

Mike arched his brow. "We--? More than one person actually cares?"

"Quite a few persons. Of course, there are quite a few of those persons who would like to learn more about your rough night ... in detail."

"Sorry, boss. Even if I could remember the details, it wouldn't change the story."

Grands slowly shook his head.

"You know, Brennen, you really set a record this time for stirring things up. I've never seen so many loose ends and dead bodies in one case. If you want to call it a case. It wasn't one you were sharing with me. Except that Reed and the Calamity Janes somehow got mixed into it. Even looking at all the corpses lying around, you seem to have killed only one of them and you shot that one with an invisible gun. Talk about confusion. And who was it that was trying to kill you? Corry–? The Rezzoros–? Or was it Sheffer herself–?"

"Pretty much all of them, Lieutenant. I promise I'll write you a nice report first chance I get."

"Including the name of the source?"

"Naming the source wouldn't make any difference to what happened. The main players are dead."

Grands shook his head again. "That Sheffer was a real shock."

"No shit. I believed and trusted her right up until she stomped the hell out of my foot and tried to dro--" Mike stopped. Shit. How would he explain the drowning? Could he even bring it up? All the bad guys who knew about it were dead. No one was left to tell about him and the Panellis. The drowning story, he decided, was best left untold. He quickly changed the subject. "What about Sergeant Pragg? I've got the impression he didn't have anything to do with it."

"He's clean, but he's a bit devastated. He and Sheffer go back quite a few years, I guess. He never had any inkling of what she was doing. Nobody did. You're a lucky man that she more or less confessed to Chief Macklin. I think proof would have been hard to come by."

"Now you know why I wasn't running around telling everyone about it."

"Yeah, I guess I can see that," admitted Grands. "You don't happen to know how she got involved with Rezzoro to begin with, do you?"

Mike shrugged, felt the resulting pain, and wished he would quit shrugging.

"She used her son's drug habit as part of the reason she went to him, but she openly admitted she was drawn to Nicky himself because ... in her words ... she 'liked the way he did things'. Oh, and she also hated her thankless job and the wise-ass men who dominate it."

"Ouch. Well, the rest of the Rezzoro family is not admitting to knowing anything about her and Nick being involved, or about Nimmer, and certainly not about any assassination plot against Chief Macklin. They believe Detective Brennen is laying the blame on them because you had it in for Nick."

"Oh good. Now I can have nightmares about them coming after me."

"I don't think you have any worries there. They know they're going to be under a microscope for a long time now because of this. Coming after a cop wouldn't be in their best interests. Besides, with the loss of their brother and with the Nimmer plan blown, the Rezzoros are pretty much dead in the water for now."

Mike eyed his lieutenant. "And how is the good Captain Nimmer taking this?"

"To say the least, he's really pissed off at you for dragging him into it. He claims, of course, that he's never had any ties to the Rezzoro clan. He especially can't believe that his fellow officers would take the word of a screwed up, two-bit cop like you over his word as a captain. I wouldn't count on him for any favors in the near, or distant, future. Be glad he's not your captain."

"Screwed up, two-bit cop? That's how the captain is describing me? That hurts," said Mike. Then, surprised, "You mean, his fellow officers actually are taking my word over his?"

"Let me put it this way, Brennen. Despite any plans that the Rezzoros might have had for him, if Chief Macklin had been killed, Captain Nimmer would not have been the replacement. I understand he has some failings that aren't widely approved of and you know he'll be under closer scrutiny now."

"I did get that impression from Polinski."

"Polinski?"

"He stopped in earlier. He's confused, too."

"I'll bet. Five dead people, two of them police lieutenants. Did he give you a hard time?"

"Not too bad. I think we came to an understanding. At least, I still have a job."

Grands gave him a crooked smile. He said, "Well, and don't let this go to your head, but I guess I'm glad you're still around, too."

"You guess?"

"Don't push your luck."

"Right."

The lieutenant eyed the food again. "Maybe breakfast will be better."

"Can't be worse," said Mike.

"I'll see you tomorrow. Be ready to do some reporting."

"Yes, sir."

Half an hour later, the food was still sitting there when Police Chief Macklin came in.

"Not hungry?" he asked.

"Starving," said Mike.

"Ah. I understand. So, Detective Brennen, I wanted to stop in say thank you for saving my life and to see how you're doing. Besides starving."

"I think I'll live...sir. How are you?"

"I admit it's all left me a bit shaken. It's not every day you get set up by a fellow police officer to take a bullet and then have to shoot that officer, a well-liked lieutenant. It's a memory not likely to go away any time soon."

"Since she was about to shoot me, I really appreciate that you didn't hesitate too long in your decision. I thank you for that. We both would have been dead, you know, if that makes it a little easier. The lieutenant was full of hate, sir. She wasn't very nice."

"I know, but I do intend to see to it that her son isn't forgotten because of all this," said Macklin. "And I want you to know that I appreciate what you must have gone through the last couple of days. I wish you would give us more information regarding it, but I'm trying to understand your reasons for keeping it to yourself. Next time you need some help, though, don't be afraid to call on your fellow officers."

He smiled and Mike returned it. It wasn't every day that the Chief of Police smiled at him like that.

Shortly after Macklin left, a pretty, young girl in a candy-striped apron came in to pick up his supper dishes.

"It doesn't look like you ate much," she noted with concern.

"I drank the milk," said Mike. He checked out the name tag. Good ol' name tags. "Tell me, Annette, is there a candy machine or something within this general area?"

"I'm afraid not. Not on this floor," said Annette.

"You giving the help a hard time already, Detective Brennen?" asked a man coming in the door.

"Clark!" exclaimed Mike happily.

Clark Thorn was in a wheelchair, another candy-striped girl pushing him. He was wearing a white robe, his right arm was in a sling. He was looking pretty chipper.

Annette quickly took the tray and left. The other girl parked Clark beside Mike's bed and told him, "Just knock on the door when you're ready to go, Mr. Thorn." And she left them.

"How you doin', partner?" asked Mike.

"Better than you, from what I've heard. Sounds like you grabbed a tiger's tail and wouldn't let go," said Clark.

"Couldn't let go better describes it."

Clark eyed the foot. "Don't tell me you were shot in the foot?"

"Lady just stomped the hell out of it."

"Don't tell me -- Sheffer?"

"Yep. But how about yourself?"

"I'm doing fine. Going home tomorrow. Guess we were both pretty lucky to survive that nasty little ambush of Reed's." Thorn cocked his head. "I don't suppose you want to share with your partner how we did survive it? I've been told that you're keeping it a secret. That and a lot of other things."

"They're lying. I just don't remember."

"Sure. Was it Sheffer behind that, too? Can you tell me any part of the story?"

"I promise, I'll tell you what I can, someday."

"Did you actually save the police chief's life?"

"More or less."

"'More or less? That's it?"

"Someday, Clark. Just know that it's been a hell of a couple of days and besides getting shot, I got threatened and beat on by a female lieutenant and her hood boyfriend and I hurt all over and I'm starving."

His partner eyed him carefully. "I heard you shot somebody."

"I did do that, yes."

"You want to talk about it?"

"No. That particular asshole deserved it. He called me names and tried to dro -- tried to kill me and grinned the whole time. When he grinned once too often, I shot him -- several times. I admit one or two bullets would probably have been enough, but I was very upset at the time. I have absolutely no regrets."

"Good. I'm glad you don't have to talk about it, because it sounds messy. I also heard Macklin shot Lieutenant Sheffer. When you asked me about her, were you having some kind of suspicions? Why were you having suspicions?"

"Clark, I'm really, really tired of people asking me questions."

"Sorry. What do you want to talk about? Oops, another question."

"I don't want to talk about anything. I want to sleep. No offense."

"Hey," said Clark. "I can take a hint. I'll stop in tomorrow before I leave."

"I'm leaving tomorrow, too."

"Oh? Who says?"

"I says. I've had enough of hospitals lately. I'll sneak out if I have to."

"I heard you were good at that, too. I'd be interested to hear--"

"Good night, Clark."

Clark smirked and rolled himself over to the door to knock on it.

"Sweet dreams, partner," said the sergeant as the young lady pushed him out the door.

Mike was looking for a comfortable position to sleep in, a challenge considering his foot and numerous aches and pains and the blood dripping in his arm, when Annette returned. The young hospital volunteer was looking sheepish and a little fearful. Getting close to his bed, she sent a wary glance over her shoulder and then slipped something out from under her apron. It was a cellophane wrapped sandwich. "It's a chicken sandwich from the cafeteria," she said. "And I'll be in real trouble if they find out about it."

Mike's eyes lit up.

"You're an angel," he said as he took it. "Will you marry me?"

Annette blushed.

CHAPTER 41

"Was breakfast any better?" asked Carl Grands the next morning.
"Worse," said Mike, "unless you like cold cereal and warm milk."
"I don't think so," said Grands with a sour face.

The lieutenant had arrived with a cassette recorder and a competent-looking stenographer, Ms. Keene. He was ready to make sure he got every word of his officer's statement.

"I'm hoping that after a night's rest, you're feeling more cooperative about giving us all the details from the last few days--"

"I'll tell you what I can," stated Mike, who was very tired of it all, "but the source who came to me was being a helpful citizen and they want to remain anonymous. Period."

"There are going to be some unsatisfied people," allowed his boss. "We are talking about five bodies. Unless you include Reed and his thugs, and the Drogan woman, then it's--"

"Come on, Lieutenant. Like I told Polinski, technically the only ones who got murdered were Corry and the Drogan woman. Sheffer killed Corry and I told Polinski to have Officer Leeds look at--"

"Yes. I know. She picked out Steve Packard as the one who sent her to the phone."

"So there you go. You've got Drogan's killer. As for Reed and his dirt bags, if someone hadn't stepped in and shut them down, it would have been me and Clark who were dead. I like to think no one is unhappy about that."

"Of course we're all glad to have you both alive and kicking," grunted Grands, and sighed resignation. "Okay. What about Nick Rezzoro and Steve Packard? Ballistics says the same guns who did Reed and…"

"I don't look at that as a bad thing. If somebody really cares about Rezzoro and Packard, tell them to send flowers."

"And there was Fred Dorn."

"I killed Fred and I won't be sending him any flowers."

"One could consider that a bad attitude for a police officer," noted the lieutenant.

"It's my personal attitude," said Mike. "The man was trying to kill me."

"And the gun you shot him with, what happen to that?"

"I was unconscious. I don't--"

The lieutenant sighed again and shook his head. It was obvious he wasn't happy with the way things were going. But, for now, he waved at Mike to begin. Detective Brennen proceeded to give him as much of a statement as he could, carefully skirting the never-to-be-seen Panellis and Tommy Bears and the attempted drowning. Things were coming to an end when Grands threw him for a loop.

"But when did Lieutenant Sheffer do that?" he asked nodding at the cushioned foot.

"When did she…?" Mike blinked. Oh shit. He closed his eyes, mind racing.

"Mike?"

His eyes popped open. "Yeah. Right. That was after I got out of the hospital…."

"When the someone got you out of the hospital…"

"Yeah. The someone. I had figured out it was Corry who was going to be the assassin and I had them, the someone, take me to Sheffer's to tell her about Corry. I thought she was on my side. Except she wasn't and I found Nick Rezzoro there. They wanted to know how I knew about what was happening and I wouldn't tell them. While they were yelling at me and asking me all these questions, she got mad and stomped my foot."

Grands looked at him. "So you wouldn't tell them who was helping you, either."

Mike gave him a weak smile. "No, sir."

"And how did you escape her clutches, Detective?"

Mike's smile became weaker.

Now Grands gave him a hard eye. "The same someone who rescued you from Reed and got you out of the hospital and helped you in the parking garage. This mysterious someone really gets around."

"Yes, sir."

"Brass isn't going to like all the blank spaces in this report, Detective."

"Sorry, sir, but the someone wants to remain blank. They aren't guilty of anything more than helping me and the NYPD."

"Right." Another sigh. "I guess that will have to do. As soon as Ms. Keene gets this keyed up, I'll have someone bring it over here so you can sign it."

"Not here. Home," said Mike.

Grands frowned. "The doctor I talked to said at least two more--"

"I'm out of here today. They pumped me full of blood yesterday and I'm going home to my own bed today. And real food before I starve."

"What about your foot?"

"I have a crutch."

"Well, I'll see what the doctor--"

"Lieutenant, I'm not staying here another night. You can maybe have a squad take me home...?"

Carl Grands' eyes narrowed. "Or maybe you could call on the someone who took you out of here the other night."

Mike's smile was crooked. "That someone doesn't work days."

"Uh-huh," said Grands.

"I want to go home," said the detective with finality as the lieutenant and the stenographer left.

He was still there two hours later, now sitting in a chair with his sore foot soaking in some kind of solution, when Clark and Etta Thorn came in. Arm still in a sling, Clark was dressed to leave, Etta pushing him in a wheelchair. His wife was still showing the strain of being a wounded cop's wife. It made her appear older than her forty-one years.

"How are you, Mike?" asked the concerned woman. "Oh my word, look at that foot. Is it broken?"

"I guess a couple of little bones were, but it's not as bad as it looks."

"Well, I'm afraid it looks awful. The two of you sure know how to scare a gal."

"I'll be fine, Etta," Mike assured her.

She leaned over to give him a peck on the cheek and said, "Thank you for making Clark wear the vest. It saved his life. But next time, you wear one, too."

Clark shrugged. "Told her that was a lost cause."

"It's not a lost cause. I will nag," stated Etta.

"That's okay," said Mike. "It's nice having a lady care about me. The last few days all the females in my life have been trying to kill me or beat me up or scratch me."

He absently touched the bandage over the scratches, which were itching at least as much as they were hurting.

"Do you know when you're going home?" asked Etta.

"Today, one way or another."

"Stubborn tough guy," said Clark. "This is what I have to live with on the job. I don't envy his doctor or his nurse."

"Well, if they do let you go, Mike, take care of yourself," said Etta. "You really don't look too ship-shape. Be especially careful getting around on that bad foot."

Clark smirked. "His cat will wait on him."

"Hey, you'd be surprised what Rambo does for me."

"I doubt it."

After they had left, a nurse came in to care for the foot and get him back into the bed.

"I'm supposed to go home," complained Mike.

"Not my decision," stated the nurse. She wrapped the foot and left him fuming.

Mike's impatience continued to grow as he waited for someone to come and tell him he could leave. When lunch arrived, the detective's grumpiness was at a high.

"I'm supposed to be out of here," he told the server sharply as she set the tray on the bedside swing table. The detective ignored her name tag.

"Not my problem," stated the short, thinnish woman. She did not look that great in the candy striped apron.

Mike lifted the cover from the plate for a look. It was a piece of chicken, a scoop of mashed potatoes, and a spoon full of corn.

"This is it?" said Mike. "This wouldn't fill up my cat! If he'd even eat it."

"Not my problem," said the woman.

She had obviously built up a strong resistance to the gripes and groans of grumpy patients. About anything. The nameless woman left, totally ignoring Mike's desperate glare.

Mike ate it. If only to quiet his growling stomach. The plate's contents, along with the slice of bread and butter, and sickly-looking green Jello, vanished in a couple of minutes. His stomach continued to growl.

At one o'clock, the doctor and a nurse came in.

"I'm leaving," Mike told them flatly.

"So I understand," said the medium-sized, rather rumpled looking doctor whose name tag said his name was Cross. "But not until I've given your wounds a look and Nurse Dormann puts on fresh bandages."

Mike's attitude brightened considerably.

"Really? I can go?"

"Didn't you just tell me you were?" rumbled Cross.

"Well, yeah, but so far everyone has ignored me."

Cross removed the bandage from his foot, carefully examining it.

"This foot will need to be soaked several times a day," stated the doc.

"Sure, I can do that."

Doctor Cross grunted at that. Next he removed the bandage on his bullet wound and looked that over. He said, "I would prefer you spend another night, but your Lieutenant Grands suggested you'd probably do better at home. Besides, the nurses are rebelling. If I let you go, is there someone who can bring you in for fresh bandages tomorrow? And you'll for sure soak this foot regularly and keep it wrapped? And stay off it as much as possible?"

"Sure. I can do all that."

The doctor was now examining the scratches. "I hope so. Your body's been through a lot and if you don't take care of it, you will be back here and you won't go home again until I say so. Do we understand each other?"

"Yes, sir, Doc. I promise I'll be good."

"I hope so," said Cross with some sharpness. He stepped back. "Everything is showing improvement. Don't do anything to rock the boat."

The man wrote on a piece of paper. "Get this from the drugstore on your way home. It's to be diluted in water for soaking that foot."

Mike took the note. "Yes, sir."

The doctor left and the slender, starchy Nurse Dormann took over, wrapping the foot and cleaning and bandaging the wound and scratches. Not as gentle as she could have been, decided Mike as he grit his teeth, but he was leaving and could live with it.

When she finished, the woman told him, "Someone will be in shortly with papers to sign and then a nurse will come with a wheelchair. Do you have any clothes here?"

"I haven't seen any of my clothes, or anything else of mine, in at least two days," grunted Mike. "But I'll go home naked if I have to."

"God forbid," said Nurse Dormann. "I'll have someone round something up for you."

It was half an hour before a bored looking young man came in with the papers for Mike to sign. Then another fifteen or more minutes before the wheelchair showed up, Nurse Sharon Jove pushing it.

"Going home so soon, Mr. Brennen?" she asked.

"It's not so soon to me," said Mr. Brennen.

"These are for you to wear." She handed him some clean and folded clothing. "They aren't much, but they should get you out the door."

"Thanks," said Mike. "I'll be sure to return them."

"Would you like help dressing?"

"Thank you. I'll manage."

"I'll be back soon, then. Be careful of that foot."

There was no underwear, which was good since Mike had enough trouble just getting the blue, drawstring pants on over his foot. At least he could easily handle the worn, long-sleeved, white shirt that buttoned down the front. He stuffed the doctor's note in the shirt pocket. There was a ragged pair of slippers for his feet. By the time he had finished, he was exhausted. Mike gave serious thought to going buck-naked once he got home, at least until he could maneuver without pain. Collapsing into the wheelchair, he was very glad he didn't have to walk out of the place.

When Nurse Jove returned, she brought along a nice set of crutches.

"All ready to go I see," she said. As she rolled him to the elevator, she told him, "There is a squad car waiting for you downstairs, Mr. Brennen. To take you home. I hope you know someone who will help you take care of yourself, because you don't look too good yet."

"I'll be fine," said Mike, but at the moment wasn't so sure.

Barbara Sammoy and Tim Barker, the officers who had helped grapple with the Fuller sisters, were waiting for him.

"How nice to see you again, Detective Brennen," said Barbara with a very nice smile.

"Except you look worse now than you did the last time we saw you, Detective Brennen," noted Tim. His smile more closely resembled a grin.

"Thanks," said Mike. "I needed cheering up."

They settled him into the back seat next to a large, brown envelope.

Barbara told him, "The envelope is for you from Lieutenant Grands. It's your ID and wallet and watch, et cetera, including your gun."

"Hallelujah. I'm somebody again," sighed Mike.

"This is quite an honor for us," said the officer as she drove away from the hospital. "Chauffeuring the man who saved the police chief."

"Maybe, if we're lucky, he'll give us his autograph," said her partner.

He was still grinning.

"How about I buy you some lunch instead?" said Mike. "Stop at the first drive through you come to."

"We already had lunch," said Tim.

"So have I, if you want to call it that," said Mike. "So I'll buy you dessert, but I want lunch."

They went through a Hardy's drive-up window where Mike ordered two large cheeseburgers with all the fixings, two large fries, and the biggest chocolate shake they had for himself. Barbara wanted nothing, but Tim ordered a chocolate shake, too.

"Thanks, Mike," he said. "This is better than an autograph."

"Should you be eating all that?" asked Barbara with concern.

"Doctor Brennen's orders," said Mike, "before I shrivel up and die."

He also had them stop at a drugstore. "I need this stuff." He handed the note to Tim. "And a nice pan for soaking feet. Please."

"This shake is getting expensive," grunted Tim.

When they got to Mike's building, Barbara put his lunch and brown envelope into the shopping bag to carry while the two officers saw to it that he got up the front steps on his crutches okay.

"You sure you don't want us to see you up to your place?" she asked once they had him in the elevator.

"Not now, but I wouldn't mind a visitor once I've rested up some," Mike told her with an inviting smile.

"Well, I'm kind of busy this week, but--" started Tim.

"Shut up, Tim," said Barbara. To Mike, "How about tomorrow evening, Detective? I'll fix you a proper, nourishing meal."

"Not too proper or nourishing," said the detective. "And maybe a little...dessert?"

"Instead of an autograph...?" said Tim.

"Lose him," said Mike.

"First chance I get," said Barbara. "You sure you can handle dessert with that foot?"

Mike just smiled.

CHAPTER 42

Brennen had to set the shopping bag down at his apartment door so he could rummage through the large brown envelope for his key. Before he could find it, the door opened and Tommy One Bears looked out at him.

"Welcome home, Detective Brennen."

Mike blinked. "Why are you in my apartment?"

"We couldn't very well visit you at the hospital, so when we heard you were checking out, we decided to come here," explained Tommy. "To see how you're doing and all."

"We?"

"Me, and your other partner."

Tommy reached down to pick up the shopping bag, stepping aside so Mike could enter. When he did, Mike saw Joe Panelli sitting on the sofa chair with Rambo curled up on his lap. The cat was obviously enjoying the stroking and scratching Joe was bestowing upon him. Sitting on the floor beside the man's feet was a small, dark green bag.

"Glad to see you, Detective," greeted Joe. "And that's a swell outfit you're wearing."

Tommy closed the door.

Mike glared. "Comfortable?"

"My right shoulder aches a little, but Doctor Anna says it isn't a serious wound. How about yourself?"

"Screw you." Mike hobbled over to sink weakly onto his couch, propping the crutches next to him. "Do you have any idea of the pile of shit you left me in?"

"Give me a break, Brennen," allowed Joe. "If we had stayed, the pile of shit would have been a lot deeper. A cop working with the Panellis? Even honest, law-abiding Panellis? And the Panellis didn't need the hassle of explaining our … relationship, either. Or where we got our information from. Nobody would have cared about what our intentions were, good citizens or not. One way or another, it would have been turned against us. Pulling out of there was the best move. Hell, you're a hero. You saved the police chief's life. How much of a hero would you have been if I'd hung around?"

That was a sobering thought. Still, "There were five fucking bodies to explain. Five. And if Macklin hadn't been the one to take out Sheffer, I don't even want to think about what the consequences would have been."

"That was a stroke of luck," admitted Joe. "But, it did happen, so there aren't any consequences to think about. Tell us, what's happening with Captain Nimmer?"

"He doesn't like me for sure and, hell, I still haven't even met the man," sniffed Mike. "And for your information, I was told that even if Macklin had been killed, Nimmer would not have been the choice to fill the job. That's a lot of dead people over a scenario that wouldn't have happened."

"You have to remember, if they weren't dead, Macklin almost certainly would be," Joe pointed out. "That part of the scenario would still have gone down. I guess you'll have to decide if his life was worth the price."

Mike grunted. "Antonio and Sylvester Rezzoro aren't happy with me, either. I trust you'll avenge my death if they shoot me?"

"Personally," promised Tommy. "But I wouldn't worry about it. They're going to be busy with more important problems than a two-bit cop."

"That makes me feel much better. What about your mysterious source?"

"There is no more source. It left the country and probably won't ever be back," said Panelli.

"There's a surprise."

It was quiet for a moment, except for Rambo's purring motor.

Then, in some amusement, Joe said, "If you traded even, my clothes for those, it was a bad deal."

"Not when you consider that yours were in pieces. They cut them off thinking I was shot underneath them. Because of all the blood. Wasn't cop's blood, though. It was grinning Fred's blood. Fred who fucking pees in the street."

"Then it's worth the loss. I appreciate your doing him in for me."

"Didn't do it for you. I did it for me. He called me a fuckin' two-bit cop once too often."

"Ouch," said Tommy. "I better be more careful what I say if that's going to become a normal reaction."

"Guess I better pass that along to my brother, too," said Joe.

"That's an especially good idea," said Mike. "Just in case he and I bump into each other sometime. Heaven forbid."

Rambo purred.

"So, no raises or promotions or medals for Detective Brennen?" wondered Tommy.

"I still have my job."

"Polinski give you much trouble?" asked Joe. "I mean, the man did ignore you when you told him about the assassination plot."

"That's my one bright point," admitted Mike. "Having Polinski ask me if I'd mentioned our little conversation to anyone and if I thought it was necessary to bring it up. I don't plan on pushing my luck, though. I've got a lot of years left before retirement."

Rambo finally got a whiff of the hamburgers and jumped down to run over to Bears. Sitting up on his haunches, the cat pawed at the sack and serenaded them with some squeaky hinges.

"He is a helluva burglar alarm," noted Tommy.

"None better...as long as the burglar is carrying hamburgers," said Mike. "Which reminds me, my food's getting cold. Why don't the two of you get out of here so I can eat?"

"Hmmm," said Joe. "Smells like just the kind of meal that an injured body needs to heal."

"Don't start. It's exactly what my body needs."

Tommy set the shopping bag next to Mike and Rambo joined it, with continued screeching and pawing. Joe stood up, brushing at the black and white cat hairs on his pants.

"An expensive pair of pants?" said Mike, grinning. "At least now they look lived in."

"I'll send you the cleaning bill," said Joe with a half-smile.

"Send it to Rambo. He can use it in his litter box."

Tommy Bears laughed. "That sense of humor must keep the bad guys smiling."

"All the way to jail. Might be you'll find out someday."

"Never gonna happen," said Tommy and opened the door.

Before going out, Joe glanced back. "Take care of yourself, Mike. Who knows, maybe we'll cross paths again."

"Not if I see you coming. And hey, don't let anybody see you leave my building. My reputation you know." The door shut. "Such as it is."

Rambo was trying to tear the sack apart. No easy chore with only one front paw.

"This is my food!" protested Mike. "Just give me a minute and I'll get you some of your own."

Man and cat both knew, of course, that the man would also end up sharing with the cat.

With much effort, the detective got up on the crutches. His eyes fell on the green sack left behind by Panelli.

"What the hell?" He went over to pick it up. "Well, it's not ticking."

Cautiously, Mike peeked in and gave a snort of surprise. It was a pair of sneakers. New, black and white Nikes. He took them out and discovered a note stuck inside one of them with duct tape. Pulling it loose, he read what was printed on it: 'You'll have to replace the key yourself.'

Detective Mike Brennen had to laugh.

FUN IN THE SUN

A Detective Mike Brennen Story

    It was eight o'clock in the evening when Detective Mike Brennen entered his building's elevator to push Three. He usually took the stairs, but with his left foot in a plastic cast for the occasion and him on one crutch, plus his left side still healing from a bullet wound, that wasn't a possibility for a while. Besides, it had been a long afternoon and early evening and he was tired.
    For one thing, the disagreeable part, he had had to wear a suit and tie and had even dug out the only actual pair of shoes he owned and shined them up. No sneakers today. Then he had had to smile and make nice -- no jokes -- because his picture was being taken with important people. And his fellow officers were watching him receive an NYPD commendation and an actual metal for saving Police Chief Andrew Macklin's life. They even applauded. He even noticed Internal Affairs

Lieutenant Marvin Polinski at the back of the room applauding. Mike had to concentrate to keep his smile from turning into a grin.

It had been an afternoon ceremony and Mike finally admitted to himself that it had been very nice. His immediate superior and boss, Lieutenant Carl Grands had been there. Also his partner, Sergeant Clark Thorn, along with his wife, Etta, and their children, Alex and Cecily. Even his aunt and dear friend, Betty Warner, had driven down from Boston. Having her there was almost as good as having his deceased parents there. She had winked at him and made his smile bright.

Afterward, he and the Thorns and Betty had gone out for an early dinner. Both Mike and Clark were recovering from bullet wounds received during that investigation and late nights were not their thing right now. It had been fun and they had had a great time.

But now he was tired.

Mike got to his apartment door and, leaning on his one crutch, was inserting his key when his mind suddenly registered the sound of low voices coming from inside. Had he left his television on?

"Come on in, Mike," called a voice. "I'm friendly."

Mike closed his eyes and frowned. He knew that voice all too well. He turned the key and went in. Tommy One Bears, in a black tee shirt and jeans and signature Western boots, was sitting in the sofa chair. His sport coat was draped over the back of the couch. Rambo the three-legged black and white cat was curled up in his lap. The tv was on low. There was a beer on the little table next to the chair.

Mike stopped and stared. "What are you doing here?"

Tommy gave him a genuine smile. Rambo purred.

"I'm here to congratulate you on your medal," said Tommy brightly. "You really look spiffy in that suit and you even have real shoes on. You are one handsome police detective."

The compliments were spoken with complete sincerity, but Mike was looking doubtful. He said again, "What are you doing here?" Suddenly he glanced around worriedly. "Panelli's not here, is he?"

"Nope, he's not. But he sends his congratulations, too." Then, "Can I see it?"

Tired, Mike pushed the door shut and hobbled over to drop onto the couch, letting the crutch drop. He stared at Tommy and started again, "What are...?"

Rambo jumped down and went to float onto the couch, sniffing the large brown envelope that held the framed commendation and the small box that held the medal. He purred and rubbed on his person.

Tommy leaned forward, resting his elbows on his knees. "I've come to offer you a mini-vacation in the sunny south. No cost. Just a quiet place to finish your recuperating."

Mike blinked. "You're bribing me to do…what? Maybe save the mayor this time?"

"You are suspicious, Detective Brennen."

"I wonder why."

"This is a bona fide offer for you to get some sun and join me on a visit to the Bears' RUNNING B RANCH in New Mexico. I think you earned it."

Mike blinked again. "Running B Ranch?"

"Owners Thomas and Sophia Bears. And me. Lots of wide open spaces. No traffic or honking horns or sirens. Peace and quiet. A great place to heal and get some color and bring back your smile."

"You own part of a ranch?"

"I do. I was even born there and grew up there."

"You grew up on a ranch."

"I did. I was a real cowboy. My grandparents first bought it many moons ago."

"I thought your folks met here, in New York."

"They did. Long time ago. My dad's folks were still alive then and working the ranch. My dad came to New York to work construction, to make some money for the ranch. It's not a big ranch so it does need some financial help sometimes to keep it going. They only run maybe a hundred head of cattle. These days, my folks also do a little horse breeding. Appaloosa horses. They've got six mares and…"

"Appa…what?"

"It's a horse breed. Appaloosas. The mares are excellent horse flesh and Mom and Dad pick out top stallions to breed them to. They raise and sometimes show the offspring and then sell them to pay for the feed and the breeding fees. They don't make a lot of money at it, but they love doing it. I'm a part owner of the ranch and I pay into it to help. I visit them five, six times a year. I thought you might like to ride along this time. I'd like them to meet you."

Mike was looking surprised. "Really?"

A crooked smile. "I don't want to shock you, Mike, but I like you."

Mike stared. "Really?"

"Really. You're a smart and clever detective and you've got that endearing sense of humor."

Still staring. "Huh." Then, "Not sure I've got time enough for a drive to New Mexico. This stupid foot is a pain, taking this dumb plastic cast on and off, and I'll be going back to work on the desk in maybe a week."

"We're flying."

The frown returned. "Not sure how that would…look. Tommy Bears buying me a plane ticket and…"

"Private jet. No tickets. Nobody would have to know."

Startled. "A private jet? You have a private jet...?"

"Not mine. A client's." The Indian sighed. "You called me a 'hired gun' once and I guess I am." He leaned back in the chair again. "In my early years, Mike, I was Special Forces. Did two tours in Afghanistan. Then I came home and used my special skills here. Most of my work is bodyguard and I'm well paid for it. Not well enough to buy jets, but some of the people I have worked for can buy jets. You saved Police Chief Macklin. I have saved a few people myself and they are grateful, and generous."

Now Mike looked at Tommy One Bears in a new light. "You guard rich bodies."

"I do. Big shot CEOs, politicians, a movie star on occasion, very wealthy businessmen, certain foreign visitors." He smirked. "I'm very good at it and I charge them a lot of money."

"So you're not really a message and delivery guy."

"Well, sometimes I make special deliveries. Last week I delivered a guy carrying twenty million dollars in cash to clench a deal for a wealthy client. It was the only way he could put the deal together.

Mike blinked. "Twenty million dollars? In cash?"

"Peanuts for this guy. But he still didn't want it stolen."

"And this guy lets you borrow his jet."

"He's one that does." Tommy shrugged. "They appreciate me."

"Are the Panellis one of those clients?"

"They are."

"Damn."

"So go to New Mexico with me. I'd love for my folks to meet a real hero."

Mike snorted. "Not sure about that." Then, "Wonder if Macklin has a jet?"

"Sadly, I think that medal and a 'thank you' are probably your only rewards from the NYPD."

"And being a cop, I shouldn't be running off in a rich man's jet."

"Like I said, nobody has to know any more than you're going someplace to heal. You don't need to give anyone a lot of details. You're going with a friend to get some sun. Or is friend too much of a stretch?"

Finally, Mike smiled. "Guess someone who has saved my life a couple of times could be called a friend. And some warm sun would be nice. I still get the chills sometimes when I think of that dunk in the river."

"Excellent!" Tommy stood up. "I'll pick you up at ten tomorrow. That gives you time to sleep in after your big day and to get packed."

"Since it's a private jet, can I bring my gun? I kind of feel undressed without my gun."

"That's one of the main reasons I travel private. Now, show me your hero awards."

Mike did sleep good, but was up early enough to get ready, packing his duffle bag. He had never invested in any actual luggage. He didn't travel much outside family visits. Like the trip to his Aunt Margo's in Albany the past weekend for her son's thirteenth birthday.

He admitted to himself that this trip did sound like some fun in the sun. He called Clark Thorn and told him that a friend had offered him a trip to New Mexico.

"What friend?"

"An old one I ran into...."

"What's in New Mexico?"

"Warm sunshine and peace and quiet. I'll be back in time to show up for work."

"I want details when you do," said the sergeant.

Mike made arrangements with his neighbor, Marj, to take care of Rambo. Mike knew she would give the cat lots of hugs and petting as well.

"You have a good time, Michael. You've earned it. Rambo will be fine."

Mike used to tell her that he wasn't a Michael. His birth certificate named him as MIKE JOHN BRENNEN. His folks just wanted it that way. But Marj 'wanted' it to be Michael, so he finally gave up correcting her.

Mike John Brennen was sitting on the front steps of his building waiting when Tommy pulled up in his Mercedes. He popped the trunk as he lowered his window.

"Toss it in and hop in," said Tommy. "Our plane is warming up, my friend."

Mike did it and slid into the front seat. As Tommy started out, the detective said, "I didn't mention that I've never flown before."

Tommy gave him a glance. "Really? Kind of like you don't know how to swim?"

"Never go anywhere. New York City is my whole life. I never was in the service. The only traveling I do is to visit family and I drive there."

"Are your folks here in the city?"

"They're gone. Killed six years ago by a drunk driver. The Panellis didn't sniff that out?"

"They weren't sniffing in that part of your life. I'm sorry about your folks. Must have been tough."

"It was. Very. If my Aunt Betty hadn't been there for me...well, I wanted to rip that drunk's heart out."

"So he survived. I hope they put him away for a long time."

"Not long enough. Ten more years and the fucking bastard will be out."

"Want me to 'dust' him for you?" smirked Tommy.

Mike smirked back. "How much?"

"For you, no charge."

"I'll think about it and get back to you in ten years."

"Deal." Then, "So, this is your first time flying. You'll be spoiled in this plane. It's very nice."

"Whose is it? Anybody I know?"

"You do, actually." Tommy Bears gave him a careful glance as he told him, "The Panelli family."

Mike's eyes almost popped. "What?! Goddamnit, Bears! That is sneaky!"

"It's a perfectly good plane. And...Joe is glad to have you along."

"What!? He's going with? If I had known that..."

"You wouldn't have come...so I decided not to mention it." Then, "Look, Mike. I know it was a rough few days, but Joe's a good guy. I really believe the two of you can be friends. I admit his brother can be a pain the ass and his father, well, Anthony lives in the past a lot. But Joe, he's a good guy and..."

"He's a--"

"Panelli. I get that. But a 'new age' Panelli. When their father went to prison, the sons did a remarkable job of turning the family around. They were never a part of the old days, you know. But they were smart and they did the right thing and saved the Panelli name. And Anthony paid for his bad years and his father's. And what with the cops' bad attitude toward them, it wasn't easy for the sons to do. Just try to cool down and give Joe a chance. He did save your life, too. More than once."

Still fuming, Mike muttered, "We'll see."

When they arrived at the private airfield, Joe Panelli was waiting to greet them. His attitude was also a little on the cool side, but he gave Mike a smile and they shook hands. "Welcome to my humble flying abode, Mike. I'm glad you decided to come along with us."

"Thanks to Tommy for the invite," muttered Mike.

"How's the foot?"

"Doing good according to the docs. I use this stupid plastic boot to help out."

"Well, come aboard and let's be on our way."

They mounted the steps to the sleek-looking jet where the detective stopped to look in in amazement. He had seen plenty of planes in movies and on television, but they hadn't looked like this. Decked out in light brown leather, it was very handsome looking. There were ten cushy seats with small adjoining tables. There was also a small circular table with seating around it for meetings or workspace or meals. There was also a counter space with a microwave and coffee maker and cabinets above.

Joe nodded at a door, telling him, "There's a small bedroom in there along with the bathroom. You can even shower if the mood strikes you."

They settled in and Mike experienced his first breathtaking takeoff. Once they had reach altitude, Joe served coffee with danishes and croissants at the circular table. With Tommy's persistence, the 'stiffness' between Mike and Joe slowly ebbed. By the end of the journey, if they weren't friends, they were at least friendly.

They landed In El Paso where Tommy had a large four-door, silver Silverado pickup waiting for them. On the front doors in red and white letters was RUNNING B RANCH flanked by red and white feathers.

"For my folks," he said.

"Very nice," said Joe.

"I'm impressed," said Mike.

"The back seat is for you and your foot, Mike."

"Still traveling in luxury," smirked the detective.

They loaded the luggage in the truck bed and were on their way.

More than an hour later, Mike commented as he stared out the window, "You weren't kidding when you said it was wide open spaces. And it's really flat."

"It would be hard to argue with that," agreed Joe.

"There," said Tommy with some enthusiasm. "The two of you agreed about something. This trip is looking better all the time."

Mike ignored the remark, saying, "I sort of envisioned mountains of majesty."

"There are mountains of majesty in New Mexico. Up north, and west. My folks' ranch is down here in the south. This country is called the Staked Plains. Because of the yucca."

"Yucca?" said Mike.

"That's what those tallish sort of tree-like plants are." Tommy waved a hand at the flat countryside.

"Lots of yucca, but not many trees," said Joe.

Tommy patiently explained, "It's cattle country. Some of the best grazing in the world. Still some big ranches in the southwest. But you won't see a lot of trees and the ones you do see are there mostly because people planted them. Otherwise you wouldn't see many trees."

"Tommy, I don't see any grazing cows, either," noted Mike.

"That's because it's open range, cattle are spread out. And it's been pretty dry this year so far. When ranchers have to put out hay to make up for the lack of grass, the cattle 'tend to stay close to the ranch headquarters and watering troughs. When it does rain, it's beautiful, but rain can be scarce sometimes. We're lucky at the Running B to have a small river that runs through the ranch. And my folks planted a lot of trees over the years so there's plenty of shade. You'll see grazing cows and horses. We'll be to Butch's in about fifteen minutes to pick up supplies, then on to the Bears' ranchero."

"Why didn't you get supplies in El Paso?" wondered Mike.

"I like to give Butch the business," said Tommy. "He needs all he can get out here."

"Certainly no traffic to worry about here," said Joe.

He had just gotten it out of his mouth when a large black limousine cruised past them at a high rate of speed. Then it abruptly cut back in front of them. It caused Tommy to brake.

Mike scowled. "That was rude."

Joe said, "There a lot of limousines out here? They don't exactly fit into this kind of country."

Tommy frowned at the impolite limo as he answered, "Might belong to one of the big ranchers."

Some ten minutes later, they arrived at Butch's. A large sign, painted in black and yellow announced BUTCH'S EVERYTHING STORE. As large as the building was, it looked like it just might carry everything. Parked out front was the black limo. A man leaned against it, arms folded across his chest.

"Damn," said Mike. "He's got the look of a New York City asshole."

"He doesn't look any more polite than his driving," allowed Joe.

Tommy skillfully backed the truck up to one of two loading docks. As he turned off the motor, the Indian gave the impolite hard ass a brief scrutiny, saying, "Now, if we were in New York, I'd feel it necessary to confront the gentleman about his driving. But, we're in New Mexico, on vacation, and I intend to be a smiling, cheerful guy, visiting my folks."

Both Joe and Mike looked at him. Bears wasn't exactly known to be a smiley, cheerful kind of guy. At least, not when it came to assholes.

Tommy went on, "Most important here, is the visiting my folks part. No need to talk shop beyond that Joe's a client friend and Mike's a cop friend. Three friendly guys on vacation. So, who wants to go inside with me to meet Butch?"

"That sounds like a friendly thing to do," said Joe, and opened his door to get out.

"I think I'll stay out here and make friends with the cheerful limo guy," said Mike, "but, hey, if you see some Western shirts, grab me a couple, would you. I'd like to fit in."

Tommy sent the guy a glance. "Just don't get yourself hurt. Making friends isn't something you're good at."

He and Joe went up the steps, to cross the wide plank porch and enter the store.

Mike frowned and muttered, "That's not true. How many cops have made friends with the Panelli family and a half-breed hired gun?"

He opened his door and slid down out of the high vehicle, carefully taking his weight on his good right foot. Closing the door, he relaxed against the truck and crossed his arms. And smiled.

"Good morning," he said with a friendly tone.

The Limo Guy gave him a bored look, and a barely distinguishable nod in return.

"Name's Mike. I'm on vacation. Great place, the Staked Plains. Lots of yucca, and grazing cows. You live here?"

Now the Limo Guy gave him a don't-bother-me look and turned his head and eyes away to take in the horizon.

"Ouch," said Mike. "I was led to believe folks down here were really neighborly. Guess not, huh."

His neighbor continued to stare at the horizon.

A large gray cat strolled out of the opened door of the store. He sat down at the edge of the wide porch and started grooming himself.

"Hey, big guy," Mike greeted him.

The cat continued to groom for a minute before looking up. Then his eyes moved back and forth between Mike and Limo Guy, giving each of them a close study. Finally he stood up, came down the steps with no small amount of arrogance, and went directly to Limo Guy. With practiced ease, Gray Cat began to rub against the man's legs.

"Get away from me," grumbled Limo Guy and pushed it away with a foot.

Gray Cat was not discouraged. He was right back, rubbing more gray hairs off onto the man's dark pants.

"Get the fuck away from me," griped the guy and gave the cat a harder kick.

"Careful there, fella," Mike's tone not so friendly. "No reason to be impolite with the kitty."

Growling, Limo Guy said, "I hate cats."

Mike carefully slid down to sit on the pickup's wide running board, his back resting against the side. Gray Cat came over and the detective began scratching him in all the right places.

"Well, that explains it then. I've heard cats have a habit of annoying people who don't like cats. They can sense it. I have a cat at home. Big black and white cat I named Rambo. He lost a leg when dogs attacked him, but I rescued him and…" And Mike went on to annoy Limo Guy with a lengthy tale of how he and Rambo had met.

Inside the store, Tommy was making introductions. "Butch, meet Joe. He's visiting us on vacation."

The burly Butch looked all cowboy from his Stetson to his boots. He shook Joe's hand vigorously. "Got no last name, Joe?"

"Don't use it when I'm on vacation," said Joe. "How about you?"

"Haven't bothered with it for a long time. My wife handles anything that requires a last name. I just stand out here and shake hands and sell things." Then, "So what can I sell you, Tommy?"

"Whatever you've been selling my folks. Mostly feed, I guess. Including for cats and dogs. Just fill up that silver pickup out there."

"Very nice," said Butch with a glance out the doorway. "But didn't you just buy them a new one last time you were out here?"

Tommy shrugged. "Man can never have too many pickups."

"That security business of yours must make a lot of money," noted Butch. "You in the security business, Joe?"

"I hire Tommy to take care of my security. He…"

"Hey, you," a voice interrupted. "Mr. Hudson doesn't have time to stand around while you're gossiping."

Butch and Tommy and Joe turned heads to look at a cool eyed blond wearing new Western clothing including a hat and boots. Behind him, at the counter, was a sharp faced man in a new, well-fitting Western suit. Boots but no hat.

"Be polite, Jordy," said Mr. Hudson. "I'm told folks out here are laid back. I'm sure…Butch is it?...will take care of us in turn."

He conjured up a smile and stepped over, offering a hand.

"Mitchell Hudson, gentlemen," he said. "Friends call me Mitch."

"Joe," said Joe, noting the man's very firm shake.

"Tommy Bears, Mitchell," said Tommy, less than pleased to shake the man's hand. "I'll stick with Mitchell since we're not friends yet."

"Bears. I believe the Bears are my neighbors to the north."

"Yeah," said Butch, also shaking hands. "Heard a couple months ago you bought Andy Miller's place. You've not been in here yet."

"Haven't had time to introduce myself around, I'm afraid. I do a lot of business around the States. The ranch is going to be mostly a hobby, though I hope to set it up so I can do a lot of my work from there."

"Hobby?" Butch arched an eyebrow. "That's a lot of ranch for a hobby."

Hudson gave a laugh. "Well, it is that, but I'm going to let the experts do the handling of it. But now, when you have a moment, I've a list to leave with you to order for me. I can promise you a lot of business, Butch. And Jordan Spike, here, is my right-hand man. You'll probably see him more than me."

Tommy gave Spike a brief glance, then said, "Go ahead and help Mitchell out, Butch. We're in no hurry."

"Why, thank you, Tommy," said Hudson.

"That's just how folks are here," allowed Tommy. "Friendly. Neighborly. Mr. Spike may have to work on that a bit."

Jordy Spike's don't-tread-on-me look made it obvious that he would need to work hard on that aspect.

Butch, making no effort to cover a grin, went to help Mr. Hudson.

"Don't think I'll be calling Mitchell, Mitch any time soon," rumbled Tommy.

"From his handshake, he likes to be in control," said Joe. "Wonder just what his business around the States is?"

"Whatever, I'm sorry to hear Andy had to sell his place," said Tommy. "His family's had that ranch for a long time and he was a good neighbor."

"Well," said Joe, "I've met Butch, and Mr. Hudson and Jordy. Think I'll pick out a couple of shirts for Mike and then go see if he needs some help making friends with Mr. Hudson's driver."

He did that and when he got outside, he found Mike had made friends with a cat. He said, "Why am I not surprised. You're not going to rescue that one I hope."

"Actually, I already did," said Mike, carefully standing up. "This nice gentleman kicked him and I told him not to do that again."

Joe and Limo Guy exchanged glances.

"Guess he needs to work on his neighborly attitude like his friend, Jordy, inside. I just met their boss, Mr. Hudson. He was chummy enough, but he does need to better train his watch dogs. Including their driving."

"Couldn't worm a name out of this fella. I did share with him the story about how I met Rambo. I think he was really interested."

"I can imagine..." started Joe.

"His name is Abe Dorn." It was Hudson, coming out of the store with Spike. "And I will try to train my men to be more neighborly. We come from an environment where watch dogs need to growl more than smile." He gave Mike a brief smile as they came down the steps and held out his hand. "I'm Mitchell Hudson."

"Mike." The detective shook the hand. "You might want to train them to be friendlier with the livestock, too."

"I'll keep that in mind," smiled Hudson. Then, "I'm having a barbecue at my ranch tomorrow evening. Sort of a get-acquainted picnic with my neighbors and some of the town folk. The Bears are already invited. Tommy and you boys are certainly welcome, too."

"Well, not sure what the Bears have planned for us, but we'll keep it in mind," said Joe.

"Excellent." Mitchell Hudson beamed. "The little get-together should help us to learn more about cowboy country." Then, "We need to get moving, Abe."

Abe Dorn gave Mike one more unfriendly glare and turned to get into the driver's seat. Spike opened the back door for his boss and then got in front next to Dorn. The limo's motor turned over and Dorn revved it up a couple of times before charging onto the road, rear tires sending a lot of dust into the air.

Mike and Joe stared after them for several quiet moments before the latter noted, "I get the feeling Mr. Dorn didn't like you. And after Tommy told you to be careful about making friends."

"I don't want to be his friend," sniffed Mike. "He hates cats. And that blond guy was a mean-looking cowboy."

With a sigh, Joe said, "Well, I also got the feeling that none of them is even a little bit interested in becoming neighborly, let alone liking cats."

Mike's eyes fell on the shirts Joe held.

"Are those mine? They look great."

In the limousine, Mitchell Hudson was wearing a frown.

"I get a sense that Tommy, Joe, and Mike, could be more than casual vacationers. Men who are a little savvy. And Tommy Bears is the son of the couple who have the Running B."

"Bears was armed," said Spike. "Joe could have been, too."

"Mike was," said Dorn. "Saw it when he got out of the pickup."

"So, maybe not so unusual out here," said Spike.

Hudson's frown did not change. "But out here, ranchers usually carry their weapons in their pickups or on their belts. I'm pretty sure they don't usually carry concealed weapons. They like to make a show of how tough they are. Concealed weapons are more usual with city boys. If they're on vacation, Let's hope they won't be here long enough to maybe be a problem. Let's just try to keep it friendly."

A wrought iron sign curved over the entrance, announcing they were entering the RUNNING B RANCH. The ranch buildings could just be seen in the distance, surrounded by trees. Rustic wood fences lined both sides of the road as they drove to the ranch headquarters.

"There you go, gentlemen," said Tommy. "Horses grazing on one side. Cattle grazing on the other. Trees ahead."

"Just like you promised," said Mike, enjoying the sight.

As they entered the yard, it was easy to see that it was all carefully cared for. The small front yard and somewhat larger back yard of the house had the only trimmed, grass lawns. Flower beds lined the front and sides of the light brown, two story house. The dusty yards around the rest of the place were clean. There were two barns, also brown in color, one large and one small. Two corrals were attached to the large barn. There was also a small one-story bunkhouse, a couple of storage sheds, and a large chicken coop and pen.

Two dogs came running when they stopped, barking with excitement. Sophia Bears came hurriedly from the house. Thomas Bears came walking briskly from the small barn. Mike and Joe watched as the tough, hard-core Tommy exchanged hugs and kisses with his folks.

"Probably would be best if we never mention this side of Tommy Bears back home," said Mike with some amusement. "Might not look so good in his job references."

Joe smiled thinly and gave a nod. "Anybody finds out he has a soft side, it could affect his business."

"Another new pickup, Tommy?" said the senior Bears gruffly. "That's not--"

"Don't want to hear it," said Tommy firmly. "Just come meet my friends. This is Mike Brennen. He's the cop I've told you about."

"Real pleasure, Mr. and Mrs. Bears," said the detective. "Good to know Tommy was hatched from such nice folks."

"And this is Joe Panelli, one of my best clients," Tommy went on.

"Very nice to meet you," said Joe.

"Our pleasure," said Sophia with a bright smile.

"And so you know," said Thomas, "I didn't want to saddle my son with a 'junior', so we went with Tommy instead."

"Not important, Dad," said Tommy with a shake of his head.

A man came from the big barn, walking toward them with a big smile as another came galloping on a black and white horse. The latter got to them first, reining to a dusty stop and coming out of the saddle.

"Tommy, you hard ass!" said the rider, grabbing Tommy's hand and also giving him a slap on the back.

The other came up to also shake his hand, saying, "Good to see you, you good-for-nothing half-breed."

"Sounds like they know our Tommy pretty good," remarked Mike.

"It does seem that way," agreed Joe.

Tommy introduced the rider, "This is Lucas Rivers. Another half-breed. Half Apache and, sadly, half white. And this Mexican bum is Quintin Santos. They're the best goddamned ranch hands in the state of New Mexico."

Both men were in their forties. Solid, weather-worn cowboys.

After the hand shaking, the luggage was unloaded from the pickup and the Bears led their guests to the house. Mike on his one crutch and carrying the new Western shirts. Santos jumped in and drove the pickup to the large barn to unload all the feed. Leading his horse, Rivers followed to help.

In the house, Sophia was almost bubbling. "I'm so excited to meet some of Tommy's friends. He always sounds like he doesn't have any."

"Job keeps me busy, Mom," said Tommy.

"We're just glad to have all of you visit," said Thomas.

A small black dog greeted them at the door, jumping with excitement.

"Stop, Poker!" Sophia tried to calm him down. "Please forgive him. He loves attention. He's mostly an indoor dog. Some cruel soul dumped him off. He was skin and bones when he showed up. We think he's a mixture of Chihuahua and Dachshund." She nodded at the stairs. "Joe, you'll sleep up in Tommy's old room. And we fixed up the spare room downstairs for you, Mike. Tommy told us about your foot and this way you don't have to climb steps."

"And Tommy gets the barn?" smirked Mike.

The half-breed smirked back. "Wouldn't be the first time."

"If he's a good boy, we'll let him stay in the bunkhouse with the boys this time," said Thomas with a crooked smile. Then, "Tommy told us you're a police detective, Mike, and got your injury from a bad guy."

"Actually it was a very bad girl and I'm glad to say she won't be stomping on anyone else's foot ever again," said Mike.

"We understand you are a genuine hero," said Sophia, "and we're anxious to hear the whole story. Right now, I'm just glad to hear you like animals. Especially cats, because you will be sharing your room with another of our indoor four-legged family members."

Thomas said, "Tommy told us about your three-legged Rambo and our Geronimo has his problems, too. He forgot to grow."

"We had to turn him into an indoor cat when the big boys outside started picking on him," Sophia told him. "He'd put up a good fight but was definitely ill-matched."

They stopped at the door of the spare room to see a yellow and white cat sprawled out on the twin sized bed. A very small cat. He lifted his head to look back at them.

"Hey there, Geronimo," Mike greeted him. "You are a little fella. My Rambo could almost swallow you whole."

Geronimo laid his head back down, not interested in Rambo or what anyone thought about his size.

"Would you like to rest a while?" asked Sophia. "If you're hungry, I can fix you some sandwiches. Thomas has a couple of venison roasts on a spit in the back yard for tonight."

Joe smiled in anticipation. "I think we'll be glad to save our appetite for that, and we've been resting a lot of hours. Be nice to stretch our legs a bit. Well, Mike's one leg."

"I can handle stretching my leg," Mike assured them.

So the Bears took them on a slow walk around the ranch yard. It was a zoo-like adventure that included horses, milk cows, beef cattle, two wandering goats, a large chicken coop, multiple cats, and the two dogs. And a large garden. The dogs followed them around as did the goats and several cats.

"These are our pride and joy," said Sophia as they came up to a fenced pasture. "These are our Appaloosa mares. Five of them gave birth this spring and had lovely, spotted babies."

They were all colors -- black with white blankets and white spots; dark brown with the blanket and spots; one mare was all white with black spots. And five frolicking, spotted babies.

"We'll show them some and then sell them," said Thomas. "Their daddies are well bred and famous in the show ring and on the track. We enjoy them a great deal."

"They are certainly eye-catching," said Mike.

"I can see why you enjoy them," smiled Joe.

When they got to the tree-lined river, Mike eyed the twelve foot span with question. "No offense, but you call this a river? It can't be more than two or three feet deep."

"Trust me," said Tommy, "in this part of the country this is a big river. And it's especially a big deal around these parts."

Eventually they settled at a couple of picnic tables in the shaded, grassy backyard. Eyeing the roasting meat, Mike's mouth watered.

"How long did you say before we eat?" he asked with a crooked smile.

Sophia laughed. "Not long, Mike. I've got stuff ready in the house. Just get comfortable and Thomas can introduce you to some of our menagerie."

"Can I help you bring things out?" asked Joe.

"That's my job. You're on vacation," said Tommy and followed his mother into the house.

The menagerie had trailed them into the yard. Thomas looked fondly around at them.

"The goats are Lucy and Ricky. They keep the weeds in check and mow the lawn for me." Thomas patted a big black dog. "This monster is Buckaroo. Buck for short. No idea what his breeding might be, but I think there's some elephant in there somewhere. The black and white one is Pecos Bill. Pecos for short."

Pecos Bill was about half the size of Buckaroo.

He glanced around at the seven or eight cats. "I won't bore you with all the cat names, but the big gray and white one is His Majesty. Well, mostly we call him King. He pretty much rules the roost here."

Shortly Sophia and Tommy showed up with bowls of food and Thomas cut the meat. Quint and Lucas came up and joined them. Stories were shared on both sides and there was plenty of laughter.

The meal was winding down when Tommy mentioned, "We met your new neighbor at Butch's."

It wasn't hard to see the change in everyone's expression. Smiles slipped away and some gloom settled over them.

"Hmmm," said Tommy. "Is there something about Mr. Hudson not sitting right?"

"Humpf! That man," sniffed Sophia.

Thomas shook his head. "We're thinking he's not going to be much of a neighbor."

Tommy eyed his father. "Oh? Mr. Hudson already stepping on toes?"

"More like stompin' on feet," said Lucas.

"Ouch," winced Mike. "Don't like foot stompers."

"That man," repeated Sofia, her tone steamy. "He finally showed up here a few days ago--"

"It's been maybe three months since he bought the place," injected Thomas.

"--and comes whipping in here in his big limousine--"

"He almost ran down Buck," injected Quint.

"--and introduces himself," continued Sophia. "All dressed up in fancy Western duds. Like that makes you a rancher. And invites us to some fancy barbeque."

"And then proceeded to make an offer to buy our place," said Thomas gruffly.

"What?" That surprised Tommy.

"Huh?" said Mike, and Joe frowned.

Thomas was shaking his head. "He shakes hands and then says he wants to buy the Running B".

Sophia humpf'ed again. "First we stared at him and then we laughed. Don't think he liked the laughing part. Like we cared."

"Did he give you any kind of reason?" asked Tommy. "I mean, he told us he bought the BOX M as a hobby. That place is almost three times the size of our place. How much of a hobby does he need?"

"Good question," sniffed Thomas. "But he'll have to make do 'cause we sure as hell won't ever sell this place."

"It was a huge surprise that Andy even sold his place," said Sophia. "And now it's called the BIG H."

"That's Andrew Miller," Tommy told Mike and Joe. "The Millers have been on that ranch since the late eighteen hundreds."

"For sure," said Thomas. "Andy told us he was thinking about retiring, but we never dreamed he would retire off the ranch. And he's got two sons, Carson and Frank, that we figured would take over."

"I know damned well that Carson thought he would," said Rivers. "Frank, maybe not so much. But we haven't seen either one since Andy sold out."

"We haven't seen Andy but once since then," said Sofia, "and he was acting distant, especially about the ranch, which isn't like him at all. He's always been a talker. It's all very strange and disturbing. Even more so now that that disagreeable man talked about wanting our place."

"Well, we've been invited to the fancy barbeque, too. Tomorrow evening, I believe," said Tommy.

His parents glowered at him, Thomas saying, "That's not going to happen. We aren't setting foot over--"

"Actually," interrupted Mike, "it might be a good idea to go. Be an excellent way to find out a little more about Mr. Hudson. As a cop, I love digging around somebody's life. Especially a suspicious somebody."

Joe smirked. "He is good at that. Digging. Someday he's likely to dig his own grave. But I agree. It is a good idea if you want to get to know more about the guy."

Tommy grinned. "If Mike and Joe are agreeing about something, it has to be a good idea." To his folks, "And I'm sure you two can put on smiles and be friendly for a couple of hours."

"He best not ask us to sell him the ranch," grumped Thomas, "or I'll pop him one."

"Yes. We both will," said Sophia.

"If there's any popping to do, I'll handle it," Tommy assured them.

When Mike woke up in the morning, the yellow and white Geronimo was curled up on the pillow beside his head. Eye-to-eye.

"Well, good morning," he said.

The cat didn't move, but he instantly started purring. Loudly.

The detective smiled and scratched the little cat's head. "Is all that noise coming out of tiny you?"

The vacationing cop rolled onto his back and stretched. It had been a long time since he'd slept so good and for so long. Sunlight coming through the window told him the morning was probably well along. He looked at his watch.

"Damn!" It was after eleven.

Shortly he hobbled into the kitchen on one bare foot, one wrapped foot, jeans, and a new cowboy shirt. He found Joe and Sophia at the table with coffee mugs

"Morning," he greeted, wearing a dopey half smile.

"Morning barely," said Joe. "We were about to start discussing funeral arrangements. Not for the first time I might add."

Mike snarled. "Funny."

"You're on vacation," said Sophia. "You can sleep all you want. And from what Joe has told me, you've earned it."

Mike eyed Panelli. "Do I want to know what stories you were spinning about me?"

Sophia gave a little laugh. "They were good stories, Mike." Her eyes softened as she studied him for a few moments. "You help people, Mike. Not just as a police officer, but as a human being."

Mike winced. "Now I really need to know what you've been telling her."

"And you obviously impressed Geronimo." The woman looked down at the cat, which had followed Mike out and now was rubbing against his legs. "I think you've been adopted."

Mike reached down to scratch the cat. "We did good together. He doesn't begin to take up as much room as Rambo. Even with only three legs mine takes his half and half of mine."

"Well, how does fresh eggs and bacon and Texas toast sound for breakfast?" asked Sophia.

"Lunch," said Joe. "It's almost lunch time."

"It sounds wonderful whichever meal it is," said Mike.

Shortly he was eating heartily when the Bears men came in.

"Decided to join the living, Mike?" said Tommy.

"I'm on vacation," said Mike around a mouthful.

They spent the day relaxing. Mostly out in the shaded backyard. At one point, it was just Mike and Joe and Tommy.

"What do you think about this Hudson wanting to buy your folks' place?" asked Joe.

"Yeah. He seems pretty sure of himself," said Mike. "Doesn't look like the type to let anything stand in the way of what he wants."

"It is curious, and bold, his interest in this ranch," said Tommy. "I'll talk to him about it when we're over there later. I don't want him pestering my folks about it. And I'd sure like the chance to talk to Andy Miller about why he sold the Box M. That ranch wasn't just property to them. It was their blood."

"I can have my people look into Hudson's background," offered Joe. "His name doesn't ring any bells with me, but if he's got money to buy a large ranch and he does business all around the country, he's got to have a name in the business world."

"I'd appreciate that," said Tommy.

"I'll be sure to mention I'm a cop at this shindig. Just to see his reaction. Maybe get a reaction from his hired help, too." Mike smirked at the last.

"You can share some of that irritating cop attitude you used around me and my family," said Joe.

"You noticed," said Mike. "I wasn't sure I was getting through…"

"On vacation!" said Tommy sharply.

They all went in the new pickup. Mike, in another of his cowboy shirts, sat up front with Tommy. Joe and the Bears shared the roomy backseat. They all eyed the large new sign over the ranch entrance -- a big "H", black against white. The seven foot high, ornate iron gate stood open, but to their practiced eyes, they saw it would lock tight when closed.

"Most of this was free range -- unfenced -- when it was Andy's place," said Thomas. "Now this Hudson has not only fenced a lot of it, I've heard he's electrified much of it, too."

"So we see," said Joe, noting the High Voltage signs on the seven-foot wire fence.

"Surveillance, too," said Tommy, spotting a camera.

"A big gate that can be locked and cameras keeping an eye on you," remarked Mike. "Nothing like a warm welcome."

Tommy was shaking his head and said, "I'm curious as hell why a man like him would buy a ranch. A big ranch. They've tested for oil here and what they found was too little, too deep to bother drilling for. And it's not what you'd call scenic territory. It's a cattle ranch, period, and I don't think it was all that profitable, was it Dad?"

"Andy certainly had his ups and downs, like we do," said Thomas. "Lucky for us, we have a son with money to invest. Andy's sons weren't in a position to help much financially, but they worked hard."

"That's why I don't understand why Andy sold out," Sophia said sadly. "He worked so hard all these years to keep the place running."

"Maybe it just wore him out, Mom," said Tommy. "Maybe the financial problems got too big."

"I don't believe that for a second," grumped Thomas.

Neither did his son.

It was more than a mile's drive to the ranch headquarters. There was a crowd milling about and talking in the large front yard of the old house, an impressive three stories. And more than a few were over at the new house, built of stone and glass. Some of the guests using a large swimming pool there. There was an old, large, wooden barn and not far away was a new, larger, metal building.

"What's he need a building that size for?" wondered Thomas.

"I surely hope they don't tear down the old house. It would be such a shame," said Sophia sadly.

A man wearing Western clothes, and a thin bored smile, directed them to a parking area.

Mike gave the guy a look as they passed and said, "Why do I get the feeling that man has never chased a cow?"

"He probably wouldn't know which end to chase," sniffed Thomas.

"That may be true, Dad, but we are here on a friendly, information gathering mission," Tommy reminded him. "Do yourselves a favor and don't get on the wrong side of a man with this much money and power. Especially since he's your neighbor."

"Well, it looks like just about every rancher in the county is here," said his father. "And Phil Hyland. Phil's our sheriff. A good man. Wonder what he knows about Hudson?"

"There's quite a few folks from town as well," said Sophia. "And there's Butch and his wife, Susan."

Tommy parked and they all got out, Mike using his crutch.

"Here comes the BIG H himself," said Joe.

Mitchell Hudson had seen their arrival. With a big smile, he walked toward them with another man -- tall, hefty, in his late thirties. He wore a mustache on a deeply tanned, rugged face. He was slightly bow-legged.

"Now he looks like a cowboy," remarked Joe.

"Kind of looks like Tom Selleck," added Mike. "If he was wearing a gun, he'd fit the bill as a Western Marshal."

Hudson and the man came up, Mitchell greeting, "Mr. and Mrs. Bears. Gentlemen. I'm so glad you came."

They shook hands all around and Hudson gave Mike's foot a sympathetic look. "Didn't realize you were injured when I saw you yesterday, Mike. What happened?"

"Nasty bad person did it. I'm an NYPD detective and catching bad guys -- and girls -- is my favorite thing. The one who did this was a bad lady and I'm glad to say she won't be hurting or killing anybody else."

If the announcement that he was a cop disturbed Hudson, it didn't show at all. "I hope it's mending well. Being a police officer gives you some slight connection with Harvey, here. I'd like you all to meet Harvey Elson. He's a former Texas Ranger from Dallas. He'll be managing the ranch for me."

There was more handshaking. Harvey's smile was more genuine than Hudson's.

Thomas wanted to know, "What happened to Andy's foreman, Al Dunn?"

"He was interested in looking for greener pastures," Hudson skimmed over the question. "Please, go and enjoy the food and we can chat more later."

The two men waved them toward the others and went off.

"He's going to chat with us later," said Tommy. "He's got that right. But now let's stuff ourselves with some of his food."

They did, filling their plates, and then Tommy's folks joined some of their neighbors. Tommy and Mike and Joe settled at a picnic table on their own. Tommy sat on one side, his eyes on the ranch compound. Mike and Joe faced the large front yard and all the people. The three ate quietly for a while, drinking bottles of beer with their food, studying their surroundings.

Finally Mike said, "Okay, Mr. Bears. I know we're out West and all but does a neighborly ranch host usually have gunmen wandering around guarding his place from his neighbors? I mean, besides our good buddy Jordy, I see at least four other guys with jackets covering holstered weapons. Jackets on a hot day. Maybe if they were wearing them like they did in the Old West it might be kind of fun, but..."

"No, Detective Brennen, it's not normal in the New West," said Tommy. "Mr. Panelli, would you like to take a stroll with me and see what happens when we wander toward that big metal building?"

"That sounds like it might be interesting," said Joe. "If Mike thinks he'll be alright by himself. I would hate for one of these unfriendly looking gentlemen to come up and stomp on his other foot."

"Not a problem. I can beat them off with my crutch. But if you fellas start hollering for help, I'm not sure I'll be fast enough to come to your rescue."

"That's okay. Sheriff Hyland is here and he's pretty reliable," said Tommy.

The two men stood up and, casually taking their bottles of beer with them, moved off. Mike arranged himself so he could watch the guys with the guns. To see what they might do.

Tommy and Joe left the front yard moving toward the new building. Mike almost grinned when two of the gunmen picked up their pace to head after the explorers, their obvious intent to cut them off.

"Where do they think they're going?"

The question turned Mike's head to see Jordy Spike come up to the table.

"Just taking a little walk to look around," said the detective. Then mused, "And it looks like a couple of your guys are going join them. That's a neighborly thing to do."

Spike didn't sound neighborly as he rasped, "Mr. Hudson would prefer that no one took any walks. Wouldn't want anyone to get hurt."

Mike gave a laugh. "You don't need to worry about Tommy and Joe. It would take a lot to hurt them. Besides, what's out there that could hurt anybody? Clear blue skies and wide open spaces--"

"Where are Tommy and Joe going?" Mitchell Hudson came up a little hurriedly and with a hint of a frown.

"That's what I was asking, Mr. Hudson," said Jordy.

"And I was just telling him that Tommy and Joe were stretching their legs. Why all the concern about taking a walk?" Mike said. He raised one eyebrow and smiled secretively. "Got one of those UFOs hidden in that big building, there Mitch? I've read the stories about Roswell, New Mexico. You--"

He had lost the attention of Mitchell and Jordy. Their eyes were on the walkers who had almost reached the new building. So Mike watched with them as one of the gunmen got ahead of the pair of guests. Gunman Number Two hung back and to one side. Tommy and Joe and Gunman Number One started talking.

"Jordy, why don't you ask Tom and Joe to join us here at the table and we can have that chat," said Hudson and Jordy went to do that.

Hudson waved at another of his wandering guards. "Owen! Do me a favor and bring us some cold beers over here. Three of them, please."

"Yes, sir," said Owen and headed for the large ice-filled tubs.

"So, how was the food, Mike? Did you get enough?"

"Can't complain, Mitch. I have to admit, though, the meal the Bears had for us yesterday was a dandy, too. I keep eating like this and I won't be able to chase any bad guys when I get back home."

"So how long will you staying here?" asked Hudson.

He sat down, his eyes on Jordy as he talked to Tommy and Joe.

"Not sure, but I still have a week or so off before I return to the job. Been a month healing my foot and my wound."

"Oh? You were wounded, too?"

Jordy, Tommy and Joe were walking back now. Gunmen Number One and Two moved back toward the ranch yards.

"I was mixed up with several different, very bad cases all at once. They all took a toll on me. But, I'm a very determined cop and managed to win the day."

"Is he bragging again?" said Tommy as he and Joe and their guard dog arrived.

Owen came up with the beers. Setting them on the table, the man moved off again.

"Thought you'd like some cold ones," said Hudson.

"I try never to turn down a cold beer," said Tommy, taking one as he sat.

"Mike didn't bore you with cop stories, did he?" Joe said, sitting and exchanging his empty bottle for the fresh one. "He never misses a chance to talk about his exciting life as a cop. That and his cat stories."

"I do enjoy sharing my interesting life," said Mike. "Something's always going on."

"So, Mitchell, what's in the big metal building?" Tommy asked out right. "Your boys seemed uneasy that we were walking in that direction."

"I asked him that," said Mike. "I was hoping it might be one of those UFOs. Like at Roswell. That would--"

Hudson forced a laugh. "Nothing so exciting. It's just a hangar for my plane. It's not here yet, of course. They're still working on the runway. I'm hoping it will be ready in another week or so."

Boldly, Joe said, "I'm curious, Mitchell. What is it you've got here that you need all these gunmen around?"

It caught Hudson a little off guard. Spike scowled.

Mitchell gave them a crooked smile. "So you've noticed some of my people are armed."

Tommy shrugged. "I'm in the security business and Mike's a cop and Joe has security for his own businesses. Hard for us not to notice. It just seems a little over the top out here on the wide-open plains of New Mexico. Not going to find too much trouble with your neighbors here."

"I see your point, of course. But, Jordy is my security man and he's very serious about his job. Even out here. I am a high-profile businessman and back in the city he was used to being prepared for the possibility of different kinds of trouble."

"What city is that?" asked Joe.

"Home base was Atlanta, but I have business dealings in a number of cities. I will consider this my home now and will use the plane for important meetings wherever needed." Changing the subject from himself, he eyed Tommy and Joe. "Since Mike is a New York police officer, I'm guessing the two of you are also from New York."

"We are," said Joe. "You could say I'm a high-profile businessman, too. And Tommy, as he mentioned, is in the security business and takes very good care of my security. We both met Mike when we were partially involved in a case he was working on. We learned Mike is a detective not to be underestimated."

Both Hudson and Spike gave the detective solemn glances, but Hudson then eyed Tommy. "You live in New York, but own part of your folks' ranch."

"I work from New York. The Running B is my home. I was born and raised there. Which brings up a question I'm curious about, Mitchell. They told me you were asking about buying the ranch. I can't help but wonder why. The Box M-- pardon me -- the Big H is the largest ranch in the area. Why would you need more land for your hobby?"

"I wasn't aware at the time that the Bears had a son who was part owner," said Hudson. "And my interest in the land was because of the river. It's just about the only above ground water for thousands of square miles. Plus, I've commissioned to build a small airport and was told your land offered some of the best area for that."

"With all the ranch land you have here, I find that hard to believe. And you have plenty of wells providing water in many areas for your needs." Tommy smiled. "More than enough to fill that swimming pool. And if you want to do some fishing, the Bears always welcome their neighbors to visit and throw out a line."

Mitchell Hudson found a smile. "That's good to know, Tommy. I appreciate that. And I can understand how attached you and your folks are to your place. But, who knows, maybe in the future you--"

"No," said Tommy, still smiling. "Never."

"This is kind of exciting," Mike couldn't resist. "Is this like one of those cowboy movies? A range war? All this land, but the guy with the biggest place is gobbling up all the smaller places. Hope it doesn't lead to a gunfight, Mr. Hudson. The three of us are pretty good shots."

Mr. Hudson turned a sour look on the detective, saying, "I don't think--"

A woman screamed. Not a hearty, terrorizing scream, but a short surprised one, from inside the old house.

Tommy instantly recognized it. "That's my mother!"

In a split second, he was up and across the yard and onto the front porch with his gun out. The Indian yanked open the screen and when he found the door locked, he opened it with a hard kick. Joe, also with his gun out, had followed on his heels and the two men charged inside. Hudson and Spike came right behind them, the latter also had his gun out.

Left sitting at the picnic table was a swearing Mike. He got up and hobbled after them but didn't bother to draw his gun. If all the firepower in front of him couldn't handle the situation, it was unlikely he could.

"I'm fine! I'm fine!" Sophia Bears waved her hands at her son. "Tommy! I'm fine!"

They were all in the kitchen, one of Hudson's sentries standing there with a startled look on his face.

"For heaven's sake!" declared Sophia, frowning angrily. "Put the guns away! Are you all crazy?"

They did look a little crazy, all standing there with guns in their hands.

"I'm sorry!" Sophia apologized and again said, "Oh for heaven's sake. I used the restroom and when I came out, I all but ran into this gentleman."

The gentleman changed from startled to annoyed. "She came into the kitchen. Guests aren't allowed past the house rest room."

Now Thomas Bears arrived in a bit of a panic. "What happened!? Sophia! Are you--?"

"I'm fine! Calm down. I'm a woman. We snoop in people's kitchens. I was just curious to see if they'd done anything in here. I'm very sorry."

Guns were put away.

"It's I who should apologize, Mrs. Bears," Hudson spoke up. "Different rooms are being worked on and Erv is in here to be sure someone doesn't get hurt in the mess."

There was more apologizing as they went back out the door.

"I'll pay for that," stated Tommy of the kicked in door.

"Not a problem. Don't concern yourself," Hudson assured him.

The crowd of guests were waiting anxiously and Sophia again explained about the ruckus. When everyone had returned to food and drink, the Bears and Joe and Mike gathered back at their picnic table.

"Does anybody here believe Mr. Hudson is protecting his neighbors from injury in this house?" asked Tommy quietly.

"I don't doubt he's protecting something, but I doubt it's his neighbors," said Mike.

Sophia looked around at the men. "Please, this was--"

"Having this many armed men guarding your ranch, and especially an old house, isn't exactly normal, Mom. Joe and I were also redirected when we took a walk toward that new building. And I haven't heard anyone offer a tour of the place. Did you hear anything interesting from anyone, Dad? Did you get a chance to talk to Sheriff Hyland?"

Thomas shrugged. "Just that everybody is still surprised Andy sold the ranch. And nobody has really talked to any of the Millers in weeks. There's also some anger about the fences Hudson has put up. I asked Phil about that, but all Hudson told him is that he likes his privacy and that he's going to be holding big business meetings here and has to keep corporate spies away." The Indian snorted. "Sounds like a bunch of bullshit to me."

Joe allowed, "As someone mixed up in big business myself, I can see some of his reasoning. What I find odd is someone like Hudson buying a place like this just to have a hobby and a place to hold business meetings. Hobby or not, ranching isn't particularly profitable and he strikes me as a man unlikely to invest in something like this."

"This is close to Mexico," said Mike. "Could he be into drugs? That's big business and very profitable and he's getting an airplane. And he's talking about building an airport."

"It's not impossible, but we're not that close to the border and I don't think he could easily fly in drugs here." said Tommy. "In this kind of terrain it would be hard to be secretive. No mountains or even much in the way of hills. An unusual amount of air traffic would be noticed."

"Well, I bet he's hiding something in that old house," said Thomas.

"Or maybe he's just an arrogant, private, rich man," said Sofia, obviously not liking the disturbing discussion. "And I'm ready to go home."

No one argued with the suggestion.

Mitchell Hudson and Jordan Spike watched the Bears' pickup leave.

"I can't decide if they're going to be a problem or not," said the former.

"It's shit luck they had to show up now. And one of 'em has to be a smartass cop," grunted Spike.

Hudson thought quietly for several moments. Finally, "This is too big and it's too late to be changing plans anymore. There's too much at stake. We'd better take care of the one loose end left, to be safe. See that it doesn't come back to us."

"Yes, sir."

"His name is Buckshot," said Quint Santos. "He's an Appaloosa and he's our senior citizen. He'll take good care of you."

It was the next morning and Mike was being introduced to a horse. A white gelding with black spots. The detective eyed the animal cautiously. The animal looked sleepy and bored.

"A senior citizen?"

"He's almost twenty years old and pretty much retired." Quint smiled. "We keep him around for visiting cops with a sore foot to ride."

"Very funny."

"Come on, Mike," Tommy slapped a hand on a stool. "Step up and get on. Because of your foot, just lay across the saddle and swing your leg over. You can't come to a ranch and not go riding."

Joe had a crooked smile. He was already mounted on a brown mare named Ginger. Tommy had his saddle on a buckskin gelding named Rebel. His folks came from the barn leading horses as well. The Bears were taking their guests on a tour of the ranch.

"It's better than crutches, Mike," said Sophia with a smile.

"Not sure about that, but…" Mike took a breath and got on the stool. Dubious, he lay across the saddle and Tommy helped him swing his leg over and settle in the saddle. When Buckshot shifted on a foot, Mike grabbed the saddle horn.

"You're good," said Thomas. A twinkle in his eye, he added, "Now we can race to see--"

"Race!?" declared Mike.

His friends laughed, Tommy telling him, "Put your right foot in the stirrup to help you balance and leave the left one hang if it makes you feel better."

Mike did that and the Bears mounted up to lead them from the yard, Buckaroo and Pecos Bill running along with them. They went down to and along the narrow river. As they rode, Mike and Joe learned all about fun things like rattlesnakes, scorpions, black widow spiders and fire ants. When the two dogs began barking furiously and circling something, they reined in, and the two tenderfeet got a good first-hand look at a rattlesnake. As the dogs circled it, the viper's rattle buzzed and it hissed and struck out at them, forked tongue flicking in and out.

"Not crazy about snakes at all, thank you very much," grimaced Mike. Then worried, "Won't the dogs get bit?"

"It's the snake that's in trouble," said Thomas. "Those two hounds can take out a rattler no problem." He pulled his rifle from the scabbard. "But I think I'll help 'em out today. We run into a snake, we do kill 'em. We lose cattle and horses to snake bites every year."

Without seeming to aim, the elder Bears raised and fired the rifle, easily dispatching the snake with one, quick shot. None of the horses were disturbed by the sound. Tommy swung down and pulled a knife from a scabbard on his belt, stooping to cut the rattle off.

"Souvenir for you, Mike," he said and tossed it up to his friend.

Mike jumped in surprise, barely catching it. He gave a shiver, eyeing the rattle almost fearfully.

"Shit. I'm not sure I want a snake's tail."

"Take it home to your cat," said Joe. "He can play with it."

The hosts respected the rear ends of their guests, keeping their first ride to an hour. They spent the rest of the day relaxing and playing horseshoes and enjoyed another meal outdoors in the evening.

Joe called his people to see what they could learn about Mitchell Hudson of Atlanta, but a return call told them they found out nothing new to speak of. On the surface, the man was a hard-nosed businessman in land and construction.

On the morning of the third day of vacation, Mike took the plunge and graduated to walking without the crutch or the plastic boot. Tommy did the honors, removing the heavy-duty bandages and replacing them with a lightweight elastic wrap. Mike pulled out a sneaker that was one size too large that he'd brought along for the purpose. With a great deal of relief, the detective took a walk across the ranch yard. He was accompanied by Tommy, Joe, several cats, and the dogs.

"I feel liberated," said Mike brightly. "I can walk like an ordinary human being again."

"You walk like a cop who's been on crutches for a while," said Joe. "Don't get over ambitious."

Mike looked at him and smiled. "Joe's worried about me."

"Well, he is the reason you got hurt," Tommy allowed.

Joe scowled at him. "He doesn't need any reminders, Mr. Bears."

"Oh, I'm not ever going to forget that," snuffed Mike. "The next time--"

"No next times," stated Joe. "The NYPD can dig out their own possible assassins from now on."

Tommy had stopped and was watching the dust of a vehicle coming in on the ranch road. "That looks like a sheriff's SUV."

They stopped and waited. Seeing them, the driver of the car came on into the barn yard and stopped beside them.

It was the sheriff himself and Phil Hyland did not look happy.

Getting out, the man said, "Got some bad news, Tommy. Maybe we should get together with your folks."

"I'll get Dad. He's in the barn."

As Tommy hurried off, a screen door banged and they glanced over to see Sophia had come out the back door.

"Might as well go to the house," suggested Joe.

A few minutes later, they were all gathered in the backyard.

Sitting at a picnic table, Sophia asked, "What's happened, Phil? You're scaring me."

Hyland took a deep breath, slowly let it out, and told them, "Andy Miller's pickup was found at the bottom of an old gravel quarry this morning. Andy was in it."

Sophia's hands went to her face. With instant tears, she gasped, "Oh dear God."

She reached out a hand to Thomas. He took it and dropped down to sit beside her. Both looked shocked.

"Have his sons been notified?" Sophia choked.

"I know Carson is in Santa Fe and I think Frank is in Albuquerque. I've sent word to the local authorities to pass on the news."

"Which stone quarry?" Thomas wanted to know.

"That old one over on the Coombs' place. Kids went there this morning to go swimming. They're not supposed to, of course, and Russ has signs up, but…anyway, it looks like he just drove off the cliff."

"Suicide? No!" exclaimed Thomas almost defiantly. "I won't believe for one minute that Andy would kill himself."

"I agree," said Sophia, tears running down her cheeks. "Andy would never do that. He loved his boys too much to put them through that."

Tommy also shook his head. "They're right, Phil. Hell, even you should realize that. You knew Andy as well as we did."

Phil scowled and swallowed nervously. "We all know these last few months had to be hard on him. Maybe too hard."

"What we know is that he's been avoiding us since he sold the ranch and we haven't seen him at all the last couple of weeks," Sophia pointed out. "And if we did see him, he barely said hello."

"Which means he was depressed," noted Phil. "Besides, how could you drive off into that quarry by accident? You have to admit there was no reason at all for him to be near that quarry."

Thomas, tears in his eyes for his longtime friend and neighbor, stated, "No suicide! And no accident, Phil."

Hyland swallowed again. "If you're saying somebody killed him, Thomas, I find that hard to believe, too. Why would anybody murder Andy?"

"Do you know how long the pickup has been there? How long he's been dead?" asked Mike.

Phil looked at him. "Well, the kids admit they were there yesterday, too, and the pickup and Andy weren't. So, whatever happened, it had to happen in the night sometime."

"You've got a homicide detective right here, Phil," said Tommy. "A very good one. Why not let him take a look while the scene is still there?"

"Well," said Hyland, "there's a detective coming from the Highway Patrol, as routine, but I guess it wouldn't hurt if you want a look. You remember where the quarry is, Tommy?"

The Indian gave him a quirky smile. "I used to be one of the kids who snuck in and swam there."

"I should go…maybe…and see…" Thomas stammered.

"No, you shouldn't, Dad," said his son. "When you pay your last respects will be soon enough."

Thomas didn't argue.

———

"I'm not sure how much help I can be, Tommy," said Mike as they drove. "I mean, I'm ready to do what I can, but things are probably done different here and…well, this is one time I don't want to step on someone's toes."

"Just take a look, Mike. Another pair of eyes can't hurt. And it will help my folks grasp the loss. I can't believe Andy would do this to himself."

"You thinking Hudson might be involved?" said Joe.

"It's a tempting thought, but just because we don't like the man doesn't mean he's a killer."

"Even if all his men carry weapons and are unfriendly," noted Mike.

"Even if," said Tommy. "Let's just have a look."

It was almost an hour's drive to their destination. Most of it over dusty, gravel roads.

"These kind of roads is why there are rock and gravel quarries on almost every ranch around here," Tommy explained. "Way cheaper than any kind of pavement or black top."

"And you came all this way just to go swimming?" said Joe. "You've got a river in your back yard."

"The river is too shallow for much more than splashing around," explained Tommy. "That was okay, but if you really wanted to swim and dive, the quarries were the place to go. And it was a much shorter trip on horseback, which was how us kids mostly got around."

"In this kind of country, where the hell did the water come from to fill a hole so you could swim?" wondered Mike.

"When it rains, it pours, and fills up the holes. Dry summers we made do with the river or the big water troughs where cattle came to drink. Those were filled by windmills from deep wells."

Coming up on the gravel pit they saw a Sheriff's SUV with a deputy leaning against it.

"Stop here, Tommy," said Mike. "Let's have a look at where he supposedly drove off."

Tommy did and they got out.

"You're the guys Sheriff Hyland said were coming to have a look," said the deputy, not a question. "He's down in the pit."

"We'll get there," said Mike, his official detective tone kicking in. "Whereabouts did the pickup go off?"

The deputy pointed. "Over that way about twenty yards."

"They didn't mark it off?" frowned Mike.

The man shrugged. "It's just tire tracks. Nothing else."

Mike and Tommy and Joe walked that way until Mike motioned them to stop and he went on alone. He circled and slowly worked his way in. He couldn't see anything amiss. No skidding, no braking. Just the tire tracks leading right up to the edge. Except…could those scuff marks be boot prints? He stooped to study them.

"Mike, can I come over to you?" Tommy called.

Mike straightened. "I'll meet you halfway." He did. "What's up?"

"We're being watched."

Without being obvious, Mike glanced carefully around. Mystified, he said, "How can you know that? There's not even anything to hide behind."

Tommy gave a light sniff. "I am half Indian. I know these things."

That earned him an annoyed look.

With a crooked smile, the Indian said, "Okay, it might look flat, but there are dish bowls in the ground where a man can slip along and lie flat without being seen. And I saw a flash of sun, probably off binoculars."

Mike took a breath. "Okay. Well, I found what look like boot prints over there near the edge that could mean someone gave that pickup a helping push. So maybe we should give whoever is watching something to think about."

He stooped and Tommy stooped with him as Mike did some pointing around. Tommy got into the act by nodding. He did ask, "You really saw possible boot prints?"

"I did." They stood up. "Now Let's make it more interesting." And Mike walked over to the deputy. "Officer, I'd like your help here, please. Your name?"

"Evan Tripp," said the man, straightening.

"Deputy Tripp, have you got a way to put up some police tape?"

"Yes, sir. I carry some stakes for that. We don't have trees or many bushes out here if we need to do that."

"Very good. I'd like you to put it up around that area where the pickup went off. Be careful not to step into that area yourself. Say thirty feet across."

"Yes, sir. I can do that. You see something important?"

"It could be, Deputy, and we don't want it to get messed up."

Tripp got busy and Mike and Tommy rejoined Joe, who asked, "Did you really find something?"

"Possible scuff marks that could be boot prints but not clear enough to be any real help. But our Indian friend says somebody's watching and I thought I'd give whoever it is something to think about."

"Aren't you clever," remarked Joe with a little snort as the three men climbed back into the pickup.

"Hey, making suspects nervous is a part of my job description," said the detective. "Even if I don't have any suspects."

"If somebody's watching, somebody is nervous, and if somebody is nervous, somebody did something," said Tommy. "And Andy did not commit suicide."

The gravel pit was deep and it covered at least five acres. Dug into the bottom of it were more holes, several of which held water. Several kids were sitting around one of those, two bareback horses dozed nearby. Sheriff Hyland's SUV was parked there along with a jeep. Laying on its side near one of the pit's high walls, was a half-burned pickup. The sheriff and another man were there and came over to meet them when they got out.

Hyland introduced the elderly man with him, the jeep and ranch owner Russ Coombs. "Good to see you, Tommy," said Coombs, weatherbeaten and in his late seventies. He waved at the pickup. "Except, not liking any of this. Seeing Andy...." He shook his head.

"I know, Russ," said Tommy.

They turned to the old pickup truck which was lying on its side. The windshield had smashed on impact and the body of Andy Miller was halfway out of it. The front end of the pickup was partially burned and the fire had blackened Miller's clothes and burned away some of his hair, but not much more than that. Keeping a careful distance away, Mike slowly circled the area. Mostly to study the body and pickup and ground. Partly to put on a show for any suspects who might be watching.

Finally Mike rejoined the others and reported, "I believe the intention was for the pickup to explode and burn when it crashed. When all it did was crash, someone purposely set it on fire and left in a hurry to avoid being seen and to be out of here when the gas tank did explode. Except that didn't happen either. The gas tank hadn't ruptured in the crash and the fire that was set at the front didn't get close enough to cause the gas tank to heat and explode. Whatever they used to set the fire just burned awhile and died out. There's just nothing around the pickup to burn. It's a rock quarry. A lab should be able to tell what kind of accelerant was used and should prove it didn't come accidently from the gas tank or anything else in the pickup." Mike took a slow breath. "Until the autopsy, we can't be sure how Mr. Miller died. I will say that the botched job with the fire makes it very suspicious. And the boot marks I saw up top…well, I think this pickup was pushed off that drop, not driven. I'm afraid, Sheriff, that I believe Andy Miller was already dead when they did it."

"Son of a bitch," said Hyland.

"Yes," agreed Tommy gruffly.

"I know he's a good friend and it's hard to see him like this," said Mike, "but you should leave him and the pickup untouched until the State's CSU can do a thorough job. I would be interested to hear what they find and about what the autopsy turns up."

"I'll do that," said Hyland with a nod. "And thanks for taking the time to help us out."

"I'm very sorry about your friend," said Mike.

Phil nodded again and went to get on the radio.

Coombs stared at the scene, sorrow in his expression. "This is a hell of a thing. Poor Andy. He deserved a lot better."

Tommy agreed, "He did, but hopefully we'll get to the bottom of it." Then, "Didn't see you at the Hudson's barbeque, Russ."

"That bastard. I won't ever set foot on that ranch again. I don't know what he did to force Andy to sell, but I do know he wouldn't have. Not willingly. I wouldn't be surprised if Hudson had something to do with this. The sonofabitch."

"I don't understand it either, Russ, but maybe don't get too verbal about it. Right now we need to keep peace in the neighborhood so they can find out what happened to Andy."

They said their goodbyes and headed back to the ranch, Joe saying, "Not sure Hudson's going to be a peaceful neighbor."

"He sure doesn't seem to be making any friends," allowed Mike.

"Well, tonight we'll come back to the pit and watch to see if Mike's little tricks with the tape and finger pointing stirs anyone out," said Tommy.

Mike frowned. "That was the idea, but how do you hide a car so you can watch from it in this flat country? There aren't any places to hide."

"Like I said, the country isn't all that flat," said Tommy. "There's lots of dips a man can disappear in. We'll ride over and it's easier to hide horses--"

"You're riding back? All the way back here? At night? In the dark?" the city cop's voice rose.

"We are going to ride back here," corrected Tommy. "And yes, it's usually dark at night."

"Makes sense keeping watch," said Joe. "Hudson's men would never consider that. When they don't see a car or pickup, they won't have any qualms about--"

"I have qualms!" interrupted Mike. "Horses do not have headlights! Can they see any better than we can in the dark? How do we even find our way back over here?"

"Mike, where's your tough, brave, nail-'em-down cop? You hunt down big bad nasties in New York City," said Tommy. "How can you be afraid of the dark?"

The brave cop's eyes narrowed. "Only fools don't worry about what's in the dark."

"You'll be fine," said Tommy.

"We have complete faith in you," said Joe.

"The two of you can go to hell."

It was dark, and cooling, and they had jackets on.

Tommy Bears checked his father's scoped rifle once more and then slid it into the rifle scabbard on his saddled horse. He also wore a holstered handgun on his belt, as did Joe Panelli. Mike Brennen wore his gun in a holster at the small of his back.

But Mike's gun, or even the darkness, weren't the uppermost thing in the detective's mind at the moment. His eyes were on the black horse in front of him.

"Where's the old fart, Buckshot?" he asked.

"Buckshot is white, Mike," said Tommy. "We need to take what precautions we can not to be seen."

"Widowmaker is almost as old as--" started Thomas.

"Widowmaker! You're putting me on a horse you call Widowmaker?"

"That was when he was young," said Lucas Rivers, making no effort to hide his amusement. "He's a pussy cat now."

Mike glared at him. "If you knew my cat, you wouldn't use that comparison. He's never been a pussy anything. And just how many widows did Widowmaker make?"

Joe pointed out, "You've really no problem, Mike. You don't have a wife."

"And it was your idea," Tommy reminded him, "to draw out the bad guys using the yellow tape and all that stooping and pointing."

"I was thinking like a New York City cop, not a Wild West marshal."

"Well, now you're both," allowed Tommy.

"Widowmaker did not make any widows, Mike," said Sophia. "That's just a name from the story of Pecos Bill. He's a gentle old horse."

Mike wasn't looking all that convinced.

Joe said, "Just get on the damn horse, Mike."

Mike closed his eyes and took a deep breath. Then, opening them, he climbed onto the stool and into the saddle. Widowmaker snorted and shook his head.

Mike took a quick breath. "What's he doing?"

"He's just a little unhappy about having to go out at night," said Rivers.

"You're not helping, Lucas," said Thomas.

"That's fine," snarled Mike. "I'm unhappy about going out at night, too. So we should get going before me and Widowmaker change our minds."

"Good idea, Marshal Brennen," said Tommy. "Let's get this posse moving."

The three-man posse moved out and had an uneventful ride, though Tommy kept them at the job a good part of the way. Mike strangled the saddle horn and gritted his teeth. Widowmaker showed his displeasure with Mike's bouncing by flattening his ears.

"I was wounded you know," Mike reminded Tommy.

"I'm pretty sure that you're healed up enough so that this little ride won't cause you any trouble," allowed the unsympathetic Tommy.

"Easy for you to say!"

Mr. Bears did give the tenderfeet frequent walking rests, but he still kept them moving.

After what seemed like an uncomfortably long time to Mike, Tommy announced, "We're there."

Now Joe was even a little skeptical. "We're there? Even I have to ask, how you can be sure?"

"Exactly," said Mike, rubbing his sore butt. "It all looks the same in the daylight and in the dark you can't even be sure of that."

"You white men need to have more faith in your handsome Sioux scout," allowed Tommy. "And as a kid I made this exact ride hundreds of times." Then, unexpectedly, "Hold onto your saddle horns, gentlemen. This is a little steep."

"What do you think I've been hold--shit!" Widowmaker was suddenly sliding down the side of a gully. Mike all but fell off over the horse's head. "You did that on purpose, Bears!"

"Maybe a little." Tommy smirked in the darkness.

"Your sense of humor with us city boys can be trying, Mr. Bears," said Joe.

They dismounted and Tommy hobbled the horses so they wouldn't wander off. From a saddlebag, he pulled out three small communication radios and three equally small binoculars.

"Lucas and Quint use the radios to keep in touch with Dad when they're out checking cattle," said Tommy. Passing them out, he gave his friends a quick lesson on how to use them, finishing with, "Keep the volume low."

They climbed out of the gully, his friends giving Mike a hand. At the top, the detective glanced around.

"No trees to hide behind," he noted sarcastically. "We going to hide in the pit?"

Tommy said, "I'm going to find you comfortable spots to lie down and...."

"We're lying down?" Mike piped up. "You tell us tales of ants and snakes and scorpions and now you want us to lie down?"

"Don't forget the black widow spiders," said Joe.

Mike snorted in frustration. "Right. This is my night for widows."

"I'll try to pick places where you'll be safe," promised Tommy, but there was another smirk in his tone.

Turning on Joe, Mike said, "Does he know he's not funny?"

"I admit he does seem to be enjoying our little discomforts out here. I'm not crazy about lying on the ground in the dark myself."

"Again, you have to have faith in your Sioux scout--"

"Fuck the Indian crap," griped Mike. "If I get bit by something, you're fired!"

Tommy spread them out around the yellow tape circle so they could keep watch in all directions. Mike found it a challenge to keep his concentration on who might show up. He spent at least as much time trying to watch the ground around him for the creepy crawly things. Not that he could see much in the darkness. Joe did his share of keeping an eye on the ground as well. It was a little unnerving knowing what was out there.

Fortunately it wasn't for nothing. About one in the morning, Tommy's voice came quietly over the radio.

"Four-wheeler coming. Pretty sure there's two riders."

"Let them get their noses behind the tape," said Mike.

"Yes, sir," said Tommy.

"Good idea," quipped Joe.

"Smartass posse," grouched Mike.

The men on the four-wheeler were obviously not worried about being seen. The vehicle's headlights were on and they were moving at a good clip. Coming cross-country, they had avoided any sheriff's car that might be watching the ranch entrance on the highway. They stopped a short distance from the tape and turned off the engine, but left the lights pointed at the encircled ground. Disembarking, they carried flashlights for more light. One carried a scoped rifle. They stopped at the tape and shone their lights over the area.

"What the hell was he seeing?" said the rifleman. "I don't see anything."

The driver, whose voice they recognized as Abe Dorn's, said, "He's a cop. Cops are always making stuff up just to be a pain in the ass."

"Well, he did that. We just bounced all the way over here on our asses for nothing," said his partner.

"Maybe not for nothing from our point of view," spoke up Mike but without revealing himself. "You boys showing up makes the night interesting."

Both men twisted and half-crouched, flashlights moving quickly in an effort to find the speaker.

"Who the hell's that?" demanded Dorn.

"Just your pain in the ass cop," said Mike. "And I'd appreciate it if you'd put the rifle on the ground. Along with any other toys you might have."

"What's this about?" Dorn continued to demand.

"Put the damned guns down! Now!" insisted Mike sharply. "You're covered, so be gentlemen."

"Shit. Fine!" griped Dorn. To his partner, "Just do it, Matt."

Matt laid the rifle down and they also pulled guns from holsters to lay them on the ground.

"We're licensed to carry," said Dorn gruffly.

"I'll bet you are," said Tommy.

He and Mike and Joe rose up from the ground, guns aimed at the two angry men.

"What the hell's going on?" Dorn once more wanted to know.

"That's my question," said Mike as they closed in on them. "Who's your buddy, Abe?"

"Matt Evers," the man answered for himself.

"Matt's a crack shot," said Abe. "I brought him out here to try his luck with coyotes."

"Did you now," said Tommy. "That's illegal this time of year."

Dorn shrugged. "Didn't know that. Just heard they were a real nuisance with the cattle. Didn't think anybody would care."

"Coyotes might," said Joe.

Tommy added, "I also don't think Russ Coombs gave you permission to be on his land, so you're trespassing."

"That's two good reasons to arrest you," said Mike. "Makes it legal for me to exercise my oath as a police officer and take you to the local authorities. And it's a reason for me to ask you why you came out to this particular area to do your hunting."

Dorn fixed his furious glare on the detective, saying, "We don't need to answer any of your fucking questions and we'll be out of jail so fast your head will be spinning."

The man was most likely right, but it would still be on record that two of Hudson's men had come nosing around the scene of a suspicious death.

Tommy went to get the horses. When he got back, he waved at the prisoners to mount Widowmaker.

"Fuck you," growled Dorn. "I'm not getting on any damned horse."

"Then you'll be walking," allowed Tommy. "And it's a good long walk to the ranch's front gate."

"Want to flip to see who gets the saddle and who gets the horse's ass?" smirked Joe.

"Sonofabitch," said Evers and reached for the saddle horn.

"The saddle's mine," growled Dorn, shoving forward.

The posse thoroughly enjoyed watching the two outlaws struggle to get onto the gelding. Mike especially so when Widowmaker bucked a little as Evers scrambled on behind the saddle.

"Either of you got wives?" asked the cop. "Widowmaker likes to keep his reputation up to snuff."

Mike gratefully rode the four-wheeler. Tommy and Joe rode their horses one on each side of their prisoners. Tommy led Widowmaker, keeping them at the trot. Dorn held onto the horn for dear life. Evers held onto Dorn for dear life. The horse's ears were flat back as he shook his head and threw in crow hops every now and then. By the time they reached the gate and the Sheriff's deputy there, Abe and Matt's language had greatly deteriorated. Mike had the deputy radio in.

When he had, the deputy reported, "They want me to bring them in and also asked that Detective Brennen come along."

"I can do that. I like to see my arrests get to the station," said Mike, smiling at the angry Dorn and Evers.

Tommy nodded and told him, "We'll take the horses and the wheels back to the ranch and come in to pick you up."

"See you later," said Mike.

Sheriff Hyland had been called and he was there waiting when Mike and the prisoners arrived. No surprise the two men refused to talk about anything and Dorn immediately made his one call. In spite of the early morning hour, Jordan Spike and a lawyer, Stuart Brew, showed up within the hour.

"This is bullshit," Spike declared. "You should be asking this damned city cop what the hell he was doing out there with his nosey buddies."

"It was an authorized stakeout," Hyland fibbed.

The sheriff had been a little out of sorts when Mike had filled him in on the night's little adventure but went along with it.

Brew sniffed. "And they caught two coyote hunters. Hardly seems worth the time and effort, Sheriff Hyland. They got us all out of bed for nonsense."

"I don't feel it was nonsense," allowed Mike. "It played out the way we thought it would. Now we're all wondering why you boys were interested in a crime scene."

"What the hell are you talking about? What crime scene?" asked the annoyed Spike.

"Don't bite, Jordan," said Brew. "They're fishing and there's nothing for them to catch. I'll get a dismissal for these ridiculous charges from the judge and we won't be back here at all. Take your men and go home."

As Spike and his two men left the building, they passed Tommy and Joe coming in. All three gave smirks to the posse members. Brew was snapping his briefcase shut when they walked into the room.

The lawyer gave them all a cold look and stated, "This was all a bunch of nonsense, Sheriff Hyland. If anything like it happens again, restraining orders will be put in place. Mr. Hudson is a very busy man and won't put up with it."

He walked out.

"I'm betting Mr. Hudson won't enjoy his breakfast when he hears how the night turned out for his men," said Joe.

Tommy gave Hyland an apologetic smile. "I'm sorry you were dragged out of bed, Phil. We were just interested to see if we'd get a nibble at our bait."

"Like I told Mike, I'd just like a heads up next time," said the sheriff. "And what exactly did this prove?"

"Technically, I suppose it only shows unusual interest by Hudson over the death of the man he bought a ranch from," admitted Mike with some disappointment.

"He did send men out," said Joe. "In the middle of the night and right to where we were waiting. That's something."

Tommy nodded. "It does beg more questions about Mr. Hudson."

"I'll keep that in mind," said Hyland. "And I'll call tomorrow morning after the autopsy, let you know what they find."

"Appreciate that, Phil," said Tommy.

They ate a late breakfast in the morning and were drinking the last of their coffee when Hyland called. Tommy answered it and was listening quietly until something made his eyebrows go up.

"What?" asked Mike.

Tommy held his hand up to wait and soon said, "Okay, Phil. Thanks a lot for getting back to us with it."

He hung up and sat back down at the table. Sophia was there, too, and joined in with the questioning looks.

"Andy was definitely dead when he went off that cliff," Tommy told them. "And you'll never guess what killed him."

"Then don't make us guess, dear," said his mother solemnly. "We're talking about a friend here."

"Rattlesnake bites. At least six of them that they found and maybe more."

"What?" exclaimed Sophia. "That's…that's almost as crazy as suicide. There is no way Andy would get himself into a situation to get even one bite let alone six."

"No man is going to sit still and allow that," snorted Thomas. "And it would have to be more than one snake. No one rattler is going to strike that many times."

"It's what killed him," allowed their son. "He had enough venom in him to kill half a dozen men."

"But they still tried to burn him?" Joe was mystified. "That doesn't make sense either."

"Yes it does," said Mike. They all looked at him and he went on, "The fire was supposed to burn him bad enough to cover up the snake bites. We were supposed to think he was killed by the crash and the fire. Suicide. Now it sounds like murder-by-snake to me." The cop shuddered at the thought. "Suspicious but not like death by bullets and a lot harder to prove murder in a court of law."

Tommy's expression was hard. "I think it's time for another visit to the Big H."

"Now, Tommy, I don't want you boys getting--" started Sophia.

"We're just going to return their four-wheeler, Mom. Least we can do after our little confrontation last night."

"I like it," said Joe. "Maybe we can discover a pen of rattlesnakes."

"I can do without that thought," cringed Mike. "What I'm more interested in doing is stirring up the two-legged snakes."

Shortly they loaded the four-wheeler into the bed of one of the big pickups and were off to maybe stir the pot a little.

The fancy gate was closed and locked this time and the eye of the surveillance camera looked at them coldly. When Tommy pushed the button for attention, an equally cold voice asked, "State your business."

Tommy smiled nicely at the camera. "Good morning to you, too. I'm Tommy Bears, along with my friends, Mike and Joe. We're here to return your four-wheeler vehicle that went coyote hunting last night."

It was quiet for more almost a minute and Tommy was about to push the button again when the voice returned.

"Just leave it at the gate," it said bluntly.

"Can't do that," stated Tommy firmly. "We really need a ramp to get it off. Just pushing it out could bust it up. That would make us look bad and..."

Another long pause, then the gate clicked and slowly opened.

"I knew that Bears' charm would get us in," said Mike.

As they approached the headquarters, they saw the man named Erv. He was in a Western hat, shirt, jeans, and boots. There was a modern holster with a gun clipped to his Western belt.

"Not bothering to hide the guns today," remarked Joe.

Tommy stopped and ran his window down, again using his smiling charm. He received none in return.

Erv pointed at the old barn. "There's a ramp for unloading over there."

"Thank you, Erv," said Tommy.

Erv did not say, "Your welcome."

Sitting behind Tommy, Mike ran his window down, too. "Good morning, Erv. How's your day going?"

Erv didn't share his day, just stepped back to glower at them.

"I think they're having a really tough time adjusting to Western hospitality," decided Joe as they drove on.

As they approached the ramp, they saw they had greeters awaiting them. Jordan Spike and Abe Dorn, also in Western wear and also wearing guns, did not look hospitable either.

Once more Tommy smiled and greeted, "Good morning, gentlemen. It's nice of you to take time to come say hi."

"Hi, Abe," said Mike. "You're looking rested after your busy night of coyote hunting. We thought we'd better return your mechanical horse in case you want to try again tonight."

"We're busy," said Spike sourly. "Unload the damned thing and leave."

Tommy expertly, but unhurriedly, maneuvered the pickup back up against the ramp. All three of them got out of the truck. Mike and Joe let the tailgate down while Tommy climbed in ready to handle the machine.

Joe said, "If I may suggest, Tommy, it would be a good idea for them to check the vehicle over. We wouldn't want it said that we returned damaged goods."

"Just unload the damned thing!" Jordy said again, still sour.

Mike had approached Dorn with a hospitable smile. "Did you report to Mitch that you didn't find anything incriminating at the murder scene last night, Abe? Or was he just pissed at you for getting arrested?"

Abe glared. "Fuck off."

Mike grimaced. "Your clothes say you're getting into the Western spirit, but you've got a long way to go to get that 'Howdy, how are you?' spirit."

Joe had moseyed up to Spike. "You seem to be on the sour side this morning, Jordy. Not used to short nights?" When he only got the sour look again, he went on to ask, "I'm curious. How'd you come up with a lawyer so quick in the middle of the night in the middle of New Mexico?"

"Mr. Brew is Mr. Hudson's personal attorney and lives here," said Spike gruffly. "Now back that thing off and get the hell out of here."

Tommy started pushing the four-wheeler out of the truck.

Mike had looked past Dorn and now cheerily announced, "Hey, Mr. Hudson is coming to say howdy."

Mitchell Hudson was walking toward them from the new house. He did not appear to have much in the way of morning cheeriness.

"Good morning, Mitch," Mike greeted. "Beautiful day, isn't it. But then, I guess almost every day is beautiful in the Sunshine State."

Mitchell Hudson did not acknowledge the greeting or the beautiful day. And Detective Brennen's expression suddenly turned cool and hard.

"You do know that two of your men trespassed on another man's ranch," he said flatly. "And intruded on a police line at a murder scene."

Tommy had finished pushing the four-wheeler out of the truck. He turned on Hudson and said in a tone colder than Mike's, "And it was Andrew Miller's body that was found."

His jaw tight, Hudson said, "I heard. It's a terrible thing, but what makes it a murder scene? I understood it was suicide. Man drove his truck off a cliff."

"The sheriff asked Mike to take a look and he determined it was murder," said Joe. "As a homicide cop, Mike's very good at determining something like that."

"And I was interested in also determining if someone would care enough about what I was doing to come take a look." Mike smiled crookedly. "And it really looked like your boys cared a lot driving all that way."

"Make what you want of it," said Mitchell gruffly, "but the only law my men might have broken was hunting coyotes. And they didn't break it because they didn't shoot any." He paused. "It's too bad what happened to Mr. Miller, but he and I finished our business months ago and I haven't seen him since. If you think it's murder, you'll have to look elsewhere for suspects."

Mike and Joe and Tommy kept their eyes on him for a few moments and then Tommy slammed the tailgate.

"Guess we're done here, then," he said.

"You are," Hudson agreed solemnly, "and I think if we are going to be good neighbors, Mr. Bears, we'd both be better off minding our own business." Then, "Give my regards to Mr. and Mrs. Bears."

The tone of voice he used for the latter did not sit well with Tommy. He said, "I'll do that. And I'd appreciate it if you never visited them again. For any reason."

The two men exchanged unneighborly looks. Then Hudson turned and walked back toward the house.

The three visitors climbed into the pickup. As Tommy started to drive off, Mike leaned out his window to look at Spike and asked, "Hey, Jordy, do you or your friend Abe happen to know where we can find some rattlesnakes?"

Spike had no response, but Dorn's scowl deepened and there was a moment's surprise in his eyes.

"Well, damn," said Mike as Tommy drove through the opened gate. "I thought they'd at least invite us to lunch."

"I'm pretty sure we've worn out our welcome at the Big H," allowed Joe. "I have to say, Tommy, that I have a little concern for your folks. I hope Hudson doesn't give them a hard time."

"And I can't help but feel that the bastard is behind Miller's killing," said Mike. "Going to be hard for Sophia and Thomas to be good neighbors when you think the neighbor killed your friend."

"I sure as hell don't like it," said Tommy tightly, "but what's to be done about it? We've got no proof that it was Hudson behind Andy's death."

"Except for the coyote hunters, which is zero help," admitted Mike.

Tommy sighed in frustration. "For now I don't see where we can go with it. And my folks are already on edge over all this, so we'll give it a rest. I do know that I'm not going to leave them alone with this hanging over their heads. I'm going to make the ranch my home until I'm sure they're safe and Hudson won't bother them."

―――――

"The cop asked you about rattlesnakes?" Mitchell Hudson said with sharp annoyance. He was in his office with Spike and Dorn. "They must have done an autopsy which means you fucked up and the body didn't burn. No wonder they didn't believe it was suicide."

"Not our fault the truck didn't burn when it crashed," said Dorn defensively. "We had to make do with--"

"And your little hunting trip in the night was another screw up," steamed Hudson. "What the hell am I paying you for?"

Dorn shifted uncomfortably. "It's that damned cop. He's--"

"There's nothing they can prove," spoke up Spike. "It's just snake bites. There's nothing to say how Miller and his truck ended up where they are. Like Brew said, they're just fishing."

"And they could end up catching something," grouched Hudson. "So I'm thinking we better have some insurance until this is over." He drummed his fingers on his desk. "The kind of people coming to this meeting expect complete privacy with no outside problems. They will not take kindly to anymore screw-ups. The Bears, and their ranch hands, aren't the problem. It's the other three we need to get to back off and I know of only one person who would make them do that."

Spike smirked. "Mrs. Bears."

"Exactly. We need to make her our guest for a couple of days but be damned sure she cannot point fingers at us. Keep her hooded and away from this house. We'll make sure the cop and the son know what could happen if they come making trouble. We'll return her when this conference is over and go back to being disagreeable neighbors."

"I'd like to butt heads with those three assholes," grumbled Dorn. "Especially that fucking cop."

"Can't afford to risk that kind of trouble," said Hudson. "Let's get through this first meeting and then see where we are. With luck the assholes will finish their vacation and go home."

Spike shook his head. "I have a feeling they won't make it that easy."

"I've got too much at stake," stated Hudson. "I've spent a lot of money to build this place and I do not want a war with the neighbors. Once this meeting is over, I will buy out the Bears, one way or another just like I did with Miller."

"And if the son won't sell?" asked Spike.

"Then he will disappear."

The vacationers spent the day fishing and being lazy. The few fish they caught, Sophia added to the evening meal. When the cleanup was finished, the men gathered in the bunkhouse for a game of poker. The game had been in progress for about an hour when Sophia stuck her nose in.

"Gentlemen, Ken Colwell called. Janet twisted her ankle this afternoon and is down in the dumps. He asked if I could come spend some time with her. I'll be back before midnight."

"Not sure I like you going out now, Mom," said Tommy, still thinking of their unfriendly neighbor.

"Don't be silly, Tommy," she said. "I run over to see the Colwells all the time. Their place isn't that far."

Mike was glaring at his dismal hand. Dismal was how his luck had been going the entire game. He tossed in his cards and stood up.

"I'll go along and keep her company," he said. "I lose any more money, I'll have to walk home."

"We came in my plane," said Joe, "and the amount of money I've won from you wouldn't buy a gallon of gas."

"It was hard-earned money," sniffed Mike.

Sophia was shaking her head. "For goodness sake, it's not necessary for you to come. What are you going to do while two women are gossiping?"

"Maybe I can gossip with the husband," allowed Mike. "Or better yet, I can sit outside and enjoy looking at the stars. I don't see them much in New York."

"Take him, Mom," said Tommy. "He's whining more with every hand."

"Very funny," grunted Mike. "I'm sure Sophia and her friend will be better company than you oafs."

As they walked toward the pickup, Sophia said, "I'd better drive, Mike. I know you boys have been drinking beer."

"Speaking of beer, give me a minute to visit the little boy's room and I'll be right with you." And Mike hurried to the house.

He did take a piss, but he also wanted to pick up his gun, clipping the holster at the small of his back. He didn't have any expectations he'd need it, but he was undressed traveling without it. Besides, a good Western marshal would never go anywhere without his gun. He was soon climbing into the pickup beside Sofia.

She smiled as she drove off. "So the game wasn't going well for you?"

Mike snorted. "The kind of cards I was getting could lead to a gunfight at the OK Corral."

"If I remember right that particular gunfight was not about poker," said Sophia.

"Hey. This is the Wild West. Don't disillusion me."

"Then I suppose I shouldn't tell you that it didn't happen in New Mexico, either."

"Then in Texas?"

"Arizona."

Mike grinned. "Guess I need to study up on my gunfights."

Out on the darkened highway, Sophia glanced in the rearview mirror and frowned.

"My goodness that car is coming up fast. And the brights must be on. Of course, fast is the normal speed out here because of the distances between places."

Mike twisted for a look back. He could tell it was a large pickup by the position of the headlights, which were on bright. And it was definitely coming fast.

"Well, hopefully he'll pass and…oh good, he's coming around," said Sophia with relief.

But when the vehicle pulled out to pass, another pickup was right behind it and closed in tight to Sophia's rear bumper. The one that had passed suddenly pulled in right in front of her and started to slow.

"What are they doing?" she said with annoyance.

Brennen wasn't liking it at all. "Sophia, the man who called…"

"Ken Colwell."

"Are you sure it was him? You've talked on the phone with him before?"

"Well, not too much. It's Janet and I who talk."

"So you really can't be sure?"

Sophia gave him a quick glance. "Why, Mike? Who else--"

Mike reached around and pulled his gun, keeping it out of sight. He was not going to use it if it meant risking the life of Sophia Bears, but he sure as hell would use it if it meant protecting her. Right now he was desperately wishing he was the one behind the steering wheel.

"I don't suppose you brought your cell phone, Sophia?" He hadn't thought to bring his.

"It's not something we usually do, Mike. Cells don't work out here."

"Yeah. Right. Let's try this, Sophia. Pull out and pass this guy."

She sent him another glance, a hint of fear creeping in. "What do you think is going on, Mike? Why…?"

"Please, try and pass him."

"Okay…"

She started to pull out. The vehicle in front immediately blocked her. She was being forced to slow, the pickups tight on her front and rear bumpers.

"Okay. Now this is beginning to scare me a little, Mike. Tell me what's happening."

Instead of answering her, he told her firmly, "Listen to me, Sophia. This is what I want you to do and I don't want any argument. I want you to slam on the brakes, jump out, and run as fast as you can. Get out into the dark pasture and find a place to drop and hide. I'm going to go out this side and keep their attention on me."

"That's crazy. You know who this is? Why do I--?"

"You just have to! It's dark. Go fast! They won't be expecting the move. They don't know I'm with you."

"They who? What--?"

"Undo your seatbelt and go!"

Frightened and reluctant, Sophia did as she was told, freeing her seatbelt. Then she unlatched the door and hit the brakes. She did a good job of pulling it off as she threw the door open, jumped out, and ran into the dark New Mexico pastureland.

Mike had undone his seatbelt and he was out his door even quicker. When he hit the ground, he skidded to a stop, brought his gun up and started firing at the back window of the pickup in front. When that exploded, the detective twisted and fired at the windshield of the pickup in back. It didn't shatter, but the bullets punched holes through it. The big problem for Mike was that he only had the one clip of a sixteen shots. When the bullets ran dry, that would be it.

There came a lot of cussing and shouting as men scrambled out of the pickups, dodging the unexpected gunfire. When a man came out of the passenger side of the pickup behind, Mike nailed him with a couple shots. The guy cried out and went down.

"Don't kill the son of a bitch! I want him alive!!" someone shouted.

Mike turned back toward the front pickup looking for more bodies to shoot at before he ran out of bullets. Instead, a bullet tore into his left thigh. With a grunt, he went to his knees. He still fired on a couple of men coming from the front and had the satisfaction of seeing one go down with a yelp.

And then he was hit on the head from behind and darkness took him.

Some impolite person poured water over his head and Mike coughed and sputtered.

"Wake up, cop!" It was Jordan Spike's snarling voice.

Mike moaned and tried to raise his hands toward his throbbing head. He couldn't. They were tied behind him.

"Get him up," said Spike, tossing away an empty bucket.

Two men grabbed Mike, one on each arm, and roughly pulled him to his feet. He gasped out in pain as he was instantly reminded of the bullet in his leg.

"Did that hurt, cop?" smirked Jordan. "That's a real shame."

"Nothing to say, smartass?" said Abe Dorn, holding onto Mike's right arm.

Matt Evers, on the other arm, gave the detective's bleeding thigh a hard punch. Mike gave a strangled cry and would have gone down again but for the two men holding him up.

"That's for making me ride a horse's ass last night," snarled Evers.

"And this..." Dorn gave the leg another punch. "...is for setting up your fucking yellow tape trick."

Spike leaned into Mike's face. "And why the hell were you with the woman tonight? You messed with us and shot up two of my men, damn you!"

"Sorry you weren't...one of them," managed Mike.

"Fuck you!" declared Spike and backhanded him.

Blood flew from Mike's nose, Dorn and Evers more or less keeping him on his feet. The detective blinked, trying to clear his head.

"You know...beating on a cop is a serious offense. So is shooting him. And I intend to arrest all of--"

Jordan hit him again. More blood flew from Mike's nose and now from a torn lip. Mike sagged. This wasn't going well. Still, he opened his mouth again when keeping it shut would have been smarter. "Okay. Now you're really...making me mad. You are...definitely...under arrest."

"Smartass cop," growled Spike and got in Mike's face again. "Just so you know, your little trick for the Bears' woman didn't work. We got her and if anyone wants to see her again, they're going to behave themselves."

Now Mike glared angrily. "You hurt her, Tommy will skin you alive. He'll probably skin you alive anyway for--"

"You don't need to be worrying about it, cop. You've caused us some trouble, but you won't be around long enough to cause us anymore," smirked Spike. Then, "Abe, cut me a piece of his bloody jeans."

"I can do that," said Dorn with a twisted smile.

Mike was pushed to his knees as Dorn pulled a knife from a pocket and flipped it open to stoop beside the bleeding leg. Mike winced as the man yanked the blood-sticky pant leg away from his thigh and sliced into it. He stifled a cry as Dorn roughly cut off several inches of his blood saturated jeans, cutting the leg along with it.

"Fuck you," hissed Mike.

"Damn. Did clumsy me give you a little scratch? I'm really sorry about that." Dorn did not sound sorry about it.

He straightened up and handed the bloody piece to Spike.

Mike sucked air to fight his pain and sent a glance around. They were inside, but it was big and empty sounding. The large new metal building. The only light came from several flashlights -- one in Spike's hand and two on the ground.

His thoughts were interrupted as Jordan ordered, "Do it."

The two words carried a wicked tone that sent a chill down Mike's spine. "Huh?"

Mike was suddenly jerked back off his knees and shoved forward and then he was falling. He gave a surprised cry and felt raw fear for what might be coming. Then he slammed into the ground, on his left side. His shoulder took the brunt, but the wounded leg took a hard blow, too. The sharp pain caused flashes of light in his head and sent it spinning.

With tears filling his eyes, Mike tried to sort out what had happened. In the limited light of Spike's flashlight, he realized he was in a pit.

"Fuck," breathed Mike and glared up at his enemies.

"Hey, cop," Evers grinned down at him. "How's your day going?"

"You feeling any of that Western hospitality?" asked Dorn with a laugh.

Jordan wore a particularly evil expression that Mike found especially worrisome.

"And so you don't get lonely down there," said the man, "we have a friend to keep you company."

He turned away for a moment and came back to hold a gunny sack over the pit. Upending it, a rattlesnake fell from it to land with a thud about six feet from Mike. It immediately curled up and began hissing, the rattle buzzing loud and angry.

Mike froze, his eyes going wide with unashamed terror.

"There's a little New Mexico wildlife for you," said Jordan, still looking evil. "Try your hospitality on it."

In spite of his terror, his eyes tight on the snake, Mike suddenly realized something. Not wanting to upset the snake further by yelling, he rasped, "You sonsabitches. This is where you had Andy Miller, isn't it? He died here, didn't he?"

"I admit we had a little fun with old man Miller," said Spike. "We tossed in a few more snakes and when they had done their job, we did some target practice and finished off the snakes before we got him out. But don't worry, we've rounded up a few more snakes and you'll get to meet them all later."

"You are sick sonsabitches," Mike hissed. "This won't change anything for you bastards. Tommy Bears will come after you and...."

Now Jordan snorted. "You think a half-assed, half-breed redskin is going to scare us, cop? We're in control here. And if mommy wants her family to stay alive and well, she'll keep her mouth shut when we let her go. She hasn't seen any faces and she won't. And we'll find a place out in the middle of a pasture to bury your hide. With the snakes to keep you company. But for now, we'll leave some light so you and your friend can keep an eye on each other."

The men disappeared from view.

In his fury, Mike forgot his roommate and yelled, "Don't hurt her!"

The snake's rattle buzzed faster and louder and Mike sucked in air and held it, eyes locked on it. Above, a flashlight had been left at the edge of the pit, the beam aimed across the hole, providing shadowy light.

Mike's eyes hung on the snake. When it finally stopped buzzing, he slowly managed to pull himself over to sit against the wall and turned his attention to his prison. About ten feet square, it was maybe seven feet deep. Not an impossible place to get out of. A six foot man like himself could jump for the edge and pull himself out. Unless their hands were tied and they had a bullet in their leg. That made it a little harder.

Mike glowered back at the snake and rasped, "I'm in a goddamned pit with a big fucking rattlesnake and I've got a fucking bullet in my leg. This cannot be happening."

The snake must have disliked his tone and started buzzing again. Mike held his breath. The snake went quiet, but its eyes never left the detective.

"Okay. Good. We're good."

Slowly he turned his head seeing the nearest corner was maybe three feet away.

Taking a cautious breath, he quietly said, "Okay, pal. I'm just going to ease back over into this corner. Be a nice guy and stay right there. Please."

Very slowly, using his good leg to push with, Mike inched his way along the wall. Tied as he was, his hands were only so much help. When his foot slipped and skidded on a small rock, Mister Snake started buzzing again. The tough NYPD cop panicked and hurriedly finished pushing himself into the corner, his eyes wide on the snake.

The buzz stopped. Mike took a slow breath.

"Son-of-a-fucking-bitch," he said. Softly.

Tommy Bears glanced at the clock again. It was well after midnight.

Thomas Bears noticed. "What? She went over to the Colwells. She has made that drive hundreds of times."

Joe Panelli eyed his friend, knowing what was really bothering him.

"Mike's with her," he reminded needlessly, but suggested, "But, maybe call Colwells. To ease our concerns."

Thomas studied his son a little more intently. "We can call them, but something else is bothering you. What?"

Trying not to worry his father, Tommy attempted to shrug it off. "I just want to be sure they're okay."

Thomas still eyed his son but picked up the bunkhouse land line phone and dialed. It wasn't too long before the scowling Sioux said, "I know how late it is, Ken. I'm here wondering if my wife has started for home yet?"

In the next moment Thomas all but turned white. Tommy grabbed the phone. "Ken, this is Tommy. Has my mother been there?"

"Like I told your dad, Sophia isn't here. You woke us up to--" said the rancher.

"Our mistake. Sorry to bother you, Ken." Tommy hung up.

"What the hell is going on?" demanded Thomas, now worried and angry. "Where did she go?"

The dogs started barking. Not much at first, then more furiously.

"Maybe that's them coming back," said Joe.

Thomas and was out the door. Tommy and the rest followed right behind him. The dogs circled them and then ran toward the driveway, dashing back and forth. A vehicle with its headlights on sat in the driveway, halfway to the main road.

"They're back," said Thomas with relief.

But the headlights weren't moving. Now overwhelming worry engulfed Tommy and he started running.

"Shit," said Joe as he and the others quickly ran after him.

Tommy didn't have a gun on him. He was at home, on vacation. But his instincts told him he wouldn't need one. Not now. Not yet. As he neared the vehicle, he saw it was one of theirs, but it wasn't running.

"Mom!? Mike!?" he yelled out, but he knew there wouldn't be an answer.

"Tommy?" Joe beat the others there.

"Passenger door," Tommy told him as he took the driver's side.

They yanked the doors open at the same time. The cab was empty except for a large brown envelope on the seat.

"What's going on?" Thomas all but demanded as he and his men arrived. He saw the empty truck. "Where's Sophia? Tommy, what the hell is going on?"

His son was tearing the envelope open, not in the least bit interested in preserving evidence. Whatever this was, he would take care of it.

"What's that?" asked Thomas as his son read the sheet of paper he'd pulled out.

Joe came around to join Rivers and Santos, looking on.

Tommy read it out loud. "Stay out of our hair and she'll be returned in two days. Call the law and you won't see her again."

"Those damned fuckers have her," the half-breed hissed.

"Hudson," said Joe in a poisonous tone.

Thomas stared in confusion. "Hudson has Sophia? Why would Hudson have Sophia? I don't understand."

"What about Mike?" asked Joe.

"Nothing said about Mike, but there's this." Tommy pulled out a piece of denim from the envelope. It was soaked with a dark substance. "This has to be his and it's soaked with blood."

"Blood?" said Lucas with a frown.

"What's that supposed to mean?" asked Quintin.

The two ranch hands were also confused. This was something outside of the world they lived in.

Thomas' face tightened. "Are they saying Mike is dead?"

"Pretty sure not," replied his son. "At least not yet. It's a warning."

"But, he is hurt if that's his blood," declared Thomas. "And what have they done to Sophia? We need to call Phil right now and--"

"That won't help Mom," said Tommy, struggling with his rage. "We need to take care of this ourselves. They obviously didn't like us putting our noses into their business. It's our fault for pushing the man. You know Mike fought back, to protect Mom, and that's what this is from."

He clenched the jean patch in anger.

"We both know Mike's a hard head and he'll fight as long as he can," said Joe. "We know Hudson's up to something and whatever it is, it sounds like it's tomorrow -- well, now today -- and then it will be over if he's saying they'll return Sophia the next day. It's got to be happening somewhere at that ranch. That's why he wants people to stay away from there with all his fences and armed guards."

"What are we going to do?" asked the worried Thomas.

"Me and Joe, and Lucas, are riding over to that ranch...." said Tommy.

"We all are," stated Thomas sharply.

"No. You and Quintin are staying here. You're our backup. You need to be ready to call Phil. We'll stay in touch with the radios. Now Let's get moving!"

They all piled into the pickup and made the short, speedy return to the ranch. There, Lucas and Quint got horses saddled and ready while Tommy and Joe picked out the weapons they would take. Thomas got the radios out.

"I don't like waiting here, Tommy," argued his father. "Sophia is in terrible trouble and I should be going."

"I cannot worry about the both of you being in harm's way, Dad," stated Tommy. "I will get Mom back, but you need to be by the phone to call Phil when we need him."

They argued some more, father and son facing the frightening possibilities of what might happen to wife and mother. Then Rivers and Santos were at the back door with the horses. Lucas wore a Western holster, a well-cared-for Colt resting in it. He also had a rifle in his saddle scabbard.

Tommy and Joe wore holsters and guns at the smalls of their backs. Tommy also had one on his ankle. Joe shoved a rifle into the scabbard on his horse. Tommy had a powerful scope rifle he had given his dad one Christmas. It went into a scabbard. He also stuck wire cutters in the saddlebags with the radios.

"Fences are electric," said Quint.

"We'll shoot them apart. We'll be too far from their headquarters for them to hear," said Tommy. "When we do that, we'll radio that it's time to call Phil. Better call State Patrol, too. Tell them Mom is gone and we believe she's at the Big H and we've gone to find her."

"If he asks why?" said Thomas.

"You don't know. Which is true. We don't know what's going on there," said Tommy. "But we will tear that place apart until we find Mom. I promise you that, Dad."

"I know. But, both of you come back in one piece," choked Thomas. "And bring Mike back, too."

"Speaking of Mike," said Joe, "when you call the sheriff, you might also want to get an ambulance or two rolling. We know he's bleeding and it's likely he did some hurting back."

"Good point," Tommy agreed. He managed a smile for his father. "We'll be in touch."

The three men rode away into the darkness and Quint laid a hand on the elder Bears' shoulder to encourage, "Tommy's a soldier, boss. He'll bring Sophia back."

Tears trickled down Thomas' cheeks as he said, "I know."

And prayed he was right.

Mike Brennen grimaced in his pain and he was making it worse. Struggling, he had brought his wounded, bloody leg up close to his left side. Making it more difficult, he'd done it slowly, so as not to upset his pit mate. Once it was accomplished, he twisted his body and moved his bound hands so he could reach his leg. He suffered the extra pain so he could rub the rawhide that bound his hands in the blood.

Mike clung to the thought that Sophia Bears would be okay for the time being. He, on the other hand, was dead -- by bullet or by snake. Or maybe both the way his night was going. So whatever was going on with Hudson, if it warranted killing a cop and kidnapping a woman, it was something big. At least to Hudson.

But the detective couldn't take the chance Sophia would stay safe. And he couldn't expect help. He had no idea if Tommy and Joe knew what had happened. Even if Hudson had sent them some kind warning, would they dare to risk Sophia's life? And he sure as hell wasn't going to lie here in a pit with a damned snake and wait to see what came next. He was in a bad position -- in so many ways -- but he was also mad. Really, fucking mad!

The strain of the position finally got to be too much. Hoping all his effort had worked, Mike let himself collapse, taking a minute to breathe. Uncontrolled tears ran down his face as he fought the dizziness and pain.

Really, fucking mad! His anger pulled him back.

Now Mike put his energy into twisting his wrists, stretching the softening rawhide. After several exhausting minutes, he began to worry that his efforts weren't going to work. But it was his only trick. So he kept struggling. At last it began slipping. Encouraged, he pulled harder, twisted harder. Then, suddenly, Mike was able to slip the rawhide off. With a groan he brought his tired arms and hands around to slump in exhaustion, eyeing his torn and tortured wrists.

Across the way, the rattler rose up, tongue flicking in and out. He didn't buzz.

"Take it easy," said Mike softly. "Let's not ruin our friendship."

He flexed his fingers. His wrists were a bloody mess and not just the blood from his leg wound. Which was still oozing some of the red stuff from the bullet hole, though Mike knew he would have been dead long ago if an artery had been hit. He looked up at the edge of the pit. Why did it look so far away? With a bad leg and mangled wrists, was he going to be able to do this?

He had to! There was no room for doubt. He had to find Sophia Bears. Besides, he really did not want to die from fucking snake bites.

Mike scanned the walls of his prison, wishing he had more light. With his height, under normal circumstances, he could have easily jumped and gotten a hold on the edge of the pit. But pushing off on a bad leg and with his aching arms and bad wrists, it wasn't going to be that easy to pull off. Still, there was a snake ready to bite him in the ass if he didn't make it.

Anxious as he was to get out of his prison, Mike made himself sit and breathe and give his arms a rest. Damn his leg hurt.

Shit! Get up and go!

Slowly he pushed up on his good leg, using the pit wall to keep himself balanced. His fellow captive buzzed for a bit but then stopped. In the dim light, Mike couldn't see the snake's eyes, but he could sure as hell feel them.

Taking in a lung full of air, Mike crouched slightly. Determined to block the pain from his mind, he eyed the edge and raised his arms above his head. And propelled himself upward.

Pain shot through his leg and an involuntary cry escaped his lips, but his hands found the edge and his fingers dug in. Clawing and scrambling, he pulled himself up. Behind him, the rattler sounded off and Mike dug in deeper. Then he was over the edge and crawling away from his nightmare dungeon. With giant relief, he collapsed, gulping air.

Slowly Mike rolled onto his back to lie there, breathing and working to get a handle on his pain. Then, with a deep breath, he pushed himself up onto his right elbow and leg, then to his feet. When the dizziness rushed back in, Mike steadied himself and pushed it away. Breathing, he took a step. Then two. It didn't take any more than that for him to realize that any fast movement was not going to be an option.

He hobbled over to scoop up the flashlight, shining it around. The light was swallowed up in the hangar's blackness, but he discovered that the pit was located in a corner. Without much hope, Mike looked around for anything he could use for a weapon. Going up against Hudson's two-legged snakes would require more than bad language. There was nothing, not even a shovel, lying around. The light did find something that stirred up his sick feeling again.

Four gunny sacks. One open and empty. Three more tied shut.

"They were ready to drop more snakes in there with me," the detective whispered with nausea.

The sound of a metal door opening came from further down the hangar. Mike's head snapped around in that direction. Someone was coming to check on him. Maybe throw the snakes into the pit with him!

At the sound of the door shutting, Mike hobbled quickly back to put the flashlight down where it had been and moved away into the darkness. The beam of a flashlight appeared and moved toward that corner.

"Hey, cop! How are you getting along with the nice pet we gave you?"

Mike recognized Abe Dorn's voice and clenched his fists. He would be dead if the man raised an alarm.

Reaching the pit and looking into it, Dorn exclaimed, "What the hell? How the fuck did you get out of there?"

He pulled a gun as he quickly swung his light around, searching. He heard a groan and his light found where the detective was lying on the ground.

"Goddammit," snarled Dorn. "Don't know how you pulled this Houdini trick, cop, but you won't do it again."

Confident with his gun and angry that their prisoner had somehow escaped their little prison, Abe tromped over to the helpless looking man.

"Did the fucking snake get you, smartass?" asked Dorn with a snort as he approached Mike.

Mike moaned again and Dorn poked him with a foot. "Don't give me any of this fake crap. Why don't you just crawl back to the pit and save me the trouble of…."

As he spoke, he jabbed at the detective again. Mike grabbed the foot and raised it high, upending the gunman and landing him hard on his back. It knocked the air from the startled and unprepared Dorn. Mike scrambled on top of him, desperately grabbing at the weapon, hoping it wouldn't go off. Then he had the gun and quickly rolled off, giving the man a knock to the head with it.

Mike lie still for a few moments, fighting the pain and breathing. Too soon he heard Dorn stirring and the detective forced himself up. He clenched the gun in his right hand and picked up Dorn's flashlight with his left. Then stepped far enough away from the gunman so the man couldn't get to him and knock him down. Mike didn't want to have another fight. He needed to save his strength for finding Sophia.

Abe slowly rolled onto knees, his hands going to his head. Remembering what had happened, he looked sharply at his adversary.

"You fuckin' cop," he growled. "What the hell do you think you're going to do? There's guards all over the--"

"Where's Sophia Bears?"

"Shit. Look at you. You're a mess. You can barely stand up." He scowled. "How the hell did you get out? Shit, how did you get your hands free?"

"Tell me where you've got Sophia Bears."

The gunman snorted. "You can hardly hold that gun. And if you fire it, Spike and the others will--"

"I'm holding this gun just fine. And if you force me to fire, it won't matter who comes running, because I promise you'll be dead," warned Mike coldly. "At this range, the smartass cop isn't about to miss."

Dorn hardened, but worry crept in. "You can't get out of here, cop. No fuckin' way."

"Move over to the pit."

"Huh? What? There's no way I'm--"

"You are going in. You can jump and pick your landing spot away from the snake. Or I'll push you in and you can take your chances with Mr. Rattler."

"You stupid, fuckin' cop," snarled Dorn, suddenly standing. "There's no way you can push me anywhere. I'm--"

Abe was sure Brennen was literally on his last leg and almost as sure he wouldn't pull the trigger. So he made a quick move on his plan to push the cop back into the pit.

But Mike had desperation on his side. When Dorn came at him, Mike moved aside, letting the man's charge take him toward the hole with its snake. Dorn put on his brakes and skidded to a stop, but he found himself hovering over the dark pit.

"Here's your chance to jump, Dorn, or I'll--"

"You fucking sonofabitch!"

Mike shone his light into the hole and picked out the snake, now curled up in a corner. "See him? You've got lots of room."

Dorn teetered on the edge and, before the man could think more about it, Mike gave him a shove. Dorn hit the ground hard and cried out. The snake's rattle started up. Dorn scrambled to the corner farthest from it.

"I'm gonna fucking kill you, cop!" Dorn's eyes were glued to Mr. Rattler.

Unexpectedly, another snake started sounding off. Dorn's eyes went quickly to the top. He saw Mike had put the gun in his waistband and was holding a gunny sack out over the edge of the pit. What was in the sack was really angry.

"How long did you keep Andy Miller in here before you tossed in the snakes that killed him, you bastard? How long before he died?" asked the detective, his own tone venomous.

The gunman glared up at him with hate. "Go to hell."

"Where's Sophia Bears?" Mike gave the sack a shake and winced at the loud buzzing it caused. He wasn't at all sure the damn snake couldn't bite him through the sack, so he held it as far from himself as he could. "I'm more than ready to let this unhappy fella join you down there."

Abe Dorn did some more swearing, but then, "She's where you can't get near her, smart ass."

"Tell me!" Mike shook the bag.

"She's in an underground room! Beneath the old house, damn you! With armed guards. You don't have a chance in hell of--"

"Where's the door to this underground room?"

"In the pantry, damn it!"

"How many guards?" Brennen shook the bag.

"One outside. One inside. They've got guns and they'll shoot--"

"Toss me your jacket," ordered Mike.

That caused surprise. "What…?"

"Your jacket. Now!" Mike shook the bag.

More swearing, but Dorn took off his lightweight, light-colored jacket and tossed it up.

"Thank you. Now lay face down."

"Huh…?"

"If I could get out of there with a bum leg, I'm sure you could do it even with that heavy, fat head."

"And lying face down is supposed to stop me?"

Mike wore a nasty smirk. "Just do it and see."

Wary, but giving the gunny sack another hateful glare, Dorn laid down, face to the dirt floor. It suddenly went dark.

"What the…?" Dorn was suddenly, seriously worried.

"I'm going to empty these three bags of angry snakes into your cubby hole, Dorn. You're going to lay there and not move and maybe they won't bite you. And I wouldn't do any serious yelling. I'm pretty sure that will really upset them."

Loud, angry, buzzing sounded and Dorn heard a thump followed by more serious buzzing. Then a second and third thump and more buzzing. It was a terrifying sound in the blackness and seemed to be coming from all around him. Unsure of where they had landed, the man froze in fear, his swearing dying away.

"Take a nap, Dorn. Maybe I'll get around to telling the law where you are. Or where your body is, anyway."

Mike moved off in the direction he'd heard the door open. He kept his light from shining into the pit as he left. He didn't want Dorn to know that when he'd dropped the snakes into the hole, they were still in their gunny sacks. He hoped the bastard died of fright.

Mike hobbled along the metal wall until he found the people-sized door next to the airplane-sized door. There he set the light down and pulled on Abe's jacket. It was a jacket they knew Dorn wore and were unlikely to give him any serious attention. Except for his limping. Badly. Painfully. Could he keep it under control enough to prevent anyone from getting too curious? Suspicious?

The NYPD detective was about to find out.

Biting back the pain, Mike opened the door and stepped out. Careful to keep the flashlight aimed at the ground, he closed the door and quickly glanced around to orient himself. No one else seemed to be near the hangar. The old house looked a lot farther away than he remembered. The good news was that there was no lighting in the large, dusty area between hangar and house. And only a couple of dim yard lights around the old house. Beyond it was the new place, well-lit even at this hour, and probably guarded by armed sentries.

Taking a deep breath, Mike moved toward the house, which had dim light in only one window. He walked slowly, doing his best to control his limp. He would have to avoid the outside lights. If he got caught under one of them, there would be no hiding his bloody leg.

He was almost to the house before sighting the outside guard. By then his efforts to hide the limp were all but gone. The leg simply wasn't cooperating.

"Hey, Abe, what's up with the leg?" The man had come around a corner of the old house. He gave a laugh. "One of them snakes bite you?"

Mike groaned and dropped to his good knee, laying down the flashlight so the beam was away from him. Keeping his voice low he mumbled, "Help me."

"Huh? What's wrong?" The guy came his way. He was almost there before he could distinguish the bloody leg. "Hey."

Mike came off his knee and hit him hard in the face with the gun. The guy grunted and staggered. Mike hit him again, harder, alongside the head, and the guard was out, crumpling to the ground.

The detective quickly glanced around, hoping no eyes were looking in his direction. Stuffing the flashlight into a pocket, he grabbed ahold of the guy's jacket and dragged him over into the deep shadows beside the house. The effort sapped at his strength, but someone would see the body if he left it where it was.

Mike took the man's gun and stuffed it under his waistband at the small of his back. Two guns were always better than one. He also took time to check pockets for keys. If the house was locked, that would be a problem. There were no keys and he could only hope it wouldn't be a problem. Kicking in a door would be noisy. Well, with one bad leg, kicking anything would be the real problem. And hurt a lot.

Mike went to the side door first. The one Sophia had used to get to the bathroom. Locked. He was about to hobble around to the back when he remembered the broken front door. Had they bothered to fix it yet? With all the guards around the place, maybe it hadn't been a priority. Of course, with the yard light at the front, if a guard or anyone at the new house looked that way, they would see him. Or maybe not from the new house. The lights around the swimming pool would almost certainly affect a person's night vision.

He chose to believe the latter and mentally crossed his fingers that another guard wouldn't show up.

Staying in shadows as much as he could, Mike crouched and limped along the side of the house toward the front. He was pretty sure crouching probably wasn't any help, but it made him feel better. He eyed that end of the porch railing. If he could get over that, he wouldn't have to approach the front steps in the yard light. Turning off the flashlight, he put it and the gun in the jacket pockets. Gritting his teeth, he pulled himself up to lie across the railing like he had when getting into the saddle and swung his good leg over. Setting it onto the porch, he sucked in a breath and brought over the wounded leg. Done. At least the porch was in deep shadow, he just hoped it wouldn't squeak. It didn't and he made it to the front door. He was relieved to find it was still broken and he slowly pushed it open, again hoping there wouldn't be any squeaks. There weren't and he gently closed it again.

Now he stood still and listened. And heard nothing.

Mike pulled out the flashlight but debated about turning it on. Dorn had said there was a guard inside the house. He needed to find the kitchen and most kitchens were at the back of these old houses. And pantries were off kitchens. He remembered his grandparents had a pantry. He had loved that pantry. It had held all kinds of good things to eat. Mostly cookies.

He sighed. Of all times to think about cookies. Leaving the light off, he moved slowly across the floor toward what looked to be a hallway. He was about to turn the flashlight on to get his bearings when someone sneezed.

Mike froze. Whoever sneezed again, which was followed by a "Shit!" Undercover of the sounds, Mike quickly moved. The guy was just inside the hallway, now blowing his nose. Mike hit him over the head. The guy started to drop and Mike grabbed him and lowered him quietly. He felt a hint of guilt when he hit the fallen man a second time -- he didn't need him waking up and sounding an alarm. His guilt barely lasted a second. These assholes had shot him! And thrown him into a pit with a snake! And kidnapped Sophia Bears! And they had murdered Miller! With snakes!

He hit the guy a third time. And took his gun. Three guns now. He was ready to make war. But not until he found Sophia.

With extreme care, Mike turned on the flashlight. The kitchen was at the end of the hall. Keeping the light shaded and low, he went in to find two doors. One led outside. He opened the other and there was the pantry. And, being a sharp detective, it didn't take him long to find the hidden door that opened onto, of course, a stairway. With all the money Hudson seemed to have, why couldn't he have put in a fucking elevator?

Gritting his teeth, Mike slowly went down, one hand on the wall -- no railing, of course -- and one holding a gun. He was sweating hard when he got to the bottom, and discovered there wasn't just a room, there was a hallway. Less than twenty-five feet in length, there were three doors off of it. One on each side and one at the far end. But no guards.

Mike glanced around, looking for surveillance cameras and was greatly relieved to see none. Out here in the hall, anyway. Maybe in the rooms? He pushed that worry aside. Either way, he had to get Sophia out.

He leaned close to the left door and listened. No sound. He tried the door. Unlocked. He cracked it and there was light inside. He stopped and listened again. Nothing. He pushed the door open another couple of inches and peeked, gun ready. He saw lockers and benches and towels. No Sophia.

Mike shut the door and turned to the other side. Again he listened. No sounds. He tried the door. It was locked.

He rapped lightly and said, "Sophia?"

It was quiet for several long seconds, then, "Mike? Is that you?"

The detective realized he'd been holding his breath and now inhaled deeply in relief. "None other. I'll be right back."

He returned to the other room and grabbed a couple of the heavy towels. Wrapping the gun in them, he went back to the other door.

"Sophia, stand away from the door."

"I'm tied to a chair, Mike, and I have a hood over my head."

Well, damn. "Okay. I have to shoot the lock…"

"Just do it. It doesn't sound like I'm that close to the door."

Mike placed the gun on the lock and angled his aim downward. With the towels muffling the shot, he blew it out.

Slipping in, he found the light on and Sofia in a chair, her wrists and ankles taped to it.

He closed the door and removed her hood, asking, "Are you hurt at all?"

"No. No." She blinked, eyes adjusting to the light. "But I've been so frightened and worried about you. Some awful men chased me and grabbed me and put this hood--" She saw his bloodied leg. "Oh, Mike! You were shot. I heard--"

"Shhhh. I don't know if anyone is close by."

She lowered her voice, asking, "Where are we?"

Mike was tearing at the duct tape, wishing he had a knife. "We're at Hudson's place."

"Hudson's? What's going on? Do you think Tommy knows?"

"I hope Tommy knows. Hudson is up to some kind of no good and he obviously didn't like us sticking our noses into it and you're paying the price."

"I don't understand--"

"They kidnapped you to keep Tommy and Joe and I from doing any more snooping. Except they didn't expect me to be in the truck with you."

Mike finally pulled off the last of the tape and Sophia stood to wrap her arms around him. "And now you're shot. I'm so sorry."

"Nothing for you to be sorry about. Now we just need to get out of here."

She turned to glance around. "Where is this?"

"Believe it or not, we're under the Miller's old house," he said, "and there's another door down here I want to see behind."

"Can we get out that way?"

"I don't know, but I'd like to see what's there before we leave."

He opened and peeked out the door. Clear. Mike took her hand to move down the hallway to the last door. He tried it and it opened, which surprised him. Evidently they considered the outside guards enough to keep a watch on things.

The room was dark and Mike felt the near wall. Finding buttons, he pushed one. Small, ornate wall lights came on around the fairly large room, their light soft. What was revealed was a long conference table surrounded by comfortable leather chairs. Several expensive cabinets were spaced along the walls, including an elaborate liquor cabinet and bar. Under their feet was a thick rust-colored plush carpet.

It all looked very high end.

"I wonder what plans our Mr. Hudson has for this kind of--" started Mike.

Sound came from the stairs at the other end of the hallway and Mike twisted around to see Jordan Spike and two more men. The detective gave Sophia a push into the room and twisted around to bring us his gun. His leg couldn't handle the sudden move and caved under him. Still, Mike got off two quick shots as he went down. One missed. The other hit the man named Erv, who cried out as he was knocked back against the wall.

Then Mike was scrambling to get inside the room, intending to kick the door shut. But Jordan Spike came fast, grabbing the door and kicking the gun out of Mike's hand. A second kick caught him in his wounded leg and he cried out as lights flashed in his head. Sophia gave off a short scream and started to go to Mike. Spike grabbed her and shoved her to the third man, Matt Evers.

"Hold onto her!" he snapped.

His head swirling, Mike still managed a, "Sonovabitch! Don't hurt her!"

"Shut up!" growled Spike and kicked at him again.

Sophia cried out. "Stop! Please! He's hurt!"

"He hasn't begun to hurt," said Jordan. Seeing the gun in the detective's waistband, he snatched it. "You've been busy, you fucking cop."

Mike's flashing lights had eased and he desperately looked for Sophia.

A radio crackled Spike pulled it off his belt to answer, "Yes, sir?"

"Did I hear shots?" came Hudson's angry voice.

"Yes, sir. But it's under control. That shadow we saw in the yard was the goddamned cop. He found the Bears woman. We've got them both."

"What? How'd he get out of the pit?" came back Hudson, still angry.

"Don't know. We'll take him back there and find out."

"No! Bring the bastard here! The woman, too, damn it! This whole mess has gotten out of hand."

"Yes, sir," said Spike and slipped the radio into a pocket. He grabbed Mike's right arm to pull him up. "You've been a real pain in the ass, cop. Including shooting up my men! I wouldn't count on pulling off anymore tricks."

"You'd be surprised how many tricks I've got," grumbled Mike, having a trouble standing. "You hurt Sophia and I'll--"

"Shut up," Spike snarled. Then, "Erv, can you make it?"

Erv was holding his left arm. "Yeah. I'd like a minute with the fucking cop, though."

"Later."

Expecting to go back the way they'd come, Mike was surprised when Spike shoved him forward toward the other end of the room.

"That way. The double doors," he ordered.

He gave Mike another push and, much to Mike's regret, he felt the third gun at the small of his back.

"How the hell many of my men have you put down?" he declared as he yanked the gun out.

"Not enough," grunted Mike.

Spike maintained a hold on Mike's shirt as the detective hobbled across the room. Matt Evers brought Sophia and Erv followed. At the doors, Spike pulled out a key to open them. Outside was a wide hallway with carpeted stairs leading up to ground level.

"More damned stairs," griped Mike. "Don't think I can handle anymore...."

"Let the lady help him, Matt," said Jordan.

Evers let Sophia go, but said, "I think we should let him crawl up."

"I agree," said Erv.

"Still not very hospitable, are they, Sophia," said Mike.

Sophia's eyes and expression showed her fear. As she gave Mike a shoulder to lean on, she whispered, "I'm frightened, Mike."

"I know. Me, too," he whispered back. "I'm hoping Tommy's coming but just in case, if I get the chance to do something, I want you to be ready to run. Hide in the dark until help--"

"Shut up!" ordered Spike.

He moved past them to open the doors at the top. They came out into what looked like an elaborate, expensively furnished dining room. There wasn't much light and they were hurried through it into an alcove of sorts. One end was all glass and faced the lighted swimming pool.

"Erv, go have that taken care of," Spike told the man.

Erv went the other direction, while the rest went out to the pool where Mitchell Hudson and another man sat at a poolside table covered with papers. Hudson stood up as the prisoners were herded in front of them. There was some surprise when Sophia boldly spoke first.

"Mitchell Hudson, what is the meaning of all this?" she demanded, struggling to keep the fear from her voice. "Whatever it is, it won't be swept under any rug. My husband and son will never--"

Hudson gave her an impatient smile. "Mrs. Bears, this has turned into a regretful occurrence. Jordy got a little carried away when I asked him to control a situation that seemed to be getting out of hand. He--"

"Like killing Andy Miller?" said Mike.

Hudson's weak smile slid away as he put his eyes on the detective." Making up ridiculous stories like that is part of the problem. I don't--"

"You've got a lot of problems," rumbled Mike. "Like kidnapping your neighbor. And shooting a cop. And throwing the cop in a snake pit. That really pissed me off." The detective's eyes suddenly switched to the man still sitting at the table. "Where do I know you from? You ever been to New York City? Maybe on a wanted poster? Or maybe you were bad news on television or in the newspapers. If you're hanging out with Hudson at this hour of the morning, the two of you have to be up to no good."

The man gave him a distasteful look with mean eyes. "A cop. This makes me very nervous, Mitch."

"Relax, Tarto," Hudson told him. "It's a controlled problem--"

"First name basis," said Mike. "That can't be good. Being on a first name basis with somebody I think is a bad guy..." Then it dawned on Mike and his eyes drilled into Hudson's guest. "Careno! Tarto Careno! You're one of the big shot heads of a cartel in Colombia. You've been all over the news lately. Damn, Mitch, you're out here in the early morning hours doing business with Careno? That's not--"

Spike jabbed at Mike's leg and the cop gasped. If Sophia hadn't been holding onto him, he would have gone down.

"You know," said Mike, gritting his teeth and glaring at the smirking Spike, "I just got done getting my foot back in working order. Now, because of you, I'll have to start all over again, with--"

"You're not going to have to worry about it," Jordan hissed at him.

"This is all crazy!" Sophia declared at Hudson. "You can't just move onto this ranch...into our neighborhood...and threaten and--"

Hudson furiously cut her off. "Take this fucking cop and lose him somewhere! And since you shot him, it can't be an accident, so make damned sure nobody will ever find him. No more quarries...or pits. As for you, Mrs. Bears, you will be our guest here until my current business is taken care of. And if your husband and son want to see you again, they will keep their distance. After that, if you want to live in peace on your little ranch, in your neighborhood, we'll have to come to some understanding."

"Understanding?" Sophia blinked. "You can't possibly..."

"Where's that sonofabitch cop!?" interrupted a loud, angry voice.

Abe Dorn and Owen came up to the pool. The former was red-faced, his eyes finding Brennen.

"Toss me in a fuckin' pit with snakes, you fuckin' cop?" he ranted. "Let me have him, Jordy."

Spike scowled at the enraged man. "Just how did he do that, Abe?"

"I did not toss him in," said Mike pointedly. "I suggested he jump in."

"He had my gun!" defended Dorn.

"And how did he get it, you damned fool?" asked Hudson gruffly.

"He got out of the pit somehow. He...surprised me."

"Do you think you can handle throwing him back in and keeping him there?" snarled Jordan.

"A pit with snakes?" Sophia looked appalled. "No!"

She turned on Hudson and unexpectedly slapped him.

"Hey!" Matt Evers reached to grab her.

"No you don't," said Mike.

Positioned as he was, the cop brought up his left elbow and smashed it into Evers' face. It was a nasty blow that instantly caused blood to squirt from the man's nose. He staggered back, bumping into the newly arrived Owen, and they both fell backward into the pool.

Not slowing down, Mike went after the surprised Spike. He put a fist into the man's stomach and when Spike doubled over, Mike grit his teeth and brought his bloody leg up to smash Jordan's face.

"Run Sophia!" Mike gasped out as pain once more engulfed him. "Run now!"

Sophia didn't want to, but she did, and she was quick despite her sixty-two years. In a second she had disappeared into the darkness.

"Goddamn it!" exploded Hudson. "Get her!"

"Shit," said Dorn and went after her.

A furious Spike, working to straighten up, swung his gun on Mike who had dropped to the ground to hold his battered leg.

Seeing the gun coming his way, Mike miserably thought, 'All the crap I've been through in New York and I'm going to die on fucking vacation in New Mexico'.

And the gun went off.

Sophia Bears ran into the darkness, running the fastest she'd ever run. Hearing the shot behind her, tears wet her face. Mike!

Then she heard horses, coming hard, and the next thing she knew, they were surrounding her. When someone jumped down and grabbed her, she started pounding on him.

"No! Let me go!" she screamed.

"Mom! It's me!"

She gasped and quit struggling. "Oh dear God! Tommy!" she breathed and briefly wrapped her arms around her son. Then pushed off, crying, "Mike! They're killing Mike! By the pool!"

Tommy instantly scooped her up and put her on his horse. "Lucas! Take Mom out of here!"

"But..."

"Now! And radio my dad that we have her!" They had already called to have Thomas send help.

"I'll take care of her!" said Rivers and he and Sophia galloped away.

Joe held out an arm for Bears to grab and swung him onto the back of his horse. They rode for the new house and the swimming pool.

Abe Dorn had already lost sight of the crazy woman. When he heard horses, he came to a quick stop. In the next second, he heard who it was and turned to run back toward the pool.

"That damned Bears is here!" warned Dorn.

Guns started going off before Tommy and Joe could reach the pool. The two men quickly came off the horse. When Joe stumbled and started to go down, Tommy grabbed him and they dove behind a hut used for changing into swimsuits. They pulled their guns as bullets chewed up the corner of the small building.

At the first lull in the shooting, Tommy yelled, "Give this up, Hudson! The law's on its way! You kidnapped my mother, you son of a bitch! And if you've shot Brennen, he's no coyote! No one will be walking out of jail this time."

"You're trespassing!" declared Hudson. "All of you! And we have every right to shoot trespassers!"

Joe snorted and said, "You really think Sophia Bears will go along with that story? Or the law?"

"You want to talk about this, we can talk about this," offered Hudson in an arrogant tone.

"We don't have any--" started Tommy.

Spike cut him off. "I've got a gun to your cop friend's head! I think you better damn well come and talk!"

"Just shoot the sonsabitches!" came Mike's very angry voice. It was followed by a sharp cry of pain. Then, "That hurts, damn you! Tommy, shoot this goddamn bastard!"

Tommy and Joe looked at each other.

"What do you think? Will Hudson shoot us or try to put a spin on this?" asked Tommy.

"It would be hard for him to put a spin on our three bodies and he knows the law is coming," allowed Joe. "I think the man believes he can still clean this up."

"We've got the damn note he sent us," said Tommy.

"Nobody signed it," Joe reminded him. "And I'll bet ours will be the only prints on it or the envelope."

"You want me to start counting!?" yelled Spike.

"Okay. If we do this, it gives the cops more time to get here," decided Tommy.

Joe nodded in agreement.

"We're coming out!" Tommy called out.

"Guns first!"

They obeyed and raised their hands to step around the hut. As they walked, they took in the scene at the pool. Which seemed a little chaotic.

Oddly, two men were climbing out of the pool, clothed, and they recognized them as Matt Evers and the man Owen. Evers had a bloody nose. Abe Dorn, his clothes wrinkled and dirty, wore a venomous glare and had a gun in his hand. Jordan Spike had a blood smeared face and looked a little worse for wear. Surprisingly, even Mitchell Hudson had a little blood trickling from his lower lip. The only person who looked unscathed was an unfamiliar man standing at the pool table.

Mike was on his knees with Spike's gun jammed in his right ear. The single shot that had been fired had only clipped Mike on the right side of his neck when he literally dodged the bullet to his head. Tommy and Joe were glad to see him alive, but he looked a wreck with a bloody head, bloody torn wrists, and a mess of a leg.

"Damn, Mike," said Tommy. "You're supposed to be on vacation, not waging war."

Joe scowled. "That's the same leg you just healed."

Mike's growl was heated. "I don't want to hear it. And this bastard with a gun in my ear, I'm gonna kill him."

"Shut up!" snapped Jordan. He straightened, lifting the gun away, but delivered another kick to the wounded leg.

Mike couldn't control his painful cry as more tears leaked out.

"Don't do that again," said Tommy in a calm, cold, threatening tone.

He and Spike locked eyes. For several moments it was as if all the others were frozen in place, watching the two men. Then Spike gave his head a shake and broke the tension. He also took an involuntary step away from Mike.

Eyes shut, Mike moaned, "I thank you, Mr. Bears. And you should know that I've waged about as much war as I probably can tonight. You and Joseph will have to--"

"You still need to shut up," snarled Spike, but he didn't kick at him.

Tommy's attention turned on Hudson. "You want to tell us how you're going to explain what's happened tonight, Hudson? The sheriff is on his way and there's no way he's going to believe any cock-and-bull story that you--"

"I think he will," said Hudson. "To begin with, you are trespassing and--"

"You kidnapped my mother, you fuck," Tommy rasped sharply. "You should understand that it doesn't matter what the cops do, I will see that you--"

"You're all fucking dead men!" Spike was still snarling. "Nobody is ever going to see you again. Any of you!"

"I want to put the cop back in the snake pit," Dorn got into it. "And I'm going to watch while the snakes eat him up."

"Snake pit?" said Tommy.

"In the hangar," Mike was glad to fill them in. "A goddamned snake pit. And Tommy, I'm sure they had Andy Miller in it the day of the barbeque."

Joe was eyeing the man next to Hudson. Now he said, "You're Tarto Careno. What the hell kind of business are you doing with a Colombian, Mitch? Wouldn't have pegged you as a drug dealer."

"Not drugs. Conferences. I'm offering high level conferences to anyone who needs complete privacy in a highly secured area," explained Hudson with some arrogance. "That's what this place is all about. To provide secrecy for anyone who wants it."

"You won't have a business if you don't fix these problems right now," spoke up a steaming Careno.

"We'll be fine," insisted Hudson. Then ordered, "Get them out of sight before our neighborly sheriff gets here. The two-bit law around here is not going to be any problem. That's another reason I chose this place. I won't--"

Owen suddenly yelped, followed instantly by the bark of a high-powered rifle. The man went down with a shattered right shoulder. Before anyone could react, Abe Dorn screamed out as he was spun around and went down from a second shot.

Now Tommy and Joe were moving. And Mike, who grabbed the distracted Spike's legs and brought him down hard on the cement. Then the two men were fighting for the gun.

Tommy quickly pulled his hideout and pointed it at a confused Matt Evers.

"Throw your gun in the pool!" ordered the Indian.

Evers hesitated and Tommy just stepped over and gave him a hard push into the pool. The gunman's second dip of the night.

Joe had snatched up the whimpering Owen's gun and turned on Hudson and his now furious client.

"No! You fools!" Mitchell exclaimed in disbelief. "You can't--"

Disgusted, Joe stepped over to plant a fist into the man's stomach. It put Hudson back in his chair.

When Careno started to rise, Joe waggled the gun at him. "I think it would be a good idea if you stayed put."

The hard look on Joe's face convinced the Colombian, but he used colorful words in his own language to complain.

Mike had got hold of Spike's gun and now demanded, "How many more men do you have here?"

"Go fuck yourself," rasped Jordan.

In a particularly bad mood, Mike fired a shot past the man's ear. Spike cried out and grabbed the ear.

"How many?" asked Mike again.

"Three on the perimeter! The ones you wounded earlier, and Erv, are in the bunkhouse, you fucking cop!"

Sirens could be heard in the distance, moving closer. Tommy and Joe had everyone on their knees. Except for Evers who was again climbing out of the pool, his gun left behind in the water. He also sank to his knees and Joe kept a gun on them all while Tommy helped Mike into a chair.

"From lousy cards to getting shot. Not one of your better nights, detective," remarked the Indian with a shake of the head.

"And trust me, getting dumped into a snake pit isn't a fun way to spend vacation time, either."

Sophia Bears and Lucas Rivers appeared from the darkness. The former carried the high-powered rifle.

Mike arched his brow. "Sophia! That was you shooting?"

"It was. I usually shoot at targets, but…"

Lucas was grinning. "The lady is a state champion shooter with that gun."

"…I was some kind of angry tonight," finished Sophia.

Joe glanced at the wounded Owen and Abe. "I can see that. And I bet you hit what you were aiming at."

"I do not kill. Even varmints like these," she stated.

Tommy relieved his mother of the rifle, giving her a kiss on the forehead. "Thanks, Mom."

"You're welcome, but I don't want to ever shoot people again." She went to Mike and gave him a gentle hug. "I thought that awful man had killed you."

"He tried." Mike touched the bloody scratch on his neck. "But I moved a little too quick for him. Damn but they've made a mess of my cowboy shirt."

"I'll find you lots of cowboy shirts," she promised.

With sirens and flashing lights, two sheriff's SUVs came to a quick stop in the yard. One had a smashed in front end.

"Doesn't look like the cops waited politely at the gate," said Joe.

"I'll make sure they've got ambulances coming," said Tommy. "And they need to get the FBI and the DEA in on this, too. I'm pretty sure they'll all be very interested in what was going to take place here. "

"I think Mike's leg needs immediate care, Tommy," said Sophia.

"Let's get him into one of the SUVs," said her son. "I'll take him right now."

Lucas helped him get Mike into the back seat of a deputy's car. Sophia climbed in with him.

"Seems like I'm always taking you to a hospital," sniffed Tommy as he got into the driver's seat.

"It's not my fault," muttered Mike.

"Be nice, Tommy. Mike is my hero," said Sophia.

Tommy moaned. "Don't tell him that."

"That's very nice," said Mike. "I'm a hero."

As they were leaving, two State Patrol cars came rushing in.

"Gonna be a busy night at the Big H," said Tommy.

Mike Brennen barely remembered the trip to the hospital followed by the hustle of doctors and nurses in the ER. Sometime during all that, they told him he was going into surgery and that was that.

When he woke up, Sophia was sitting beside him reading a magazine.

"Hey, lady," he croaked, throat and mouth dry.

She looked up and gave him a bright smile, putting the magazine aside. "Hey, back. I'm so glad to see you open your eyes."

"I'm glad to see you. Are you okay? Did they check you over?"

"I'm just fine. Couple of bruises is all. You sound a little rough, though." And she helped him get a drink of water.

"Thank you, lovely lady. I guess they must have patched me up okay."

"You did give us some concern for a while," Sophia admitted. "You lost a lot of blood, young man. And those terrible men were very hard on you. But Tommy assured me you have a strong will. We've been taking turns watching over you."

Mike frowned. "How long have I been out?"

"Almost three days."

"Damn."

"I'm afraid all that moving around on your wounded leg caused some problems and they had to do some repair work. It was worrisome, but seeing you awake makes me feel much better."

The door opened and Tommy and Joe came in.

"Don't tell me he's finally awake," said Tommy.

"We knew it had to happen sooner or later," quipped Joe.

Sophia gave them a scolding look. "Behave yourselves. I won't have you picking on my hero."

Tommy snorted. "Hero? He's been laying around in bed while we did all the hard work."

"He didn't get out of all of it, though. A lot of people are waiting in line to get his story," said Joe. He counted on his fingers. "The sheriff's office…the State Police…the FBI…the DEA…"

"Stop," begged Mike. "Just tell me you got all the bad guys rounded up."

"Rounded up, but it's going to be a courtroom battle when it comes to Hudson," said Tommy. "He's got a pile of lawyers."

"Unless his future clients want to look for a little vengeance," Joe pointed out. "Mr. Careno is particularly unhappy."

"What about the ranch?" wondered Mike.

"It's been overrun by every law enforcement agency you can think of," said Tommy. "But that ranch foreman, Harvey Elson, was for real and didn't know anything about Hudson's other business. He'll be taking care of the ranch itself for now. Then we'll see if we can't get it back for Andy Miller's sons."

"That would be a great happy ending," said Mike.

"A happy ending is that all my boys are safe and sound," said Sophia.

"And that my mother is safe and sound," added Tommy. "You get any more new neighbors, I want to know about it so I can check them out."

She laughed. "I promise you that."

Much to his dismay, Mike spent another week in the hospital and spent a lot of that time talking to lots of branches of the law. He also got in touch with his partner Clark Thorn and his boss Lieutenant Carl Grands, to explain how he got mixed up with more bad guys and ended up with a bullet in his leg. He winced at their response to that.

When he did finally get out, again on crutches, he got a welcoming party at the Bears' Running B. That was followed by several days of being cared for and well fed by Sophia and Thomas, who thanked him many times over for watching over his Sophia. He also had to make several more trips back to the hospital so they could keep an eye on what had been a bad wound. After five days they gave him the okay to return to

New York as long as he stayed in touch with the doctors and started his rehabilitation.

So he said his goodbyes to Sophia and Thomas and Quint and Lucas and all the animals. Especially Geronimo.

"Please come back," said Sophia.

"Only if you promise no more nasty neighbors and snakes."

"Promise!"

On the drive back to El Paso, Mike worried, "After everything that's happened, it's not exactly a secret anymore that I was in New Mexico with Tommy Bears and Joe Panelli."

"So, your friend Tommy took you to visit his folks at their ranch. You didn't know I was going to come along," said Joe. "No big deal."

"Not so sure about that."

"Just roll with it," said Tommy.

"Right."

But it all worked out. Mostly, everyone just wanted to hear about what happened and about his dealings with the FBI and DEA and about riding the range in New Mexico. Mike made the most of his adventurous night at the Big H and the snake pit. He skimmed over the presence of Joe Panelli and no one cornered him on it.

He spent over a month rehabilitating and then was on desk duty until his leg was in working condition again.

"Think you can handle getting back on the job again?" asked Clark Thorn after taking a call.

"Trust me. I am so ready," declared Mike.

"Then let's go get a murderer or two."

It was several months later that the threesome had to return to New Mexico for Mitchell Hudson's trial. Fortunately, his battery of lawyers didn't help him much. The murder of Andy Miller, the kidnapping of Sophia and Mike, and the attempted murder of a cop proved to be too much for him to beat. His plans for the specialty business didn't help much either. He and Spike and all the men involved found themselves locked away for a long time.

After that, it took some time, but the happy ending did work out for Andy Miller's sons. It was discovered how Hudson had threatened and manipulated Andy Miller to get his ranch. Then Miller had gotten stubborn and decided he was going to take it all to the authorities, leading to his murder. So eventually, with the help of lawyers provided by the Panelli family, the ranch was returned to the Miller family again. Shortly after that, the Bears and all the neighbors attended Andy's funeral when his ashes were brought home and laid to rest on the ranch he loved.

Back in New York City, Detective Mike Brennen chased bad guys.

Made in the USA
Columbia, SC
26 October 2025

eb0e5b7a-1d04-4685-b6a0-de6c2c33778fR01